Secrets And Assumptions

by

Jane Drager

Secrets And Assumptions

Cover Art by *Kristian Norris*

The Wild Rose Press, Inc.
PO Box 708
Adams Basin, NY 14410-0708
Visit us at www.thewildrosepress.com

Publishing History
First Crimson Rose Edition, 2016
Print ISBN 978-1-5092-0931-6
Digital ISBN 978-1-5092-0932-3

Published in the United States of America

After a deep breath, Teegan

rounded the corner into the living room, gun aimed and finger on the trigger.

Anna's head shot up. She cursed audibly but kept her gun pointed at Budd, her body rigid, her gaze like razors. The smile changed into a nervous twitch.

She's not so cocky while staring at the barrel of a gun.

Anna's nostrils flared. "If that damn rifle hadn't run out of bullets, I'd have pumped every last round into you from the ridgeline."

"Lucky me." Fate was on her side.

Anna's gun hand shook. "So, you wore a vest after all. You have a nasty habit of foiling my plans, Miss Fancy Pants." The cords on Anna's neck showed a heavy pulsing as she nodded toward the hallway. "The agents secured the house and barn when they arrived. How did you get in?"

That's right. Keep her talking. "Budd had instructions to unlock a back window the moment he arrived." She flashed a quick glance at Budd to see him staring, mouth ajar. *Oh, God, what he must think.* She approached, gun aimed at Anna's head. "You're finished, Anna. Give up."

Anna's gaze darted to the door. "Don't take another step, or I put a bullet into Budd's chest."

Teegan stopped. "You know I won't let you do that." Her finger itched to squeeze the trigger. *Come on, bitch. Make my day.*

The copter sound intensified, vibrating ground and cabin. Reinforcements were close.

Panic emanated from Anna's eyes as her gaze shifted from the door to the ceiling to Teegan.

Dedication

To my editor, Leanne Morgana,
for your patience and skills.

Chapter One

Budd Richardson frowned as he surveyed the bundled lump huddled near the airplane window. His seatmate. A woman. *Just what I need to complete my day.* First, a traffic jam blocking the roads to the O'Hara airport made him scramble through security only to discover an indeterminable flight delay. That had kept him in the terminal waiting area in stifling July humidity because the air conditioning sucked. Then came a half-riot between two sets of parents over some stupid child's toy.

The hour hit the three o'clock mark twenty minutes ago. Any longer and he'd be driving to his meeting straight from the Vegas airport. The frustration was enough to make a grown man cry.

Now, this. He was grumpy as hell and in no mood to be civil to anyone, male or female. He wanted some much-needed shuteye. Budd waved his hand to catch the attention of a male steward.

After the man fought his way up the crowded aisle, he stood with a quizzical lift to his brow. "Can I help you, sir?"

Budd waited while a portly man squeezed him against the seatback, nearly pushing him onto the seat in the process. He glared at the man's wide back before turning to the steward. "Any possibility I can change to the other side of the plane?"

"I'm sorry, sir, but the flight is booked solid." To another passenger further up the aisle, he said, "That's right, ma'am. In the overhead. Don't jam it in too hard." He cringed when the woman had done exactly that. He rolled his eyes and then gave Budd a practiced smile. "Vegas is a popular summer destination for you folks in Chicago."

"I live in Vegas, and for the record, I hate Chicago. Everything about this business trip has been a fiasco." He hadn't meant to take his annoyance out on the man. So what if his client was an overbearing pain-in-the-neck who owned too much property in Nevada? No one cared, least of all the steward. "Do you think anyone will switch?"

A sly grin curled the corners of the man's mouth. "Trust me, sir. You won't want to change your seat. You'll understand why soon enough."

Budd narrowed his gaze at the steward and then shifted it to the sleeping bundle. "Did she board with the rest of us?"

"She boarded in Philadelphia and fell asleep during the layover. Hold onto your libido, sir." The steward inched his way down the aisle.

Libido, hell.

Budd stuffed his briefcase in the overhead compartment and slammed the lid before flopping onto his seat. Surrounding passengers banged the overheads as if the latch refused to hold. *Bing, bang, boom.* The guy behind him whacked it four times.

The bundle never stirred. She had her face turned toward the shaded window and buried under the blanket. Deaf as a stone. Or dead.

That was a pleasant thought.

Oh, come off it. He enjoyed the company of a woman as much as the next man. His attitude was the problem.

The seatbelt sign dinged as the plane taxied toward the runway.

A flight attendant checking for buckled belts stopped alongside. She leaned in and nodded toward the bundle. "I'm afraid I'll have to wake our sleeping beauty. She looks so comfortable."

Comatose was the word. She hadn't moved, even when the plane bounced as if the wheels fell off a curb. Budd stopped the attendant from reaching across him. "I'll do it."

"Thank you, sir. Please make sure she has her belt fastened and backrest forward."

Now, he had a good reason to see who hid beneath the blanket. The steward's words caused an insatiable curiosity. Budd nudged her. "Hey, sleepy head." Dead. No doubt about it. *It might be a pleasant flight after all.* He nudged again and prayed she didn't come up swinging. "Yo!"

The woman woke with a start and turned, her loose chestnut hair whipping onto her face. A pair of teal marbles fluttered in rapid succession, struggling to focus.

Sweet heaven! Her eyes were extraordinary in color, a beautiful blend of blue and green with tiny specks of gold around the pupil. His mouth went dry. "We're taking off." Damn, his voice squeaked. He coughed. "You need to fasten your seatbelt."

The woman tossed the blanket to the floor and raised the backrest. Her hands wrestled with the two ends of the belt, both of which were buried beneath her butt. After a quick click of the clasps then a soft cry of victory, she yawned and settled back, rigid.

Between the blanket and her movements, he caught a whiff of her perfume. Very nice. Subtle. An intoxicating blend of…some kind of flower. Or spice. He hadn't the foggiest idea how a woman's perfume was concocted. As long as it smelled nice and wasn't poured on.

"Wow, I passed out." She suppressed another yawn. "Thank you."

"You're welcome. Do you always sleep so soundly?"

"I have a reputation for sleeping through hurricanes."

Her voice had a rich tone of maturity, smooth and seductive, the kind a man loved to hear after a rousing night of sex. She looked in shape with softly-defined arm muscles showing under short sleeves, a flat tummy, and proportioned breasts. For a change, a woman with some meat on her bones. The opposite of his usual social fare with their breast implants, butt implants, and God only knew what else implanted. She wore casual clothes of T-shirt, blue jeans, and sneakers. An off-the-rack variety. No wedding band. No jewelry in fact. Only a silver watch with diamond studs surrounding the clock face, expensive and out of synch with her attire. "On vacation?" He glanced at her posture. She still sat rigid, like a schoolgirl waiting for punishment.

"No, going home."

A Vegas resident. She'd recognized him. He was certain of it.

As the plane bounced along, her rigidness eased somewhat. She opened the shaded window to look onto the runway.

Budd pretended to do the same. Any man in his right mind wouldn't stare out a window with such a stunner nearby. Her age, at a guess, was early thirties with an exquisite profile of small nose and lightly glossed lips pieced together by flawless tanned skin. Perfectly shaped brows matched the chestnut color of her shoulder-length hair with a slender neck completing the picture. He searched for a scar. A mole. Anything to break the illusion of perfection. He found nothing. Not even a pierced ear.

The plane revved for takeoff.

Sucking in a breath, she pressed her head to the backrest and clamped her eyes shut.

He cocked his head toward her, his voice low. "We're at the mercy of the pilots."

Her hands gripped the armrests. "That's very reassuring." She scrunched her face. "I hate flying."

"I have a pilot friend who tells me takeoffs are the most dangerous part of the flight. Full gas tanks, explosion time."

She narrowed her gaze. "You are not helping matters."

He adjusted the airflow over his head. "I'll hold your hand on the way down."

"Gee, I can't wait."

Her smile was brief, but he caught the curl and chuckled at her sarcasm. The plane leveled off. "There, see? Nothing to it."

"I should have taken a bus," she mumbled.

A few minutes later, the seatbelt sign turned dark.

"Oh, good. I need to freshen up." She stood to get by.

A face worthy of a sculpture, a shape muscular but lean, a Vegas resident. And more. She had a fluid movement as if she trained her body to move without waste, a movement he recognized. She was a showgirl, and *that* was his usual fare. The realization conjured images of the lifestyle he'd chosen, one full of one-night-stands and non-committal relationships. He shifted to let her pass.

Halfway up the aisle, she turned and met his gaze, her hand hesitating on the lavatory door while she gave a subtle bite to her lower lip.

A flight attendant broke the spell by scooting around her with an armload of pillows.

His seatmate cast her gaze downward, shook her head slightly, and entered the restroom. The entire scene reminded him of the women who pretended *not* to know him, the ones who passed by hoping to catch his eye but played their coy game to the hilt. Obviously, she was another one.

The woman didn't belong in first class. Showgirls rarely made enough to keep themselves afloat, let alone waste money for an expensive plane ticket. They fell over each other to date him, because they lived like a queen at his place…for a few nights anyway. Her watch had to be a gift from a grateful suitor, probably one of many. "Awake now?" he asked when she rejoined him.

"Barely." She re-buckled her seatbelt. "I guess I was more tired than I realized. Are you on vacation?"

Still playing the coy game. *I'll go along.* "Heading home, like you." He fussed with his trouser crease. "You haven't been in Vegas long. I still hear a Philadelphia accent."

She groaned and lowered her head. "I've had

several people tell me that. I never knew Philadelphians had an accent until I transferred out here."

"Which was when?"

"Two months ago. I promised to return for my mother's birthday, and that's what I've just done. Now, it's back to work."

Two months? Enough time for a beautiful woman to acquaint herself with the Vegas dating scene. "Yes, we have our bills to pay. Which casino?"

"Casino?" She half-turned in her seat with a cocked brow. "I work for the Smith Tool Company outside of town."

Not a showgirl then. Too old perhaps. Or her career was sidetracked by an injury. "I know the place. The factory is sitting on some prime real estate. Actually, I helped Frank Smith negotiate the land deal."

Her head snapped, slapping a thick strand across her face. She tucked it behind her ear. "You did?"

That got her attention. "I only handle high-end clients, and Frank is about as high-end as they come. I assume you worked for him in Philly?"

She grabbed the blanket and gave it a haphazard fold. "Yes. I had a different job back east. I agreed to come and get the place started. He assured me the job was temporary. I don't believe him." With no place to put the blanket, she dropped it to the floor.

"I'd believe him. Frank's a nice guy. I liked him the second we met. Are you operational yet?"

"Not quite. Three more months, if we're lucky. Then I'll head back to Philly."

A flight attendant rolled a liquor cart alongside his seat. He ordered white wine. She ordered Irish whiskey on ice. He quirked an eyebrow and stared at her glass.

"Strong stuff for a woman."

She sipped. "Not strong enough. We still have to land."

His curiosity flew into overdrive. Her curvy shape, her beauty, and now her choice of liquor spelled showgirl. *Why would she lie about working for Frank Smith? I know a dancer when I see one.*

Ah, of course. An ex-showgirl from the east coast recruited by a wealthy man to fulfill a sexual dream. He had to give Frank credit for nailing this one. "What do you *do* at the Smith Tool Company?" *Besides sleep with the boss.*

She swirled the ice cubes in her glass. "Paper shuffler mostly."

He rotated in his seat to study her. "I had you pegged for the factory area."

Her head tilted as she met his gaze. "Why?"

"Your hands show strength. You look like you can handle a tool." *And a man's body parts.* Most of his women wore nails sharp enough to cut off his balls. Her nails were trimmed short. A pleasure to see.

She studied her hands while splaying the fingers. "Yeah, I can handle a tool, and I've worked in the factory, but right now, my job involves paperwork. A ton of it."

Paper shuffler equaled file clerk with no skills. Hence, mistress. The perfect setup. He faced forward to sip his wine. "My entire career involves paperwork. I never get away from it. The wealthy generate more than usual."

"As opposed to the poor peons, you mean?"

The sarcastic tone surprised him. He elaborated. "They want to keep the money from cousin Bob, that

8

sort of thing. I also handle a prevalence of palimony contracts from rich men to their mistresses and sometimes the other way around. The whole process gets ridiculous at times." But a profitable one for his firm. Pre-nups, divorces, last Will and Testaments a mile long—all generated big bucks.

An odd expression spread onto her face. Her back stiffened while a slow gaze scanned him from head to toe. "I gather you were Frank Smith's lawyer?"

For some reason, her scrutiny unnerved him. Showgirls displayed gratitude for his attention, not this careful dissection of his torso. "I'm considered one of the best in Vegas. You should know that." He sat forward and toyed with his glass. "I can't go anywhere without someone recognizing my face."

"Well, this is your lucky day, counselor. I haven't the foggiest idea who you are." Her head tilted. "You our mayor or something?"

Damn her. Too outspoken and brash for her own good. He shifted in his seat. "You don't need to act naïve. Everyone in Vegas knows me."

"Naïveté isn't what I'm expressing. I have no idea who you are except a man full of himself. Big deal, you handle high-end clients. A realtor can make the same claim to fame." She lifted her glass in a gesture of salute. "Before this drink fogs my brain, anything else you want to say to impress me?"

She thinks this is a game. He finished the last of his wine in one gulp. "I don't need to impress you. I'm stating a fact."

"Which is?"

"If you live in Vegas, you know who I am. Don't deny it." Dear Lord! When was the last time he argued with a woman over his fame and fortune? He should cut the subject short before he put his foot too far down his throat.

A faint grin twisted the corner of her mouth while her body rotated fully to face him, her gaze probing into his soul.

He'd like to kiss that grin off those luscious lips, maybe swallow her whole, and then spit her out. *Get your head together, man.* No woman got the better of him, not in the courtroom, and certainly not on a plane. He stared at the seatback in front of him.

"Let me guess." With one finger, she tapped her chin, a thoughtful expression passing onto her face. "You're a headliner at one of the casinos."

His hand gripped his glass. "Don't be absurd."

"Why not? It wouldn't be the first time a lawyer entered showbiz. I'll bet you can belt out a good tune...I know!" Grinning, she snapped her fingers. "You operate a popular wedding chapel."

Game, indeed. He growled at his empty glass but kept his lips clamped shut.

"All right, that wasn't it either. Then, enlighten me. I'm new in Vegas. I barely have my stuff unpacked. Should I be asking for your autograph?"

One more barb and explosion was imminent. He scrutinized her with a glowering gaze.

She responded with a fluttering of her lashes. "Did I bruise your ego?"

A flush of heat traveled from the center of his gut all the way to the top of his head. At any second, he could explode. "I have enough experience to know when a woman is lying."

"Oh, so now I'm a liar." She shook her head. "You

are full of yourself, counselor. What's it like to feel so self-important?"

"Something you can't possibly know." He held his glass in the palm of his hand while contemplating whether to hurl it at her head. The glass was cheap-ass plastic, though. No weight, no pain. *She'd sue anyway.* "You're jealous."

"Hardly. I have this aversion toward snobs. Maybe you should change your seat."

His head snapped as he narrowed his gaze. "I already tried. As you see, first class is full. People like you shouldn't be up here."

Her eyebrows shot halfway into her hairline. "People like me?" She pinched her off-the-rack clothes. "Poor and underprivileged, you mean? I put on my deodorant this morning. Go find an empty seat in coach."

Smart ass. "I might suggest the same for you."

"Oh, but I wouldn't change my seat for the world. I like sitting here with the high and mighty. It makes me feel"—she paused, pursing her lips—"important." She threw back her head with a flair.

A put-on for sure. The woman wasn't shy. She'd come out with fists swinging if necessary. "This boldness of yours, is it a Philly trait?"

"South Philadelphia to be precise. We learn early in life to watch our backs. Maybe I should become a lawyer and enter your world of hoity-toity."

"I am not hoity-toity." Despite his annoyance, he smiled. He couldn't help it. No woman had stood up to him like this one. "You'd make a formidable opponent."

"Wow, a compliment from a man full of

assumptions."

"My assumptions are usually correct as I assume Frank paid for your seat."

"Nope." She sipped her drink. "I mortgaged my house to buy the ticket. Next assumption."

"You're Frank's mistress."

Her beautiful mouth fell open. Seconds later, she slapped it shut. "Explain your reasoning."

"I think you're a showgirl from the east coast casinos sent out here away from his wife, either to resist temptation or for a dalliance when he visits. He's got the money for both."

"Except he's super loyal to his wife and family. My dumb luck."

"Ah, so you've tried. I'm not surprised. He's a hard man to pass up." *Aw, shit.* He was acting like an idiot. So what if she was Frank's mistress or anyone else's for that matter? What the hell was in his wine? He cleared his throat. "I apologize for the indiscretion."

She acknowledged with a roll of her eyes, swallowed the last of her drink in one gulp before grabbing a magazine from the seat rack.

Well, I made a fine impression. He needed another drink, maybe a stronger one to help dull his senses. *And maybe some tape to seal my lips together.* He had liked Frank Smith, and whatever the man fancied in his spare time was a privilege afforded the wealthy.

For the remainder of the flight, he tried his utmost to ignore her, but the scent of her perfume drifted toward his nose, and he'd glance in her direction. He'd catch her doing the same, their gazes meeting only to quickly divert. Sparks flew with his woman, something electric and tantalizing, vibrating every nerve in his body. An odd feeling, foreign even. Unfortunately, he wasn't sure if he wanted to hump or strangle her to death.

Good-looking women had never rattled him. They passed in and out of his life like candy tasted then tossed aside. With this one, he wanted a long, luxurious savoring. She intrigued him, a woman with wit and a lot of guts.

After the plane taxied to the terminal and stopped, he stood to retrieve his briefcase from the overhead. She followed his movements like most women eyeing their next sexual encounter. "Is this your backpack?"

"Yes." She stood as he tugged it from the compartment. Their gazes locked. She took a step back and promptly bumped her temple on the overhead. She winced, whether from pain or embarrassment, he wasn't sure. He handed her the backpack.

She slipped the strap over one shoulder and slid past him to join the exiting passengers while he fought the urge to run after her. *Don't be a fool.* He'd be stepping on Frank's toes, and he liked the guy too much. Besides, Budd Richardson had plenty of women to occupy his nights. One more and he'd need a bigger book.

Oh, hell. Maybe I should talk to a shrink. He grabbed his briefcase and, without closing the overhead, hurried for the exit. Everyone and their mother blocked his path, especially the people walking four abreast, stretching from one side of the bridge to the other. He almost plowed through them like a bowling ball after pins. Once free, he caught up to her in the crowded terminal. "Can I give you a lift?"

She shifted her backpack to her left shoulder. "My

car's in the lot." A half-smile touched the corner of her mouth as she met his gaze. "I'm surprised you offered."

"Me, too. Not enough blood in my brain."

The words generated a low chuckle from her throat.

A small boy ran past him followed quickly by a man who scooped him into his arms. The child screamed with delight.

"Do you have a reason for keeping pace with me?"

He shifted his gaze from the child to her. "I'm debating whether to apologize or not. I made a crappy first impression."

"That you did." She looked at him while her fingers tightened on the backpack's strap. "You're judging a book by the cover, counselor. The contents can turn into a good read. I'm not who or what you think I am."

"I'm not a snob either."

"Now that, you'll have to prove."

Budd turned right at the terminal junction, but saw that she continued straight. "Luggage pickup is this way," he called.

"I'm carrying my luggage."

No luggage, no clothes, no money. He wasn't wrong about her at all. *Does it matter?* "Wait, I don't know your name!"

She turned to face him while walking backward.

He welcomed the opportunity to scan her one last time and liked what he saw.

"We're even, counselor. I don't know your name either."

This wasn't the time or the place to debate the truth. The damn woman tantalized him with a sparkling

14

gaze, and she was about to walk out of his life forever. "Budd Richardson."

Her lips curled. "Nice to know. I'm Teegan Smith, Frank's daughter."

Chapter Two

Gotcha, big boy! Teegan bit her tongue to control the laughter about to burst from her throat. Budd Richardson stood mute, mouth agape, eyes wide. His expression was priceless. He was fun. If anything, he helped make a boring flight tolerable.

Her father had talked about the lawyer he used in Vegas—a nice guy, head screwed on straight, money of his own. The words flowed through one ear and out the other, not enticing her curiosity. If he'd said Budd's name, well, no matter.

Her old man had a nasty habit of playing matchmaker, always claiming to have the perfect man in the wings. *Uh-huh.* Over the years, he'd arranged one too many woof-woof dates, and at the first indication of matchmaking, she'd close her ears and nod like a bobble-head. As if his daughter was incapable of attracting a suitable male. She had a long list…when she remembered to look at it.

Budd, without a doubt, tops every man I've ever met, and I'm not stretching the truth any.

When she'd opened her eyes and focused on his face, she swore the plane crashed, and her spirit floated toward the heavens with his dreamboat of a face to stare at along the way. His chiseled jaw showed the faintest trace of stubble, and she resisted the urge to feel whether the stubs were fuzzy-soft or pinchy-firm. His sky-blue eyes conjured images of soaring up, up and away into cloudless oblivion, and sandy hair—a touch of brown, a touch of gold—cut to perfection, reminded her of the beaches along the Jersey shore. His lips looked kissable-soft when they weren't pressed with sternness, which was practically their entire flight. If her imagination failed to invoke the most erotic sexual fantasies, then she hadn't a female hormone left in her body. The man was downright stimulating. Period.

Then, he opened his mouth and spoke. Spoiled everything.

Her tolerance for snobs was a step above bigots but not a very big step either. Budd Richardson had exhibited the classic characteristics of a man who believed his shit wouldn't stink. The I'm-rich-and-you're-not attitude that irked her to no end. Not to mention his assumptions so totally off-the-wall ridiculous. He should write a book with chapter one detailing his biggest inane statement about her being Frank Smith's mistress.

Wait 'til I tell Dad.

She'd almost kept quiet about her identity, but the man nudged up her curiosity a few notches. Was it his habit to put on airs with all women or was she the lucky one? And who was he to think himself so high and mighty that she should know him because she lived in Vegas? *Pul-lease, give me a break.*

She'd grown to adulthood with many men like him, pretending to be important, famous, or the most wonderful lover in the world. Teegan Smith wasn't easily swayed. For a man to impress, he'd have to make a pizza from scratch with pepperoni and plenty of cheese. Even a nice—

What the frig—

Two firm grips had clamped onto her arm and whipped her with a force to send her backpack and purse flying. She crashed into the wallboard, the impact tumbling chunks like an avalanche onto her head, back, and shoulders.

A woman screamed. Several others cried out. Too many feet approached to distinguish which two belonged to the assailant.

"Honey, are you all right?"

"Somebody call the cops!"

"Is this what we can expect in Vegas?"

"Where's security when you need them?"

Voices and noise clouded her thoughts, throwing her into utter confusion. Someone helped her into a shaky stance. Another brushed off the wallboard pieces.

What happened? One minute, she was laughing to herself, the next, she shook away wallboard dust.

"Anything broken?" An old woman had asked the question.

Teegan shook her head stupidly, too stunned to use words.

A tall man shoved his way through the crowd.

The sandy hair and blue eyes forced her to focus.

"Good heavens, Ms. Smith, who did this?"

The million dollar question. "I have no idea." Other than a robber who envisioned her backpack and purse as easy targets. She looked around for the items.

Budd turned to the crowd. "Anyone witness anything?"

"Over here." An elderly man stepped forward wearing a flowery Hawaiian shirt with his beer-belly stretching the lower buttonholes. "A woman in a blue jacket grabbed onto her arm and tossed her like a sack of potatoes into the wall. Then, she took off like a bat out of a cave down the terminal." He pointed a fleshy arm. "I don't know which way she turned after that."

Budd craned his neck and scanned up and down the terminal. "What kind of blue jacket?"

"One of those sweatshirt kind. She had the hood up and was wearing a pair of big-ass sunglasses. I thought Vegas was eighty degrees outside."

The man spoke as if he stood at the opposite end of a long tunnel. Even the voices of all those gathered had a muffled tone. Teegan knocked the side of her head to clear any wallboard dust from her ears.

"Anything else?" Budd asked. "Can you describe the woman?"

The man scratched his bald head. "Sure. Small build, brown hair—I think. Fast as a whip. Someone with a screw loose, no doubt. I thought we only had those in Chicago."

Security arrived. One guard took the man aside for a repeat of the description and then relayed the information over his radio. Another guard dispersed the crowd.

Budd brushed small pieces of debris from her hair. "Maybe you should go to the hospital."

Maybe she should tell her father Vegas was no safer than Philadelphia. "I'm fine. Only shaken."

A guard handed her the backpack and purse, intact.

Not a robbery then. *All right, what other explanation do I have? A personal attack?* No, she agreed with the old man—someone with a screw loose.

"We'll need a statement from you, ma'am."

Blinking a couple of times, she focused on the

guard. A nice-looking man with the shoulders and chest of a weightlifter. She should fake a faint and fall into his arms.

"I'll go with you," Budd said.

Whoa, that snapped her attention to the present. "No, Mr. Richardson, thank you, but it isn't necessary. I can't tell them anything."

"Well, I can. I have a good idea who attacked you." To the guard, he said, "I want a copy of the surveillance photo sent to Detective Sergeant Reeves of the Las Vegas Police Department. He needs to hear about this."

Teegan touched his arm. A jolt of electricity shot through her fingers and straight down to her toes. Surprised, she dropped her hand, met his wide-eyed gaze, and her breath stopped. *Did he feel the spark? Was it the carpet?* She searched his face for an answer, but a scowl appeared. *Well, well, I've got a Jekyll and Hyde here.* His expression had changed from startled to restrained with a simple bat of the eye. She shook herself. "Who was it?"

His upper lip rose into a sneer. "The woman who's been stalking me for several months. I may be wrong, but the description matches. Photos should confirm my suspicion." His face relaxed as he met her gaze. "Are you really okay?"

The sincerity in his voice caused a momentary flip of her heart. "I'm resilient." *And embarrassed as all get-out.* The assailant had caught her off-guard and all because her mind was preoccupied by this dreamboat of a man standing alongside. Given her background and training, she failed Observation 101. "You don't have to accompany me, Mr. Richardson. I'm sure you have someplace to be." *Like your throne in a castle.*

"I feel responsible." He frowned.

The guard stepped in. "I'll notify Detective Reeves, sir. You should proceed toward the baggage claim area." He indicated the direction with a wave of his hand.

Budd hesitated with his gaze shifting from her to the guard and back again. Anger flashed within the blue until his shoulders gave slightly, and he nodded. "All right, officer. I'll proceed to baggage claim. I've a conference with the mayor tonight, and I've got to get home to change. See that she's personally escorted to her vehicle." He handed the man his card. "Any difficulties, call me."

Bushy eyebrows rose as the guard read quickly. "I should have recognized you, sir, but yes, I'll see she gets out of here safe." He slipped the card into his breast pocket. "This way, ma'am." He touched her elbow.

Teegan glanced back at Budd who watched, his mouth tight with a deep frown creasing the bridge of his nose. As her gaze met his, she felt an unmistakable tug, as if he pulled on some unseen chain. The same sensation had hit her on the plane, but she ignored it. Now, the feeling was powerful, an attraction far beyond anything she'd ever experienced. She broke the hold by shifting the backpack on her shoulder and forcing her attention forward.

A stalker, eh? Who was this woman? And why attack a total stranger who happened to be walking through the airport terminal?

Chapter Three

Ah, if life was more simple. If he could twitch his nose and make everything right…

"You're paying me good money to sit and twiddle my thumbs, you know."

Budd turned from his large picture window. He had been staring at nothing in particular, a boring high-rise view of mid-morning Las Vegas. Even in daylight, lights glittered, never to dim. His legal assistant's voice had broken into his thoughts. "I'm sorry, Denise. Where was I?"

"Dear Doug." She sat with pen poised over her notepad, waiting.

He cocked his head. "Go on."

"That's it. You said it five times."

He stuffed his hands into his trouser pockets and jiggled the loose change. Maybe he should buy a small change purse like his Uncle Henry used, save the wear and tear on the lining of his pockets. *Like I can't afford a new pair of trousers.*

"Hello?"

Dropping his chin, he focused on his shoes. They needed a good polish.

"Budd?"

He shook himself. "My mind's wandering. Let's start over." He turned back to the window and squinted from the sun's glare. "Dear Doug. The groundwork for your new hotel…"

Too many tourists this time of year, all gawking at the opulence. An ambulance siren filled the air. Red flashing lights fought their way through the thick Vegas traffic below his window. People stopped to stare. An age-old custom where hats came off and heads bowed as the horse and wagon rode by.

"I can go home and do a load of laundry."

Did she speak Swahili? He faced her. She had taken her usual stiff-backed chair off to the side of his desk, always ignoring the more comfortable leather chairs in the front. Something to do with better back support.

She tapped her pen on her notepad. "I've never seen you so distracted. Are you feeling okay?"

Budd flopped into his thick leather chair with a grunt. "I can't concentrate."

"No kidding. What's the problem?"

A constant vision of teal marbles staring dazed after her crash into the wall. Denise was more a friend than an employee, but he couldn't tell her everything. "Jet lag, I think."

She waved aside the comment. "You hardly ever get jet lag. Was it the interview this morning?"

"No. I managed to get through it without making a total ass of myself." *Which was a small miracle given my state of mind.*

"Then why don't you take off the rest of the week? Give yourself a nice vacation to relax. You've earned it."

He straightened his silk tie. "I've too much to do. My trip to Chicago put me a week behind."

"Nonsense. You have partners and eager associates

at your disposal. Let them earn their salary so the boss can take a break." She paused to fuss with her skirt. "You have an appointment this afternoon at two. Afterwards, you're free to do as you please. Use the time to go to the cabin."

A tempting suggestion. His cabin was the culmination of years of planning from a carpenter's dream to reality. The project had become a secondary home, a place of solitude and peace—foreign words in this city of opulence. The paparazzi, always eager for a scoop, never gave him an inch of free space. One of these days, they might stroll through the door and make themselves at home.

He drummed his fingers on the desk. "I do need to get some work done." Sheetrock, border trim. A half dozen tasks.

"There! A spark in an otherwise staid expression. You made me wonder what happened in Chicago. You attended a business meeting with a wealthy client, not his funeral. If you…" She tilted her head, brows raised. "Am I boring you?"

Budd jerked. "What?"

"Maybe you should leave now. Your concentration spans all of two minutes." She leaned forward. "Is anything bothering you?"

"No." A bold lie. He had spent the entire night staring at the ceiling because of Teegan Smith. Frank's daughter. Who would have believed she'd be so beautiful? "Any news from Sergeant Reeves?"

Denise gave him a blank look, her glossed lips ajar.

"What's the matter?"

She shook her fly-away auburn hair. "Sergeant Reeves is due here in ten minutes."

Sitting upright, Budd stared back. "Why?"

"He said he has important news and asked to stop by. Remember?"

"No. When did you tell me?"

She blinked. "I didn't. You told *me* before I sat down to warm this seat. He called on your cell phone."

"Oh, yeah." Maybe he'd had a stroke and didn't know it. Or Alzheimer's. It explained his memory lapse. *Hell, I'm only thirty-something...shit, thirty-four.* He swiveled to face the window. "I met a woman on the plane."

"So, what else is new? You're a magnet where women are concerned. That's why they call you Vegas' Most Eligible Bachelor."

His hand curled into a fist on his thigh. He hated the title. The definition implied a willingness to get snared. He wasn't the least bit eligible.

"What about this woman?"

Swiveling the chair, he faced her. "She kept me awake all night."

Denise wagged a finger. "You know the rules, Budd Richardson. I have no interest hearing about your sex life."

"You misunderstand, Mrs. Callahan. She kept me awake, but she wasn't with me."

Denise stared, brown eyes wide to popping. "Are you raising my hopes? I've known you for a long time, and no woman has driven you to distraction. What's her name?"

"Teegan Smith." He shot her a furtive glance. "Frank Smith's daughter." He hit a key on his computer. A picture of Teegan appeared, showing a face with a beautiful smile and bright eyes. Distraction was too mild a word. Never in his life had he lost sleep over a woman nor had he wished for her sudden appearance beside him. *A man can dream.*

Denise gasped and flew around his side of the desk for a close up. "She's Frank's daughter? The man's a behemoth! How could he father a woman so gorgeous?"

Indeed. Budd had researched Teegan online and read every detail available. The information was professional, nothing personal to reveal the woman, why she obsessed his thoughts, or why this insatiable appetite to discover every aspect of her life. No woman had ever caused such turmoil. Normally, his interest in the opposite sex died after a romp in bed.

Denise pointed to the computer screen. "You date beautiful women all the time, Budd. What's different about this one?"

Damned if I know. "Besides being the daughter of one of Philadelphia's wealthiest men?" He stared at the screen. "She has a Ph.D. in metals chemistry, which she achieved at the ripe old age of twenty-six, has a reported IQ higher than Albert Einstein, and holds so many patents she doesn't need her father's money." He sighed and leaned back in his chair. "She's out of my league."

"And that's bothering you?" She crossed her arms over her chest. "You're no slug, Budd. You built this law firm from the ground up, despite the odds against you. You're no longer the poor boy from the other side of town struggling to be noticed in this lawyer-infested city. You should be proud of your accomplishments." She patted his shoulder and returned to the chair near the desk.

He followed her movements while drumming his fingers on a pile of papers. "My success has nothing to do with this. You know how I feel about the children of rich parents. Nothing but spoiled brats. They like to spend Daddy's money." He pointed to himself. "In college, I was nothing more than an object of ridicule to those bastards."

"But a minute ago you told me Teegan has her own money."

"Doesn't matter. She grew up rich." Pursuing Teegan would be a lesson in futility, a lesson he'd learned a long time ago.

Denise shook her head. "You're making assumptions again, Budd Richardson. If you remember, Frank fooled us. He was a down-to-earth man. So much so, I invited him over for dinner with the family, which he loved. A regular meat-and-potatoes man. His daughter may surprise you."

"I doubt it. Offspring follow a predictable pattern."

"Oh, like your showgirls are so unpredictable? They call when they need a meal or a place to spend the night. Give me a break." Shaking her head, she shifted in her seat and tugged at her skirt. "I can't believe she intimidates you."

"She does not!" Holy shit, the words sounded so high school.

"If you don't have any desire to approach her, then why lose sleep?"

Pride. Man-genes. Stupidity. He cleared his throat. "I made a total ass of myself on the plane. I assumed she'd heard of me."

"Ah, so now we get down to the nitty-gritty." Her brown eyes brightened. "She didn't know you at all and bruised your ego. How long has she been in Vegas?"

"A couple of months."

Denise rolled her eyes. "That explains it. She's not familiar with your face. You're not on the news every night nor in the newspaper every day." She leaned forward, pen pointing toward the computer. "Your meeting this afternoon involves the Smith Tool Company, you know. The Vegas Environmental Group wants you available to answer questions while they inspect the place."

Oh, hell, I knew I had something to do this afternoon. He stared at the pile of papers on his desk then at his wristwatch. Driving to the other side of the city for an unnecessary meeting was a total waste of time. His brows creased into a frown. "Why are they bothering? The plant isn't operational yet."

"It's a preliminary inspection to assure they're following code. You can send an associate. I'm sure they won't mind."

"No, I'll handle it. I need a chance to redeem myself." *Why* was the question. Not like he had room in his little black book for another woman, least of all Frank Smith's daughter. He took a long, lingering look at Teegan before hitting a key to turn the screen black.

He had vowed never to get involved with a rich-bitch. They'd demeaned him incessantly throughout college because of his low income roots. Now that he had money, he couldn't keep them off. They fell over him in embarrassing ways—too much alcohol and drugs, exploiting their bodies, not the type of women to write home about. The names of showgirls filled his date book, the poor and needy ones who repaid his generosity with sex. "Forget about the letter until I return from the meeting. Maybe my mind will be clearer." Or totally befuddled.

A soft tap on the door interrupted. The firm's receptionist poked her head through the opening. "You have two gentlemen to see you, sir. One is Sergeant Reeves from LVPD. He said you are expecting him?"

"Yes, Christine, send them in." He waved Denise back into her seat. "Stay put. I want you to listen, in case I don't retain any of it." Which was highly probable at this point.

Detective Sergeant Michael Reeves strolled through the door like a bully entering a playground. He moved with a confident swagger, a don't-tempt-me-or-I'll-break-you-in-two arrogance. A burly man's man in every sense of the word. Military buzz cut. Muscled chest. Proper suit and tie. Budd had liked him the moment they met at the mayor's inauguration.

The man behind him was older by about twenty years with a weathered face that endured too much stress. A mop of gray hair covered his head, an unruly mess, as if he stepped in the center of four fans and threw the switch. Oddly enough, the back edge and sideburns were freshly trimmed while the top was left to do as it pleased. His suit fit a small frame, a beanpole in contrast to Mike. Budd stood to shake their hands.

"This is Jeff Andrews, the regional director for the FBI," Mike said.

Budd cocked a brow as he reached across the desk to grasp the older man's hand. "I assumed you were here about my stalker. Mr. Andrews, my assistant, Denise." He motioned toward the leather chairs. "Sit down, gentlemen." Budd resumed his seat.

Both men acknowledged her presence and took a

seat opposite the desk. Jeff Andrews placed an expensive leather briefcase on his lap.

"Yes, we're here about your stalker," Mike began. "Some interesting developments surfaced."

"In that case—" Budd withdrew a pink envelope from his suit jacket and handed it to Mike. "This was on my windshield this morning when I came out of the coffee shop."

Mike read aloud. "*'Don't think I'm not watching you and who you're with. I know where you are every second of the day, even when you take a trip to Chicago. The time has come for us to be together again. Don't fight it, Budd.'*" He handed the note to Jeff. "You realize by now this is someone you know."

Budd shifted on his seat. "I know a lot of women, but I have to admit, I'm not familiar with one who matches her description."

Mike glanced briefly at Jeff Andrews and then sat back to cross his thick legs. "Let me explain why we're here, Budd. While you were in Chicago, Denise got another letter. She handed it over to me, and the lab picked up a nice set of prints. You'll be happy to know we identified your stalker."

About bloody time. He stole a glance at Denise.

She shrugged. "Yes, I told you while you stood at the window."

Nothing had registered this morning, like a fog followed him as he performed his morning rituals. Small wonder he found his way to the office without getting lost.

Jeff Andrews clicked both latches on his briefcase, opened it, and extracted a photo. He slid an eight-by-ten glossy across the desk. "Look familiar?"

Too familiar. The photo was of a plain-looking woman with straight brown hair and vacant eyes. She hadn't changed much over the years except for a few wrinkles around the mouth. "It's Anna Kincaid." Saying her name hurt, even after all she put him through.

"She escaped from the Nevada State Mental Hospital several months ago," Jeff continued. "She killed a night shift orderly who resembled her, took the employee's place, and then walked right out the door and into the woman's car. The identity of the victim was masked because of repeated blows to the head and face, making a facial ID impossible." He unbuttoned his suit jacket to ease the pull at his waist. "Since the death occurred in Kincaid's room, the powers that be assumed another inmate killed Anna in a rage, and confirmation of identity was delayed until the following morning. By that time, Kincaid had disappeared." Jeff grimaced while shifting the briefcase on his lap.

"You can use my desk." Budd pointed to the corner.

"No, it's okay. My grandson waffled my leg with a plastic bat. I've got a bruise the size of a melon." Jeff rubbed his left thigh. "Anyway, Kincaid made a series of carjacks along the way. She ditched one car then picked up another, usually by force, beating people in the process. Two victims are still in the hospital. We tracked her to Vegas, and Mike's hit confirmed her presence." He leaned forward, his gaze stern. "We think she's come to settle a score, Mr. Richardson."

What a friggin' nightmare. He had hoped she'd be locked away forever. He gritted his teeth and glared at the two men. "I've been getting threatening letters for the past month. Why hasn't she approached me? Even more important, why wasn't I notified of her escape? I'm the reason she wound up in the nut house." He fought the urge to slam his fist onto the desk. He'd only hurt his hand, and Anna had caused enough pain.

Jeff ran a hand through his mop. "A pure bureaucratic blunder, Mr. Richardson. They allowed Kincaid to work in the file room. She was never to be left alone, which I'm sure is exactly what happened, and obviously had a chance to change her records. The notification section was blank. In the staff's defense, they claimed she was a model inmate, always performing her tasks without complaint. In fact, they expressed doubts about whether her diagnosis was correct."

Mike uncrossed his legs and leaned forward. "LVPD was notified of Kincaid's escape, but the report went to street patrol, not the detective bureau. I saw the A.P.B. when her fingerprints popped up."

"With that said—" Jeff slid more photos across the desk.

Budd spread the snapshots for a better view. Most showed the assault on Teegan and the crowds in the terminal, all black and white and taken from a security camera's high angle. One picture caught his attention, so Budd picked it up and held it. The image showed him and Teegan walking through the terminal. She had her head turned away, but her lips revealed the faintest curl of a smile. She was, without question, the most beautiful woman to cross his path.

"Kincaid was the attacker," Jeff said. "The description matches. The photo you're holding, do you know her?"

He pried his gaze from the picture to look at Jeff. "Teegan Smith. We sat together on the plane." He slid the snap across the desk. "Why would Anna attack her? I go out with a woman at least twice a week. Nothing ever happens to them."

"Excuse me," Denise said while leaning forward. "Will someone show me what Anna Kincaid looks like so I can stop her from coming through the door?"

Mike smiled at her tone. "Sorry, Mrs. Callahan." He handed her the photo of Anna.

Denise gasped as her eyes widened and she tapped the image. "This woman was hanging around the lobby! Budd, you had to see her."

Since he'd found Anna's little notes on his windshield everywhere he went, he shrugged at the news. "I've been using the back entrance for the past two months, mainly to avoid paparazzi." He swiveled to face the two men. "What now?"

Jeff gathered the photos and placed them in his briefcase. "First of all, we need to discover how Kincaid knew your flight arrival time. Possibly she hung around the airport, but I don't see that happening without Security getting suspicious. She also needs food and shelter. She can't do either without money, and we don't have any robbery reports matching her description." He closed his briefcase, secured the latches, and placed the case by his chair.

"She has no known relatives," Budd said. "Her mother died a few years back, and the proceeds from the house funded Anna's care. I'm not sure if she still has friends."

Jeff rubbed a hand down the length of his tie. "Yes, we uncovered those facts and are working on any possible links to old classmates. In the meantime, I'm here to offer you twenty-four hour protection."

Just what he needed, no privacy whatsoever. "I'll think about it when I get back. I'm heading to my cabin tomorrow."

Jeff narrowed his gaze. "Where is this cabin?"

"In the desert hills."

A frown formed. "If she follows, then you'll be a sitting duck. Maybe you can delay your trip."

Oh, yeah, right, for a woman half my size. One side of his mouth lifted into a sneer. "You're asking me to put my life on hold when you have no idea what Anna will do. She's had ample opportunities to kill me if that's her plan. Besides, I take a rifle along."

"But can you use it? Are you capable of putting a bullet in your ex-girlfriend?" Jeff attempted to cross his legs, winced, and returned his foot to the floor. "Not many people traverse such a fine line, Budd. Squeezing a trigger isn't easy when death is the outcome." He rubbed his thigh.

"I can handle her."

Denise cleared her throat. "Don't you think they should know your cabin is smack in the middle of a dead zone for cell reception?"

Both men glared at Budd.

Oh, good grief. His gaze flicked upward before returning to the men. "Yes, it's true. No cell coverage for forty miles. I have a CB in my vehicle for emergencies."

"Our cars can monitor CB frequencies but not talk on them," Mike said. "For any crisis, we need instant communication."

"I'm not asking for your protection."

Mike held up a finger and leaned forward. "We want to catch her, Budd, before her death toll rises. To do that, we need to keep an eye on you." He sat back. "Give us a few days to install the radios."

Budd clenched his jaw. He hated when people told him what to do. He'd made it through life on his own and would continue until old and feeble, and no one, not even Mike and Jeff, could convince him to take protection. Like any good lawyer, he forced his voice toward a calmer tone. "In this modern age, the radios should be a digital input. What's the problem?"

Mike's mouth twisted to the side with a half-fast sneer. "I can't take my men off police frequencies to talk on CB. The tech guys have to set up the radios so they can jump between frequencies."

Budd shot to his feet and paced behind his chair. "Well, I'm not waiting around. If Anna follows me to the cabin, then so be it. I've known her since we were kids. I can talk to her."

"Don't be so obstinate," Denise argued. "They want to keep you alive."

Shooting her a quelling look, he held up a finger. "That's assuming she plans to kill me."

Jeff chuckled as he toyed with his tie. "I don't think she'll love you to death, Mr. Richardson."

The pacing stopped, and he shrugged. "Look, I didn't get where I am by being afraid. I'll compromise. I'll leave the day after tomorrow. I'll stay the whole weekend, but your men must have their own means of comfort. A self-contained trailer perhaps, or even a tent. They can camp out on the main road at the entrance to my property. Take it or leave it."

"How far to the cabin?" Mike asked after

exchanging looks with his partner.

"About a half mile."

"Really, Budd, that's—"

Jeff nudged Mike's arm. "We'll take it." He stood. "If you don't want protection, then at least hire extra security around the office building."

"I don't own the building, Jeff. I rent the entire fourth floor. Tell you what. I'll hire a guard for our office. We can position him by the elevators and stairwell. I don't want any of my employees to get hurt." He pointed to Denise. "Make a note." Nodding, she quickly scribbled in her notepad.

"Acceptable," Jeff said as he pushed to his feet.

Budd walked around the desk to shake their hands. "And don't forget to install a good antenna to get some range. Otherwise, you'll be talking to no one."

What had possessed Jeff and Mike to believe Budd Richardson was a man to cower from Anna Kincaid? The woman had caught him with his back turned once. Never again.

No sooner had the men exited when Joshua Feinberg and Edward Connors hurried through the door. Their names shared the placard for the Richardson, Feinberg, Connors law firm. Budd had recruited Josh first, an old friend from law school. He was the brilliant strategist in the courtroom, but he lacked any semblance of attractiveness. He kept his wiry black hair trimmed short along with a black beard to hide the acne scars from his youth. His worst shortcoming was his eyesight. Normally a contact lens man, today, he wore his bottle glasses with the heavy black frames. They made his dark eyes look like round balls behind the thick lenses.

Denise slipped to the edge of her seat as if to stand, but Budd gestured with an open palm for her to wait. He circled his desk to retake his seat as Josh and Ed approached. With a finger, Budd motioned toward Josh's eyes. "Where're your contacts?"

Josh nudged the frame up his nose. "The wind blew sand in my face and a grain got under my contact. I scratched half my eyeball before running to the bathroom for a rinse. Hurts like the dickens."

"Not enough to stop his antics in the courtroom," Ed said with a grin.

Ed Connors, in contrast, was a Budd Richardson wannabe. Blond and good-looking, he wowed women jurors until they agreed to everything he said. Josh emphasized facts, but Ed flirted. He had aspirations to become the next Vegas' Most Eligible…if a social disease didn't get to him first.

"Weren't those cops?" Both frowning men spoke in unison.

"They were here about my stalker." Budd explained in detail as the men flopped into chairs.

"I remember Anna," Ed said. "She was plain, definitely not the type we see on your arm these days. Do you remember her, Josh?"

Josh rubbed his beard. "Vaguely. Small, right? Your Anna-swap was around the time Sue filed for divorce."

Those weren't happy days for Josh. Still in law school, he had asked his wife to wait for children until he graduated. She quit the pill and surprised him. They divorced six years later because of financial difficulties.

"What do the cops have up their sleeve?" Josh asked.

Budd glanced at both men. One of these days, he'd get the shock of his life to hear genuine concern instead of two men seeking juicy gossip. "They want me to have a bodyguard."

Ed chuckled. "That's a date killer. Did you agree?"

"It's Anna." Budd shot him a glare. "I'm afraid of neither her nor what she has planned." He drummed his fingers on the desk. "I will hire a guard to protect the employees, however. Now, gentlemen, I hate to rush you out, but I need to get some work done with my assistant over here."

Budd stared at the open office door after they left. Anna. Of all the women who might have been stalking him. They'd had some good times together before insanity hit.

"You're being unreasonable again," Denise said. "I know I talked you into going to the cabin, but I spoke before we heard about this escaped nut. Who's Anna Kincaid?"

"A bad memory." The same sad, empty feeling settled in his gut whenever his life with Anna surfaced. Not a year passed without an old school chum asking about her, and he hadn't a clue what to say. As for Denise, his friend and confidante as well as assistant, she deserved to know. He swiveled in his chair to face her. "We grew up together. Same neighborhood, same schools. We dated off and on through high school and after. The yearbook committee labeled us as most likely to marry, and she took it to heart." He swiveled toward the window to stare at the clear, blue sky. "When Anna realized I had no intention of marrying her, she put a knife in my back."

Denise gasped. "You never told me!"

He turned back and waved aside the comment. "Anna was before your time. She was convicted and locked away on an insanity plea."

"If she aimed to kill you once, she'll try again. Why don't you want protection?"

"I won't give up what little privacy I have. Now that I know who's following me, I'll look over my shoulder more often."

Denise rubbed the bridge of her nose before meeting his gaze. "I know the cabin is your sanctuary, Budd, but it's isolated. Even the agents parked at the end of the road will be too far if she shows up from another direction." She held out an open palm while one eyebrow lifted. "Maybe you'll consider the satellite service we talked about."

The cabin was a long way from being finished to worry about a permanent means of communication. He loved the solitude it offered, the feel of the breeze coming through the valley, the awesome silence with no traffic or planes. The whole atmosphere created a happy threesome—him, his dog, and nature.

But the news caused his jaw to tighten to the point of discomfort. If he wasn't careful, he could crack a few dental caps.

Denise stood. "Anything more before I go?"

"Huh—oh, no, Denise, nothing else."

Except maybe a blood pressure pill or a good stiff drink. Anna Kincaid was back in his life, and for five years, he had put her out of his mind. Neither had made any effort to correspond because prior to the knife attack, she'd made his life a living hell, always following like a puppy or appearing at his door at the worst possible time. He was older now with a different mindset and could handle her better, convince her to return to the mental institution and continue her therapy.

In the meantime, he had a meeting to attend and a reputation to salvage with one Teegan Smith.

Chapter Four

Teegan Smith entered the Smith Tool Company fighting a yawn. Somehow, she'd driven through the late-morning traffic without a crash since she squinted more from sleepiness than sunlight. Employees passed with smiles and hellos, some from the office, others from the factory. She had known their names once. Right now, her brain was caffeine deficient. She couldn't quite shake the jet lag.

Yeah, some excuse. A good night's sleep would do wonders, but curiosity had gotten the better of her, and she flipped on the computer when she should have gone to bed. She stayed glued to the chair, researching this pompous ass who was gorgeously handsome, the man who made her breathless and sweaty, all within the short span of eye contact. The hours passed unnoticed until the screen became a blur. When she hit the bed, she envisioned every known obscene sexual position invented by the human race. Him on top. Her on top. Biting. Tasting. A sexual feast. Even now, she shuddered at the tempting visions.

Budd Richardson's entire life history was available for preview on the web. He had become Vegas' classic poor-boy-makes-good story, detailed for any writer to produce a movie-of-the-week. The newspapers had plastered the Most Eligible Bachelor label on him, even though he declared his desire to remain unhitched.

Every snapshot was the same with a glamorous actress/showgirl hanging on his arm like their career depended on the photo shoot. They posed for the cameras with flirty smiles and tilts of the head, sticking out their chests to show the world their boobs while he scowled like an old sourpuss.

After watching dozens of taped interviews, Teegan understood his you-should-know-me speech. Budd had earned the local legal expert honor, the go-to man for answers. The public adored him, and the paparazzi fueled their ravenous appetite with covert shots. Small wonder the man had attracted a stalker. The bane of any public figure.

"Dr. Smith, you're back!"

Teegan stopped in front of her assistant's desk, plunked her briefcase on the corner, and leaned against it like the case had the strength to hold her upright. She was in no mood to do any work and looking at perky little Claudia hadn't helped matters. With an effort, she stifled another yawn.

The little blonde leaned back in her chair, all smiles. "When did you fly in?"

"Yesterday. Give me ten minutes before you come in for the lowdown." She sounded all western after only two months' time. If she wasn't careful, she might shout a yee-haw.

Teegan strolled into her office, thinking how nice a bed would feel right about now. Nothing special. A bed with a pillow. Maybe two pillows. Cozy blankets for an air conditioner on full blast. Maybe an extension to the closet…

Oh, fish sticks. She tossed the briefcase onto the desk, ignored the mound of papers waiting for her attention, and turned to stare out the window.

The desert and the mountains. A combination that never failed to put a catch in her throat. Forbidden, yet fascinating. Barren, yet picturesque. The desert surrounded the industrial park while the mountains created a gorgeous backdrop off in the distance. Varying shades of brown and gray colored the landscape with intermingling pieces of green. A majestic sight.

She hadn't expected to fall in love with the southwest so quickly. Vegas, in her mind, was a town of bright lights and gambling, not wide-open spaces and breathtaking scenery. The company built the new plant on the edge of town in an area designated for industrial development. Theirs was the third building in an area meant for eight, all on flat open desert with an asphalt highway running through for the inevitable big delivery trucks. The view from her window was a spectacular example of untouched nature with the desert rising into cloud-catching mountain peaks. With any luck, she'd enjoy the scene for the duration of her stay before a yet-unknown company built a monstrosity behind them to block everything but the tips of the mountains. Then, they'd probably paint the walls purple so she'd vomit every time she glanced out the window.

Could she leave such magnificence at the completion of her job? And what about the change of seasons? What were they like? Hot to hotter? Granted, the dismal loneliness overwhelmed her at times. She'd never been away from her family so long—her two brothers and their wives, one cute-as-a-button nephew—and of course, her parents. Her friends were back east, too. She knew no one in Vegas except employees. If she dragged her butt out of the office and socialized a little, met new people, dated—all normal activities for a thirty-one year old—she'd conquer the loneliness. Her last date was when? Six or seven months ago? Maybe longer. Her vagina wouldn't know what hit it.

All Dad's fault. Her father had yanked her out of the lab to become a desk jockey. From a comfort zone of test tubes and Bunsen burners to…oh, all right, another comfort zone of time tables and challenges. Once the plant went online and her workload lessened, she'd have the opportunity to explore more social possibilities…someday…maybe.

A soft tap on the door interrupted.

Claudia stuck in her head. "Ready for me now?"

Ten minutes so soon? "Not really, but come in anyway." Teegan settled into her large leather chair and yawned.

Claudia took a seat opposite the desk and flipped through a notebook, reading page after page. She relayed the progress in the factory, the new hires, and the supplies trickling in.

Important stuff a chief operating officer should know. Teegan watched Claudia's mouth move but absorbed nothing. Her mind drifted to the dreamboat from the plane, the man who had every female in Vegas panting. Teegan blamed her rambling thoughts on Claudia's dangling blue earrings that shook with every head movement. They resembled Budd's sky-blue eyes. "Pull the paperwork for this place, Claudia."

Claudia's small mouth fell open. "You talking about the deed? The legal department in Philly has it."

That was true. *Silly me.*

"Shall I call them? They can fax a copy."

"No, let it be. I don't know why I asked in the first place." She hadn't screwed her brain in right this morning. So what if Budd was her father's Vegas liaison? Dad had needed an expert to deal with the shenanigans of politicians who wanted jobs but not the factory. If she hadn't been in the middle of a Russian drilling project, calculating the strength for a drill bit to tunnel through two miles of rock, she'd have been with her father and met Budd.

And brushed him off sooner.

"That's it for now." Claudia closed her notebook and placed it on her lap. "Aside from the meeting at two this afternoon, your schedule is clear." She tilted her head. "You look tired, Dr. Smith."

And I feel like shit. "I shouldn't be tired at all after my mini-vacation." She yawned, raising a hand to cover it. "Is Bill here?"

"Yes, ma'am. He said to call when you head to the meeting."

"Good. I'll let him handle the tour of the factory. My synaptic waves aren't connecting. Have you ordered the refreshments?"

"Everything's arranged."

"Okay then. That's it."

The rest of the day involved paperwork, a ton of it. A few days away from her desk and her inbox grew a mountain of white.

As the two o'clock hour approached, Bill Campbell, the general manager, poked in his head. "The vultures are gathering."

His oblong face had always struck her as unusually long, but he was the nicest man she'd ever met. "Come

45

in, Bill. How's the plant look?"

"Spotless." He stepped inside. "I'm glad they're inspecting us before we get started. Makes for a better impression." He fussed with his tie. "The mayor and several councilmen showed up, and I won't be surprised if a state senator wanders in. Several are campaigning for re-election, you know."

"That's why you're here, Bill. I don't have the patience to deal with them." An inherited trait from her father. Luckily, Bill Campbell had the perfect temperament. He was a good family man with strong values, six kids, three dogs, ten chickens, and one goat. If anyone could handle bureaucrats and the crap they threw, Bill was the man. "Give me five minutes to freshen up, and we'll head in together."

Chapter Five

Budd's gaze wandered around the conference room of the Smith Tool Company, sweeping over the carpet, the furniture, and lighting as if searching for a flaw. The room had none of the opulence usually found in a multi-million dollar business. No sparkling gold hardware on the double doors, no famous paintings on the walls, or expensive portraits of board members. Instead, several photos of young Irish dancers hung, along with Highlanders playing bagpipes. *An odd selection.*

Then again, Frank Smith wasn't like most millionaires. The man had refused caviar because it stuck in his teeth, and he hated the taste of wine. A fat burger with a beer kept him happy along with a Little League ball game and plenty of hot dogs. An ordinary man living with ordinary likes and dislikes. How many men passed the quality onto their children with so much money up for grabs?

None I know.

In college, the rich bitches had flashed their diamonds like a carrot on a stick, assuming he would trail behind them with a drooling tongue. Many men had obliged only to have their egos crushed like bugs.

Budd Richardson wasn't one of them. Anna Kincaid had filled his time, and they dated for many years. He'd felt comfortable with Anna, a woman from

47

his neck of the desert. They had some fun times, too, until their easy friendship turned into something akin to being stuck like glue. She obsessed over every minute of his time, what he was doing, who he was with until he felt smothered. They argued constantly, and she accused him of cheating when he threw his client confidentiality clause into her face. Nothing he said or did made a difference, and he called it quits. She, of course, had other plans.

While he waited like everyone else for the queen bee to arrive, he sipped from a water bottle to squelch the acid overload rumbling in his stomach. *I can't be nervous, right? I'm a been-around-the-block guy who knows the route.* More likely, his nervousness was from the aggravation of sitting twiddling his thumbs when he had so much work waiting on his desk.

All right, I'll admit it. I'm nervous, and I shouldn't be. So what if she hates my guts?

For some reason, her acceptance of him mattered, and he had no idea why.

"Yo, Budd!"

He had taken a seat toward the back, hoping to blend into the oval conference table, but his face was too familiar. Everyone knew him. Those who didn't were quickly introduced but followed their own agenda and wandered off. A councilman approached to gab about his re-election prospects, a subject in which Budd had no interest because the man was doing a lousy job. The mayor sucked up to the environmental president, making promises he had no intention of keeping. A committeeman with a pendant for booze and loose women asked for legal advice. Budd gave him the address of a clinic in Henderson that specialized in

STD, a discreet location shared with him by many wealthy men with the disease. Women gathered in circles, whispering among themselves while glancing his way. *Drawing straws, no doubt, to see who should approach after the conference.*

Same old, same old.

A perky blonde hurried through the door, carrying a tray of sandwiches. She placed it on a cloth-covered side table alongside the coffee machine and an array of sweets.

Then she turned to the crowd with a practiced smile. "Ladies and gentlemen, Dr. Smith said to grab what you want. The tour won't take long, but she doesn't want anyone to pass out from hunger."

Ha, ha. Very funny. The crowd hit the table like vultures.

Budd checked his watch. *Why am I sitting here? I don't need redemption.* So what if she's Frank Smith's daughter?

No, the FBI visit had caused his sour mood. Jeff Andrews had this cockamamie idea about Anna out to kill him. *What a crock of shit.* She'd left notes on his vehicle everywhere so she obviously followed his movements. If she'd planned to kill him, what was she waiting for? An invitation?

I should have listened to Denise and sent an associate.

The side door to the conference room opened. Teegan Smith stepped through wearing an impeccable lavender suit which emphasized her lovely curves. Even in high heels, she glided across the floor with the same fluid movement, crossing the room as if she floated on a cloud. The woman was so full of grace he wanted to genuflect.

She headed to the podium and smiled at the crowd. "Thank you for coming. If you will, please take a seat." Her gaze scanned the many faces and spotted him. One eyebrow arched, and she winked.

The woman was stunning. If she wrapped herself in a burlap bag, she'd still stop a bus. Her face alone caught a man's attention with its soft angles and flawless skin. Couple it with the sparkling teal marbles and beautiful smile, and the woman took a man's breath away. Like now. *Admit it. Deep down, I couldn't stay away.* He had to see her again, even if she shunned him. The woman consumed his thoughts, and that, more than anything, created an insatiable curiosity.

"Good afternoon, ladies and gentlemen. I am Dr. Teegan Smith, the chief operating officer of this facility. This gentleman next to me is Bill Campbell, our general manager. He will be your tour guide and the one to whom you should direct your questions. I'm here to bore you with a little history of the Smith Tool Company."

A man next to her? Well, golly gee. The woman commanded the attention of the room, and the man behind her was nothing but a blurred shadow.

Bill Campbell resembled a man with more legs than body, tall and skinny with a shirt collar dangling like a cow's neck, making his tie resemble a noose. He wore a wedding band on long, thin fingers, which for some reason was a wonderful sight.

Teegan spoke with a daughter's pride of the accomplishments of her father, the grandson of poor Irish immigrants. Budd's ears clicked into standby since his concentration centered on the woman at the podium.

The word sophistication came to mind. She was polished with the right touch of makeup and jewelry complementing the form-fitted business suit. No huge rocks covered her fingers, and no glittering diamonds circled her neck. Instead, a small pearl hung on a gold chain, drawing his gaze to the open collar of her shirt and the cleavage so conspicuously hidden. A gold-colored watch covered her wrist, sparkling with diamonds, dressier than the plain silver watch she'd worn on the plane. Her voice, smooth and seductive, mesmerized the crowd, and only when she had shifted away from the podium was the spell broken.

"That's all for now. I'll be here when you return should you have questions." She waved the tall man forward. "I'm sure Bill will give you an exceptional tour."

The crowd chattered as they filed from the room.

Budd stayed in his seat, watching Teegan. She matched the gaze with the faintest trace of a smile. When the last person disappeared, he stood. "How's the shoulder?"

"A minor bruise. No biggie." She stepped around the table. "I take it you're the lawyer for the group? Shouldn't you be with them?" She tilted her head toward the doorway.

He strolled toward her. "They can ask questions when they return. I almost didn't come since I made a complete ass of myself on the plane."

"That you did." She headed for the food table. "Have you eaten yet? I missed lunch, and I'm starving."

She loaded a plate with half sandwiches, potato salad, and pickles before taking a bite of one sandwich and pouring a cup of coffee. She glanced his way, one side of her mouth bulging. "Don't let me eat alone, Mr. Richardson. Otherwise, I'll go and hide in my office."

He chuckled as he followed with sandwiches and coffee to the conference table. He wasn't hungry, but for the sake of keeping her in the room, he'd stuff a horse down his throat. He sat in the chair next to her. "Who are you, Teegan Smith?"

She glanced up with a cocked brow, both cheeks bulging like a chipmunk. "What do you mean?"

"You're not like any woman I've met. You have money but don't act like it. On the plane, you were so casual I swore up and down you didn't belong in first class. Yet, here you sit, every image the successful businesswoman. Which one are you?"

"Neither." She wiped her mouth. "I belong in a white lab coat with a pencil stuck behind my ear." She swallowed her food with a swig of coffee. "I'm not a highfalutin rich-bitch, if that's what you're asking."

"I had you pegged as a showgirl."

"Yes, I know, which, I might add, I considered a real compliment." She forked some of the potato salad into her mouth and, after a few quick chews, tilted her head and gave a crisp nod. "Not bad."

An ordinary woman bred from an ordinary man. Both wealthy in their own right. Neither flaunting it. Denise was right—Teegan Smith was like her father. Who would have thought he'd meet such a creature? He bit into his sandwich. "Your opinion of me can't be very high."

She sipped her coffee before responding. "It isn't. I hate snobs, Mr. Richardson. I grew up with enough of them." After dabbing a napkin over her lips, she stood. "I'm getting another sandwich. Want any?"

A woman who liked to eat. He never believed he'd meet *that* type of creature either. He held up an open palm. "I've got enough." He waited for her return and stared at the pile of half sandwiches on her plate. "Most women I know eat like birds. They order expensive meals and let the food sit untouched. Irks the hell out of me."

"Well, I love food. All kinds. I'm happy my metabolism is keeping up. Otherwise, I'd be big as a house." She opened a sandwich to inspect the inside and grimaced. "Oh, dear. I picked up a tuna and cheese, much too fishy. I don't want the aftermath on my breath." She set it aside.

He smiled at the casualness of the statement. He didn't want the odor on her breath either. "You look comfortable at the podium. I'd say you're a natural for a boardroom."

Frowning, she held up a warning finger. "Don't tell my father, please. I'd like to make this COO stint short. For the record, I'm comfortable at the podium only because I give lectures around the world."

"Yes, I know. I looked you up online."

Her gaze twinkled. "I did the same with you."

Well, what do you know? He had a shot with this woman after all. His confidence soared. "I'm flattered…and surprised."

She bit into a pickle. "I figured you had a reason for acting so high and mighty." She chewed. "Vegas's Most Eligible Bachelor. Quite a label."

"Hmmpf." He tore into his sandwich.

She stopped chewing. "This is a touchy subject for you, isn't it?"

He stuffed the remainder of the sandwich into his

mouth, chewed but swallowed most of it whole. He surprised himself by not choking to death. "A female reporter plastered the label on me a few years ago. I was already well known in the city, but overnight, my privacy disappeared. Paparazzi follow me like leeches, and because of the constant coverage, women call me for dates. They want to be seen out and about for publicity. The only peace I get these days is when I head to my cabin." He gulped the last of his coffee.

"Maybe you should get married."

He nearly sprayed the contents of his mouth all over the table. Swallowing, he stared with widened eyes. "What?"

"You heard me. Get married. The label will no longer apply, and people will lose interest. In order for the reporters and paparazzi to get their scoops, they'll need another eligible bachelor to take your place." Setting down the sandwich, she sat back and laughed. "You should see your face! Is marriage such a cardinal sin?"

Taking a deep breath, he shook himself. "You took me by surprise, that's all." He wiped his mouth with a napkin and pushed aside his plate. "I have no intention of getting married. I tell my dates straight up so they won't get any ideas."

"Then you like the notoriety more than you admit."

He shook his head while wagging a finger. "Not necessarily. Bachelorhood has its advantages. I'm not tied down with one particular person."

She inspected another sandwich. "In other words, you change partners like you change bed sheets."

His gaze narrowed. She'd made it sound perverse. Most men applauded his lifestyle. He leaned toward her to a make a point. "Women usually push for marriage."

"That's because women aren't into one-night stands. They like stability rather than uncertainty, but I understand your reasoning. The male sex instinct is primitive in nature, the-impregnate-the-herd mentality. The exact reason females in the animal kingdom raise their offspring alone."

Good heavens, how true! Her tone wasn't a bit sarcastic. More likely, she spoke as the brainy scientist. He peered at her. "Are you always this logical?"

"I can be worse." She wiped her mouth. "I have to ask one question, however. I'm sure my father talked about me. After you found out I worked for the Smith Tool Company, why didn't you ask if I was his daughter?"

"Because you look nothing like your father. And before you say anything else, he showed me a picture of your mother. You don't look anything like her either."

A faint lopsided grin curled her lip. "Explanation accepted. My two brothers look like my father, but I resemble a great-aunt on my mother's side. This aunt was the only other mathematical genius in the family. I inherited her genes." She gulped half her coffee and then stared into the cup. "This stuff isn't strong enough today. I can't quite shake the jet lag." With the back of her hand, she hid a yawn.

"You should be used to flying if you travel around the world. Your fear's ridiculous, too."

"What can I say? I like Irish whiskey." She snickered into her coffee cup.

He wasn't fooled for a second. Her fear was real. She had white-knuckled the arm rests on the plane's landing. "Maybe you need some time off."

As she chewed, she held up a finger. "I just spent four days in Philly, cut short, I might add, because of this meeting. I have to go through the whole process again with the EPA once we go online. Probably next month."

"Excellent! Then you have time for a trip to my cabin. I'm leaving day after tomorrow for the weekend."

Her sandwich paused midway to her mouth. "You're jumping the gun here, counselor. We don't know each other well enough."

"We'll remedy our situation at the cabin. We'll be alone—you, me, and my dog."

Her mouth fell open. "Are you crazy?"

"Yes, probably." He chuckled at the wide-eyed look on her face. "The cabin isn't finished yet, but the exterior is done. Most of the remaining work involves the interior. I estimate a couple more months to finish, depending how often I get out there." He brushed a crumb from her cheek. The gesture was light and quick, but the feel of her skin sent a shiver of pleasure straight to his groin. She gave no reaction since the shock of his offer hadn't worn off. "The cabin's livable. Bathroom and kitchen are done. I'm working on the secondary bedrooms. Think you can help me with wallboard?"

She blinked and leaned back.

"You'll be the first woman I'm taking to my cabin. I'm hoping you won't blab its location to the media."

Again, she blinked, mouth ajar.

Budd broke into laughter. He hadn't been charmed by a woman in a long time. "You're nothing like I expected, Dr. Smith."

She snapped her mouth shut. "I'm used to bold

propositions, but you've earned a spot at the top of the list."

"Most women would jump at my offer." He flashed a grin.

"Most women don't think you have a screw loose. And call me Teegan."

"All right, Teegan. I can see you'll take some work." He leaned forward and urged her to do the same. A whiff of her perfume toyed with his senses, the same subtle scent from the plane. "I should reveal a few things before you commit to a visit. I have only one bed, but a full-size sofa sits in the living room. The cabin is in an isolated location in the desert. No one around for miles. It's also a dead zone for cell coverage. If you need a working phone because of your position, then you're out of luck. For emergencies, I have a CB in my SUV."

He took both her hands in his. Like her arms, they showed strength with a buildup of muscle on the thumb side, not the pampered type so common for a woman of wealth. Her skin also revealed tiny scars. He rubbed his thumbs over them and cocked a brow in question.

"One can't be a chemist without breaking some glass," she said with a shrug.

This was her one flaw. Otherwise, the woman personified perfection. He squeezed her hands. "Another thing, Teegan. I've had a woman stalking me, the same one who attacked you at the airport. She's a woman I dated a long time ago. LVPD and the FBI are both working the case."

Her hands slipped out of his as her eyebrows tightened toward the bridge of her nose. "FBI? Why?"

"She killed an orderly to escape the mental

hospital." He shouldn't have made it sound as if Anna was on the ten most wanted list. If he had his brain screwed in right, he shouldn't have mentioned it at all. He leaned back with a heavy sigh. "She has always been under the assumption I promised marriage."

Teegan crunched on a pickle while giving him a steady gaze. "A woman doesn't assume such a move unless you gave probable cause."

Lawyer speak. *Impressive*. "I didn't. She was crazy then, and she's crazy now. She took the rejection hard by putting a knife in my back."

"Ouch." She ran a finger along the rim of her cup, her gaze distant.

An odd reaction. Most women would be all over him with sympathy, begging for details. Teegan's demeanor was *too* calm, a woman unfazed by his near-death experience. He'd seen the response many times in the courtroom, the result of newscasts inundating viewers with countless clips of violence, but this was his personal story. He'd expected a slight teary-eyed look.

After several long seconds, she glanced up. "The cops have you under surveillance?"

"Yes." He grabbed her cup and his own and walked to the side table. "I refused their bodyguard offer, but I have no choice about them following me." He refilled their cups and returned to his chair. "I noticed you drink your coffee black. So do I." He placed her cup on the table.

"Um, Mr. Richardson—"

"Budd."

She crossed her legs.

Whether intentionally or subconsciously, he didn't

care. They were as gorgeous as the rest of her, long and slender with muscled calves.

"My father will be upset if I get caught in some crossfire."

"Yes, I know. I shouldn't have asked you." Nor could he resist. The chances of Anna going after Teegan were a million to one...well, maybe a hundred to one.

"You shouldn't go to an isolated cabin with a loon on your tail, Budd. Why haven't the Feds talked you out of the trip?"

He sipped his coffee. "We compromised. That's why I'm leaving the day after tomorrow. And I've one more point for you to consider, Teegan. I have a Rottweiler who doesn't take easily to the women I bring home."

Her gaze narrowed. "You're tossing me an awful lot of variables, Budd Richardson, mostly negative. If your stalker doesn't kill me in a blind rage, then your dog might take off my leg. Is that what you're saying?"

"Yeah, I guess I didn't think things through." Hormones before common sense. *She must think I'm as loony as Anna.* He ran a hand through his hair then glanced at her with a grin. "You look like a woman who doesn't frighten easily."

"One can't work around heavy metals and be willy-nilly." She fingered her cup while studying him. "Let me get this straight. You're asking me to your cabin to help with wallboard and not for a weekend of wild sexual intercourse, correct?"

"Both if you're up to it."

Her eyebrows arched. "I appreciate your honesty. However, your ex-girlfriend's jealousy level is extreme.

What would she do if she found us together in your cabin?"

"We'll probably die."

She burst into laughter, uncrossed her legs, and tilted forward. "Tell you what. If you survive your excursion with all limbs attached, give me a call." She lifted the pen protruding from his shirt pocket and wrote her cell number on a napkin.

Returning the gesture, he wrote on the back of his business card before replacing the pen in his pocket. He extended the card. "Office number on the front, cell number on the back, in case you change your mind. And one last important detail before the tour group returns." He took her chin and guided her lips to his own. He'd caught the surprised opening of her mouth and savored the softness boasting of coffee with a hint of mayo. He probed for more.

At first, she hesitated but soon countered with a probe of her own.

He separated from her lips while brushing a finger across her cheek. "Damn, Teegan, you taste good."

She responded with a subtle bite of his lower lip. "You're tasting ham and cheese on rye."

The woman gave him chills from a simple kiss. He shuddered at the possibility of a full assault. *I can only hope.*

"How do you know I'm not seeing another man?" she whispered, her brows furrowed.

"I don't. So, come clean. Are you seeing anyone?"

"No."

"Would you like to see me?"

"I think you already know the answer to the question."

Chapter Six

The conference had ended without a hitch. All questions were answered, no problems surfaced. Everyone was pleased as they departed back to their normal routines.

Teegan relaxed at her desk with Budd's business card rotating in her hand. His kiss had ignited an inferno in her gut that had yet to fade. Why? She'd dated dozens of good-looking men. Their kisses were nice but hardly worth a fire.

Maybe the jalapeño peppers had caused it. She'd thrown one too many on a ham sandwich, but hey, they were good, roasted to perfection. The heat woke her up, and she hadn't yawned since. Unless the kiss got her blood rolling. *Oh, yeah.* Images of mind-boggling sex in an isolated cabin with a handsome dude activated juices not easily squelched.

A soft tap sounded on the door before Claudia stepped inside. "Two gentlemen to see you, Dr. Smith. Mr. Jeff Andrews said to mention his name."

"Jeff?" *Well, this is a surprise.* "Send him in, Claudia." Her mind raced through the newspaper headlines of the past few weeks. Counterfeit casino chips discovered at the annual poker tournament? A cut-and-dry case if she remembered. How about the woman who had fallen from the top floor of a parking garage? *Pushed maybe*? How about Budd's case with his stalker slash ex-girlfriend? That seemed a trifle cut-and-dry, too. She stood as the two men entered her office.

The man she knew from so long ago appeared as frazzled as ever. His hair was grayer, his face a tad more wrinkled, but his gray eyes were as sharp as the day they'd met. Teegan hurried around her desk. "I haven't seen you in ages." She wrapped her arms around him and squeezed. "How's your wife?"

He kissed her cheek. "Patient considering we moved twice in the past five years. This is Detective Sergeant Mike Reeves from LVPD."

Whoa! A hunky man took her hand. His chest was so broad she wanted to rip open his shirt to see if his bulletproof vest was underneath. *I'd better get out and start dating if Budd and Reeves are typical Vegas men.* Teegan motioned toward the two chairs in front of her desk. "When did you leave D.C., Jeff?"

The two men unbuttoned their suit jackets as they eased onto the seats.

"A while back," Jeff said. "I'm regional director for this area."

"Congratulations." She settled in her chair and swiveled to face them. "The FBI regional director doesn't leave his office unless he has a good reason. What's up?"

He opened his briefcase and slid a photo across the desk.

The photo was of her and Budd walking through the airport terminal. She held the photo and marveled at the clarity.

"You make a nice couple."

Jeff flashed his notorious sissy-ass grin, the one

with the I-know-something-you-don't-know smirk. She eyed him through narrowed lids. "You're up to something. Why don't I trust you?"

As he shuffled papers within his briefcase, Jeff chuckled. "Well, I do have this seedy reputation."

"Uh-huh. Budd just left here."

"Yes, we know. He's under surveillance." His expression now sober, he slid another photo across the desk. "That woman is after him. Her name is Anna Kincaid. She's the one who attacked you."

Teegan replaced the first photo with the second and studied it. An automaton stared back. No smile, brown eyes showing an emotionless void, straight brown hair looking like straw. "Budd told me she killed an orderly to escape."

"That's correct. She made a series of carjacks to reach Vegas. Several people ended up in the hospital, two were critical." He scratched his ear, his gaze downcast. "I received word about an hour ago that one victim has died. Those make two murders to pin on her head." He looked up. "I'm afraid we'll have more before the case is resolved." He took back the photos.

Mike raised a staying hand. "You might want to leave Anna's with her."

Teegan shook her head. "It's not necessary." She paused for only a second. "Although, I'd like to keep the other one."

Jeff flashed his grin again and slid the photo across the desk. "Something about you two, wouldn't you say?"

Budd's face was the surprise. As they walked, he watched her, lips slightly parted, gaze intense, his attention riveted while she stared off to the side, oblivious. She'd seen the look before…when a man knew her name. So many times, men had fallen at her feet when images of money and good times danced in their heads. She handled them better than the ones frightened by her high IQ. Consequently, serious relationships never developed beyond two people having a night out. But at the time, Budd hadn't a clue who she was, and her heart skipped a few beats to see his interested expression.

"That snap brought us here, Teegan." Jeff closed his briefcase and placed it on the floor. "Catching you and Richardson together was a stroke of luck." He leaned forward, his hand on one knee, gaze alert.

She recognized the look but would be damned to acknowledge it.

"Richardson wants to go to his cabin the day after tomorrow, Teegan. It's located smack in the middle of a dead zone."

"Yes, he told me." She turned to Mike and raised an eyebrow. "Do you have a lot of dead zones out here?"

"Too many," he answered. "Mostly in the desert areas where population is scarce. Our cops do better with two-way radios rather than cell phones, but Budd has a CB. Those frequencies are too low for our standard equipment."

"Below twenty-seven megahertz, if I remember."

Jeff nudged Mike's arm. "Didn't I tell you? Photographic memory." He tapped his forehead. "She sees something, and it's in her brain forever."

Yeah, even a useless fact like CB frequencies. "It's a curse," she told Mike with a half-hearted shrug.

"Anyway"—Jeff continued—"Budd's allowing us

one day to install CBs in our vehicles."

Teegan picked up her pen and fiddled it between her fingers. "How about giving him a two-way cop radio? It would save a lot of time and effort."

Mike shook his head. "Cop radios operate on a repeater system. Towers are installed throughout the county along major roads, and they receive a signal from the police car's antenna. Budd's area is totally desolate, no phone or electric lines, no cell towers, nothing—probably the most desolate in the entire tri-county area. A CB is the best option because its antenna has a greater range. Only a few hours are needed to program the cars with the CB frequencies and install a bigger antenna, but we used the excuse to keep Budd in town."

"A satellite phone then. I understand several companies serve the area."

"A satellite phone would take too long to set up and too expensive for such a short period of time," Jeff answered. "We have the CBs in the storeroom, quick to grab and install." He tugged on his ear. "Our big dilemma is Richardson won't let the agents near the cabin. He wants them to remain down on the road."

"Oh." She pursed her lips. *A foolish move, indeed.*

"We took a preliminary look at the area." Mike opened a leather folio and shuffled through papers. "A fly-by to study the terrain. He's as isolated as he said. Kincaid can trek in from any direction." He handed her several aerial photos from different altitudes.

Teegan spread them on the desk. Budd had built his log cabin in the middle of nowhere with mountains to the rear and desert stretching right and left. The front faced off-set to the main road with a large barn nearby, and next to it stood a stainless steel water tower. Budd had created the perfect getaway, a place to leave the city behind and enjoy the peacefulness of his surroundings. She pointed to a rectangular box. "Is this a generator?"

"Yes. He has to create his own electricity. Propane powers it."

She studied the photos. "The cabin's roughly nine hundred meters from the main road."

Mike's mouth fell open. "How did you calculate so quickly?"

"Mathematical genius," Jeff said with a wink. "She can tell you your shoe size."

Both men looked at her, eyebrows raised.

"Thirteen." She hid a smile.

Mike slapped his mouth shut. "Wow, and yes, the drive is a half mile long."

Jeff snickered and nudged Mike's arm. "Believe me now?"

Obviously, Jeff and Mike had some sort of debate going about her abilities. She shot Jeff an irritated glare.

Jeff wiped the grin off his face and cleared his throat. "Look, Teegan. Budd won't let the agents stay in the barn. He wants them down on the road, which makes for ineffective surveillance. This strategy will get him killed."

"What do you expect me to do?"

"Delay him. Keep him here in town. We'll stand a better chance of catching Kincaid with a lot more eyes on him and his movements. We don't know how she discovered Budd's plane arrival time, but we're working on it. If she knows where his cabin is, she could be waiting."

Muscles tensing, Teegan chewed her inner lip. "None of this sounds right, Jeff. Do you know what Anna plans to do with Budd?"

Both men exchanged glances.

Mike tugged on his suit jacket to move the edge away from his hips. "We can only assume she wants to finish what she started years ago when she pierced a knife into his back."

"She'd have done it by now, don't you think?" She dropped the pen and drummed her fingers on the desk. "Budd's told me briefly about the knifing, but what's his history with her?"

"High school sweethearts, sporadic dating throughout his college days."

"Then, she has something special planned." Leaning back and gazing toward the closed door, she flattened her lips. "Budd should realize this. Yet, he refuses protection. Why?"

Jeff tugged on his ear. "We've considered several possibilities. According to Mike, Budd has refused personal protection from the beginning when the letters started. The fact the stalker is Kincaid hasn't changed his mind. I'm hoping you'll uncover his reasoning."

Fat chance on that. "You know, Jeff, you keep tugging on your ear, and you'll look like an elephant one day."

Squirming in his chair, he squinted. "My lobes should be down to my knees by now. Don't change the subject."

He caught that, huh? She chuckled softly. "Your best bet is to set a trap to lure Anna into the open." She mentally analyzed several scenarios before she caught the glint in Jeff's gray eyes. *Sneaky little devil.* She peered through one eye. "You're using me to draw out Anna. She'll recognize me from the airport and fly into a rage. In other words, I'm the bait to lure her into the open. Is that your plan?"

He grimaced then nodded. "Pretty much."

"And how do you propose I keep Budd in Vegas?"

"Come on, Teegan. When was the last time a man refused your request?"

Well, since he put it like that…

She shook her head. "You know how my father feels about these special assignments. He'll ream your ass when he finds out you recruited me *again*."

His posture straightened. "Then you'll do it?"

Unwilling to answer yet, she held up a finger. "I'm not sure." Teegan tapped the bobble-head on her Philadelphia Eagles souvenir. *Yes or no*? Oddly, the little guy shook to and fro, not up and down. *So, he's saying no.* Yet, the excitement of a new assignment grew inside her. Should she? She wanted to. Then again, she didn't. She wasn't cocky enough to think her analytical brain was superior to every criminal Jeff threw her way. And she'd be a fool to match wits with a woman on a personal vendetta. She gave Jeff a long look, still not convinced she knew everything. "Why does Anna warrant so much of the FBI's attention when more dangerous killers are still on the loose? What aren't you telling me?"

Jeff fussed with the crease on his pant leg before meeting her steady gaze. "The murdered orderly was my administrative assistant's daughter."

Question answered. Kincaid had murdered one of the family. Unfortunately, Teegan faced more indecision and glanced at the policeman before refocusing on Jeff. "You realize this is not my usual forte."

"I want you to keep Budd in town, nothing more. Kincaid is dangerous, and I expect you to use every ounce of your training. Our men will be in the background at all times, waiting for Kincaid to make her move."

Again, Teegan hit the bobble-head. "Budd already asked me to the cabin."

"Teegan, that's perfect!"

"I said no."

He leaned forward in his seat. "Why?"

She shot him a glare. "I don't make a habit of going to isolated cabins with men I don't know."

A broad hand swept the air as Jeff smiled. "He obviously doesn't think of you as a stranger."

The glare intensified. "He's Vegas' Most Eligible Bachelor, Jeff. Women fall at his feet. I'm not one of *those* women."

"Ah, well, too bad. Budd's attracted to you, and before you go off on me, why do you think I'm here? I can assign a more-experienced female agent, but that photo shows the sparks arcing between you. Look at him, Teegan. If Budd isn't a man ready to drag you to bed, then I need glasses."

Jeff was right. The sparks had flown on the plane. Her IQ dismissed the attraction as a statistical improbability, an incalculable hypothesis to be ignored. *People do not fall for each other in a few hours' time.*

Her argument anyway. After a lifetime full of male deceit, she ignored whatever emotions they stirred—Budd Richardson included.

Yeah, right. His kiss still seared her lips. Like any

woman, she'd wanted more, but the returning tour group interrupted. They had swamped him with questions all the way out the door. "I don't have time for this, Jeff. The factory is about to go online."

Jeff stood, his lips tilted downward in a pout. "Okay, if you won't help, then we'll do without you. I'm sure my assistant will understand."

"Careful. I'll put an Irish curse on you."

Jeff chuckled while he placed his briefcase on the chair and checked the latches. "I'm appealing to an age-old guilt complex, Teegan." He shot her a sideward glance. "Is it working?"

Clearing his throat, Mike stood. "They tell me you're a real ace for the FBI, Dr. Smith. How long have you been a special operative?"

She thumbed a gesture toward Jeff. "Since this guy recruited me in college. I haven't been able to hide from him since. I'd help more if my father wouldn't have heart palpitations worrying."

Jeff stepped around the desk, took both her hands, and urged her to stand. "I know you said no more assignments, Teegan. I'm requesting your services as a friend. I want to put this bitch behind bars before she hurts anyone else. That person might be Budd."

"It can also be me, damnit. You're asking me to risk my neck for a man I just met."

"No, I'm asking you to help catch a woman's killer."

Oh, crap. She couldn't deny the growing intrigue of working undercover. And something different to do besides paperwork. She sighed heavily. "All right, I'll see what I can do. Under no circumstances should Budd be told." She hugged him. "I'll need a weapon."

Grinning, he held her at arm's length. "Let me guess. A Beretta Pico."

Teegan tapped her nose and winked. Her favorite weapon. The gun fit anywhere, even a clutch purse.

"You know I can't simply give it to you. You have to be tested and qualify."

"I'll get her through." Reeves smoothed a hand along his tie. "Stop by the downtown police station in the morning, Doctor. I'll make sure you have access to the range."

Assuming she had enough skill in her to hit the broad side of a barn.

"Oh, yes, I almost forgot." Jeff reopened his briefcase and extracted a manila envelope then handed it to her. "Kincaid's file. Maybe you'll see something we missed. We don't know where she's staying or how she's feeding herself. She steals cars then ditches them the same day. The woman's cunning. Mike's arranged twenty-four-seven surveillance on Budd so they'll keep a sharp eye out, but we still want to keep him away from the cabin. That's where you come in. But be careful. So far, the woman hasn't used a gun."

Shaking her head, Teegan rolled her eyes. "Gee, your concern for my safety is heartwarming." She escorted the men to the door. "One last request, gentlemen. Don't you dare breathe a word of this to my father!"

****

Dear Lord, what had she gotten herself into? Should she risk her neck for Budd Richardson? He was a ladies' man, a man-about-town, one whom women strived to conquer. What would he care if she died in the process? He'd merely draw a line through her name in his infamous little book.

I'm after a killer who murdered a member of the law-enforcement family. A murderer stalking Budd, a woman who thought nothing about hurting complete strangers to accomplish her goal. *Not my usual assignment for sure.* Espionage was more up her alley, national security stuff, the danger-to-all-mankind scenario. Although, Jeff had asked only to keep Budd in Vegas. What was the harm in that?

Assuming I can do the job without gushing over him like an idiot.

She flipped open Anna Kincaid's file, glanced at the front and side view photos, and skimmed through the papers. Psychiatric evaluations, supervisor reports, statements from everyone within the institution except the janitor. Her concentration sucked, and she slapped it shut. *Maybe a nice walk around the building will help me focus.*

Teegan kicked off her heels and slipped on a pair of bright red sneakers, a clash with her lavender suit, but too bad. She often took walks around the building, and the red sneakers were the clue to the staff to let her be until she returned. She waved to Claudia on the way out the door.

What to do, what to do? Keep Budd in Vegas. Lure Anna. How can I possibly accomplish both goals without throwing myself at the man? She'd rather take a one-way trip to Mars.

Budd wasn't worth the trouble. Granted, he'd kissed her in the conference room and a hot quiver pulsed through her veins like a stream of molten metal. Big deal. The feeling meant nothing except maybe as an indication she should get out a little more and stop depriving herself of some wonderful man/woman togetherness.

Enough. Relax. Don't think. She gulped in a deep breath and marveled at how dry the late afternoon air was. Back east, the July heat and humidity created an outdoor oven. That meant frizzy hair days with clothing sticking to the skin, jumping from an air-conditioned car into an air-conditioned building, downing ice water like no tomorrow. Here in Vegas, the heat was endless. Yet, she walked without developing a sweat. A good thing, too, because she hadn't included a shower in the office plans. A HAZMAT containment room existed in the factory, which included a shower, but the boss wasn't supposed to sweat.

Bedroom and shower. A definite part of any future expansion plans.

The contractors had done an excellent job constructing the building. The frame was metal, the exterior white brick to reflect the hot sun. The loading dock with four bay doors faced the rear. As she turned the corner, she heard the distinct whine of the forklift inside the bed of a tractor-trailer.

Two men stood to the side and waved as she passed, one was the foreman, supervising the unloading. The parking lot was half empty, but by this time next summer, all the slots should be filled, and she should be back in the Philadelphia lab.

Can't wait. She was a chemist and a damn good one, not a paper-shuffling COO.

"I was hoping you'd come out, bitch."

Teegan's heart jumped, and she whirled toward the terse voice.

A short woman stepped from between two parked

cars. She wore a blue hoodie with dark sunglasses.

The same description from the airport. Teegan recognized the straight nose, the sharp point of her jaw, and lifeless hair. Anna Kincaid. The clever woman had strategically confronted Teegan away from the loading dock doors.

Teegan glanced toward the closed side doors, hoping to see someone step out. Not a soul in sight. "You talking to me?" A typical South Philly response. So classy.

"Yeah, I'm talking to you. You were walking with Budd at the airport." She cocked her head and pouted. "Did I hurt your precious body?"

With a swift gaze, Teegan sized up her adversary. Anna was no more than five feet tall, slim build, a toothpick appearance with no curves. Her hands held no weapon, and nothing bulged beneath her jacket. A verbal confrontation. *Yeah, I'll take it.*

No choice really. She had no gun, no handcuffs, and her self-defense skills were a bit rusty to say the least. Jeff hadn't recruited her in recent years, and her physical activity amounted to a night of vigorous sex— of which she hadn't had in months. "What do you want?"

Anna stepped forward. "The same two men who visited Budd walked out of your building. They're cops, aren't they? Don't deny it."

Teegan faced Anna while crossing her arms on her chest. "I have no reason to deny or confirm your questions. I don't know you."

"Well then, know this, bitch." She stepped closer while throwing her chin toward Teegan's face. "Budd Richardson is my man. You're to stay away."

The woman's eyes blazed even through the sunglasses. "If you're implying he came to see me, you're wrong. Mr. Richardson was here for the news conference along with everyone else. If you had better observation skills, you'd see that." *Oh, brother. Why don't I antagonize the woman more?* "How did you know I worked here?"

"Because I recognized your car from the airport. That's why I stuck around. You're another Vegas hot-shot with your fancy Audi." She stepped back, finger waving. "I caught how he looks at you. He's not like that with other women so I need to break your spell."

Spell? What century are we in? Sighing heavily, she dropped her arms to her sides.

Again, Anna invaded Teegan's space and glared up through dark sunglasses. "I suggest you keep your distance if you know what's good for you."

Oooo, big threat. But that was typical South Philly, too. So was her reaction not to back down. With arms remaining by her sides, she clenched her fists and inched closer.

Anna backed away, brows halfway up her forehead. "Wow, a rich-bitch with spunk. I like that. You strike me as a woman who won't be afraid to get her nails dirty."

"Right on that one, dear. I don't like what you're implying about me and Mr. Richardson."

Anna whipped off her sunglasses and met Teegan's steady gaze. "Stay away from him. I'm warning you."

Teegan stared into the eyes of a cold-blooded killer. She hadn't any fear of Anna, but her muscles tensed in anticipation of an assault. *Who would have thought Anna would come to me?*

Breaking eye contact, she searched the area for another human, someone who could help restrain this woman but saw no one, not even an unfamiliar car. "How'd you get here? All these cars belong to the employees." But when she looked back, she spoke to no one. Anna was gone.

"You okay, Dr. Smith?"

Three factory workers had stepped from one of the building's many side doors for a break. *Oh, now they come out.* She approached them. "Anyone see the woman talking to me? I have no idea how she disappeared."

One employee, a young man with blue-tinted hair, pointed toward the road. "She took off on foot. More likely had a car parked on the highway."

"Well, if you ever see her again, call the cops and then call me. I don't want her hanging around."

Anna Kincaid's appearance had decided one nagging debate. Teegan now knew what she had to do.

Chapter Seven

Budd Richardson ripped into his hamburger like a starving Neanderthal, squirting ketchup, mayo, and relish out the sides and onto his fingers. He hadn't enough napkins on the table to wipe the mess, and so what? Food had a way of relieving the aggravation from a frustrating morning. Now, here he sat, in a busy burger bistro with lunch crowds pouring in, creating too much noise to rattle his nerves and force him to eat without chewing. *I may stroke out after all this.*

Sgt. Reeves had assigned a seasoned surveillance team to watch his house, two trained professionals, and they had missed the whole show. Hell, they'd miss neon signs and flashing lights, and the sloppy burger was the best coping tactic on the planet, provided he didn't choke to death. Along with a mouthful of burger, he'd shoved three fries into his mouth without realizing.

The intruder had to be Anna. She had disconnected the motion sensors and thrown black drapes over the outside cameras, effectively disabling the security system. Then, she broke into the garage and caused havoc with his SUV. The Mercedes was left untouched, which shocked him to no end. He'd called Reeves to rant. The man was all apologies, giving the old get-to-the-bottom speech. Like Mike's words eased his blood pressure. Budd hadn't wanted the tail in the first place, but what incompetence!

He tore into a pickle and squirted juice into his eye, causing his eyelids to clamp shut while one side of his face winced from the burn. *Great. Now I'll need a corneal transplant.* With a clean edge on his napkin, he dabbed the area.

At least, the cameras weren't destroyed. Removing drapes and reconnecting sensors was nothing compared to the damage to his SUV. Last night, he had loaded the vehicle with the wood trim, tied a half dozen long planks to the roof, and heaved two five-gallon buckets of plaster into the trunk. All the supplies had to be unloaded in order to get the SUV out of the garage and repaired. If he ever—

Budd froze, hamburger poised mid-bite. His anger vanished, and he shook his head to clear his vision to ascertain she wasn't an illusion. The most beautiful woman in the world had stepped out of a silver Audi and into the bright afternoon sunlight. She wore a tank top with shorts to reveal plenty of tanned skin, making him drool. Hardly work attire. He gulped his soda to swallow what remained in his mouth and hailed as Teegan passed through the busy entrance. The teal eyes widened, and she flashed a smile that melted his bones as she meandered through the crowd toward him.

"What are you doing here?" they said the words in unison and laughed.

"Join me." He waved toward the opposite chair.

"Let me get something to eat. Any recommendations?"

"The hamburger for starters. You order in the beginning of the line. By the time you reach the cashier, it's ready."

Bob's Burger Bistro was a cafeteria-style

establishment with enough selection to feed the fussy. Why they called the place a bistro puzzled him, but the place was popular along the Strip for tourists and locals alike. The interior contained simple wooden tables and chairs, crammed together to accommodate as many patrons as possible.

Teegan slid her tray along the wide, metal tubes while talking to the food servers behind the counter, pointing to something behind a glass partition as if she'd completed the routine a hundred times.

Her nose wasn't in the air nor did she use a condescending voice, a woman not only with beauty and brains but one confident in her chosen path and the world around her.

She returned a few minutes later with a loaded tray.

A burger, potato wedges, coleslaw, peach pie, bottle of water, milk shake, and some brown stuff he couldn't identify. The woman had a healthy appetite. "How'd you find this place?"

She had returned to the table with a wad of fresh napkins on her tray and handed him half while pointing to his crumbled pile. "My brothers make a mess, too." She dunked a potato wedge into a cup of sour cream and took a bite. "A couple of people at work raved about the food. Since the place is along my errand route, I stopped in to give it a try."

"Let me guess. You can't cook."

"*Au contraire, mon ami*. I love to cook as much as eat." She cocked her head, the teal sparkling. "Dare I dispel another assumption?"

"I sit before you humbled." The woman was full of surprises, and her napkin gesture was a little more endearing than he cared to admit. He cleared his throat and pointed to a small side dish. "What's with the goo?"

She pushed the brownish food around with a spoon. "It's supposed to be apple crisp. I think they left off the crisp." She scooped a small amount and tasted. "Good though. What are you doing here? Isn't today your off-to-the-cabin day?"

He swallowed the contents in his mouth. "A slight delay. Someone punctured three of my tires overnight. Sidewalls. Total loss. The worst part is they got in through my garage side door, bypassing every alarm sensor installed." He sipped his soda then grabbed a fresh napkin to wipe his mouth. "The tow driver took forever to drag the vehicle out and up onto his flatbed."

"You should have cameras installed."

"I have them. They were deactivated. Even the dog missed the intrusion, and he's usually good at sounding an alarm. Nothing else was disturbed, and no attempt to break into the house via the garage access door. The security firm monitoring the cameras saw nothing, only a shadow. Puzzling." He sipped his drink before continuing.

"My SUV is at the tire shop down the block. Naturally, they didn't have my size. Hence, lunchtime while I wait for their call. I was boiling mad until you strolled through the door."

"Glad to oblige." With a two-handed hold, she took a bite of her burger and rolled her eyes. "Wow, this is good." Still holding the burger, she lifted a pinkie finger and pointed toward his plate. "I see you like your meat to bleed."

"Medium rare. They cook it perfect every time. Yours is overdone."

She shook her head. "I have an aversion to oozing blood." She placed the burger onto her plate and looked around. "This place has more windows than walls. Aren't you afraid of being spotted by the paparazzi?"

"I won't cower in the corner, Teegan. I've learned to face the challenges in my life, paparazzi included."

"How about your stalker?"

"Her, too." He licked ketchup from his finger. "Since I walked here, I may have a temporary reprieve from both, but be forewarned. Paparazzi have a habit of showing up unexpectedly. They have this uncanny radar that sends out a signal whenever I'm with a woman. Like now." He finished the last of his burger.

Paparazzi be damned. What a beautiful day it turned into! All his troubles had flushed down a drain at the sight of this woman. Her face, her body, the sound of her voice. No one had ever transformed his mood so quickly. The feeling was mind-boggling. And scary.

"You know, Teegan, I almost backed my Mercedes out of the garage, but I wasn't sure how the underbelly would handle the dirt road to the cabin. Not to mention I didn't want to strap wood planks to the roof nor do I have a CB radio installed. Someone obviously knew this. I'm glad I let it sit."

She unscrewed the cap on the water bottle and took a swig. "What's the matter with the dirt road?"

He wiped his mouth and sat back. "The Mercedes only has a six-inch clearance, and I've got some good ruts running down the drive. I'll take a chance busting the oil pan. Besides—wait a minute." He sipped his drink to wash the last of the burger down his throat. "Let me give you a lesson on surviving an excursion into our wonderful southwest." He leaned onto the table.

"The desert consists of coarse sand, gravel, and rock. Anytime you leave a packed road, the wheels sink in, and you'll find it impossible to get out. Without proper tires and four-wheel drive, the car will be stuck until a tow truck arrives. Those of us who live in the area know too well how dangerous the situation is. Keep my lesson in mind when you go out exploring. Nothing will spoil your day faster than getting stuck in the heat." He bit into his pickle. *Garlic, pal. Nothing worse than garlic breath*. He debated spitting out what remained in his mouth, but he'd already eaten half before she arrived. "Want some pickle?"

She pushed several potato wedges to the side and pointed. "Got my own."

All right! Two garlic breaths intermingling into one. Perfect. "Why aren't you working?"

She bit into the pickle and chewed before answering. "If I work a Saturday, I'll take a weekday off. The free time helps maintain my sanity. Can I taste a fry?" She grabbed one from his plate without waiting for an answer and munched. "Not bad." She searched out the window. "You forewarned me about the paparazzi, but I'm more worried about strange females lurking." She met his gaze. "Am I safe to sit with you?"

"I assume you're referring to the loon in my life. I won't let her hurt you."

"But she's roaming around somewhere."

"Don't know. Don't care. My surveillance team will spot her if she—" He stopped to hold up a finger. "Let me rephrase the statement. The team didn't see my intruder cover the cameras. So, I'm not full of confidence they'll spot my loon before she plunges another knife in me." He munched on a fry. "Fate has gripped the back of my neck, Teegan, and I can tell you, I'm not a strong believer in fate."

She looked up, cheeks bulging. "What are you talking about?"

"You and I. Three times in one week. I considered this morning as bad luck. Now, I'm not so sure. What are the odds of another chance meeting?"

She chewed. "Are you asking me to do the math?" She opened a packet of mayo and spread the creamy sauce onto her burger then followed with a packet of relish. "Statistically, our trend can be easily broken. Your trip to the cabin, for example."

A depressing realization. This woman was worth her weight in gold. Could he possibly put her off until he returned?

Whoa, boy. Listen to yourself. Women fell at his feet every day of the week. Why should this one warrant more attention?

Because her beauty was not a product of skillfully applied makeup. She sat before him with the barest trace of powder on her face, her skin glowing as natural as a snow-capped mountain. Unlike his showgirls with their thick eyeliner and false lashes, he'd recognize Teegan in the morning when her eyes fluttered open. A diamond among charcoal.

Budd glanced toward the entrance, and his gut clenched. His worst nightmare had walked through the door.

Ed Connors, plastered with the smile that bowled over women, sauntered to the table, eyeing Teegan like she was a raw piece of meat. Even worse, Teegan's head snapped with a quick double-take.

Ed stood directly at her side, his gaze scanning every square inch of her chest. "I spotted this stunning creature through the window and hurried in to save you." He extended a hand to Teegan. "Ed Connors, Budd's partner." He held onto her hand and whistled. "Gorgeous eyes."

Teegan looked at Budd, brows high. "Do you need saving?"

Budd sneered. "Ed's taken a few unwelcomed females off my hands, but you are not one of them." He glowered at Ed, hoping his partner would take the hint. "Don't you have someplace else to be?"

Ed's smile flickered as his thumb caressed the top part of her hand. "Where'd you find her, Budd?"

"Release her hand, and I'll introduce you."

He and Ed had been friends for a long time, but this wasn't one of those buddy-pal moments. He barely controlled the urge to rip out Ed's spleen. He wiped his mouth. "This is Teegan Smith, and no, she's not a showgirl. Why are you in this part of town?"

Ed released Teegan's hand after one final caress. "Nice to meet you." Turning toward Budd, he said, "I have an appointment with a client. Weren't you going to the cabin?"

"A slight delay."

"I can see why." He winked at Teegan.

Budd crushed a fry in his hand, spewing the potato plus ketchup onto his palm.

Teegan grabbed one of her napkins and thrust it into his hand, her gaze sparkling.

He gave her a one-eyed squint before turning to his partner. "I'm not inviting you to sit, Ed. Don't be offended, but I'd like you to leave."

Ed backed away, hands raised in surrender. "Right. Another time, Ms. Smith."

As she watched Budd clean his hand, Teegan chuckled. "If I didn't know any better, I'd say you wanted to be alone with me."

He threw the soiled napkin onto his tray along with a half dozen others from the burger. "That is one dead-on assumption, woman. He may be a partner, but I am still senior."

Her gaze followed Ed as he paid for his purchase at the cashier.

Was she interested in the Budd Richardson wannabe? How would he know? Even more important, why would he care? Regardless, something boiled in his gut besides food. Anger about Ed. Uncertainty about her. He hadn't felt such a conflict in years.

Teegan crumbled her napkin before picking up another. "When will your car be ready?"

Never with any luck. He washed down the wishful thinking with his drink, double-checked for Ed's departure from the parking lot, and sat back in his chair, feeling victorious for some reason. "I'm waiting for their call. The tires need to come from some warehouse in Henderson. I think the same sloth who towed my vehicle is the same one dispatched to get the tires." He checked his watch. Two hours had passed, and the service manager promised to call in an hour. "I might be eating dinner here."

Nothing would annoy him more...unless she stayed with him. "I can reach my cabin in about an hour and a half. Once my car is done, I'll go home to reload my supplies, suitcase, and dog. Maybe I'll get out of Vegas before dark."

He hated to arrive after sunset. Once, a coyote had surprised him by sleeping on his front porch. The creature had the audacity to snarl like he owned the place. On another trip, a rattlesnake made its nest near the generator. A big shock that night. "Do you live nearby?"

She swallowed before answering. "Since I'm still finding my way around, I don't have an answer. I live ten minutes from the plant. A nice easy commute."

"That puts you in the older part of town. My old neighborhood. And Anna's."

Eyebrow arched, she forked some coleslaw. "Who's Anna?"

"My loon. Anna Kincaid. We lived a few blocks apart."

She wiped her mouth. "Let's talk about her for a minute. What's she want from you—hey!"

"You had the gall to steal one of my fries, so I'm reciprocating by tasting your peach pie." Grinning, he cut a piece with his fork and slipped the succulent pastry into his mouth. "Not bad, but it has a touch too much cinnamon."

"Cinnamon is good for you. Have another bite." She took the plastic lid off her milk shake, unsheathed a plastic straw, slipped it in, and stirred. "So, what about this Anna person? What's she want?"

He licked his fork. "The cops think she's out to kill me. If that's the case, I'd be dead by now."

Teegan wagged a finger. "Not necessarily. She may want the Romeo and Juliet scenario. You know, he dies, she dies, they live happily ever after in the heavens above. To accomplish this, she has to get you alone. From your reputation, you're hardly alone."

"That's why I love my cabin so much. Hold on a minute." He used the tip of his finger to wipe mayo from her lip. If he was closer, he'd use his tongue. She watched with unreadable eyes. Everything about her was attractive, even an expressionless face.

Maybe his digestive juices were robbing too much blood from his brain. That would explain why this one woman had him mesmerized.

"Not to sound preachy, Budd, but you shouldn't go to the cabin alone."

"I already invited you." His cell phone rang, but he ignored the shrill.

Her lips curled into a smile. "Your car might be ready."

"I don't want to break this trend we started, Teegan." He slid his tray to the side and leaned across the table. "How about I take you out Friday night?"

Her fork paused midway to her mouth. "You asking me on a date?"

"Yes. Dinner and dancing. How's it sound?"

She sat back, her face bright. "Wonderful. I haven't seen the inside of a casino since I moved here. What about your trip?"

"I'll go next week and take you with me."

"Oh." She wiped her mouth. "Don't jump to conclusions. I may not be in the mood to put up wallboard."

His invitation to the cabin shot out of his mouth before his brain had a chance to consider the consequences, but to hell with analysis. She sounded interested, and damned if that didn't brighten his day. As he took her hand, he smiled. "Work will not be on my mind if I've got you in my cabin."

"Is that a fact?" She squeezed his hand. "I can handle more than a tool, big boy."

Her innuendo shot a bolt of pleasure straight down to his groin. "Maybe I should amend our date to this evening. I'm not sure I can wait until Friday."

"You have to wait, Budd. I've got a conference call tonight, and they usually last several hours. Tomorrow night is new employee orientation. We'll leave our time together for Friday and let the anticipation build."

If the bulge in his pants was an indicator, his anticipation should develop into a full-blown frenzy.

Chapter Eight

Mission accomplished.

Teegan had learned early in life from her wise and wonderful mother that if a man saw skin, he dangled his tongue for more. She not only achieved the cancellation of Budd's trip, she now had a date with the most gorgeous man to cross her path in months.

A giddiness surfaced. She had the unmistakable urge to call her mother and gush—like a teenager who snared the coolest guy on campus, ready to brag to the entire world. Except this wasn't school. She was on special assignment, and everything else took a back seat.

A fact not supported by her stimulated libido.

As she and Budd headed for the exit, she glanced out the windows, a cursory inspection to avoid a deadly confrontation with a crazy woman. According to the FBI profilers, Anna wouldn't miss a detail of Budd's daily activities. She'd note his every move, the people he was with, the stores he frequented.

The surveillance team had eased back to allow Teegan full rein to establish herself as a target with the hope that Anna hadn't picked up a rifle and now aimed from a rooftop somewhere. *I need to have my head examined for doing this.* She turned to face Budd as he held the door for a little old lady with a cane. "Can I give you a lift?"

He made sure the woman was clear of the door before releasing. "No, thanks. The shop's only down the next block, and I should walk off this anticipatory energy you caused. I'll escort you to your car, though."

Her breath hitched. She'd have to be blind not to see his arousal. *Oh, what I wouldn't do to drag him home and pop that sucker from his pants. Love in the afternoon. Can't beat it.*

So much for focus.

Only a few empty slots remained in the crowded restaurant parking lot, too packed to spot a lone woman waiting in a car. Anna could be anywhere—in a nearby store, across the street, whatever vantage point suited her. Teegan reached her car.

Budd slipped his fingers over the door handle. "Teegan—"

Surprised at the croaked tone of his voice, she met his gaze and inwardly gasped. His blue eyes burned with a desire she hadn't seen in a long time, as if the sunlight fueled the fire. He pinned her to the car and captured her mouth like her lips would escape him, thrusting his tongue deep. The maneuver caught her completely off-guard, and a certain thrill arose within her chest.

Not because of eagle-eyed Anna, but because this man created indescribable sensations, a tidal wave of emotions from a thundering heart to astonished pleasure. Like the feel of his hard erection pressing against her abdomen, how his body imprisoned her against the car—no embrace, hands firmly planted on the car roof. He hadn't given her a chance to utter a cry of protest. Not that she would. They stood in the middle of the parking lot for all the world to see. She grabbed the front of his pale green shirt to hold him in place.

She had denied the attraction while talking with Jeff, but she couldn't deny the sensations now. Budd's kiss flushed the blood to the surface of her skin, causing a surge of arousal in a part of her she'd sworn had shriveled and died. His tongue probed while his male hardness created reactions that flew her hormones into a rage.

Heat surrounded them. Her knees weakened, her eyesight blurred, and her breathing had become erratic, gasping into his mouth in short, excited puffs. She responded with equal probing, not giving a hoot who gawked and ignored the possibility of passing out from the hot afternoon sun. She wanted this moment to go on forever.

Still with his hands on the car roof, he placed his forehead against hers and sighed.

With trembling fingers, she stroked his cheek before dropping her hand to his chest. "That was the best dessert I've ever had." He kissed her forehead and lifted his head with a gaze so tender she almost melted onto the asphalt.

"Let's call this the appetizer." He traced a finger along her jaw. "Dinner, dancing, and then dessert. Trust me when I tell you I won't keep my hands on any car roof Friday night."

"Yes, why did you do that?"

"If I had wrapped you in my arms, I'd have lost control, Teegan."

The innuendo sent a shiver of pleasure down her spine. *Two nights away. How can I possibly concentrate?* "You make me forget where I'm going," she whispered.

A faint smile touched his lips. "You make me forget my own name."

She brushed her lips against his before using both hands to push on his chest. In two more seconds, she might drag Budd into the backseat of the Audi. "Go on. Get your car. We gave everyone enough of a show." Including the men listening through the transmitter taped between her breasts.

"Friday," he said with another gentle touch on her chin. He glanced back with a smile before leaving the parking lot.

Somebody give me a fan! Or at least a cold bucket of water, not to mention knee braces and a bronchodilator. Her body shuddered at the idea of mind-blowing sex with a man too hot to touch.

Her gaze followed him as he strolled down the street, hands in his jeans pockets, whistling, his tush drawing her attention. *Nice.* But she wanted more than a taste of his lips or the feel of strong arms around her body, more than a one or two-night stand. She wanted love and the happily-ever-after scene, a companion to talk to, share a bed, eat dinner with—all the good stuff that encompassed a real relationship. *A little soon for those kinds of thoughts.* He could turn into another thanks-but-no-thanks kind of guy. *Like usual.*

Teegan closed her eyes to force her pounding heart to calm down. Friday was definitely too far away. So was a release for the floodgates down yonder. She opened her eyes and, while pretending to fuss with her clothes, took a good look around.

All right, enough of this. Focus.

Had Anna seen them? Would she follow Budd to the tire shop or confront her new adversary?

Instincts picked the latter. Anna had given her warning, and Teegan disobeyed. Therefore, punishment was the only course of action.

She pushed herself away from the car door with an effort, as if he had glued her to the metal, checked her knees for stability, and nodded with satisfaction at a full recovery. *The man is a good kisser, for sure.*

A vehicle caught her eye at a strip mall across the street. A gray sedan faced the restaurant while the other cars alongside faced the stores. The lone occupant slumped in the driver's seat, barely high enough to see through the steering wheel. Was the driver Anna or was someone waiting for a shopper in one of the stores? "I have a possible sighting. Stand by for confirmation."

Teegan stepped into her car and started the engine. As a precaution, she grabbed her little Beretta from her purse, chambered a round, and slipped the gun into its holster before clipping her weapon to the back of her shorts waistband, careful to conceal it with her tank top. After adjusting the rearview mirror, she studied the car and caught movement in the front seat. The occupant, a woman, had straightened to see over the steering wheel. She wore sunglasses, and a blue hoodie covered her hair.

"I've got Anna in sight, guys. Budd already left so she's waiting for me." *Predictable as a magnet on metal.* The bitch would target her competition before moving on Budd. "Anna's parked across the street from the restaurant in front of the Everything For A Party store, gray sedan, older-model Ford. I can't see the license plate. I'll wait for backup." She opened her sun roof.

Her cell phone rang, and she glanced at the screen.

Jeff Andrews.

"Delay as long as possible, Teegan. We're right behind you."

But Anna had started her car, and the vehicle inched from the parking slot. "She's on the move, Jeff."

Not willing to let her get the upper hand, Teegan tossed the phone onto the passenger seat, started the Audi, and glided over the asphalt, carefully watching for Anna's next move. Both parking lots had an entrance and an exit. The strip mall's exit faced the restaurant's entrance, and the gray sedan crawled toward the curb. Four lanes of heavy cross-traffic prevented a quick getaway.

Without waiting for a clearing, the sedan shot across the street toward the restaurant's entrance, causing cars to squeal and swerve. As Anna's car hit the incline, the metal underbelly scraped on concrete, throwing sparks in every direction.

The crazy bitch aimed straight for her!

With no place to go except into traffic, Teegan threw her body onto the console as the sedan crashed into both driver-side doors, shattering glass and crushing metal, slamming the Audi into a nearby utility pole, effectively crushing all four doors. The impact created a surreal sound, one reminiscent of a movie scene with glass and metal flying coupled with the hiss of exploding airbags. The ensuing silence was deafening, like she had entered a vacuum where all sound ceased to exist.

Anna jumped from her car and gave Teegan a crooked grin. "Gotcha, bitch!" She ran toward the back of the burger restaurant.

Had Anna just thrown her a challenge?

Too dazed to move, Teegan watched her run. Her heart raced, her breaths blew in choppy jerks, but she shook away the feelings and grabbed the door handle. "Oh no, you don't." *Where in the universe is my brain? I can't open any of these doors.* She scurried through the open sun roof, jumped to the asphalt, and took chase.

Boy, am I glad I wore sneakers today.

"Anna's on foot. I'm behind her. Rear of restaurant. One street over." *I hate running.* The last time she ran was…well, never. "Making a left. I'll need oxygen." *Damn, I'm out of shape.*

If she was chasing Anna through the streets of Philadelphia with its many alleys and side streets, she'd have lost her two blocks ago. Here in Vegas, the entire city had a wide-open appearance with sand and palm trees at every turn. Following Anna wasn't hard, but the distance between them increased with each block. According to Anna's file, she had broken several sprinting records at the mental hospital's Special Olympics so running after her wasn't a bright idea. *She's a friggin' cheetah.*

Teegan's chest ached from the strain of sucking in much-needed air. She'd never been the athletic sort, maybe a little touch football with her brothers, a swim or two in a pool, but nothing strenuous. Except sex. She loved strenuous sex. *Best exercise in the world.*

Anna sprinted into a casino, the local kind with a cowboy on a rearing horse in flashing lights.

"I'm entering the Horseshoe Casino. Someone needs to go around to the rear."

Teegan stopped inside the main entrance, fighting to control heavy breaths by bending over onto her knees. *I am so not into this.* She let her vision adjust to the interior surroundings before straightening.

The darkness struck her first. Rich mahogany wood was everywhere from the beams on the ceiling to the wooden floor beneath her feet. The only lights came from slot machines and twinkling lights around the bar. People had turned to stare as if she was an impending coronary about to collapse on the floor. No sign of Anna. She had disappeared into the crowd. *I wanted to see the inside of a casino, but not like this.* Teegan stepped outside into the sunlight.

Two cars screeched to a stop alongside the curb. Men in dark suits jumped out.

Teegan approached. "I lost her inside. This could be one of her local haunts with friends inside waiting to bash out my brains. I'm not in the mood. Tell Jeff I'm heading back to my car."

Another time, another place...destined to meet again.

Taking her time on the return trip, Teegan rounded the corner of the burger bistro to see a cop reach through the broken window of her car.

He straightened with her purse in his hand while talking on his shoulder mike.

Aw, damn. He eyed her approach with enough suspicion to raise a guilt complex for littering the glass onto the sidewalk.

"Is this your vehicle?" His voice growled the words.

"Yes, sir, it's mine. I chased the woman who hit me." She pointed in the direction behind the restaurant.

"Not very bright, ma'am. Both of you left the scene of an accident. Stand over here by my car, please."

Oh, brother. A regular beat cop. And her with a gun in the small of her back.

He dumped her purse contents onto the hood of the cop car, rummaged through her wallet, and extracted her driver's license.

As was the norm, she had nothing to identify her as a special FBI operative. Only a gun. *This is definitely a tricky situation.* "You might want to contact Detective Sergeant Mike Reeves, Officer. He'll explain everything."

The officer shot her a squinted glance before strolling to the driver's side of his car.

A brown SUV drove into the lot sporting four spanking-new tires. Budd jumped out, his eyes wide as he surveyed the Audi and gray sedan. "Holy crap, Teegan, who did this?"

Muffling a groan, she met him halfway so he wouldn't overhear the cop on his radio. "Some crazy woman, the same one from the airport." She assessed the damage to the car. One side was totally demolished, the other side bent inward from the utility pole. "I'll need a new car, and this one's only two months old."

Frowning, he touched her arm. "Are you hurt?"

She rotated her head side to side. "Surprisingly, no. I managed to lie down before impact." Except the console might have left a bruise on her rib cage. No biggie.

"Where'd Anna go?"

"She ran. The cops are after her."

The officer ambled back. He handed Teegan her license and purse. "The gray sedan is stolen, ma'am. I'll have an insurance report for you by tomorrow. The form will include the address of the yard where we towed the vehicles. Sign here, please."

She signed and accepted a copy, wondering how in the hell she'd get to work in the morning.

"Just stop by the station and ask for me. Everything will be ready. Do you need a ride?"

She glanced at Budd and raised an eyebrow.

"I'll take her home," Budd said. "See that Det. Reeves in Homicide gets a copy of the report."

"I'll do that, sir."

Teegan patted Budd's arm. "Let me get some stuff from my car first." She popped the trunk with her key fob, surprised to see it worked on the first try and used the cover of the raised hood to sneak the gun into her purse before rummaging for the personal toiletries strewn all over the trunk rug. *I knew I should have tied these damn plastic bags.* Her hands shook, and she fumbled the shampoo container, then the deodorant, and finally, a catch-me-if-you-can game with a bottle of rubbing alcohol. Three bags total, all items accounted for. She placed them into the back seat of his SUV.

But he placed his body between her and the car door to stop her from stepping into the front seat. He picked glass from her hair. "That was a close call, Teegan."

If he only knew. "I guess Anna caught our kiss in the parking lot." *Anna will be out for blood now.*

"I'm sorry."

"For what, kissing me?" While marveling at the gentle gaze studying her face, she touched his cheek. "I enjoyed every second." *Eat your heart out, Anna.*

His brows creased together into a frown. "Get in the car. Otherwise, I'll give her more to worry about."

She should have peeked inside Budd's SUV before

agreeing to the ride home. The vehicle resembled a contractor's truck with rags and maps sticking from the door compartments. Everything imaginable filled the cup holders in the console except cups. Dust had accumulated on the dash board, and Lord only knew what covered her seat. She expected to find nails on the rug—oh, nails were indeed underfoot. "Do you realize your interior is loaded with dog hairs?"

He flashed a boyish grin. "Rommel is only allowed in this vehicle. I keep a roller brush in my office to get the hairs off my suit every morning." Leaning forward, he turned the ignition.

"You could drive your Mercedes to work."

"I could also clean my car." He shifted the vehicle into gear and eased toward a secondary exit on the side street. "The Mercedes is for dates—like you. Give me your address."

She relayed the information and watched his lips curl downward. She almost laughed. "That's not such a pleasant look."

"I know exactly where you live because I grew up only a few blocks away." He slowed for a stop sign and glanced both ways before continuing. "This will be the first time in seven years I'm returning to my old neighborhood. You may see me shudder."

"Then you'll know where I live when you pick me up on Friday." She pointed to the radio under the dashboard. "Is this your CB? Where's the antenna?"

"I'll attach the antenna at the last minute because the length exceeds the height of the garage. A good antenna is the key to an effective CB."

After a few more miles, he maneuvered through the streets of her development. The area had sprung to life back in the hey-days of the nineteen sixties when Vegas casinos grew from the sand. Every house was a rancher, all built from the same blueprint—some with rock gardens on the front lawn, others nothing but stone, still others, like hers, a mixture of tumbleweeds and sand. Several willow trees offered some shade, most were gnarled instead of weeping. A building over two stories was rare. Rarer still was any deviation to the flatness of the land. "This one is mine." She pointed to a faded, yellow-sided ranch-style house.

He eased the SUV alongside her curb. "I'm heading to the police station to talk to the man handling my case. I don't want Anna near you again."

"I doubt we'll stop her." She leaned over to kiss him lightly on the cheek. "Thanks for the ride." She slipped out the door and grabbed her bags from the back seat. "I'll see you Friday."

"Friday."

He waited for her to open the front door before he blew her a kiss and drove off.

Chapter Nine

Teegan's Friday night date with Budd pleased Jeff Andrews to no end. The man was beside himself with joy, because now he had time to develop a plan to trap Anna Kincaid. *Hurrah, hurrah!*

Teegan had her doubts. Throughout her Friday workday, despite the constant interruptions, meetings, and phone calls, she allowed her mind to drift back to Anna Kincaid. Something about that woman bothered her. Exactly what, she couldn't say. Her eyes maybe, not a craziness but more like an under-appreciated sanity if such a description existed.

Anna ran as fast as a whip on sure-footed feet, which enabled her to slip into the casino and out another door without anyone paying her any mind. She'd lived her life in Vegas and probably knew the layout better than elected officials, and perhaps still had friends willing to help her through a jam. Above all, Anna had the advantage over Teegan Smith, a newcomer to Vegas, a woman who barely knew her way around the city streets without the help of a GPS.

One fact is a certainty. If Anna doesn't kill me, then my father will.

Teegan had been down this road before, a stretch full of dangerous curves. She was a year into graduate school at Louisiana University when Jeff suckered her into uncovering the identity of a documents thief. Not just any ole documents. The Feds were searching for the perpetrators who sold copies of the Department of Defense blueprints detailing a very special weapon. Her covert assignment uncovered an espionage ring involving three students, foreigners on temporary visas, and one faculty member, the greediest bastard she'd ever met.

Like a fool, she'd agreed to a second assignment to find the whereabouts of stolen mercury from a government warehouse. That led to a third and fourth assignment until her father begged her to stop. The man had worried about guns pointing at her head or knives slitting her throat when she hardly had contact with the perpetrators. But from the moment she'd scraped a knee after falling from her bike, he always worried about his little girl. Needless concern—a father's job.

But Anna Kincaid's case was different, a stalker turned murderer after a man to do Lord knows what. Torture then kill? Force him into marriage? Kiss him until he submits to her demands?

Budd had refused police protection. Why? Granted, Anna had ample opportunities to kill him, but shouldn't he be more wary after her first knife attack? What rational thought lurked in the back of his mind? Yes, men with big egos believed themselves capable of solving any problem, especially physical. Her two brothers and father had taught her that marvelous piece of insight. *Maybe Budd is too macho for his own good—like Dad.*

Teegan threw down her pen and sat back then swiveled her chair to stare out the window. Despite the mound of paperwork waiting on her desk, she couldn't concentrate on anything but Anna Kincaid. She had pored over Anna's file, read dozens of psych evaluations, and reached the same conclusion as the experts. Anna was not crazy. Her lawyer bargained for an insanity plea to keep her out of prison. A classic defense. Now, Anna was on a vendetta to get the man who locked her away.

Oh, God, what a mess I'm in. Because one undeniable complication had developed. She and Budd had a powerful attraction, like two magnets struggling to stay apart. The feeling had started on the plane and only grew with each encounter. Every touch, every eye contact, had generated an overwhelming urge to mate— primitive, yes—but undeniably strong. Never in her dating history had a man hit her so hard nor so fast. At first, his pompous attitude was an excuse to dismiss him, but even her father gloated from time to time. Male ego again.

Like I don't have one.

Not blatantly obvious anyway.

After fighting a lack of concentration, Teegan gave up and left work in her brand new Audi, white this time, sleek and beautiful. Her date with Budd was several hours away so she stopped at a local convenience store, grabbed a plastic basket, and wandered the aisles, checking off her mental list of supplies. Eggs, milk, cream. A few munchies. *The oranges look good.* She sniffed a few and placed them in her basket then paused to study the array of bread selections.

A shadow approached. "Budd prefers rye." Ed Connors, wearing a gray business suit with matching tie, stood alongside, sipping from a large cup of coffee.

The man had movie-star qualities with his chiseled

face, blond hair, and blue eyes. Hands down, he was more handsome than Budd with arrogance more prominent. His smile was a devastating advertisement for great dental care—bright, white, and sparkling. He also had a way of making a woman feel naked with a simple sweep of his gaze.

"Ed Connors, Budd's partner." He extended his hand.

"Yes, I remember." She took the firm handshake and, like before at the burger bistro, he held on a tad too long. Fighting not to grimace, she pried away her hand. "What are you doing here?"

"I had a hankering for a cup of coffee."

He showed her the cup like she was blind and couldn't see. "The first time we met, you wore shorts and tank top. Today, it's business suit and heels. Beautiful then, beautiful now."

She stiffened. Ed's appearance in a business suit and tie at a convenience store buried within her development struck as an odd coincidence. Only locals patronized the place. "Do you live nearby?" She hoped not. A too-close-for-comfort scenario.

"Just passing through. I don't know what made me look you up online, but I'm glad I did." He slipped one hand into his trouser pocket and leaned against the shelving.

Her mind raced. Was her address posted on the web? Certainly not on the Smith Tool Company website. The county tax records perhaps, but local governments were notorious for their inability to keep records up-to-date.

His smile broadened. "You've made quite a name for yourself, Teegan Smith. A metals specialist with a doctorate. Fascinating. No wonder Budd's smitten."

"I wouldn't say he's smitten, Mr. Connors."

"Call me Ed."

She'd rather not call him anything. She moved down the aisle while picking up one bread loaf after the other, squeezing for freshness.

"Your date's tonight, right?"

"Yes." And if she didn't eat something soon, the butterflies in her stomach might pop out of her mouth. "How'd you know?"

He chuckled into his cup. "The news is all over the office. No one can keep a secret. You know, office gossip, water cooler talk. Look." He took out a business card from his shirt's breast pocket and shoved it in her hand. "If your date with Budd doesn't work, give me a buzz."

The man had brass balls. Teegan turned the card and stared at the Richardson, Feinberg, Connors imprint with Ed's cell number already included. The man probably never slept, if everyone called his personal phone. She wanted to toss the card back into his face, maybe shove it down his throat so he'd choke to death. She eyed him through narrowed lids. "Don't you think you're stepping on Budd's toes too soon?"

"I doubt it. He's not the serious sort. He'll show you a good time but never more than a few dates. That's his way."

She lifted one eyebrow. "You said he was smitten."

He sipped his coffee and swallowed quickly. "A figure of speech. He isn't the type to fall head over heels for a woman."

The statement confused her. Budd had put a lot of emotion into his kiss. If he gave so much with every woman, then he sent quite a few mixed messages. *No wonder Anna claimed he promised marriage.* For a man determined to remain single, he should kiss with a little less passion. Not like she had to worry. If history repeated as usual, her men lasted for a few dates before becoming uneasy with her brain.

"Number fifteen!"

"That's me," she said. "My lunchmeat order is ready." Teegan grabbed the rye bread then headed for the cash register.

Ed followed like a puppy on a leash.

The woman cashier looked at Teegan's purchase then cocked her head to the side.

"Twenty-seven sixty-two." Teegan dug into her purse for her wallet.

The cashier scanned the items into the digital register. "Twenty-seven sixty-two." Her slim shoulders slumped.

Ed stared, eyes wide.

The cashier laughed at his expression. "She does this to me all the time. A mathematical genius. I can't trip her up." She placed the items in a bag and handed it across the counter. "See you next time, Dr. Smith."

Ed followed Teegan out the door.

Would he follow her home, too? She approached her car door but stopped to look back at him right behind her.

"You have a legitimate super brain," Ed said. "What's it like to be so smart?"

Like many men before him, he had spoken with a tone not complimentary but not quite sarcastic either. Borderline nervousness was her description. A man unsure how to handle a smarter woman. She forced a smile. "I'm too analytical."

"Oh? Can you analyze me?"

She already had him figured out, but to keep the peace, she stifled a laugh and grabbed her door handle. "I don't understand men at all." Which was a bold lie. Between her father and two brothers teaching her the tricks up a man's sleeve and a mother adding her two cents, she'd had Ed pegged as another ladies' man at the burger restaurant.

Ed lifted the lid on his coffee cup to view the contents. "Do you live nearby?"

This man was getting on her nerves. Too pushy, too…coincidental. "Yes."

"In this neighborhood? Come on, Teegan, be straight with me. This isn't a place for a woman like you. Where? I know the area well enough."

Obviously, since he'd found a convenience store off the beaten track. "Nearby."

He flashed another brilliant smile. "I get the message. Sorry." He swallowed the last of his coffee and tossed the cup and lid into a nearby bin. When he turned back, he stared toward the street and started. His smile faded as the blood left his face.

Teegan followed his gaze to a dilapidated Chevy Impala parked alongside the street curb, spewing black smoke out the tailpipe. The occupant, a woman wearing sunglasses with a blue hoodie over her hair, fixated her attention on the store's entrance…on them.

Ed gasped and staggered against Teegan's car, blue eyes wide to popping. "She's following me!"

An interesting statement, although unlikely. *Play it cool.* She turned toward Anna's car and feigned a frown. "Who is she?"

"Her name's Anna. We had a few dates, some fun times. Budd's old girlfriend. Jealous of a fly touching her man. She's stalking me, too." He moistened a pair of dry lips.

"Well, sorry to hear that, Ed, but let me be on my way." She stepped into her car.

He grabbed her elbow and leaned close. "You can't leave me. I want her to see me with another woman."

She jerked her elbow from his hand. "Why, so I can take the bullet?" The man's complexion had turned to white ash. She wasn't certain whether to offer him sympathy or laugh herself silly. Instead, she patted his arm. "Relax. Maybe she has an issue with your law firm. You should tell Budd." *So I can get the hell out of here and chase the bitch.*

"Yeah, I'll tell him all right. Unlike Budd, I'll gladly accept police protection."

With a rumble, the Chevy took off down the street.

His gaze followed the smoke trail. "That woman scares me. I'm sure Budd told you about her." He wiped sweat from his brow. "I don't like this. We only had a few dates. Nothing serious. She hooked up with me years ago when Budd started with other women. A payback to make him jealous."

An interesting little tidbit. Jeff should know about Anna's earlier shenanigans. "Did it work?"

"No. Budd was done with her and didn't care. Anna refused to unhook her claws and went nuts." He took a step away and craned his neck to see down the street. "I'm slowly getting a reputation like Budd's, and women like Anna are a real nuisance. She'd never make my hot chick list."

"Careful. That kind of statement might get a knife

in your back." *From me this time.* She reached to close her car door, but Ed still stood in the way. She wanted to slam it against him to give him a hint to bug off.

He fidgeted, running a hand over the front of his shirt. "You're right. Don't repeat what I said to anyone. The truth is I'm in the running for Most Eligible Bachelor should Budd decide to tie the knot, which is unlikely. I'd hate for Anna to ruin the reputation I'm building."

Ed was tedious, filling her with tidbits of information she'd rather not hear. He had confirmed everything she'd read online about Budd Richardson, but tonight, she wanted to forget all the gossip and hearsay and have some fun.

"Seriously, Teegan, Budd only gives a woman a few dates before he moves on. Call me. You won't regret it." Finally, he moved away from her car only to hop into a red Jaguar in the next parking slot, roared the engine, and, with a wave, squealed from the lot.

Teegan scanned the immediate area for the Chevy and sighed. An opportunity lost.

She was aware of Budd's history with women. His habits were well documented on blogs, interviews, and news reports. He'd broken a few hearts, but no one labeled him a bastard. *Afraid to burn the bridge, no doubt.* She hated women with no backbone, allowing themselves to be used until someone better came along. *And what am I doing?*

A job, damnit, with fringe benefits. She closed the car door but hesitated, with her finger over the power button.

Ed's appearance had created an interesting happenstance. Was his arrival pure luck or a calculated move? Had he followed her from the office? If so, why…other than the obvious male conquering gene? If, by chance, he hadn't followed and simply saw her pull into the convenience store lot, then what brought him to this particular part of Vegas so far removed from any major route?

Anna's old neighborhood. And Anna had passed by. An interesting circumstance indeed. Leaning into the seat, she picked up her phone and called Reeves.

****

For two days, Budd struggled to grasp some semblance of concentration. He apologized right and left to the clients who sat before him, using the excuse of not feeling well until he finally told Denise to reschedule everything for the following week. Maybe by then, he could piece a conversation together without sounding like an idiot.

Never in his vast experience with women had one affected him so drastically. An incomprehensible confusion fogged his brain, something akin to an emotional rollercoaster since Teegan activated feelings he hadn't believed possible. She created an insatiable hunger. A physical hunger, yes, but an emotional one, as well. She'd given so much with a simple kiss, and an overwhelming wave of contentment flooded his core.

And Anna had nearly killed her. She'd intentionally rammed her car into Teegan's because of a kiss. Would Anna try again and succeed? He'd asked the question of Mike Reeves, and the big man merely shrugged in answer.

"You with me, Budd?"

Josh Feinberg's voice jolted him away from his thoughts. The bespectacled man had been sitting

110

opposite the desk, babbling about his latest case. Josh was the best strategist in the business, but right now, he spoke in a foreign tongue. Budd hadn't understood a word out of his mouth.

Ed Connors burst in, breathless, gripping the doorknob like he'd snap it in two. His beet-red face combined with his blond hair and eyebrows gave him the appearance of a lit torch.

"Anna's following me!"

Budd stared at the slightly disheveled man with his hair wind-blown and tie askew. "You ran up four flights of stairs?"

"Yes, I ran. The elevator takes too long." He stepped in and paced. "What should I do?"

"Calm down for starters." He motioned toward the door. "Maybe you should keep this conversation private."

Ed continued to pace, his gaze darting around the room as if Anna would materialize out of the book shelves. Josh jumped up to close the door and then reclaimed his seat.

Budd rolled his eyes at Josh's faint smile. "Why would Anna follow you, Ed?"

Ed's pacing stopped with a jerk. He stared while a finger touched the beads of sweat forming on his upper lip.

"What do you mean why? We dated and slept together."

"As you have with all my women." He leaned forward on the desk. "How about you, Josh? Did you date Anna, too?"

Josh chuckled as he fussed with his trouser crease. "Remember, I was married at the time you two were swapping bedmates. That's why I'm the brilliant one. I *studied*."

Budd sat back and gave Ed a long look. "I'll tell Sgt. Reeves about this. He'll want details."

"I'll tell him myself." He turned toward the door.

"Yo, whoa! What's the hurry? She threaten you?"

Ed stopped, his gaze to the floor, shoulders slumped. He glanced back with a weak grin. "She scared me."

What a wimp. "Where'd you see her?"

Ed chewed his lip.

A familiar delay tactic Budd recognized from law school when Ed mentally pieced together an argument for an answer he didn't have.

Ed unfastened the top button on his shirt and tugged his tie away from his neck. "I'm sorry, Budd. I was cutting through your old neighborhood when I spotted Teegan entering a convenience store. I usually wait for the okay, but damn, she's a wide cut above the others."

Budd tensed in his chair. "You hit on her?"

"I simply said hello. We talked a while. Then, Anna rode by."

Budd's blood boiled in his veins. He slammed his fists on the desk and shot to his feet. If the desk wasn't in the way, he'd have strangled Ed with his bare hands. "She's off limits, Ed! Do I make myself clear?"

Ed threw up his hands in surrender. "Clear enough. I know I should have waited—"

"Off limits, damnit! And Anna wasn't following you. She was watching Teegan." He grabbed his cell phone from the desk and made a quick call to Reeves to relay the information. Finished, he disconnected, tossed the phone onto his desk pad, and ran a hand through his hair. "Mike will stop by to talk to you. Give him details, hear me?" *Of all the brazen, stupid, idiotic—*

Ed hadn't done anything new, but this was the first time Budd wanted to tear him into tiny pieces. Teegan wasn't a showgirl out to make a name for herself. She had class plus brains and beauty, not to mention he hadn't given Ed the go-ahead.

Budd sucked in a deep breath to help alleviate the blood pressure about to squirt out his ears and turned toward the windows. *Maybe I should punch his face. That will help.*

The reaction was foreign. For some strange reason, Budd felt a possessiveness toward Teegan, as if no man had the right to look at any part of her...especially Ed, the man with roaming eyes, hands, and tongue. He faced his two partners and frowned at Ed's continued pacing. "Sit down because I want to discuss something with you and Josh."

Josh grabbed for Ed's arm as he passed and held firm. With a nod of his head, he motioned toward the chair alongside. "You're more nervous than some of my clients."

Once Ed settled on the seat, both men turned their attention to Budd.

Thank God for Josh. He was the quiet one, the calm between two storms. The trait came in handy— like now. Budd sighed heavily and flopped onto his chair. "I want to offer Bailey a partnership."

Both men stared, wide-eyed.

Josh shook himself first. "Why?"

"He deserves the promotion. He's bringing a lot of money into the firm because of his divorce specialty."

Josh uncrossed his legs and sat forward, his gaze intense through the thick glasses. "I'm against the move. Another partner is technically a pay cut for the three of us."

"Well, here's the kicker. I want to reduce my load without overburdening either of you."

Josh's dark eyes grew wide. "Because of this woman?" He sat back.

"No, because my cabin is almost finished. I'd like to spend more time there." *With Teegan.* He inwardly jerked. Had he actually thought that? No woman would tolerate such an isolated location without phone or TV available. Heaven forbid. And a rich one at that. *Don't assume, idiot. Ask her.*

He should break his habit of assumptions. She might surprise him and love the solitude.

"Why not take time off whenever you want?" Josh suggested. "Let Ed and I handle your load. I can use the extra money."

Ed gripped the arms of his chair and glared at Josh. "I'm not anxious for any additional work. I have a social life. You don't."

Josh held up a finger. "For your information, I'm doing okay in the dating department. I refuse to brag, that's all."

Ed quivered his legs in a rapid up-and-down motion as he sat with his hands rubbing the armrests. He no longer had the beet-red face, but his gaze darted as if he was trapped in a cage.

Budd rolled his eyes. "Calm down, Ed. I'm tempted to beat you to a pulp, but I won't since you're so upset."

Ed snapped his gaze toward Budd. "Huh? No, I'm

not worried about you. It's Anna." He slapped his knees to stop the quiver. "I wouldn't hurry to the cabin with Anna breathing down your neck, Budd. If she traps you in the middle of the desert, she'll end your life for sure." He jumped to his feet. "I need a drink. Anyone?" Without waiting for a reply, Ed hurried to the wet bar, poured a hefty shot of whiskey into a glass, and gulped the spirit in one swallow. He slid into his seat again. The quivering legs continued. "What makes you believe Anna was watching Teegan?"

"Because Anna attacked her at the airport, and Teegan was only talking to me. Then, she slammed her car into Teegan's at the burger restaurant, nearly killing her."

Ed's mouth fell open. "Why didn't Teegan say something? She had to recognize Anna. I sure as hell did."

"She probably had a thousand reasons why. For one, Anna ran from the car accident. Maybe Teegan didn't get a good look for a proper ID."

Ed stared at the wet bar and licked his lips. "Plausible." He met Budd's steady gaze. "Then don't you think it's risky to date while Anna's on the loose?"

Josh glanced from one man to the next, his gaze squinting behind the glasses. "You two make Anna sound like an animal. Suppose she had justification for killing the orderly? Need I quote some of the horror stories we've heard from institutions around the country?" He scratched his beard. "We should treat all information as hearsay."

"Bullshit to your hearsay," Ed complained. "You can't justify purposely crashing your car into another. I think her upstairs compartment is skewed." Arching an eyebrow, Ed tapped the side of his head. "She's crazy."

Josh waved away the comment. "I'm keeping an open mind. I don't know why she's after Teegan except for a jealousy factor. What do you think, Budd?"

Budd drummed his fingers on the desk. "Anna should come forward and talk to us. If she's a victim of the system, she could cop a defense plea."

"You're both nuts." Ed shifted in his seat. "You can't justify her attack on Teegan."

"I'll discuss the matter with Mike," Budd said. "Otherwise, we can debate the subject all day." He leaned forward on the desk. "I want you to think about Bailey. The sooner we sign him on, the more time I can spend at the cabin. I won't talk to him until the two of you give the okay. Mull it over this weekend and let me know Monday."

"Assuming you survive your hot date tonight," Josh said with a grin.

A knock sounded on the door before Denise popped in her head. "Am I interrupting?"

Budd swiveled to face her. "What's up?"

"Everything is set for tonight. Do you want to pick up the roses, or should I have them delivered?"

"Have them delivered and tell the florist to make sure the flowers are fresh." Nothing, not even a wilted bouquet would spoil his plans for Teegan tonight.

Chapter Ten

If anyone challenged Budd to write a list about the annoyances in his life, he'd write the cell phone at the top in bold letters. He hated the incessant interruptions, and from the time he walked through the courthouse doors and drove back to the office, he'd answered one call after another. He vowed then and there not to give his cell number to anyone ever again, only the office phone. *Enough, damnit.* He stepped into his building's elevator with the phone plastered to his ear.

With his phone in one hand and a briefcase in the other, he took advantage of the only other occupant in the elevator for assistance. "Four, please."

His women would be first and foremost on the cutoff list since they were the majority of the calls. They offered invitations to parties—premiere events, grand opening ceremonies, wherever a studio sent a camera crew. Like he had the slightest desire for more exposure. The paparazzi made his life unbearable now. On a daily basis, they gathered outside the courthouse doors, followed him on dates, even once into the john. Shocked by such a blatant intrusion, he'd almost peed all over the guy.

The one voice he'd love to hear was Teegan's. Naturally, she had more important things to do other than pick up a phone for some idle chit-chat. All right, this last buzz was Denise. She usually had something important to say, but he was in the elevator for crying out loud, almost with his foot inside the office door.

The elevator stopped with a lurch. He glanced up to see the light lit for the seventh floor. *Great.* Missed his floor. "I'll be a few minutes, Denise." *Unless the contraption plans to swallow me alive.*

"Funny how you can count on people to be oblivious with their surroundings while on the phone. You never double-checked to see if I pressed the fourth floor button."

His head snapped to the other occupant, a woman in a blue hoodie, standing by the buttons, her hand on the emergency stop.

"Anna!" Good grief, he gasped like an idiot.

She lowered the hood and twisted her lips into a grin. "Hi, Budd."

What now? He wasn't afraid of her, but her proximity was too close for comfort. "How'd you get past security at the entrance?"

"Oh, please, anyone can study their habits and slip by." She folded her arms across her chest and leaned against the elevator wall. "Day in, day out, they follow the same routine. No deviation. That's because some moron in a front office gives them a checklist to follow so they don't have to use their brain." She motioned toward his hand. "Put away the phone, Budd. We need to talk."

He glanced at his phone to discover Denise had already disconnected. Had she heard anything to alert Reeves or at least security on the ground floor? With his luck, probably not. He slid the phone into his suit pocket. "I've no desire to talk to you, Anna."

She hadn't changed over the years. Still small,

maybe a hundred pounds, no more. Same long, brown hair, a tad too dull and lifeless. She had a few more wrinkles around a pair of brown, emotionless eyes. Some people called them laugh lines, but she wasn't the cheery type. Her lips had the same crooked smile from so long ago—a sneer exposing two side teeth. When he was younger, he thought her smile was the sexiest he'd ever seen. Now, the sinister twist caused a shiver.

"I followed your career, Budd. You've made quite a name for yourself. Every man envies you. Every female wants you in bed. How's it feel to be so famous?"

"Fame is a curse." He remembered the day he vowed to take on the snobs of Vegas. He had busted his ass waiting tables for a Saturday night dinner crowd when Shirley Beckett chastised him in front of the entire dining room. Her father had millions invested in a casino, and she was the typical spoiled brat with her curved nose in the air and bottle-red hair lacquered to withstand a tornado. She'd come into his restaurant and purposely requested one of his tables, taking great pleasure in reaming him from top to bottom about not enough ice in her water glass, not enough salt in the shaker, not enough artificial sweetener at the table—everything and anything to make him hustle.

At one point, he wanted to dump the entire salad bowl onto her lap but bit his tongue and took the abuse, because he needed the job. He hadn't waited on her again, even when she insisted. And no big loss either. She was a lousy tipper.

"Yes, I see the smugness on your face, Budd. You achieved everything beyond your wildest dreams. Fame, fortune, and status." She tucked a strand of long, brown hair behind her ear. "We had a good camaraderie."

"Until you stuck the knife in my back."

She wagged a finger. "You forgot to write the word loyalty on your list. That was me, you know."

He snorted. "You wanted marriage, Anna. I was still struggling with my career."

He wasn't about to turn into another Josh Feinberg. Josh married too soon and had a child shortly thereafter. Following the divorce, the poor man couldn't afford a newspaper. Budd had helped him renegotiate the divorce settlement so he'd have money to buy a sandwich.

He scanned the ceiling of the elevator to see if, by some miracle, the building owner fixed the busted camera. No such luck. Still without a lens or a red light. He scowled at Anna. "Did you flatten my tires?"

Her brown eyes widened to show red within the white. "Why would I do that?"

"You tell me. Someone broke into my garage and punctured three of my tires."

"Not me, honey-baby. I'm sure you've made plenty of enemies over the years."

Honey-baby. He inwardly shuddered at the pet name. He'd hated the tag in high school and sure as hell hated it now. A quick glance at the floor numbers again. Would anyone notice the elevator sitting stationary? Or how about Denise? Would she wonder why he's taking so long?

Fat chance on all of the above. He had a habit of having lengthy discussions with other business owners in the building. With four elevators covering sixteen floors and constantly on the move, people wouldn't question one out of order until a second one broke down. "What do you want, Anna?"

She shifted onto one foot as she uncrossed her arms and stuffed her hands into her jacket pockets. "The answer is obvious, Budd, but not here, not now. We have a lot of catching up to do. This visit is to prove I can reach you anytime I want, despite those two idiots following you everywhere." She cocked her head. "You never came to see me in the hospital."

Well, duh. "You tried to kill me. What possible reason did I have to visit?"

She shook her head. "See what I mean about loyalty? You don't know the meaning of the word. Why'd you hook up with a rich-bitch?"

He stared and stepped back toward the opposite elevator wall. "I'm not seeing anyone."

"You kissed her in the parking lot."

The hair on the back of his neck stood on end. He wanted to grab Anna's head between his hands and pound her against the wall to knock some sense into her thick skull. Her attack on Teegan was totally unjustified and so juvenile, like high school all over again. He glared at Anna's smug face. "You almost killed her."

"And done you a big favor in the process. I can't believe you're dating a Vegas snob. You despised them in college, but I guess you forgot."

"No, I didn't forget. And I'm not dating her." *Yet.* "Besides, she's different."

She gave a harsh laugh. "You're one of them now, just another Vegas snob with his nose in the air. You rejected me because I wasn't good enough anymore."

He gritted his teeth. "You wanted marriage. I didn't. You're the one who couldn't wait."

"For what? I'm not stupid. You were calling it quits after all our years together. I'm sorry I didn't use a longer knife."

If she had, she wouldn't be having this conversation with him in an elevator. He'd be six feet in the ground.

In retrospect, he'd handled her badly. He just signed Ed on as a partner, and the pair wanted to celebrate. Anna insisted on tagging along. He politely told her to climb a flagpole and flap around to make herself useful. And he'd said that *before* any liquor touched his lips. A month later, she put the knife in him.

He clutched his briefcase to his chest. "Okay, you've come to kill me. So, do it."

She snickered while adjusting the zipper on her jacket. "I'm not going to kill you. I had plenty of opportunities before this. We need to spend some time together, that's all."

A friendly chat perhaps? And then what? Would she say goodbye forever before the court locked her in a cell for murder one? "Why'd you kill the orderly, Anna? Was she abusing you?" Something flickered in her eyes. Pain? Anger? *Maybe Josh is right.*

With a finger, she brushed away a loose strand of hair from her face. "Like you really care. Don't play me for a sap." She flicked her straight hair off her shoulder. "The system sucks as anyone will tell you. And this isn't the time nor the place for our conversation. We can't hold the elevator all day." She looked up at the floor numbers. "I will make arrangements for our discussion." She released the elevator stop button.

The car continued its upward journey.

"Look, Anna, you're in a lot of trouble. Surrender to the cops, and I'll help you."

"Oh? Like you helped put me in the loony bin? Get real." She flipped up the hood to cover her hair.

"Your lawyer filed an insanity plea. I had nothing to do with the court's decision." He contemplated slamming the alarm button to attract security's attention, but what was the use? The elevator was heading upward, and security was on the first floor. By the time a response team arrived, they'd find Budd twiddling his thumbs while Anna strolled out the front door. *Unless I hold her.* But what if she was armed?

He shot her a probing gaze. "The best I can do is keep you off death row, Anna, but you have to turn yourself in first. I can't bargain otherwise."

The elevator stopped.

Anna exited on the eleventh floor but held the doors in the open position. "Thanks for the offer, Budd, but I won't turn myself in. I think I'm smart enough to stay one step ahead of the cops." She glanced up and down the hall before fixing a steady gaze onto his face. "And one more point to consider. Be careful with this rich-bitch. She isn't what she seems."

Teegan? She was the most transparent woman he'd ever met. He matched her steady gaze. "What are you saying?"

"I can't figure her out yet. When I do, I'll let you know."

His gut tightened. "I want you to leave her alone."

"And I want her to leave *you* alone. I'll be in touch."

The doors closed on Anna's sneering face.

A cold chill traveled the length of his spine. What

part of Anna was the girl he knew? Her bitterness hadn't mellowed over the years. *But she only wants to talk.*

And I've got an island in the middle of Lake Mead to sell. Without question, her visit breached the security the police meticulously arranged. With a tight fist, he slammed the button for the fourth floor and then yanked out his cell phone to call Reeves.

Chapter Eleven

Teegan had several hours to ready for her date. She started with a long soak in the tub then a hard scrubbing of her hair to wash out all the doubts accumulating. She agonized over her decision to date Budd, and in particular, her acceptance of Jeff Andrews' assignment. Keeping secrets from Budd was one matter. She hadn't known him long enough for a guilt complex to surface. Keeping secrets from her father rubbed against the grain. From the time words flowed out of her mouth, she'd told the man everything—some of which he'd prefer not to hear. Sure, not every detail of her social life, but about school, work, and now, her COO job. Since she talked to her father every other day, she had practiced the patient art of self-control.

Was she doing Jeff a favor by delaying Budd? Anna could easily remain in the shadows and plan a course of action for when the FBI and LVPD dealt with some catastrophic event, like a school shooting, or a bombing at one of the casinos. For months, she had successfully avoided arrest, so what were a couple more weeks when her obsession had festered over five years?

I can't possibly stay undercover when the factory goes online unless I'm doing this case for selfish reasons.

The thought was a valid one. She wasn't adverse to Budd's effect on her body. For two nights, she'd dreamt of him, their evening to come, what they might do, and where they'd end up. Every conceivable emotion emerged to put her into a sweat. Apprehension. Fear. Anticipation. Above all, exhilaration. Of the men in her life, none had caused such turmoil. Her stomach stayed in a constant knot. She could barely eat, sleep, or think.

Why? What was so different about Budd that rattled her Einstein brain? She'd met men like him before—a borderline-obnoxious man full of arrogance and good-looks. She'd slept with them, too. So, why the butterflies? Anna?

Maybe. The danger of the assignment. An unpredictable woman capable of slipping through the cracks. Anna wanted Budd and wouldn't stop until she got him. Well, Teegan Smith wanted him, too.

The man occupied every thought passing through her mind, and she hardly had the concentration to get ready for their date. After slipping on her dress, she rushed around with no clue why, rearranging knickknacks for no reason whatsoever, fighting off the urge to cook something to settle her nerves, which was ridiculous since she couldn't eat anyway. *Damn good thing I'm not working in the lab.* She'd be toying with formulas. One wrong move and poof! A mushroom cloud over Vegas.

The doorbell rang, and her breath stopped. He was here, and their night was about to begin. She slipped on her high heels and scanned the bedroom. Everything was in order...not like a man gave a shit about the décor. She hurried to the living room.

A special night deserved a special dress, and at the dress shop, a sleek black jersey knit had caught her eye. As soon as she closed the zipper, she gasped at the mirror for the dress showed every God-given curve. Low cut to expose some cleavage, slit up the side to reveal half of her thigh, a fitted waist to emphasize rounded hips. She couldn't resist. *No one can label me bashful.*

She'd adamantly refused to wear a transmitter even after Jeff told her about Budd's elevator encounter. This was her night, and she wanted to have a good time without eavesdroppers chuckling over an intimate moment. Bad enough they listened to Budd sucking out her lungs in the bistro parking lot. So, not tonight, thank you. With a final calming breath, she threw open the front door.

Budd's eyes nearly popped out of their sockets as his gaze traversed her body in a slow, seductive sweep.

"You look fabulous!" He swallowed hard. "I think I've become your slave." He stepped in and slipped his arms around her, crushing her close to his chest. "I'm so glad someone punctured my tires." He clutched the back of her neck as his hot lips captured her mouth.

He stole every ounce of resistance with a simple flick of his tongue, causing her body to go limp in his arms. Tiny atoms exploded with the sensations of pure pleasure as his lips slid over her lipstick, tingling her taste buds with anticipation. Without the slightest push, she could satisfy her hunger by feasting her eyes and mouth on him. All night. On a bed. No sleep, just wild, passionate sex. Unfortunately, Jeff's meticulous arrangements wrenched her back into reality. The sooner Anna was behind bars, the safer for Budd.

His hand on the back of her neck forced her to recognize the nakedness of her neckline. She'd been so busy rearranging knickknacks, she'd forgotten her jewelry. She brushed her lips across his cheek. "We might be late for our dinner reservation." She traveled back to his mouth and bit his lower lip while her fingers unbuttoned his suit jacket to slip her hands inside, not in the least willing to let him go. Solid chest muscles greeted her touch. *God help me.* She squeezed before pushing away. "I forgot my necklace."

His hands slid down her body, caressing every curve along the way.

She shuddered from the trail of heat left behind.

"You're right. I promised you a night on the town…unless you want to cancel everything and stay here." He cocked an eyebrow and waited.

Oh, wouldn't she love to do that. She wanted this man on some cool bed sheets and soon. "I'll get my necklace." *And a fan, damnit.*

When she returned, she found him standing where she'd left him, his gaze studying a small white envelope in his hands. He wore an Armani suit of pale gray, beautifully tailored to fit his solid frame.

He looked up and extended it. "This was on your doormat. I slipped it into my pocket, because I had every intention of grabbing you."

She accepted the envelope and turned it over in her hand, an invitation-size envelope with no writing on the outside, the flap tucked and not sealed. She extracted a handwritten note and read.

You run like an old lady, and I'm not surprised. The rich rarely do things for themselves. This isn't your neighborhood. You don't belong here and don't belong with Budd. I've already given you one warning. Stay away from him, or you won't see your next birthday!

Well, well, Anna had followed her home after all,

probably from the convenience store. Teegan slipped the card into her purse, grateful that Budd had occupied his attention elsewhere.

"Is this your family?" Budd pointed to the framed photos on the wall. "I recognize Frank, of course."

She stepped behind him, slipped her arms around his waist, and placed her chin on his shoulder. "Yep, my mom and dad, my two brothers, their wives, and my one nephew. That's our house in Philly. Nothing special, a big town home." She sniffed the aftershave on his neck, an intoxicating spice, and resisted the urge to bite his neck. Otherwise, they'd never get out of here. "Dad wasn't a show-off. Neither was Mom. My brothers and I are the same."

"Then your older rancher makes perfect sense even though the size and neighborhood doesn't fit someone with your bankroll."

"You can't beat a ten-minute commute, Budd, and for now, the house suits my needs." Her lips brushed his neck. "I'm in a temporary position, if you remember. I had no need to fuss."

She had fallen in love with the small rancher with its faded yellow siding the second she stepped from the realtor's car. Cute little bushes surrounded the perimeter of the exterior that drooped from lack of water, but they'd blossomed into healthy scrubs after a few weeks of tender care. The interior had a wide-open look because of a living room which merged with a kitchen. Two bedrooms, one bath, no basement. A perfect size since she was hardly home to use it. Leasing wasn't an option, so she'd purchased it outright. Shocked the pants off the realtor when she hadn't haggled.

Still with her arms around his middle, she turned Budd to face her. "Thank you for those." She nodded toward a bouquet of red roses.

He wrapped his arms around her and pulled her close.

We'll never get anywhere if this keeps up. But she loved being in his arms, loved the feel of him against her body, all muscle and man, loved how all her nerves fired at once. *I have a job to do.* She had to keep herself focused, even though visions of two people on a bed wouldn't go away.

Her fingers straightened his tie. Powder blue to match his eyes, his silk shirt was a soft cream. Handsome no matter what color he wore.

Her hands trembled, a reaction that still puzzled her. She'd been around the block a few times with some of the most handsome men in Philadelphia, but she took a slow, leisurely stroll with them. For some reason, she felt as if she sprinted with Budd, leaving her breathless and shaking. Not an unwelcomed feeling, just…strange.

He grabbed both her hands and held firm while a slight curl lifted the corner of his mouth.

Too noticeable, damnit. So much for my sophisticated PhD persona. She met his focused gaze and cleared her throat. "I'm out of practice." No exaggeration. The plans for the new factory had taken away her social time. Being this close to a man who caused her heart to skip made her feel like a school girl on her first date.

He kissed her hands and encountered a string of pearls draped over one thumb.

"Would you mind?" She handed him the necklace. "I can't get the clasp together." Since she'd suddenly grown ten thumbs. Hard to believe she had aced the gun range. Turning, she faced a wall mirror.

His eyes grew in size as he stared through the mirror. "You want me to touch your shoulders? Teegan, please, I'm having enough trouble keeping my hands off you!"

A thrill coursed through her veins at his words. Titillation plus. A woman couldn't ask for a nicer compliment. Even better, he took an inordinate amount of time to hook the clasp, and his fingers brushing against her skin caused shivers of delight to rock her core.

He grumbled in protest and smiled at the same time. "I didn't agree to a night of erotic torture, you know." He fingered the spaghetti straps that were a pretense for holding up the dress. His gaze danced back at hers through the mirror.

"Don't you dare break them!"

A low chuckle rumbled in his throat as his hands traced along the soft skin of her shoulders.

Goose bumps sprang to the surface while she fought to control short, rapid breaths. She closed her eyes and shuddered from the sheer pleasure of his warm touch.

With one hand, he lifted her hair away from her neck. "I had to tell the police my plans for tonight. I hope you don't mind." He swept feather kisses along her shoulders. "They wanted me to wear a transmitter. Can you believe they'd make such a request?" He bit her neck.

Dear Lord in heaven, I'll never make it.

"They're assigning a female cop to keep an eye on you. Of course, if you don't want to go..." His lips suckled the side of her neck.

Her heart thundered in her chest. The anticipation of being alone with this man was too much to bear. In five more seconds, she'd be lost in pleasure. Teegan whirled to plant her lips on his while grabbing both his butt cheeks in a tight grip.

He reciprocated by clamping onto her butt and pushing her belly against a rising appendage. Heat surrounded their bodies as tongues danced, the air crackling with sensuality.

She had never been so sexually attracted to a man where an unbearable emotional frenzy threatened to rob all her self control. She wanted him, damnit, but thoughts of Jeff and his plans slapped her back to reality. With reluctance, she broke away.

Budd stared with wide eyes. "Dear Lord, are you sure you want to leave?"

"Consider my lips your cocktail. Dessert comes later." She threw a black shawl around her shoulders, grabbed her purse, and hurried him out the door before she changed her mind.

So, their night began. Finally, a date.

Budd drove along the infamous Vegas Strip among bright lights and traffic pointing to the various casinos along the way. Every casino had an eye-catching scene—whether strobe lights or multi-lit fountains, all exteriors brightly illuminated to attract passersby. Some casinos were monstrous in size, looking like a city unto itself, which was understandable. If customers lose themselves on the inside, they'd never find the outside and leave.

People strolled on the sidewalks, snapping photos—some dressed for a night on the town, others in casual attire, tourists on vacation, families out for a summer-night view of the city. She hadn't seen much of the Vegas nightlife, and this was a great way to start.

Budd had chosen a five-star restaurant off the Strip, separate from the many establishments affiliated with the casinos. The maitre d' led them to a round booth against the wall with a table big enough to seat six people. She and Budd slid toward the center, a more intimate arrangement than to shout across such a large table.

Soft music played overhead, barely audible. No bustling food servers. No clanging dishes. A peaceful atmosphere with colors of greens and blues as the backdrop. Dim overhead lights gave some illumination, but to read the menu, several lit candles on the table had sufficed.

While waiting for their orders, they sipped perfectly-chilled wine with an appetizer of artichoke pâté and wafers. Budd had his arm around her shoulder and caressed her skin with the tips of his fingers. She leaned against him with a hand on his thigh. They hadn't stopped touching each other from the moment they'd left her house, and she loved every minute. "This is nice, Budd. Do you come here often?"

"Actually, only once before. I brought my parents for a celebration dinner after I passed my bar exam. I charged the meal and stretched the payments over several months." He chuckled softly then, just as quickly, his faint smile disappeared and his gaze became distant as he absently rubbed two fingers up and down the wine glass stem. "My dad died three weeks later. I hadn't a chance to tell him I'd been offered a position at the most prestigious law firm in the city." He shook himself, lifted his wine glass, and sipped.

"I didn't stay with the firm long. They catered to the wealthiest clients in Vegas, blatantly ignoring two-thirds of the people in this city. That was wrong." His gaze followed a food server moving stealthy across the room, two plates in hand. "I approached the boss with the possibility of starting a satellite office for the poor, but he laughed at the suggestion. Not long after, I quit and started my own firm. Josh joined a year later. We grew from that point." He toyed with his glass and gave her a quick sideways glance.

"I know I sounded all pompous on the plane, but the truth is I handle the wealthy, Josh mid-to-upper middle class, and Ed's in charge of seven associates working the poorer districts, people like my parents who hadn't two pennies to rub together." With a finger touch on her chin, he turned her head toward him. "You called me a snob on the plane. I'd like to believe I've changed your mind since that meeting."

She squeezed his thigh and enjoyed the feel of the hard muscle under the trouser fabric. "You have." She kissed him lightly.

A curl of a smile tugged his lip. "Thank you. Anna made the same accusation this afternoon. I don't think I've changed her mind."

Jeff and Mike were livid when Budd called about Anna's appearance in the elevator. In turn, Jeff phoned Teegan to request she stay especially vigilant. *What a joke*! If he only knew how easily Budd distracted her. One touch and her mind flew to a bedroom. However, Budd deserved a reaction to his news, and she gave him a wide-eyed quizzical look.

He touched her hair. "She got past security and met me in the elevator. Reeves went ballistic. He's the detective handling my case. I knew all along Anna had no intention of killing me."

"What does she want?"

"To talk. She said she'd set the time and place."

Yeah, a time and place to kill.

The food arrived. He had ordered shrimp, lightly browned. She ordered lobster smothered in butter. The conversation flowed to casual topics. Casino headliners. The ever-growing city limits. He discussed politics, she chemistry. She tasted his shrimp and rolled her eyes as the crustacean melted in her mouth. She almost stabbed his hand when he reached for a piece of lobster, but she reluctantly allowed him a bite.

Sitting so close, constantly touching, feeding each other forkfuls of wonderful food—each action bordered on the erotic. She struggled with the conflict of completing her assignment and the arousal Budd caused. She swore she'd hump him right on the table before the dessert arrived. What would he say about a woman with her precious Beretta in her purse ready to protect him from a cold-blooded killer?

Only Budd was convinced of Anna's benign talkfest. The powers that be—herself included—believed otherwise. If Jeff's plan succeeded tonight, he'd have Anna Kincaid belly-aching from a jail cell without Budd being the wiser about the FBI's special operative.

If the plan succeeded. The thought of failure caused her gut to wrench.

Budd glanced at his watch then motioned to the waiter for the check. With a light finger, Budd touched her chin. "We, my lovely one, have another stop to make."

That stop was—by Budd's definition—the coolest dance club in Vegas. The place was packed, the music loud, the whole atmosphere electrifying. He led the way through a horde of gyrating bodies crowding a strobe-lit dance floor.

Teegan let the music take her. Up until tonight, fun had become an obsolete word. She allowed so little time for personal indulgences since arriving in Vegas, and this man was an indulgence she couldn't resist.

The method of dance where two partners jerked in front of the other with a space of about a foot between them wasn't her style of dancing. She loathed the idea of being detached when so much fun could be derived from a touch as simple as a hand. She slipped her right hand through the fingers of his left, placed her left hand with clutch purse onto his shoulder, and closed the distance between them, using the rhythm of the music to force him to synch with her movements. His wide-eyed look almost made her laugh.

"Teegan, what the—"

She placed her finger against his lips to silence him. Speech was impossible so she motioned for him to follow her lead. He followed beautifully, matching her rhythm including a few kicks as if they had practiced a routine. Men rarely took the time to learn how to dance. Most hopped around like apes courting a female, never impressive enough to warrant a second glance. But Budd performed some impressive steps. She only wished she had another way to conceal her gun. Without the clutch purse, she'd have both hands free to traverse his body, but a sexy dress hardly left room to hide a pistol.

A slow song with its lower decibel level allowed her a chance to speak. "You dance very well."

"You're even better. Where'd you learn to move so well?"

She squeezed the hand holding hers close to his chest. "My mother dragged me kicking and screaming to the dance studio when I was seven years old, because my brothers turned their little sister into a tomboy." She whirled around him to make a point, using no more than five seconds to leave his arms. "I fell in love with dancing from the start, after the initial pouting, of course. I finally left the studio behind when I transferred to Louisiana State."

He tilted his head, his gaze twinkling. "I wasn't far off calling you a showgirl. Even on the plane, you moved with the grace of a dancer. Why didn't you turn pro?"

She shook her head, body, and everything else at the suggestion. "Too much hard work. I'm inherently lazy for such a demanding career."

"But you pursued your doctorate, which you obtained by the age of twenty-six. I'd say that's hard work." He smiled. "You continue to amaze me, Teegan Smith."

"Does my brain amaze you, too? Most men run in the opposite direction when they discover my IQ."

"I'm not like most men."

A whisper kiss brushed her nose as his hand slid to the small of her back, creating a flood of tingling chills. She silently groaned.

"I'm okay with a genius in my arms, Teegan." He guided her away from another couple. "I made my success on my own with the brains in my head so I possess a reasonable IQ along with my good-looks." His playful gaze sparkled.

She kissed his nose. "Your pretty face isn't my only point of interest, Budd Richardson. I also have this growing fascination to see your body." *All of it, and soon.*

His eyebrows arched. "Do you now? In that case, I'd like to start a full-fledged relationship. I want to discover the intimate details that make you unique."

Her mouth fell open. *Did I hear right?*

"What's the matter?"

She slapped shut her mouth. "You said a word I've never heard from a man's mouth. Men run from relationships, not initiate them." Maybe he was pulling her leg. She cocked her head. "Isn't this conversation a bit premature? We're on our first date."

"I always like to put my cards on the table. I'll admit I've never used the R-word with another woman, so I'm causing an awful lot of disappointment by taking you on full time."

"Most men would call you crazy."

He held up a finger. "The word is lucky. If the liaison doesn't work, then we'll go our separate ways." He lifted her hand to his lips and gave a light kiss to her knuckle. "Look on the bright side. I already know your father."

Teegan laughed, released her hand from his, and slipped her arms around his neck, swaying in rhythm with his hips. Her lips brushed his, a soft, easy touch of which he returned while his arms squeezed her to his chest. When she met his gaze, she gasped at the burning intensity that turned her knees into mush. Was she ready for a man with such a strong sexual pull?

A new song started, one with a distinctive rumba beat. Rumba was one of her specialties, but she refused to release her arms from around his neck.

Until now, she had never experienced such an overwhelming yearning from any man. Logic said the feeling was hormonal, a genetic predisposition to propagate the species. Her heart argued otherwise. One of these days, she might listen to her heart and tell her brain to take a hike.

"Hesitant?" He leaned close to her ear. "I felt your back muscles tense."

"I'm more shocked than hesitant. I never expected such a request from a confirmed bachelor."

"To clarify, Teegan, I'm offering a get-to-know-you proposition. You understand my views about marriage."

But he had no idea about her opinion on the subject. She wanted the whole package someday. A family to call her own, a man who wasn't afraid of her brain or her money. Should she waste time with a man who had announced his intention to stay single from the get-go? Right now, she was his toy to be played with then discarded when boredom set in.

At thirty-one, she wasn't in the mood for games. "Let me think about your offer, Budd." Maybe his definition of relationship was a little skewed. Besides, she had her secret role to consider and Ed Connors' bold statement about Budd's dating habits. The relationship could end faster than Superman's speeding bullet. However, a fling including a bedroom romp wasn't out of the question. She gave one last sway before placing her palms flat onto his suit jacket. "How about something to drink? I'm parched."

"I thought you'd never ask." He stopped her from leaving his arms. "Before we proceed further, I need to lay down a few ground rules. You have to let me win at chess once in a while. I'll get cranky if you always win."

"No need to worry, Budd Richardson. I don't know how to play chess. Never learned."

Eyes wide, he stepped back, a hand to his heart. "I assumed all geniuses played chess?"

She flicked a finger under his chin. "Not this one. I grew up like a normal kid. We played football on the lawn and baseball in the park, but no chess. I was the only one in the family with a genius-level IQ and got no special treatment."

He rubbed his hands and gave a twisted grin. "Good. I won't teach you my tricks."

Budd took her hand and cut through the crowd toward one of three bars. *Like plowing through a herd of cattle going in the opposite direction.* The dance club spanned the dimensions of a football field. Tables and booths outlined the perimeter of the dance floor, all occupied. A balcony with more tables overlooked everyone. Each bar was staffed by two bartenders with servers picking up orders as fast as they were placed on the counter.

The main entrance had a set of wide-open double doors with a constant influx of patrons. Teegan counted six exit signs, three restrooms, a stage with a DJ encased in glass, and two staircases leading to the balcony. The place was a security nightmare.

Anna had a vast selection of nooks and crannies to hide, but dozens of eyes monitored the activity. Jeff had prepared a trap akin to the Secret Service protecting the President.

But would Anna place herself in this environment to get to Budd? Logic said no. Too dangerous. Too many variables. Anna needed Budd alone for their 'talk'. Why risk getting caught before she accomplished her goal?

While waiting at the bar for their drinks, Teegan scanned the perimeter of the club, allowing her gaze to take in one group after another until settling on a cluster of boisterous elderly men in the far corner. They looked out of place with their gray hair and wire-rimmed glasses standing next to a bunch of spiked-haired twenty-somethings. The tall, handsome one stopped her dead.

Their gazes locked, and his face broke into a wide grin.

Her gut twisted. *No, no, no*!

Chapter Twelve

Teegan's father plowed through the crowd like a bull after a matador, creating a path where male and female alike stared with wide eyes and opened mouths. Powerful in size with shoulders to make a tailor cry, the six-foot-five giant commanded attention without trying.

What should I do? She had never lied to her father. If he discovered Jeff Andrews had recruited her for another assignment, he'd blow a gasket and explode the white clouds of hair puffing from the sides of his head. Then, the sides would match the top, and he'd be completely bald and blame her. She wanted to bolt, make an excuse to hide in the ladies room, anything to get away. Another part of her wanted to jump into his arms.

The latter won.

As he neared, he stretched out his arms, and she flew into them with a joyful screech. *Two handsome men in one day. How lucky can a girl get?*

His arms loosened. "Gee, it's only been a week since I put you on a plane, Princess."

"I miss you anyway." She kissed his cheek.

Once again, he squeezed her before dropping his arms. "All of us miss you with your mother and me fighting for the top spot, but I can see you're doing okay." He turned to Budd, hand outstretched. "Nice to see the two of you together. Am I a matchmaker or what?"

Budd stuttered on words that never quite came out of his mouth as he stared with raised brows at the older man.

Teegan glanced from Budd to her father. "What are you talking about?"

With a slight cough, Budd slipped his arm around her waist to draw her to his side. The move was a possessive one, a don't-touch-she's-mine maneuver that got her heart thumping.

"When Frank was in Vegas for the land acquisition, he had this bright idea we'd make a great pair and tried every trick in the book to get me to Philly. I said no because I envisioned you as a big behemoth like him. His photo—"

She chuckled softly and stopped him by placing a hand on his chest. "Let me guess. He showed you the photo of an eight-year-old with two missing front teeth."

"Bingo!" He wagged a finger at her father. "A man shouldn't entice a guy with the picture of a child. He'll get the wrong idea."

She frowned at her father while placing a hand on her hip for emphasis. "Really, Dad, you need to carry a more current photo."

He grinned. "I love that photo. I want to be buried with it."

"Trust me, you'll get your wish." Without leaving the comfort of Budd's arm, she reached for her father's large hand and tugged. "What *are* you doing here? Why didn't you call?"

"I called several times, but voicemail kicked in. I arrived a couple of hours ago for a meeting. A spur-of-the-moment thing."

She shot him a one-eyed glare. "I'm supposed to be your liaison on the west coast. You've been ordered by the doctor to go easy because of your blood pressure."

"We're not having that kind of meeting, Princess." He nodded toward the elderly bunch by the bar. "My army buddies are planning a reunion before we drop dead from old age. At last count, only seventeen of us are left. I'm with five of them now." He turned her hand in a cavalier fashion and kissed her fingers. "Will you honor an old man with a dance, that is if Budd can let you go?" He looked at Budd with a cocked brow.

Budd pouted. "I may not want to." With a heavy sigh, he dropped his arm. "I reluctantly release you."

Oh, good grief. With both hands, Teegan grabbed Budd's jacket lapels and put their faces nose-to-nose. Their breath intermingled. "I'm yours for tonight, counselor. Not even my father will change my mind." She kissed his beautiful mouth. "Hold the pucker until I return."

Her father's style of dancing was more of a shuffle to the rhythm of a Frank Sinatra ballad, slow and leisurely without any fancy footwork. Perfect for the man who hated dancing. Funk rock blared through the loudspeakers, shattering eardrums with a loud bass background. While the crowd jerked and swayed, she and her father looked like two ballroom rejects moving in slo-mo. Once he steered her away from the loudspeakers, he stretched his full lips into a grin.

"Sorry to interrupt your date, Princess, but I couldn't resist. You stepped through the door and every one of my buddies commented. Half of them can't believe you're my daughter." He glanced toward them and waved. "What's going on with you and Budd?"

"Nothing at the moment."

His bushy eyebrows lifted. "What do you mean nothing? The man's infatuated. The look's all over his face. Yours too, I might add."

She patted his arm. "Don't get any ideas. We're on our first date, and he already made his confirmed bachelor declaration."

"Aw, that ain't nothing but a defense mechanism kicking in. A man uses the excuse when he feels himself sinking. I said the same words to your mother. Two weeks later, I couldn't live without her." Grinning, he squeezed her hand. "She's gonna love this story."

Her mother would be ecstatic. She viewed her genius daughter as an ongoing marriage challenge, the last of the three children unhitched. Teegan was more career oriented than her brothers, smarter and wealthier than most men in their social circle, and never out of the lab long enough to show the world her face. Her mother constantly tricked her daughter into a social gathering where, by some stroke of luck, a match-made-in-heaven waited. Some men were okay, others so-so, but as was the norm, her IQ had sent them flying. Hence, a long-term suitor never materialized.

Teegan expected nothing different from Budd. He'd ask her on a few dates, share a few lonely nights, and then he'd split like every man before him—running for cover to protect a fragile ego. His speech about a full-fledged relationship was a crock of bull, and no woman in her right mind with a normal IQ would believe a word. The man had, after all, a reputation with the ladies, not to mention Ed Connors' confirmation of the fact. If she kept everything in perspective, she should emerge unscathed.

"Look, Princess, I know you don't want to stay on as COO, but you're doing a great job. The plant is four months ahead of schedule."

She rolled her eyes. "I belong in a lab."

"Nonsense. You're a natural for a front office...oops!" He bumped into another couple and glanced over his shoulder. "Sorry."

Back in Philly, she had run a lab with ten employees. They'd spent time together, partied, and had fun. This COO stint was different. She oversaw the operations of a factory plus forty employees, and the list of duties grew every day. As the big boss, she faced an awkwardness fraternizing with the employees. She didn't belong and never would because of her position on the ladder.

"What do ya say, Princess?"

His words jolted her back to the present. "I'm not here to discuss work, but I'll humor you and consider the offer." *Not very hard either*. She shook away the mood and forced a smile. "I'm surprised to see you in a place like this."

"No more than me. Peters—" He pointed with a quick jerk of his thumb. "He's the one with the sick hairpiece. He recently divorced after thirty-five years and suggested we hang out for a while."

She studied the group, and spotted a man dressed in a leather jacket with an open collar white shirt and neck surrounded by gold chains. "You talking about the man flirting with the spiked-haired woman?" Dear Lord, his hairpiece resembled a worn moleskin doormat!

"That's him. The stupid shit thinks every woman's

gonna fall at his feet."

Yeah, with laughter.

The music changed. Hip-hop this time. He was still in slo-mo.

Her father's hand tensed on her back as his gaze stared over her head, darting from one side of the dance floor to the other.

He motioned with his chin. "Two men are following Budd. They followed him to the men's room, and now, they're following him back. They look like cops." He nudged her and gave a one-eyed gaze. "Anything I should know?"

The man was too observant. She sighed. "Budd's being stalked by a woman. She claims he promised marriage."

His eyebrows arched. "What's she gonna do, hold a gun to his head until he agrees?"

"She might." No sense telling him the whole truth. She stared at the buttons on his shirt.

He lifted her chin, his gaze penetrating into her soul.

"If the woman wants Budd, she won't think too highly of you being in his arms." He nodded in Budd's direction. "With those guys watching Budd, who's watching you? Unless you intend to move in with him—like tonight—you'll get caught in some crossfire."

Her father had always worried about his little girl. Growing up, with her telescope in the back yard, she knew he pretended to read the newspaper at the dining room window, ever vigilant of her and her surroundings. She smiled. "The cops are watching me, Dad. A female is part of the team. She's here in the crowd somewhere."

He glanced around, his gaze searching. "All right, that makes me feel better. As thrilled as I am to see the two of you together, I'd like Budd to put his love life on hold until this nut is locked away. He's endangering his dates." He squeezed her hand.

"The police have everything under control. Some of the best are watching us." *Famous last words.*

Her father narrowed his gaze. "I'm holding one of the best in my arms. I know you, daughter, and know what you're capable of. Are you involved?"

She toyed with his lapel and shrugged. "Not like you think. They asked me to keep him in Vegas for a few days. He wanted to take a trip, and they weren't ready."

"Well, you've succeeded. I don't think he'll let you go anytime soon. Then what?"

"That's it. My job is done. They're hoping to capture her tonight."

"In this crowd? Don't make me laugh."

She silently agreed. Impossible for the Feds to take Anna, impossible for Anna to take Budd. Too many people and too many variables. The entire scenario sucked. Teegan squeezed the hand holding hers. "Please don't mention this to Budd. He knows nothing about my history with the FBI."

He kissed her hair, muffling the grunt rising from his throat. "Where was he going that they were so fired up to keep him in town?"

"To his cabin somewhere in the desert." With a tug on his arm, she stopped him from backing into a couple.

"Ah, yes, nice place. He took me there."

"He did?" Well, this was a pleasant piece of news.

"Tell me about the place. It sounds like a wonderful getaway."

"That was a year ago and still a big construction project. I helped him carry a shit-load of wood into the house, and we nailed some of the floors together. I suspect he's got the place pretty much done by now." He bumped into another couple and winced. "Sorry."

They were as far as possible from the loudspeakers. Any farther and they'd be out the door on the patio. She chuckled into his chest.

"What's so funny?"

"You. Do you want to dance outside?"

"Too obvious, huh? Look, Budd's not taking you to the cabin, right?"

"He asked, but I said no."

"Good. Someone has to keep a level head. He should stay in town until they catch this woman." He snapped his fingers and pointed. "You can do one of your fancy dances to entice him."

Teegan pulled away and stared. "What are you talking about?"

"Our forty-fifth wedding anniversary, remember? You danced with your date, and the place went wild. You can move, Princess."

She smirked. "My date was a dance partner from the studio. If I performed the same routine with Budd, I'd have the man humping me on the dance floor. Besides, I won't make any sensations with this crowd. We can hardly move."

"All I'm saying—"

"Yes, I know what you're saying. You're a dirty old man."

Sex was never a taboo subject in their house. Her

parents laid the facts on the line to their three children, explaining in detail better than the sex education her school had offered. To this day, her parents had an active sex life with the bedroom door always locked. *I should be so lucky.*

"You got condoms?"

She jerked back. "Dad!"

"All right, too personal."

"No, too loud." She gave her father a quick squeeze then broke away. "That's enough, Mr. Smith. I love you dearly, but I'd rather have Budd's arms around me."

And put the condoms to full use.

****

As Budd's gaze watched Teegan and Frank cut through the thick crowd, he salivated at the movement of her hips swaying in rhythm to the beat of a bass as if she danced while walking. She wasn't doing anything special. Just a nice gentle swing of her legs in time with the music, her arm hooked into her father's. Such a simple motion made him hot and breathless, and the blood pulsed through his veins like a rushing river, causing heat to rise from his collar.

A thrill of idiotic pride swelled in his chest, because Teegan attracted every man's attention, some with their heads snapping so fast, their dates slapped their arms. He wished traffic would freeze for at least ten seconds so he could enjoy the view. He was a lucky man. And she was his for the night. *Damn, what a feeling! And to think I had refused to go to Philly.*

If Frank had showed him a current photo, especially the one online, he'd have beat the old guy back to the east coast. In comparison, father and daughter shared nothing in physical similarities. Somewhere in the gene pool maybe but not on the exterior. Frank was a true black-and-white man—black suit, white shirt, white hair, black eyebrows. Teegan had color with her beautiful teal eyes and chestnut hair complemented by smooth, tanned skin.

Tonight, when she had opened her door, she caused his tongue to fall halfway down his throat. Her dress showed the voluptuous curves of a mature woman, and his heart pounded through his rib cage like a Saturday morning cartoon character. Even now, his heart thundered just watching the fluid movement of the woman heading his way.

"You using this stool, sir?"

He turned to a young man holding a drink. "No, go right ahead." Budd couldn't sit still if he tried. He took Teegan's glass from the bar along with his own and carried them to a nearby pedestal table with a surface wide enough for four glasses and not much else.

A familiar head of blond hair caught his eye, bobbing to the rhythm of the music like his skull rested on a spring. Their gazes met, and Budd groaned. First Teegan's father, and now him. *Is there no mercy from the heavens above?*

Ed Connors sauntered through the crowd, half-dragging an overly endowed woman on his arm. He nodded toward the dance floor. "Who's Teegan with?"

"Her father."

Ed's date leaned on him like her high heels tipped her over. He unlocked her arm from his and turned her toward the bar with a bold slap on her rear.

"Order some drinks, will you, babe?"

The woman wiggled her tight ass all the way to the

bar.

Budd checked for Teegan's approach, but a young couple stopped her, all smiles. The delay could give him enough time to shove Ed out the door. He threw Ed a glare. "I don't believe in coincidences. Did you ask Denise about my plans?"

"Nothing is a secret at the office, Buddy boy. You should know that." As he stared in Teegan's direction, he released a soft wolf whistle. "She is something else, Budd. How about we swap dance partners?"

Budd's neck hairs bristled. For years, he'd tolerated Ed's lecherous behavior and often found him amusing but not tonight, and definitely not with Teegan. He growled into Ed's face. "You touch Teegan, and I'll break every bone in your body. I'm still pissed you approached her at the store."

Ed flashed a smirk that made Budd's hand curl into a tight fist. One more remark, and he'd knock all the dental caps out of his mouth. "Go away, Ed."

"Wow, you're hot for this one." He held both palms up in surrender. "I'll back off until you're done. She's fair game after that." He strolled toward the bar to rejoin his date.

Budd wanted to scream. The man was a great trial lawyer, but his tactics to grab Budd's leftover women before offered was getting out of hand. On a first date even. *Like I'll let his slimy hands touch her.* Women were a dime a dozen in Vegas so Ed should have no difficulties occupying his nights. Once Teegan moved on, fine, but until then…

Budd inwardly jerked. Ed and his behavior had never bothered him before. Why now all of a sudden? Or maybe Teegan's hesitation at his relationship offer irked him, but a short-term fling was his plan. A few nights at her place, a few nights at his. A give and take for awhile before boredom took its toll. That's why showgirls were the perfect date. They had dreams of their names in bright lights and a star on the infamous Hollywood Walk of Fame. They were no more interested in settling down than he was.

Unless Teegan had more foresight. Dating while Anna lurked in the shadows smacked of imprudent behavior, but what was he to do? Let Teegan slip through his fingers? Any man, even those with one eye and a foot in the grave, wouldn't let such a beauty escape. He'd clarify his relationship offer later when they were alone.

Teegan and her father approached.

"I hope I made my army buddies jealous as hell," Frank said. He extended his hand. "Budd, you take care of my little girl."

"Count on it, Frank. By the way, your company's tools are getting heavy use. They hold up well."

"You can thank my genius daughter. She knows her metals." He flicked a finger under Teegan's chin and smiled. "Enjoy the rest of the evening, you two."

Teegan grabbed her father's arm. "Dad, will I see you before you leave Vegas?"

"Sure. Me and the guys should work out the details for this reunion by tomorrow afternoon. Then I'll pop into the plant to see how things look."

"You'll need my key. We won't do Saturdays until we go online." Her brows creased together into a deep frown. "Tell you what. Give Bill a call. He can show you what's new."

Frank glanced from his daughter to Budd, his gray

eyes twinkling. "Yeah, no problem. I expect you'll be busy for awhile. I'll call sometime Sunday morning. You should have your phone on by then." He patted her hand and turned to leave.

Budd stopped him with a raised hand. "Keep your buddies away, Frank. I'm not sharing Teegan with anyone else."

Frank winked and headed toward the DJ. Teegan's gaze followed, her face as blank as a sheet of paper. "Hey, I'm over here."

She started and turned, an awkward smile stretching onto her lips.

Budd lifted her drink from the small table and clicked his glass to hers.

Without hesitation, she gulped half the liquid then gasped, sputtered, and coughed as her eyes watered. Squinting, she held the glass at arm's length. "What is this?"

"Irish whiskey. Want something else?"

"No. This tastes like cheap bourbon." She slipped a hand inside his suit jacket and leaned against him, her eyes distant, looking without seeing.

Frank's interruption had the effect of a cold bucket of water, dousing their fire to a stream of smoke. Although Budd enjoyed her gentle scratching on his chest, he doubted she recognized the erotic effect it caused. A turn-on for sure, but she was still a mile away. He wrapped an arm around her waist to hold her close to his side. "Is everything okay, Teegan?"

The teal focused on his face as a wisp of a smile curled her lips. "Having a father show up in the middle of a date is a bit of a mood buster. I changed from dance partner to little girl in ten seconds flat."

"No matter what age, you will forever be his little girl. I think every father feels the same." He sipped his drink and puckered. The heat of his hand had melted the ice and diluted the drink. The liquid tasted like a metal pipe. "Now, I know why your drink tasted so bad because mine's the same." He placed his glass on the table and then squeezed her close, their faces nose-to-nose, breath intermingling, her exotic perfume taunting. He had no idea what the scent was, but he loved it just the same. "As for the dance partner, she's still in my arms. You're doing a number on my libido in that dress." He took her glass and placed it on the table. "What do you say we get back on the dance floor? You can teach me a few more moves before we call it a night." He slipped his fingers over her hand and guided her into the crowd as a song by ABBA began.

Teegan stopped in her tracks, jerking him to a halt.

Budd looked back, puzzled at the sudden resistance, only to be greeted by a sparkling gaze.

She stretched to whisper in his ear. "Let me show you what happens when your date nearly becomes a pro dancer."

The tone of her voice, low and sultry, vibrated every nerve along his skin. He stared at the face of a little devil with a grin twisting one side of her mouth. "I'm doomed, aren't I?"

"Yes, Budd Richardson, you are doomed."

He followed her lead, a style of dirty dancing, brushing against his body in ways he'd never imagined. Time and again, she'd swing her leg out the side slit of her dress drawing his gaze downward. Then, his head snapped back to feel her hot breath leaning close for a whisper kiss. Every movement, every touch was so damn effective, he couldn't take his eyes off her. She threw him into sensory overload, and the flush rising from his shirt collar was enough to drive him to a cold shower.

At each tempo change, she pressed against him, forcing his body to sway with hers. Then came a subtle tug on his belt. The feel of her soft breasts against his chest, the idea of her hand so close to his rising erection—both activated a physical awareness never experienced with any woman. Teegan had stoked the fire to a furnace blast. "You're killing me, Teegan."

"That's the whole idea."

The tempo change repeated. Again, she leaned close. This time, he held firm, controlling her sway and hiding the obvious protrusion in his pants. He wanted to take her now in the middle of the dance floor. To hell with her father or anyone else watching. His body was on fire. This beautiful, sexy genius was his for the night, and he would have a feast.

He stopped her, halting all motion. Their gazes locked, and they stood in this position until a smile glowed from her gaze. He leaned close to her ear. "I bought fresh condoms."

She traced her tongue on the outer perimeter of his ear then whispered, "So did I."

Chapter Thirteen

Teegan clutched Budd's arm. She hadn't meant for such a death grip on his jacket sleeve, but emergencies squelched finesse. She patted his arm to get his eyebrows down. "I have *got* to go to the ladies room before we leave." Otherwise, one bounce in the car and she'd be embarrassed for life.

"We're closer to this one." He pointed and, with a hand on her back, guided her through a thick throng.

"Yo, Budd, over here!" a male voice hailed.

A man with black hair and matching beard with equally black eyes stopped them. He stood with other men—all casually dressed, drinks in hand, rocking in rhythm to the music—and staring like she was a double-decked hamburger.

Budd's hand tensed on her back. "This just isn't my night." He sighed heavily. "Come on. I'll introduce you." Budd took her hand and guided her toward the group. "Teegan Smith, meet Josh Feinberg, my other partner."

Her first impression was a presentable enough man with a slim build, wearing a dark blue suit with an open collar blue shirt. He squinted and batted his eyes as if the overhead lights were too bright, just like her Uncle Johnny's habit when his contact lenses caused irritation. After a round of introductions, Teegan exchanged pleasantries, but with a bladder ready to explode, she had no interest in small talk. Excusing herself, she continued toward the restroom.

After passing through the lounge section with its plush chairs and full-length mirrors filled to capacity with weary women, Teegan entered a wash area with stalls converging from opposite sides. Women were lined along the sinks fixing hair, adjusting makeup, some even washed their hands. Every door in the place banged open or closed as women hurried in and out, clicking heels on hard linoleum, and chattering. Teegan found an empty stall, locked the door, and placed her purse on the ledge behind the toilet. She couldn't lift her dress fast enough.

The toilet cubicle resembled a closet with a door stretching from floor to ceiling. The sides had a six-inch opening at the bottom to prevent a sneak peek at the feet in the next stall with the top high enough so a tall woman in four-inch heels wouldn't pop her head up like a cow. Privacy plus. A chance to catch her breath and absorb the solitude the cubicle offered.

A constant flow of traffic passed by the door. Toilets flushed, voices spoke, their words indiscernible since the music bounced around the walls as if the ladies room sat inside a speaker. She'd never had a phobia about crowds, but a steady diet of Vegas clubs could give her one. For years, her life had centered on classrooms and laboratories with the occasional night out with friends. Her best dates were with men in a quiet corner of a five-star restaurant, sometimes a bedroom romp or an overnight stay.

Budd was definitely on his way to both. She intended to keep the man in her bedroom until tomorrow afternoon, maybe evening…if he was willing.

Oh, he'll be willing, all right, or my name isn't Teegan Smith.

He had thrown her a curve ball with his full-fledged relationship offer. By definition, the word meant commitment, but a man with no interest in changing his bachelor status should never make such an ambiguous statement. *Maybe he needs a good dictionary.*

And she needed her head examined if she agreed.

A thump hit her door and startled her. Her gaze automatically darted to the latch to check its security. Not an uncommon occurrence in a nightclub. A woman with too much alcohol in her system, unable to walk a straight line, would lose her balance or worse, fall off her high heels.

Heels...

A strange quiet had descended. No movements outside her door, toilets quiet, no doors banging. Other than the music, not a sound of activity reached her ears, as if her side of the lavatory had emptied. Totally unheard of in a busy nightclub. Instincts alerted, Teegan rushed to adjust her dress.

"You had fair warning, bitch! I'll make sure you stay away from him."

Shit!

Teegan whirled to grab her purse when the first bullet pierced the door. A burn hit her waist, and her recoil reaction slammed her against the side of the cubicle. Her back arched as muscles contracted to ease the pain of a thousand nerve endings complaining. With no time to waste, she ignored the sting, yanked her purse from the shelf, and dropped to the floor before a second shot shattered the tiled wall. Then a third. She fumbled with the purse snap and removed her gun as a fourth bullet cracked the toilet. Covering her head with her arms, she waited for the next shot. *I'm a friggin' target.*

Since chambering a round on her first encounter with Anna, Teegan removed the safety on her little Beretta, aimed at the door, but hesitated, ears straining to hear over the beat of a bass. No fifth shot? With her heart racing and blood pulsing in her ears, she rotated her head to peek into the stalls on both sides, half-expecting to see Anna's feet.

Anna was too short to jump on a toilet and shoot over the side panel, but she could aim her gun and fire through the six-inch opening at the bottom. But no feet. *My lucky day.* With quivering fingers, Teegan touched the area where the bullet seared her skin. Blood covered her hand. Much too close for comfort.

All right, Anna, where are you? Did she run, or was she lingering to take her final shot?

While hugging the side wall, Teegan slithered to her feet, ears alert for any sound other than music. With a trembling hand, she reached across the door, unlatched the lock, and gripped the handle. *One, two, three.* She yanked. The damn door was jammed. She tried again. A rattle but no luck. Without a sufficient opening between stalls, the only way out was up. So much for praising the privacy of the ladies room. And where was everybody? How could a busy lavatory become vacant so quickly?

She kicked off her heels and jumped onto the toilet to look cautiously into the next stall. The door was ajar, allowing a partial view of the corridor. No sign of

Anna. No sign of anyone. "Hey, help!" The music drowned her voice. And more. The odor of smoke hit her nose. *This just isn't my day.*

With a grip on her gun, Teegan swung a leg up and over to the next cubicle, thankful for the slit in her dress. She dropped to the floor and, with gun ready, squatted while peeking out the stall door, first down one side, then the other.

White smoke billowed from the main wash area. The trash bin more likely, full of wet towels to generate more smoke than fire. And where was Anna? Hiding in one of the stalls waiting with her next bullet? *All right, do something. I can't squat here all night.* The smoke thickened by the second, robbing her air, burning her eyes. *Where the frig are the fire alarms?*

Teegan stepped from the stall, her gaze darting in all directions. Anna had jammed a mop handle into the grip on her door. She yanked the mop free, opened the door, and then grabbed her purse and shoes. Eyes watering, she coughed. The damn smoke was burning her throat. She coughed again and hurried for the wash area.

Where was the female cop? Shouldn't she have followed into the ladies room?

No time to think about it. Too hard to breathe.

The sprinkler system sprang to life. Seconds later, fire alarms blared. Between the smoke and water spray, she struggled to see more than three feet ahead. Something caught her foot. She slipped on the wet linoleum and fell flat on her ass to see two legs sticking half-in, half-out of a stall door. Blood smeared the woman's dark hair.

Teegan gave the surrounding stalls a quick

inspection before placing the gun in her purse. She dropped her shoes, placed her purse under her armpit, and clutched the woman by the arms. "Help me, somebody!"

Teegan pulled the woman away from the stall, but she was dead weight, and the water made a slippery grip. Time and again, she repositioned her hands only to lose her footing and slip. Her eyes stung from the smoke that refused to clear so she tilted her head upward to let the water sprinkle onto her face, all the while coughing to clear the burn in her throat. A lightheadedness swept through her along with the unmistakable urge to vomit. *Why isn't anyone running in to help?* The room whirled, and she collapsed to her knees.

"Teegan!"

Budd swooped her into his arms and hurried for the exit while another man in a security uniform did the same with the injured woman.

Firemen burst in carrying extinguishers. In the hall, chaos reigned. People ran screaming, pushing, shoving while a man's voice over the Public Address system encouraged everyone to stay calm and proceed in an orderly fashion to the nearest exit. No one listened.

Budd grumbled about the human race's inability to hear at critical times, but he moved with the crowd, straight out the door with her still in his arms, and into the fresh night air.

No man had carried her in his arms since she was a little girl, and the one man she remembered most was her father. The sensations of strength and security rushed to the surface, but with Budd, she felt more. Of what, she wasn't sure. Maybe the knight-in-shining-armor syndrome. Regardless, she enjoyed every second, despite coughing into his shoulder.

He set her down. Where, she had no clue, but surprisingly, she still carried her purse under her armpit. She placed it alongside and went into a coughing fit.

A paramedic slapped an oxygen mask on her face, which gave her the sensation of suffocating. She tore off the pliable plastic and coughed some more.

With gentle fingers, the medic slipped the apparatus from her hand and placed it back on her face. "This is necessary, ma'am. The air will help you catch your breath."

Resisting the urge to remove it, she sucked in the steady flow of cool air.

"That's right, ma'am. Deep breaths. It'll push out the carbon monoxide. Keep on the mask until I return. Have you any injuries?"

She waved aside the question. She wasn't about to tell him about the bullet wound with Budd sitting alongside.

After a few minutes, her brain cleared. She rested on a stone parapet with her head on Budd's shoulder, his arm around her protectively. She was drenched. Despite the warm night, a chill scurried under her dress, and she shivered. Budd removed his suit jacket and wrapped it around her shoulders, transferring his body warmth from the jacket into her. She hadn't felt anything so wonderful in a long time, and the heat seeped through her damp dress, arresting the chill. Her head leaned right back on his shoulder.

Fire trucks with flashing lights filled the parking lot. One after the other pulled in with sirens blaring, firemen jumping from the cab, grabbing hoses, extinguishers, and axes. Cars not blocked in squealed out like on a getaway. Almost everyone talked or texted on a cell phone. "Well, this made for a memorable date."

He kissed her damp hair. "You scared the living daylights out of me."

"Sorry, but thanks for coming to my rescue." The memory of being carried in his arms lingered, a thrill despite a brush with death.

He adjusted the suit jacket, tucking it closer to her neck. "No one's allowed to smoke inside the building, not even in the restrooms. Some ass probably tossed a lit cigarette into the trash."

"The ass was Anna."

He grasped her shoulders and stretched her to arm's length, a sharp glare emanating from his gaze. "How do you know?"

The sudden movement twisted awake her back wound. Under the facemask, she winced. "She told me to stay away from you." She lifted wet hair from her forehead. *I must look a fright.* "Is my father okay?"

He shook her shoulders. "Don't change the subject. Which way did Anna go?"

Returning the glare, she shifted the oxygen mask to the side of her face. "How would I know, Budd? She locked me in the stall." She hadn't meant to sound so angry, but Anna Kincaid won this round. The damn woman had successfully ruined their date, nearly shot Teegan in the back, and turned her fifteen-hundred-dollar dress into a rag. *And I didn't do a damn thing to stop her*! She repositioned the mask and sucked in a large breath to calm her agitated nerves.

Budd's grip relaxed, and he patted her shoulder.

"Yes, you're right. I'm sorry." He wrapped one arm around her and eased her head onto his shoulder. "I don't know what to tell you about your dad, Teegan. The fire wasn't a danger for anyone in the main ballroom. The sprinkler system caused the panic."

Two men in dark suits approached. A tall one with blond hair introduced himself and the man alongside, both Federal agents.

Neither name registered in her brain.

"Can you tell us what happened, Dr. Smith?"

What is it, every intimate moment is to be interrupted tonight? She lifted her head and selected her words carefully while describing the scene. For Budd's benefit, she left out the part about not having a chance to shoot back. She also omitted the bullet burn on her back. Budd's arm tensed on her shoulders anyway.

"We weren't far from the restroom," the agent said. "We didn't hear the gunshots over the music." He stared at all the activity in the parking lot before returning his gaze to her. "The woman you saved was your tail, Dr. Smith. She followed you into the ladies room. How Kincaid knew she was a cop is another one of our unanswered questions."

"Of all the restrooms in this club, how did Anna know which one I'd use?"

Before answering, he tapped the earpiece in his right ear and listened. "It's possible she saw your direction and ran ahead. We don't know, but we'll study the security footage to find out for sure. Our men covering the loading dock saw her exit and chased her for six blocks then lost her. Cars have surrounded her last known location."

Anna got away, of that Teegan was certain. Jeff

had made careful plans with every possible scenario, but Anna outsmarted the Feds. Somehow, she arrived at the club undetected. "Is the woman agent okay?"

He rubbed the back of his neck. "She sustained several blows to the head. Once we get inside the building, we'll search for a weapon. Her service gun is missing. We'll know if Kincaid used it when the crime scene unit pulls the bullets from the wall."

Budd's arm jerked across her shoulders like an uncontrollable spasm. She glanced his way to see nostrils flaring and a gaze blazing at the agent as if the poor man was the cause of tonight's mayhem. The heat he generated was enough to dry her dress in minutes, and she leaned closer to absorb every molecule. "The ladies room went from busy to vacant in a short span of time. I don't understand why the traffic stopped."

"Simple," Budd answered. "Almost as soon as the door closed behind you, a woman placed a yellow floor sign redirecting women toward another restroom. She was dressed in a black uniform like the rest of the employees. She had to be Anna."

"You didn't recognize her, sir?"

Budd shrugged. "I paid no mind. I assumed she worked in the club."

The second agent excused himself to take a phone call. He returned a minute later. "Sgt. Reeves and Agent Andrews are coordinating the search area for Kincaid. They want to talk to you when they're done, Mr. Richardson."

Budd wrapped his arm tighter around Teegan's shoulders. "Teegan needs to change so we're not waiting around. Tell them to call my cell when they're ready."

"I'll relay the message. Thankfully, Dr. Smith came out of this okay."

Except for one important detail. She dreaded Budd's reaction, but the words had to be said. She lifted a finger. "Well, actually—"

"What the hell happened?"

Every head turned toward the bellowing voice.

Her father approached, face flushed, looking mad as a hornet. *Oops.*

Budd held up his hand. "We're good, Frank. Calm down."

"How can I calm down with my daughter sitting with an oxygen mask on her face?"

Teegan forced a smile. "Relax, Dad. I breathed in some smoke. They want me to suck in fresh air for a while." She scanned him from head-to-toe. "Are you okay?"

"Hell, yeah. We were standing by the exit when everything hit." He squinted, his stance still rigid. "Word is you and another woman were trapped."

Amazing how stories circulated. "Not trapped. She was hurt."

"Someone set the fire?"

"Yes."

He fidgeted. His jaw ground on his dentures while fists opened and closed in rapid succession.

"Dad, I'm okay."

"I'll stop by later."

She glanced at her wristwatch. "It's after midnight. No, you won't stop by later." That was all she needed to top the night.

Her father fidgeted. "I'll take you home then."

Budd stood to his feet.

She immediately felt his warmth disappear and tugged the jacket tighter.

As he matched her father's steady gaze, Budd yanked on his pants belt with a gesture akin to a boxing duel. "She's staying with me, Frank. I've no intention of letting her out of my sight."

Her father glared as his gaze shifted from her to Budd and back.

Budd stood his ground, not in the least intimidated. The whole scene looked more like a territorial dispute with two males fighting over the lone female. She loved her father, but she wanted Budd to win this one.

After another minute, her father's posture relaxed. He bent to kiss her damp hair. "Call me after you get some rest."

Budd watched him leave then smiled. "I do believe the man loves you."

Teegan chuckled as the medic returned to remove her mask.

"That should do, ma'am. If you don't mind, I'd like to take a small sample of blood to see where your carbon monoxide level is." He pricked her arm and withdrew blood into a small syringe then fed the fluid into a portable analyzer. He nodded his approval as numbers flashed onto a screen. "You're good to go. Will someone be with you tonight?"

"Yes," Budd answered. Glancing down, he pointed to Teegan's feet. "Where are your shoes?"

"Still in the ladies room, and that's where they'll stay." She should let the medic look at her back. She wasn't a contortionist capable of bending over to see her own wound. Hell, no one knew of the bullet burn yet. She took Budd's offered hand and stood, suppressing a grimace as her back muscles recoiled from the pull on the wound. "I need—"

"You need to get warm. We're heading to my place."

"But I—"

"No buts. Let's go." With an arm around her shoulder, he led her toward the car.

She glanced toward the parapet to see the medic loading his gear onto the back of an ambulance. "Budd, wait."

"Don't get all shy on me now, Teegan. My place and that's final."

Why was this man putting words into her mouth? She was a highly intelligent woman who made important decisions every day. *And is too tired to argue*. Not to mention she felt like a used washrag. Anna had caught everyone off-guard including Jeff's special operative. A fine help she was.

She had the best excuse in the world. Her concentration sucked. Hormones had taken control of her synaptic pathways and danced the samba inside her vagina, begging for a partner to join in. She wanted Budd, and Anna was an afterthought. Actually, no thought at all.

A silence filled the car as Budd drove, broken only by the hum of the engine and tires.

Teegan rested her head against the seat cushion, staring at nothing in particular, utterly exhausted. Their wonderful night had turned into a shambles. She adjusted his suit jacket still covering her shoulders. "Did your partner get out okay?"

He braked for a turning vehicle. "Partners. They

were both at the club. I'm sure they're fine."

An odd coincidence. She lifted her head and glanced his way. "Do they show up often on your dates?"

"Tonight was a first for both of them." Without removing his gaze from the road, he took her hand. "I'm sorry about this, Teegan."

His touch generated a jolt of awareness, like his skin was a lifeline to safety and comfort. She squeezed his hand. "It's not your fault."

"Yes, it is. I've put you in danger. I'll never forgive myself if you get hurt. Your father won't forgive me either." He passed a slow vehicle. "Maybe I shouldn't have asked you out."

"I agreed to the date, Budd, even after you told me about her. But she has a gun now. You won't be safe until she's caught."

"You won't be safe either unless we terminate our association."

"My brain concurs."

He looked at her with a slight tilt to his head. "What's your heart say?"

She smiled as she leaned her head onto the seat cushion. "No way."

"My heart agrees." He placed his hand back onto the steering wheel. "I've never made such a statement to a woman."

His words had a warming effect, short-lived since she was too sensible to take it seriously. "I'm flattered, but driving me to your place won't help. Anna will go ballistic."

"My house is safer. I have Rommel."

"Hmmm—yes. That is a factor to consider." She

rotated to face him, surprised at how well her wound felt. No pull, no sting, only a slight twinge. "I survived four bullets and smoke inhalation tonight. I'm not keen on your dog chewing on me like a piece of meat."

He glanced in the rearview mirror. "I won't let him hurt you. He'll stay in the patio with a door flap for easy access into the yard. I truly believe he's the reason Anna hasn't knocked on my door."

That could change once Anna sees Budd's house guest. Teegan straightened in her seat and faced forward. "What bothers me is how Anna knew which restroom I'd use. All three are spaced accordingly, and no way can anyone cross to the other without fighting the crowd."

"Maybe Anna got lucky and was in the vicinity."

And maybe her Einstein logic fell into a neutral zone. How had Anna known she cracked the skull of a cop?

Of course! While pretending to be an employee, Anna had shooed everyone out of the restroom, but the cop, because of her assignment, wouldn't leave. Then the next question, how could a trained officer, one who should have Anna's face imprinted into her mind, let Anna sneak up behind her with all the mirrors on the wall?

Too many questions, and I'm too tired to figure out things. Another day, another time. She stifled a yawn. "I had a wonderful evening, Budd, despite Anna."

A tender gaze swept over her. "Me, too. I'm hoping we can salvage some of our night."

But the fire was gone, extinguished…again. She hadn't the energy to reignite the torch.

Chapter Fourteen

If Budd had lived his life in Teegan's neighborhood with his attitude of the poor and underprivileged as his environment, he'd escape as quickly as possible and choose an upper-scale district far removed from his low-income roots.

She could have bet money and won.

His development consisted of mini-mansions in Spanish-style stucco complete with clay-tiled roofs and arched doorways. Nearly all had a U-shaped driveway paved with interlocking bricks, a three-bay garage, and mounted cameras watching over manicured grounds. As per the norm in Vegas, people forced the desert to grow grass so they could mow the lawn every week then waste water to help the blades regrow, repeating the process again and again while complaining about high water bills.

Teegan preferred her lawn of clumped weeds. She paid her neighbor's nephew to care for it any way he pleased. One day, she'd caught him snipping the weed stems with a scissor because the mower created a dust cloud.

Budd's house was smaller than the others, one-level, still Spanish design, but with a two-bay garage. A trimmed lawn gave the exterior an elegance with its precise edges and grass blades of equal length while a rock garden with an array of cactus plants reminded one of the desert nearby. The property had a certain charm that placed it above the others in the area. She wasn't sure why, maybe because Budd owned it, and her respect for him had increased tenfold since they'd met. He'd accomplished a lot in his life, all on his own, with two feet firmly planted on the ground. A rare quality in men these days. Most in her circle had the benefits of a wealthy parent.

A brown wrought-iron fence surrounded the back portion of the house where a large male Rottweiler stared through the spiral spindles, his gaze glued to her side of the car. The dog looked all muscle and head and big enough to swallow her whole. He barked a few times to call attention to himself and licked his chops, as if eyeing his next meal. Not a good sign.

As Budd held open her door, she stepped gingerly from the car while anticipating the dog's flying leap over the fence. "I hold you responsible if I lose a limb."

The dog paced the length of the fence and whimpered, his front paws stomping the ground whenever he entered a turn, a movement more playful than chew-to-kill. "He doesn't sound ferocious."

Budd scowled at the dog. "Rommel never whimpers. I'll let you inside before I check him. Maybe he hurt himself."

She glanced up and down the dark street. "Aren't you afraid Anna will toss in some poisoned meat?"

"He's trained to take food only from his orange bowl." Budd adjusted the suit jacket covering her shoulders and escorted her toward the front door. "If Anna tries to hurt this dog, I'll kill her personally." He placed the key in the lock and swung open the door. "Make yourself at home. I'll put him in the patio for the night."

She touched his arm. "I should meet him, Budd." She had no clue why. A little voice said *make friends with the potentially meat-devouring dog.* Go figure. Her dress was already ruined so she might as well let the animal have a field day.

Budd debated, shifting his gaze from her to the side of the house and back. "All right, we'll see how he acts, but be forewarned. In the past, he hasn't liked the women walking though my door."

She stepped into the house and closed the front door.

A spacious living room greeted her. Two plush sofas faced each other with an oak coffee table between, four end tables with lamps, a small table by the door with unopened mail waiting. A fireplace stood on one wall with a carved mantel of walnut, decorated with a line of framed photos. Mirrors covered the opposite wall, making the room look twice its size. Every color was coordinated in browns and tans and not a touch of the Spanish look on the interior. The man had money and spent it. She had a ton of money but chose to do a hodgepodge job of decorating. Ironic.

A formal dining room stood off to the side of the living room, its cherry wood table and chairs covered with books and papers. She suspected the room was used more as an office than for entertainment since bachelors rarely had dinner parties.

The sound of nails hitting linoleum attracted her attention. She turned as Rommel trotted through an archway and stopped where the carpet met the dining room.

One hundred and thirty pounds of power stared at

the intruder. He had the traditional markings of black coat with brown sections on his chest, face, and paws.

She had always loved the breed for its incredible intelligence, but he was bigger than usual, which caused some concern. *He'll smell the blood on my back and think I'm his next meal. Oh, dear.*

She swallowed hard and forced a smile. Like the dog gave a shit that she had good dental care. "Well, hi, fella. Budd tells me you don't like his women."

Rommel approached to sniff her outstretched hand.

"Maybe you like the smell of smoked meat." Since the odor of burnt trash penetrated every pore in her body.

Budd stood in the archway staring, his mouth agape. "Well, I'll be damned."

She glanced at him, daring to look away from the massive jaw. "This guy isn't ferocious at all. What kind of women do you take home?" She scratched Rommel's head. "He seems okay with me. Maybe he smells your jacket." She slipped the heavy material from her shoulders and handed it to Budd.

Rommel sat on his rump by her feet and stared up.

Budd took the jacket and extended a sleeve. His eyes widened. "Teegan, blood's on my sleeve!"

"Oh? Probably from the injured woman." She tickled Rommel's ear.

He inspected the jacket. "Blood's on the inside, too." Tossing down the garment, he gasped. "You're hurt!" He ran over to examine her back. A soft cry escaped from his throat.

She winced as he pulled the stuck material away from her wound. "One of Anna's bullets grazed me. I'm sorry. I'll get your jacket cleaned."

"I'm not worried about the jacket. Let me take you to a hospital." He took her elbow and urged her into the living room.

"No, Budd, I'm okay. The hospital can't do any more than clean the area and give me a tetanus shot. Since I had my booster injection before moving here, I'll take a shower, and then you can cover it with gauze, assuming you have some." His frowning gaze stayed glued to her back. She placed both hands on his cheeks and raised his head. "I'm okay, really."

A tender gaze met hers. "Teegan—"

She placed a finger on his lips. "A little soap and water, peroxide, and gauze. Do you have the last two?" His gentle nod brushed his lips against her finger, causing a shiver of delight at such an intimate gesture. "Then, that's all I need."

Budd's cell phone chirped to indicate a text message. He hesitated at first then, with a slow movement, removed the phone from his trouser pocket and read. A pained expression passed onto his face.

Teegan tugged on his tie. "Don't assume, counselor. You should realize by now I don't frighten easily."

He scanned her from head-to-toe then showed her the message.

I won't miss next time. Stop seeing her if you value her life.

Teegan sighed heavily. "The cops haven't caught her." *Absolutely no peace with this woman around.*

Budd tossed the phone onto the coffee table. It promptly rang. He glared at the caller ID then snatched the phone from the table and answered.

"Yes, we're still awake." He checked his gold wrist

watch. "Give us forty-five minutes, will you? We barely got in, and we smell like smoke. Right, see you later." He cursed under his breath. "We're getting visitors. The two men in charge of my case want to talk to us." Again, he tossed the phone onto the table and turned, his gaze darkening. "Teegan—"

She expected an apology for another interruption, not a man with a slowly growing smile.

"Would you say your dress is ruined?"

"Without question."

"Good. I've been dying to do this all night." He grabbed the two spaghetti straps on her dress, snapped them from its stitching, and stood back, eyes glowing. Nothing happened.

She laughed. "You don't expect my dress to fall off, do you?"

"It does in the movies." His lips twisted into a pout.

She pinched his chin. "The material's form-fitted, Budd. I poured in my body." The poor man looked so disappointed.

He gestured for her to follow. "Come on. You'll use the guest room. It has its own shower."

She followed him down a long hall where she passed a family room with a giant television screen, an office, a laundry room, and finally the bedrooms.

He stopped by the hall bathroom and indicated for her to wait. "I'll leave some clothes for you on the bed. But first—" He walked directly to the medicine cabinet and grabbed the peroxide and gauze before continuing into one of the bedrooms.

The entire evening had taught her the breadth of frustration, sexual and otherwise. First, her father cooling the heat by disrupting their date. Then Anna starting her own brand of fire. Now, Jeff and Mike. She wanted everyone to leave them alone, because she wasn't sure how long she'd keep her eyes open.

The shower helped. A careful inspection of the wound through the mirror showed a three-inch burn about a notch below her waist. Bleeding had stopped, but serous fluid oozed in a struggle to form a scab. She dabbed the area with gauze soaked in peroxide and nearly bit off her lip to suppress a cry.

Wrapped in a towel, Teegan stepped from the bathroom to see sweatpants and a T-shirt waiting on the bed. She slipped on the shirt and then the pants, thankful for the loose elastic band resting easily below her waist.

A tap sounded on the door.

"I'm dressed."

Budd walked in followed by Rommel. The dog's tongue dangled as he smiled up at her, happy as a lark, and dispelled any last thoughts about hating all his women.

Budd gave the dog a long look. "Of all the years I've had Rommel, I never once had him take so quickly to a woman. I've had my dates lock themselves in the bathroom with sheer fright." He sighed heavily. "I couldn't find a reason why he whimpered except maybe for you."

"I guess he likes me." She scratched Rommel's head. "I almost became a veterinarian, you know, but I found I had to stick my arm up the ass of a cow. I changed my curriculum the next day."

He grunted in answer. "Get on the bed. I've got gauze and tape for your wound."

At the mention of the bed, she felt her heart give a little double flip in anticipation, but hey, the cops were coming. She lay on her belly and lifted the shirt to expose an already too-low waistband.

He knelt beside her and lowered the pants further.

"The wound isn't down that far, counselor."

"You have a beautiful butt." He bit the cheek.

Her pulse quickened, and she groaned into the spread. "You're supposed to be my doctor."

"I'll get to it." He bit the other cheek.

"You've got company coming."

"I'll let them wait on the doorstep." He ran a hand under her shirt straight up her spine.

Goose bumps galore. She wanted his hand to do more, like stroke around to the front.

"Soft and smooth," he murmured. "And no underwear. Very nice and highly erotic." He taped the gauze over the wound. "Do you have pain, Teegan?"

"Just a burn feeling, like I backed into a hot iron."

"She almost killed you."

He had croaked the words, and her heart melted. To know that he cared, even just a little, filled her with a warmth far beyond anything experienced. She rotated her head to peek back only to see his jaw set like granite. "But she didn't kill me, and for that, I'm grateful. Am I done?"

He kissed both butt cheeks and adjusted her sweatpants. "You're done."

With lightning speed, she flipped him onto his back. "Too bad your visitors couldn't wait a few more hours." She lunged at his mouth and gave him a taste of what was to come, provided they were ever left alone. She lifted her head and grinned. "Don't look so surprised. I've got two older brothers who wrestled."

He immediately flipped her onto her back and pinned her arms overhead. "I won trophies for wrestling." He continued the mouth assault, suckling and biting to make her wish Jeff and Mike had car trouble.

Budd released his hold, and she wrapped her arms around his neck to draw him close.

Rommel put his head on the bed and nudged his cold nose against her arm.

She smiled at the dog. "I'm glad to see Rommel accepting my physical abuse of you."

"Honey, I'll lock him away if he protests."

The doorbell rang.

Rommel ran from the room voicing his presence.

Teegan sighed into Budd's mouth. "I hope they don't stay long. I'm fighting sleep." And the undeniable desire to hump him…now!

"I'll do my best." Budd kissed her nose, jumped off the bed, and hurried from the room.

Teegan entered the living room as Jeff Andrews and Mike Reeves strolled toward the sofa. Both looked tired with dark circles around the eyes, shirt collars unbuttoned minus neckties, but suit jackets remained. A long day, no doubt, and not finished. Budd introduced her, and she felt like the biggest phony this side of the Mississippi. She settled on the opposite sofa and curled into the corner.

Jeff sat forward and glanced from the still-standing Budd to her. "I'm sure you won't be surprised to hear Kincaid got away. Please tell us the details about tonight, Dr. Smith."

Teegan told them, leaving out nothing, not even the

smell of smoke lingering in her nose.

He cocked a brow. "We have no report about your bullet wound."

"That's because my father showed up. He was already upset, and I didn't want to cause more worry."

Jeff shot her a fleeting look which she returned with a sharp glare, a warning of sorts since Jeff knew her father all too well. He relaxed with an easy smile. "That was the man you were dancing with, I assume. And you, Budd. Tell us your side."

As he talked, Budd paced slowly before them, as if he spoke in front of a jury while presenting his client's case.

Teegan let her gaze wander lazily over him. Whether in a suit or blue jeans, he wore his clothes like a model on a runway, not too tight but enough to show the physique underneath. The pale blue shirt sleeves were short, allowing muscled arms just enough space before straining again the fabric. Thick thighs bulged beneath the jeans, an extension of the firm tush she grabbed earlier. Sexy as hell. Most lawyers she knew had a wide, flat ass from sitting all day.

Budd caught her watching him. Only a few seconds passed before the front of his jeans swelled, and he dropped to the sofa cushion while giving her a fierce look.

Priceless. She almost burst into laughter.

"I assumed everything was under control," Budd complained to Jeff. "How did Anna get in the club?"

"We're reviewing camera footage. I'll let you know what we uncover." Jeff tugged on his ear. "She's an elusive woman, one of the best I've seen in a long time."

"Well, I don't know what your plans are, but Anna intentionally targeted Teegan tonight. She's bound to show up on her doorstep."

"Oh, wait." Teegan ran for the bedroom. She extracted the envelope from her purse, ran back, and handed it to Jeff. "Anna already followed me home." She retook her seat on the sofa.

Budd shot to his feet and snatched the envelope from Jeff's hand. "This was the one I picked off your doormat, right?"

"Don't get angry. I didn't want to spoil our evening."

Budd read quickly. "I don't understand this 'you run like an old lady' comment." He looked up, brows wrinkled. "When'd she see you run?"

Did I tell him I chased Anna for eight blocks? She scanned her memory banks. "I guess she saw me hurry into the restaurant to buy a bottle of water." *What a friggin' liar.*

"Damnit, Teegan. You should have shown me this earlier." He jammed both hands on his hips. "Don't you realize how dangerous this woman is?"

Well, duh. He sounded like her oldest brother when she'd accepted a date with a biker-friend. Her friend was a pussycat on two wheels, but her brother made him out to be a gang leader with no scruples or respect for women. Hell, the biker dude lasted longer than her other beaus, much to her brother's annoyance.

Jeff pointed to the sofa. "Sit down, Budd. You're making me nervous."

With a smile, Teegan patted the cushion.

Instead, Rommel lumbered over and sat on his rump by her feet.

Budd continued to pace.

Mike leaned forward. "All the experts agree on one fact, Budd. Kincaid will kill you. How and when are the questions. She'll also kill anyone in her way as evidenced by her attack on Dr. Smith tonight. We can't let you go to the cabin."

The pacing stopped as Budd glowered at Teegan. Retrieving the phone from his pocket, he showed Jeff and Mike the latest text message.

Mike wrote on a notepad. "I'll put a trace on her number. Maybe we'll hit a jackpot. Excuse me." He hurried to the kitchen while taking out his cell phone.

"Teegan and I will call it quits for a while, Jeff." Budd sat next to her and took her hand. "I don't like the idea, Teegan, but I don't want Anna to take another shot at you."

Just my luck. Find a nice guy…

A heaviness settled in the center of her chest at the prospect of another relationship ending too soon. Logically, his words made sense, and she faced a heart/brain argument again. In hindsight, she could have kept Budd in Vegas another way—like break his leg, but her own greed for physical contact overruled.

Budd's gaze flashed at Jeff. "Anna's had plenty of opportunities to kill me. What's she waiting for?"

Jeff shrugged. "The right place. The right time." He fussed with his suit jacket. "Our big concern is how Kincaid knew about the nightclub. I had every door and window covered, but she got in anyway." He sat back against the cushion, tapping his notebook on his thigh. "We know, of course, your assistant made the reservations for the restaurant and nightclub, also your flight reservation to and from Chicago."

Budd's mouth fell open. "I don't believe Denise would tell anyone."

"I don't either. However, if she wrote a note and left it on her desk or in the trash—"

"The cleaning service," Teegan said with a snap of her fingers.

"Right. We'll check. Either Kincaid is part of the service or she has a friend feeding her the info. We might use the setup to our advantage."

Shaking his head, Mike returned. "Anna used a disposable phone which is currently offline. She left you with no way to respond to her demand."

"Like I would," Budd grumbled. His gaze shifted from Jeff to Mike. "I hope you gentlemen come up with a plan, because I finally met a fantastic woman, and I'm not sure how long I can stay away." He squeezed Teegan's hand.

"Then consider this," Jeff said. "Have Dr. Smith move in with you. We can watch you both while we toss around a few ideas."

"That's a great suggestion!" Budd slapped his knees and shot to his feet, his gaze sparkling.

Jeff and Mike followed, and the three men hovered in discussion.

Teegan rolled her eyes at the male gesture that was inbred from eons of evolution. *Leave the female out. Don't let her worry. Men at work.*

Good grief.

Sneaky Jeff. He had connived a way for Budd to get his twenty-four-hour protection. "Excuse me, gentlemen. I noticed no one asked my opinion."

"It's a wonderful solution," Budd said, turning to reveal a bright gaze. "We'll work out the details."

"Then don't forget the one where I go to work every day and work long hours. You can't expect me to hide either. And don't forget the big question." She tucked a strand of hair behind her ear, deliberately waiting for their undivided attention. "Why would I want to move in?"

The men stared.

"Anna is after you," Mike said.

"But if Budd and I break up, then Anna'd have no reason to come after me."

Jeff shot her a piercing look.

Had he expected her to ignore her responsibilities to guard Budd Richardson? She matched his glare. "You know I'm right."

The man's shoulders slumped, and he sighed. "Yes, you're right. Maybe you can put on a display for Anna before leaving. You know, tell Mr. Richardson to go to Timbuktu, a big blowup as you're going out the door."

Not a bad suggestion, but definitely not her style. She scratched Rommel's head. "That's assuming she's watching. A big crap shoot, Mr. Andrews."

Budd stepped between them. "I want a detail on Teegan until the media publicizes our breakup. I'll use them to my advantage this time."

"That won't be a problem," Jeff said. "Come on, Mike. We've got work to do." He opened the front door.

Budd spread his arm across the door's opening to stop them. "We're approaching daybreak. Do you think you can delay her tail until Sunday afternoon?"

The two men mumbled their apologies on the way out the door.

She smiled to herself. "Sunday, eh?"

"Yes, Sunday. Anna isn't the only one who wants you."

"Is that a fact? I'm hoping in a very different way."

"Oh, it is." He urged her to stand and slipped his arms around her. "Everyone and their mother kept us apart tonight. Absolutely ruined date night for me." He nuzzled her neck.

She suppressed a yawn. "I could use a long nap."

He bit her earlobe. "You'll need one by the time I'm done."

Her nerves fired with his words. She couldn't remember the last time she pulled a day and night sex marathon. "What about Rommel?"

Budd glanced down at the dog who stood by their feet watching. "He's not allowed in my bedroom if that's what you're asking."

"That is exactly what I'm asking, counselor."

Their gazes locked. Budd pinned her against the wall, and his lips captured her mouth, exploring with a greed of too many interruptions. His tongue probed, tasted, and probed some more, sweeping inside her mouth as if to tickle her tonsils. He jammed his body against hers, his hips gyrating with need, his hands roaming the length of her, stimulating every cell until she lifted her mouth to gasp for air.

Dear Lord, what am I in for? Never had she met a man filled with such intensity, oozing sex like a faucet, all directed at her.

Budd slipped her shirt over her head, and his hot hands grabbed her breasts and massaged as his lips traveled the curve of her neck and shoulder.

The man lost none of the heat from earlier. His

touch seared her skin, and she shuddered from sheer pleasure.

Teegan threw back her head and let him have her.

Chapter Fifteen

Budd took her with the greed of a man desperate for human contact. Never in his experience with women had a passion overwhelmed his control. He wanted her like an animal in heat, here, now, and if he didn't calm down, he'd drop her to the floor without the comfort of a bed.

Teegan deserved a slow, seductive exploration, a savoring like no other. An unparalleled bonding. Even in thought, heightened ecstasy. *Hell, I'm losing my mind.* His thoughts were scattered, nothing organized except for one word...Teegan.

He suckled her lips as his hands slipped into her sweatpants to ease the waistband below the taped gauze.

Her lips responded with an equal greed as her fingers tugged at his belt, struggling to unloosen the buckle.

He could let her win, let her strip him naked without an iota of resistance, but he gripped her butt and jammed her hips against his hard erection to stop all movement. "Not yet, beautiful." He muffled any reply with his mouth.

He had prayed Jeff and Mike left before she faded. Sleep had clouded her eyes. Even now, a glaze covered the teal, but he recognized the look of a woman lost in pleasure, her moans soft and barely audible.

After carrying Teegan into his bedroom, he placed her on the king-size bed, and stripped off her sweatpants. The allure of such an exquisite body with her lovely curves and soft skin froze him. She was everything he had hoped—from delicate to dangerously toxic. He'd enjoy a slow death with such a woman by his side. "Teegan, you take my breath away."

She held her arms outright, and he slipped into them, enclosing her in an embrace that made his heart hammer against his rib cage. As he gazed into her eyes, he stroked the soft curve of her breast. "I'm going to taste every square inch of you."

Smiling, she reached for his zipper.

"Oh, no, you don't." He clamped onto her wrist and held firm. "Me first." Nothing was more erotic than to be fully clothed with a naked woman waiting to be devoured. "Me first to taste, to touch, to have you. Acceptable?"

A dumbfounded look passed onto her face that almost made him laugh, the overwhelmed-into-silence reaction with eyebrows slightly raised and mouth ajar, atypical for a woman with a computer brain. Every male gene in his body kicked into the proud zone, and he vowed to give her the ride of her life.

He showered her with whisper kisses starting at the neck and continuing down to the crease between her breasts. Pink nipples protruded, hard against the round softness touching his cheek. He gently suckled each breast before traveling back to her neck to sniff her hair. The scent of a shower replaced the perfume. His own soap and shampoo. On her, the fragrance drove him wild.

More whisper kisses on her eyes, her nose, and

cheeks. Her mouth brushed his as he passed, but he gave only a teasing kiss in return. He pulled back with a grin.

She eyed him through a narrowed gaze. "I didn't realize I entered a torture chamber."

"I've dreamt of this night ever since we met on the plane." He nibbled her neck.

"Can you at least get undressed?"

He met her gaze. "These jeans are controlling the part that desperately wants you. Once I'm free, I'll rub you raw until you cry uncle." He lifted a strand of hair away from her face. "We lost a lot of time tonight, Teegan. Other than feeding Rommel, I've no intention of leaving the bedroom."

He muffled her response. The faintest taste of her lipstick remained, and he kissed her lips until they became plump and pink. His hand roamed from one breast to the other then downward, sliding across her hip to the upper thigh, causing an increase in her breaths that told him he was on the right track. The softness of her skin was beyond description, like gliding along the edge of a cloud so sensual he almost broke down and cried.

She wiggled against him. A frustrated sound escaped from her throat, and he realized she was struggling to unbutton his shirt. He lifted his head to meet her gaze.

"If you don't take off these damn clothes…" She unbuttoned the remainder and opened his shirt to expose his chest. "There! At least your skin will touch mine."

He chuckled softly and stood to strip.

She watched while wetting her lips, her eyes

widening as he exposed himself fully. "Oh, my." The words fell out of her mouth. She reached to take him into her arms.

But when he returned to the bed, he clamped onto both her outstretched hands and raised them over her head. He held firm as he kissed a path down her belly and bit her pubic hair.

"Budd—"

"Shhh." He spread her legs and fondled her sex. Moist heat waited.

While arching her back, she groaned. "Please let me touch you."

He released her hands. Her fingers clamped onto his hair and urged his head downward. *The woman knows what she wants.* His tongue probed her moisture.

"Oh, God!" Her fingers tightened, and she came with a fierce tremble and a groan.

He expected her to rip his hair out by the roots, but instead, she drew his head toward hers. He looked at her face anticipating a glow of satisfaction, but the teal marbles were dark with desire. For him. For what he provided.

He shuddered. The woman was in a class by herself. He slipped on a condom and drove himself to her core.

****

Teegan floated in and out of a dreamlike state, oblivious of time and space. Her brain registered the world around her, nothing more, except for sated exhaustion. She was in a man's bedroom full of heavy furniture, the scent of his spicy aftershave lingering on the pillows, the fading odor of heated sex on the sheets. Daylight seeped through closed draperies, but the hour—*oh*! He had turned the clock away from the bed. *Sneaky little devil.*

An incredible joy encircled her, like a cozy blanket on a cold, winter night. No man had ever explored every crevice on her body, touching with warm fingers to make goose bumps scream. When he'd consummated, he felt so right, not just in the physical sense, but through an emotional bond so powerful, the feeling shook her core. She hadn't encountered anyone like this man. His passion flooded her senses with every thrust, every kiss, causing her to peak and ebb with emotions firing to full blast from wonderful to the ohmygod.

A fabulous experience.

She was alone in bed.

The door was ajar, and Rommel's massive head nudged through the opening. His bright brown eyes watched her.

"Good morning." What time was it anyway?

Rommel whimpered in response but remained at the door.

She hadn't had a date like this in ages. For months, her life had involved work. Finalizing the plans. Coordinating the contractors. Moving away from Philly and getting the project started. Budd had pushed all that aside and awakened the woman lying dormant. He put to rest—at least temporarily—the scientist/COO.

Budd moved about somewhere in the house, drawing Rommel's attention away from the bedroom.

Teegan listened to the exchange between dog and master with a wonder building inside her. The wonder changed to the speculative questions that had plagued her since high school. Would Budd be like so many men before him, the ones who had entered and left because of ego, unable to handle her brain or money? She'd dated successful men, some more powerful than her father. None had given her such a night to remember.

Vegas's Most Eligible, dear. Don't forget his reputation.

Yes, all right, Budd was a man with a lot of experience in the bedroom, raising the biggest question of all. Was Teegan Smith an exception in his harem, or had she merely earned an entry into the bachelor's infamous black book along with all his other women?

A depressing notion. Even worse, how many more women were to follow? She wasn't naïve enough to think Budd would settle for one when a bevy of hungry females waited.

Still naked, Budd strolled into the bedroom.

Her breath caught to see the size of him unhindered by clothes or bed sheets, a perfect example of manhood. No chiseled abs but the muscles on his upper chest bulged, his tummy flat with no love handles, his legs long with thick thighs and muscled calves. Yes, a very attractive man. Her hands never had the opportunity to explore his body, but now her gaze consumed him. She liked what she saw.

"Well, good afternoon." He closed the door on Rommel before sliding under the sheets. "I'd say you got all of two hours sleep." He leaned over to brush a kiss across her lips.

She touched his freshly-shaven cheek, his spicy aftershave intoxicating her senses. She would never smell it again without thinking of him. "Did you sleep?"

"No, I watched you. I've never done that before. You're beautiful, Teegan." He lifted a lock of hair away from her face and caressed the strand between his fingers. "I got coffee started."

To hell with the coffee. This was the first time a man made her feel so damn special. Yes, all right, he probably said the words to all his women, but she'd like to think otherwise...for the time being anyway. She took the hand holding her hair and kissed his palm. "I won't ask you to elaborate on your comment, but I am surprised, since you're such a man-about-town."

He smiled gently. "No woman has kept me awake before. For some reason, I was afraid to close my eyes and wake to discover you were only a dream."

Well then, maybe she deserved two lines in the black book or maybe a star next to her name, something to differentiate her from the others.

Budd bent to kiss her nose. He followed with a light kiss on her lips. Not satisfied, his finger lifted her chin while his tongue probed deeper into her mouth. He leaned back with a heavy sigh. "You do have a way of turning me on, Dr. Smith."

"And so quickly, too." She broke free of his arms and hopped onto her knees. "My turn, counselor."

She shoved him onto his back and glided her fingers across his muscles, tracing the bulges as if he was a sculpted statue. She licked one ear followed by the other then slipped to the curve of his neck to kiss and sniff the aftershave, across his chest, his nipples until she paused to let his chest hair tickle her nose. From the corner of her eye, she glimpsed his hands rising toward her breasts. She held up a wagging finger to stop him. "Not yet. Hands to the side, counselor."

He groaned and dropped them. "You're torturing me."

"Payback time." Torture for her, too, but she kept the words to herself.

He shuddered when she touched his shaft. The appendage was as hard as a piece of metal and set to explode. She'd rather cause the explosion inside her, so she grabbed a condom packet from the nightstand and deliberately read the printing on the label.

"God help me," he murmured through a clenched jaw.

A snicker escaped from her throat as she ripped the packet and rolled the condom onto his shaft, carefully brushing her fingertips against his sensitive skin. He wasn't the only one with experience in the bedroom.

He clamped onto her wrists. "Now, woman!"

Torture complete. She slithered into position and drove him home, thrusting his erection deep inside her core. With a low groan, she threw back her head and closed her eyes while his hands clamped onto her hips and held firm. Their earth-shattering release hit simultaneously, and she collapsed onto his chest.

She'd never had a lover who gave so much with a combination of gentleness and power to rocket her to the moon then help her float back down. Each time, a potent sense of wonder hit. Her heart overflowed with happiness because, for the first time in her life, she felt a connection to a man beyond the physical aspect. This man was the one.

Really? The thought surprised her. She couldn't possibly be falling in love, right? She understood reality. The man was a confirmed bachelor with a potpourri of women, and she had no intention of hanging around until he changed his mind. Her pride wouldn't allow such a demeaning notion. *I'll get over him. If necessary. Like always.*

The aroma of coffee permeated the house as if they made love at a coffee shop, and the enticement forced her butt from the bed. She carried two cups back to the bedroom where he waited, propped against the headboard with pillows behind his back. She had thrown on his pale blue shirt, unbuttoned, and his lips curled as she handed him a cup. "Calm down, Romeo."

His dark gaze traversed her body. "You look good in my clothes."

"I'm glad because I need them to wear home." She sat near the headboard with two pillows propped behind her back and sipped. "Drink your coffee. You need fluid."

"Yes, doctor."

"And I'm a metals chemist, not a medical doctor."

"Yes, ma'am."

Pleasure bubbled through her, and she burst out laughing.

****

Budd's heart fluttered with an uncontrollable thrill, all because of the woman smiling into her coffee cup. Everything about her caused his heart to perform gymnastics in his chest—beginning with her swollen lips from too many kisses, to her teal eyes twinkling like bright stars in the sky, and then her face with the glow of a sated woman. Of the females he'd placed on his bed, none had such a profound effect. Why?

Damned if I know.

Sex was a man's easy release, mechanical at times and often frustrating when the woman insisted on more after he powered down, but with Teegan, the reverse had happened. He couldn't get enough of her, and the feeling scared him. Even now as he sipped his coffee, he wanted to have sex with her day and night for the duration of time. Not feasible, of course, but the idea was a pleasant one. That's what a full-fledged relationship was all about, right? Sexual euphoria. A man couldn't ask for two better words.

"What are you thinking?"

He shifted onto his elbow to enjoy the view of a woman with an open shirt. The material hid her breasts except for the soft mounds toward the center, and with an effort, he looked upward to meet her steady gaze. "How fate threw us together. How you've corrected a misconception I've had about the children of rich parents."

"Oh?" She sipped and swallowed quickly. "Let me guess. They had their lives handed to them on a silver platter."

"Something like that." He stared into his coffee. "I worked my ass off in college, because my parents didn't have two nickels to rub together. While I waited tables and stocked shelves, I endured constant mocking from my rich classmates. Worst days of my life."

She lifted a strand of hair away from his forehead. "But you accomplished so much, Budd. You should be proud."

"I am." He let the steam from the coffee tickle his nose. "I've got a successful law firm with two partners and ten associates. None of my rich classmates work for me either. I had the distinct pleasure of turning them away."

One night in the storeroom while on break from a

demanding boss, he'd written his goals on a dirty receipt. The goal at the top of the list was to be the envy of every man in Vegas. He'd achieved that and more. Some of the most beautiful women in Vegas graced his bed. He had money and fame, the respect of his profession, and political connections. All were the achievements of a successful and powerful man. No one made fun of him now.

"Anything wrong? You seem reflective."

He cocked his head and gave her a stern look. "Yeah, I'm reflective. It's about how you shouldn't sit in front of me with an open shirt." His gaze drifted to the soft mounds peeking from the shirt, real breasts, not the implants that squished like overcooked gelatin. Teegan's fit his hand perfectly, were smooth, and oh-so delicious.

He took her cup along with his own and placed them on the nightstand. Sliding closer, he fingered the collar of the shirt. From the collar to the back of her neck, easing her forward with a gentle nudge. His skin brushed hers, creating the reaction he waited to see. He used the collar to pull her protruding nipple toward his mouth.

She released a soft groan. "Ummm, are you looking for a little more lovemaking, counselor?"

"I'm looking for plain, simple sex, woman." He hated the word lovemaking, although Teegan had made the word sound less obscene. She activated an emotional connection far beyond any he'd ever experienced, and each climax forced him to question his sanity and his reasons for not pushing her out the door. He'd held beautiful women in his arms often enough. So, what made Teegan Smith so different?

That was his problem. He wanted to know why Teegan affected him beyond the sex-with-a-beautiful-woman fling.

Ultimately, his gurgling stomach cried for substantial food. He dragged her to the kitchen for sandwiches and coffee. They had thrown on clothes. Why, he wasn't sure except the gesture seemed the right thing to do.

As she chewed a sandwich, she glanced down at his dog sitting patiently by her chair. "Rommel looks happy."

Rommel stared upward with adoring eyes.

Budd sighed while slathering more mayo onto his bread. He took a bite and pushed the food to the side of his mouth. "He hasn't left your side since you stepped from the bedroom. Look at him! He loves you." He chewed.

She scratched Rommel's head. "Your assumption he hates all your women flew out a window. What else can I do to dispel your myths?"

Despite himself, he smiled. She was a special woman who had entered his life and made it fun again. He hadn't known the word was missing either. He swallowed the food in his mouth and leaned over to taste her lips. Ham and cheese on rye with coffee. Delicious.

Snarling, Rommel ran from the kitchen.

Budd's head snapped toward the doorway. "His intruder alarm. Let me look around."

The exterior motion sensors activated the spotlights and lit the early evening surroundings. Both agents watching the property were crossing the street toward him. Budd's pulse quickened at the prospect of Anna close by and met the men at the front door. "Well?"

"We don't know why your lights came on, sir. We'll look around back."

Anything could trigger the sensors. Humans, animals, large bugs. Budd returned to the kitchen.

"What's up?" she asked.

"Nothing obvious. They're checking the rear. Rommel makes the same snarl when we're up at the cabin, usually for an animal." He shoved the remainder of his sandwich into his mouth and gathered the dishes, practically swallowing the food whole. "I hope you don't mind, Teegan, but I'm heading for the yard to exercise Rommel while we still have some light." He gulped the last of his coffee and placed the mug into the sink.

She dabbed her mouth with a napkin. "No problem. I'll wash the dishes while you two play."

He'd rather let Rommel run around in circles by himself, but to miss a romp two days in a row would be akin to punishment. He'd bought him as a puppy, and they'd been constant companions since. For Rommel to accept Teegan when he'd rejected so many others proved how special she was. The news made him a happy man. Happier still to feel so comfortable with her. Maybe he should ask her to move in permanent.

Whoa, pal, think this through.

Yes, an asinine idea. While he put on a pair of sneakers, he called Mike Reeves. "What arrangements have you made for Teegan?"

"We'll have a car ready to follow her home tomorrow…*if* she leaves tomorrow."

"Thanks, Mike. That makes me feel better."

A whole lot better. Anna must not hurt Teegan

again.

After an hour of roughhousing, Budd entered the living room to find Teegan sound asleep on the sofa. She looked peaceful, oblivious to Rommel's cold nose on her hand. '*A reputation for sleeping through a hurricane.*' He believed the quote for she hadn't stirred except for the rise and fall of her splendid chest. He stroked her hair before lifting her into his arms. Without question, she was finished for the remainder of the night.

Chapter Sixteen

"Don't get all mushy on me," Teegan complained, suppressing a smile. She hadn't expected to see Budd's sentimental side surface with all his sighing and swooning. Exaggerated, of course. Otherwise, she'd have bet money she slept with a little boy.

"I can't help it. You're beautiful when you sleep." From behind, he wrapped his arms around her and kissed her neck.

"Don't start. I'll burn something."

He squeezed her waist before releasing her to pour coffee into their cups.

The whole scene was too domestic. A man and a woman fixing a late breakfast together—she at the stove, he placing the food on the table, a dog nearby chomping his kibble from an orange bowl. A paper sat unfolded on the table, waiting to be read. Saturday's paper. Sunday's edition rested on top of the mail he had yet to open from Friday. She had never experienced such a flood of contentment after one date.

"I must say you make fantastic-looking omelets." He dropped onto a chair at the table while eyeing the food on his plate.

She licked butter from her finger. "I'm a chemist. Cooking is chemistry." She scraped steaming home fries onto a platter, placed the dish on the table, and joined him. "Help yourself."

Cooking had a way of taking her mind off the bedroom. Like in the lab, a little of this, a sniggin' of that, and pray the outcome produced the desired result. She loved cooking. The early hobby of intermixing ingredients was the beginning of a fascination with science and, ultimately, a career in chemistry. Of course, having an appetite worthy of a gladiator helped since she never stopped at just one course. Three or four courses were her norm, even after a hard day at work. She'd whip up a hearty meal in no time.

Budd tasted the omelet and rolled his eyes. "Wow! Where'd you learn to cook?"

"My mother." She buttered a piece of toast. "I can sew, too, but that's one task I truly hate."

Oh, crap. So much for the frenzied lovers. What happened to her dream of a wild, passionate weekend?

Only in romance novels. Humans weren't built to rub their sex organs raw. The woman took the brunt because of the condom, enjoyable, yes—to a point—but one reached a limit eventually. As proof, she shifted on the seat. "I'm surprised you let me sleep last night." She shot him a teasing grin.

He crunched on some toast. "Please, Teegan, I'm not an animal. You were exhausted." He washed down the bread with coffee and winked. "We'll have other nights."

The comment lifted her sinking mood by a notch. The weekend was almost over. Her hormones had calmed, and reality sank in and lingered. This was as far as she'd go with Budd. He hadn't said the words yet, but the speech was inevitable.

"Have you considered my relationship offer?" He dug the spoon into the home fries and placed a hefty portion onto his plate.

The words surprised her. Most men prayed the woman suffered from a hearing loss when the relationship word slipped from their mouth. She watched him from over her coffee cup. "Let's talk about your offer for a minute. I need to understand why you asked." She sipped her coffee. "You have a reputation in the city of being a ladies' man. Every woman and her mother wants to marry you. Yet, you told me outright you're a confirmed bachelor." She rested her cup on the saucer and leaned toward him for emphasis. "I've no desire to be used for a while then tossed aside to make room for the next woman." She sat back, bracing herself for a quick retort, but he continued to chew his food unperturbed—if he'd heard at all. "Won't it be better if we date occasionally?"

"We're dating now."

"But a relationship implies exclusiveness. We're too early for that." She picked up her fork and sliced through her omelet.

He munched on a strip of bacon, his gaze staring through the archway toward the dining room. "You make a good case. To be honest, I'm not sure why I asked."

"Then let's drop the idea for now. Maybe one day the words will have meaning." *Yeah, when America colonizes Jupiter.*

The doorbell rang. Rommel bolted to the living room, growling.

Budd glared at the wall clock. "This better not be Reeves. He's supposed to call first." He pushed back his chair and stood then pointed. "Don't go anywhere."

A familiar voice boomed from the living room, and

she hung her head and groaned. Her father followed Budd into the kitchen.

He wore his usual black suit with open collar white shirt, black shoes, black socks. Her mother had desperately tried to make him wear something with color but to no avail. Teegan forced a smile. "Hi, Dad. Did you call?"

"Of course." He surveyed the contents on the table. "Sorry to interrupt, but since you're not answering your phone, I figured you were still together. How ya doing, boy?" He ruffled Rommel's head.

Teegan gestured toward a chair. "Want something to eat?" The way her father ate, she hadn't prepared enough food.

"No, thanks. I had lunch with the boys." With a smirk curling the corner of his mouth, he waved a hand over the table. "I see you're still on breakfast." He handed Budd a white envelope. "This was on your doormat."

Budd's face changed to granite. He shot a glance her way and opened the envelope.

Recognizing the envelope size, she stood to read along with him.

She survived my trap. Miss Fancy Pants thinks she's smarter than me, but we're not done yet. You and I belong together, and no one, not even your inept surveillance team, will keep us apart.

Cocky bitch. And she had indeed slipped by the men.

Budd excused himself and left the kitchen.

Her father lifted a black brow. "Bad news?"

"His stalker likes to leave little love notes." She again gestured toward a chair. "I'm guessing he's screaming at the two men out front. Want some coffee?"

"Yeah. The stuff at the hotel was a few coffee beans too light." He pulled out a chair and flopped onto the seat.

She grabbed a cup and saucer from the cabinet and reclaimed her seat. While pouring, she studied her father. He had dark circles under his eyes with red infiltrating the white portion. His eyelids drooped, and more than once, he concealed a yawn with a large hand. She handed him the cup. "You look tired, Dad. Did you stay up all night?"

"Not *all* night. At least half." He took the cup and sipped. "I didn't expect to see you so perky."

"Perky?" She chuckled as she continued with her omelet. "Hardly an appropriate word."

"All right then, content. That fits."

Yes, content. And happy to set the scientist and work aside. She had experienced a night of rejuvenated emotions and would cherish her weekend with Budd forever.

Budd returned with a sneer twisting his lip. "What good is a surveillance team if they can't see a woman walk up to my front door?" He banged his chair away from the table and sat. Mumbling an obscenity, he stood, banged the chair again, and sat.

Teegan patted his arm. "Calm down. When there's a will, there's a way. She obviously found a blind spot."

He shoveled in a mouthful of food, muffling a reply.

Teegan bit into her toast. "So, Dad, what brings you here?"

"My flight leaves in a few hours. Since you wanted

to see me before I left, and you wouldn't answer your phone, here I am." He spread his arms out wide.

"Sorry. I haven't checked my messages."

"Yeah, well, I suspect you were busy. I guess you haven't had time to read the Sunday morning paper either." He whipped out a newspaper from his suit jacket. "Ta-da! I'm in the midst of royalty." He slapped the newspaper with the front of his hand. "Look at this. It's the biggest headline in the Entertainment section."

Teegan grabbed the paper and gasped at the photograph of her and Budd on the dance floor. Budd held her close, their gazes locked, smiles bright, and faces glowing. The headline read: '*Mystery Woman in Arms of Vegas's Most Eligible. Eat Your Heart Out, Ladies*!'

"Oh—my." She shared the paper with Budd. "At least someone took the shot before I turned into a rag doll."

While chewing, Budd took the paper and held it at arm's length. "What a phenomenal shot, probably the best I've seen."

Frank beamed. "My famous daughter. Now, a Vegas celebrity. I love it."

She groaned as she picked up her fork and shoveled food into her mouth. She chewed before speaking. "I never expected our relationship to be a secret, but I hadn't anticipated to be thrust into the limelight so soon. We were on our first date!"

"Relationship?" Budd asked with a slight tilt of his head. His blue eyes twinkled.

She waved aside the implication. "A simple word, counselor."

"Better get used to the paparazzi, Princess. You

two photograph so well, the press won't give you a moment of peace. I'm taking several copies home for your mother. She'll be thrilled to death."

Budd had warned her, but she'd forgotten about people eager to snap a photo. By this time tomorrow, her name would be front page news. *Shit.* Her gaze wandered back to the newspaper in Budd's hands.

"Hello? Earth to daughter? Anyone gonna feed an old man?" He passed a hand in front of their faces. "All right, Earth to counselor? Got any cookies?"

Budd shook himself and handed the paper back to Teegan. "It's a fabulous shot, Frank."

"How about a piece of toast then, something to go with my coffee?"

"Huh? Oh, yeah, I got cookies. You're welcome to some of our…er, breakfast." After crossing the floor, he grabbed a package from an overhead cabinet and tossed it onto the table. He flopped onto the chair and dug into his food.

"Great, chocolate chip." He opened the package and shoved a cookie into his mouth.

Teegan handed the paper to her father and then finished the food on her plate. She smiled at Budd. "Obviously, Anna put the note on your doorstep before reading the Sunday paper." She nodded toward the newspaper. "That photo will send her into a rage."

Her father swallowed the cookie with a mouthful of coffee. "You talking about that woman? Ouch, I just burned my lip." With a napkin, he patted his lips and glanced at Budd. "No, I'm not a mind-reader, son. Teegan told me on the dance floor."

As if adding insult to injury, he again took a large gulp of hot coffee. The man had a leather esophagus. If her mother was here, she'd shove an ice cube into his mouth without so much as a yawn since he had a habit of rushing his food.

Her father leaned across the table to draw Budd's gaze. "This stalker started the fire, didn't she? That's why I came here and not Teegan's place. I figured you'd protect my daughter."

Poor Budd had his mouth full and chewed rapidly to answer, but Teegan beat him. "I'm not staying, Dad."

Budd leaned forward. "I offered, Frank. I've got a spare bedroom in case she doesn't want to put up with me every night."

"Not a bad idea, Princess." He elbowed her arm.

Her mouth gaped. She wasn't the type of woman to move in with a guy because of fear, however enticing enjoying sex without commitment might be. "No," she said.

Budd's cell phone rang. He checked caller ID and answered. "Yes, we saw the photo. She'll go ballistic all right. When?" He glanced at the wall clock. "Yes, fine. See you then." He tossed the phone on the table. "That was Mike Reeves. He and Jeff are on their way. They want to discuss several plans of action."

Of which she wanted to hear none. Her job was finished. She'd kept Budd in Vegas as requested, had a wonderful weekend with him, but the Anna Kincaid problem was now in Federal hands. Jeff had skilled agents for the job. She stood. "Time for me to leave."

Budd grabbed her hand. "They may want you here."

"I doubt it. If they have any questions, they know how to find me. After this photo, we'll need a just-as-public announcement about our breakup."

"Agreed. I'll arrange a press conference but talk to Jeff first." He squeezed her hand. "I'm not willing to make this announcement, Teegan, but I need to keep you safe."

She smiled and touched his cheek. "It's the best solution." And the only one unless she consented to be his bodyguard. Hell, that was beyond the scope of her training. She swept a finger against his lips before dropping her hand and turning to her father. "Can I hitch a ride in your limo, Dad?"

Her father finished the last of his coffee. "Of course."

Teegan ran to retrieve her clothes and purse, rolled everything into a ball, and returned. She handed the bundle to her father and nudged him toward the front door.

He pointed to her bare feet. "Where're your shoes?"

"Still at the nightclub." She nudged him again.

He glanced from her to Budd then cleared his throat. "I'll wait in the limo."

Budd wrapped his arms around her in a tender embrace.

Something about the man's touch melted her bones, and she leaned into him to absorb every last second of contentment, suck in his scent, and revel in the hard body that had hovered over her for most of the weekend. His forearm rested against the gauze covering her wound, causing a twinge, but what was a little discomfort when she wouldn't see him until the Feds caught Anna Kincaid?

"You don't have to go," he whispered. "I can drive you later."

She stroked an open palm across his cheek. "It's better this way, Budd. We'll get together when everything is over."

"I may not want to wait."

She kissed him. "We both have to wait. Maybe we shouldn't have moved so fast."

His arms tightened. "Regrets?"

"No regrets." She lightly brushed her lips to his and stepped from his arms. "Be careful."

"You, too. Watch your back. Don't let Anna sneak up on you again."

As the white limo left Budd's driveway, she experienced a wave of irritation, an unexplained anxiousness that tightened her throat. An odd sensation. As if she was being pulled...no, ripped from a foundation. She wanted to leave, and then she didn't. Why? A need to protect him? *Like I'm such an expert.* Or had the feelings stemmed from an overwhelming flood of warmth from a man who changed women more often than she changed her bedsheets?

I'm not making a bit of sense. In truth, she hadn't felt so loved in her entire life and wanted the feeling to go on forever, but he couldn't possibly love her. Infatuated maybe, but that soon would pass. *Let's say he's the best sex partner I've encountered.* A more straightforward assumption.

Was Budd's lovemaking—or rather, sexual prowess—the reason Anna refused to let him go? The lover extraordinaire, unwilling to share him with anyone else? A distinct possibility. The woman had gone to great lengths to make the Feds look like inept fools. She slipped into the nightclub undetected despite Jeff's precautions, and she had approached Budd's front door even with the surveillance team watching. Anna was full of surprises. *So, what's causing the irritation? Cunning Anna, or the Feds' inability to catch her?*

Neither. Teegan fought a growing frustration for leaving Budd...period. Her heart had said stay, but she'd heard the subtleties in Budd's voice. Despite his relationship offer, their weekend was a session of sex. She'd known it going in, and *that's* why she couldn't stay. Pride prevented her from being a man's toy.

Was it so wrong to want real love? Not the love of a man after her money or a well-paying job at the Smith Tool Company. She wanted a man who desired *her*, who had his own feet on the ground, his own career and goals. Budd was such a man, but—

"We're being followed, Mr. Smith." The driver motioned with his head while staring into the rearview mirror.

Teegan turned to look out the rear window. A dark sedan with a male and female occupant kept their distance. "We're good, driver. They're following me."

She had the high IQ in the family, but her father was the smarter one. He always hired a driver to chauffeur him whenever he traveled. She was dumb enough to rent a car and fight traffic.

"Now," her father began, "the 'Jeff' Budd mentioned isn't by chance Jeff Andrews?"

"Yes." Knowing how her father felt about her FBI assignments, she inwardly cringed. Jeff Andrews was synonymous with danger, but if she played her cards right, she'd avoid another fatherly lecture.

He shifted slightly on the seat. "Why is the FBI involved? She cross a state line?"

She explained the details of Budd's case.

Her father's black bushy eyebrows formed a deep crease at the bridge of his nose. "You told me your job was done."

"It is."

"Except now the nut is after you, and why we have a car behind us, and all this hoopla about Budd making a public announcement." He opened the newspaper and tapped a finger on the photo. "She won't believe any announcement, Princess. You're in love with Budd. The look is all over your face. Budd's, too. I'm not blind, and neither is anyone else."

She dismissed the comment with a wave of her hand. "We're not in love, Dad."

"Oh—right, and I don't own the Smith Tool Company. This woman will be out for blood." His frown deepened as he studied her. "What's on your mind?"

"Too much, unfortunately. I don't want Budd to get hurt."

"And what do you propose, something to make your old man worry?"

She slid across the seat and placed her head on his chest while wrapping her arms around his massive chest. "I love you, Dad."

With his arm tugging her closer, he kissed her hair. "I love you, too, Princess, but I know where you're going."

"No, you don't. I have nothing planned. As for my relationship with Budd, that will stay on a back burner until this woman is caught."

"She wants to kill him, doesn't she?"

"The FBI thinks so." Her stomach clenched at the thought.

Her cell phone chirped to indicate a text message. She retrieved the device from her purse and read with a sigh escaping. *The inevitable message.*

"Trouble?" he asked.

More than she would ever admit. "It's Budd. He wants to know if I'm home yet."

"Good. He'll keep an eye on you." He checked his watch. "My flight leaves in two hours. I want you to hire a twenty-four hour bodyguard."

She bit back a retort. "I'll consider your suggestion." After all, the man loved her and couldn't help being overprotective. Even so, she wished he wouldn't treat her like a twelve-year old.

"You'll do as you're told, Teegan, because we both know reality. The Feds don't have the budget to keep up surveillance. If anything happens to you, I'll tear apart the state to find this woman."

The limo eased alongside her driveway. She clutched her bundled clothes and leaned forward.

Scowling, her father pointed a finger in her face. "Get yourself protection today. Understand?"

"Yes, sir." She kissed him as the driver opened the door. "Say hello to Mom for me. You won't tell her any of this, right?"

"Hell, no. I'll show her the newspaper, and that's all."

Her gaze followed the limo until it disappeared around the corner. Then, she took out her cell phone to re-read the message.

—You're dead meat, bitch.—

Chapter Seventeen

Teegan's mind raced like a train engine on full steam. She'd spent a morning getting ready for work with too many interruptions. First, a new bag of coffee resisted every effort to open, and she promptly split the seam and spilled half the compressed contents on the floor. Then, she popped a vitamin pill only to miss her mouth...twice! Finally, a professor at MIT had forgotten her different time zone and called while he was on coffee break. For her, she was late for the office.

Exhaling a slow deep breath, she paused by the front door. Otherwise, she'd drive like an Indy 500 hopeful and catch every cop along the way. She patted her body to verify that underwear hid beneath her suit. *All right, I'm ready*. Briefcase. Cell phone. Food stuff in the fridge. Coffee maker off. She stepped out the door. *Check for flat tires*. Her car sat in an open driveway. Until Anna, she hadn't thought a garage necessary.

While backing onto the street, she spotted the surveillance team halfway down the block, the same one from yesterday. Different occupants, same car. A fat lot of help they'd be if Anna entered through the rear of the house. Without security cameras or motion detectors, the damn bitch would waltz right through the door. *Why bother with high-tech equipment when I have no intention of staying?* Only one man would keep her in town, but he'd have to say the right words. Marriage, commitment…love. Three words every woman wanted to hear.

She peeked into the rearview mirror at the sedan two car-lengths behind. Her father was right. Surveillance was a costly expense in an agency budget. Who was she to bleed the taxpayer's money? The case wasn't a matter of national security nor would the situation endanger thousands of lives. The world wouldn't miss Teegan Smith if Anna shot her dead. Nor Budd for that matter, even though people considered him a local celebrity. He and Teegan had the bankroll for a personal bodyguard, and contrary to her father's demands, she hadn't so much as picked up the phone book to read a list of the city's security firms. *When I get to the office.*

The thought went by the wayside as soon as she stepped through the office door and saw the mound of paperwork waiting on her desk.

She hated Mondays. Her desk could be spotless on Friday afternoon, but sometime over the weekend, paperwork grew from the desk pad. Who the hell came in on a weekend just to open mail? Some little gremlin, no doubt, born and raised to make her life miserable. She had no time to think about security, the Federal budget, or Budd…well, almost no time. Budd popped into her mind often, like every second she glanced at the blue flower vase on the sofa table and envisioned his similar-colored eyes. Or the image of a slow smile passing onto his lips whenever they touched. She missed him already.

By late morning, she wasn't surprised when Claudia announced the arrival of Jeff Andrews. He lumbered into her office looking a little worse for wear with prominent crows-feet stretching from the corners of his bloodshot eyes. His shoulders slumped as if his suit jacket contained weights instead of shoulder pads, and his hair was its usual post-cyclone hit. She hurried him toward the sofa where he collapsed with a heavy sigh, refusing her offer of a shot of Irish whiskey. She sat at the opposite end and waited.

"Now that your father is out of town," he began, "I need to toss a few ideas at you."

"My job is done, Jeff. I kept Budd in Vegas like you asked."

"Yes, you gave us enough time to set a trap."

"Of which she slipped through."

"Like a sieve." He crossed one leg over the other and brushed lint from the trouser material. "Sometimes I feel like I can't plan worth a damn."

Jeff was the smartest man she knew, but something about Anna... Teegan couldn't put her finger on what gnawed in her gut. "Anna's got my phone number now."

His head snapped, flying hair in every direction. "Is this public knowledge?"

"The phone number? Not really."

He ran a hand through his hair.

The cyclone look changed from a category five to a three. "When was the last time you slept?"

"Saturday afternoon." He suppressed a yawn by shaking it away. "Budd told me he planned on making a public announcement on tonight's news about your brief love affair. One date, good times, that sort of thing. A declaration of sorts to put himself back into circulation." He shook a finger her way. "The photo in the newspaper is the talk of the town."

Yeah, no shit. Everyone in the office had seen the photo. This morning when Teegan walked through the door, she endured a thunderous round of applause. The big boss was dating Vegas' Most Eligible. Golly, gee whiz. She'd made her own declaration to the staff, and Budd's announcement to the press should substantiate her statement.

Hopefully, Budd's words would be more convincing than her own.

"I don't care what the two of you say, Teegan. Kincaid won't believe a word. The photo in the paper guarantees it. She might be skeptical, but considering she's got inside information, she'll know soon enough."

She rested her arm onto the back of the sofa and passed her fingers through her hair, tugging more forcefully than intended. "But our relationship *is* over, Jeff. I won't waste my time with a man who uses women like I brush my teeth. Budd claims my IQ isn't a threat, but how about my history with the FBI? I'm keeping a whopper of a secret from him."

He waved aside the statement. "He doesn't need to know, and since we can't find out how Kincaid is getting her info, I recommend keeping your part in this quiet." He shifted on the seat to face her. "We studied the camera footage from the nightclub. Kincaid got in through the loading dock at eleven in the morning while a liquor truck delivered supplies. She never left."

Teegan's mouth fell open. "She stayed all day?"

"Yep. We found her hiding spot. A stall in one of the ladies' rooms. She even brought food and drinks." He unbuttoned his suit jacket to ease the pull on his chest. "After carefully studying the footage, we tracked her movements within the club. She wore a black outfit as Budd said, stolen from an employee's locker. Teegan—" He shot a quick glance in her direction. "We found evidence she prepared for whatever ladies' room you used."

Interesting. "She was after me." The words flowed so softly, she hardly heard her own voice. She cocked her head. "What kind of evidence?"

"Weapons of opportunity. Mop handles broken in half with their tips sharp as swords, a few lead pipes. All stored for easy access. Unfortunately, she obtained the ultimate weapon, a gun." He paused and watched her.

Jeff's information confirmed what she'd felt all along. Anna would dispose of her competition before moving again on Budd. The burger restaurant had proved it. Anna stayed to confront Teegan when Budd walked wide-open down the street. So, Budd's words tonight would be wasted.

What is it with this woman? Why would Anna bother with Teegan Smith, take a chance getting caught before reaching her objective, namely Budd? Some untold challenge or, more likely, something to prove? Teegan toyed with the pillow propped against the sofa back. "She never attended college, right?" She looked at Jeff. "I'd like to see her high school transcripts."

"No problem. I'll get you a copy." He met her gaze then frowned. "What do you have in mind?"

"I'm not sure." She gave a slight shrug. "A hunch, I guess. She's wasting too much time on me, and I'd like to know why."

"Mental instability."

"No, it's more than that, Jeff. I just can't explain it

right now." Something about the way Anna spoke on their first face-to-face encounter in the company parking lot. *'A rich-bitch with spunk.'* Was that the beginning of her challenge, pushed to a limit? She shook herself. "Any luck with the cleaning crew?"

"Not yet. We're also checking Budd's staff. Only Ed Connors admits to dating her. Otherwise, nada."

Someone was connected, and that someone had fed Anna tidbits of information to enable her to thwart the Feds. Budd's legal assistant? She definitely had the advantage. Teegan bit her inner lip. "Both Budd's partners were at the club."

"We saw them. I think half of Vegas showed up."

Memories of their last dance floated into her mind, the heat of his hand on the back of her dress, his aftershave so close to her nose. Just the thought of him activated a longing for his touch. *The relationship that will never be.* She inwardly sighed. "Where do we go from here?"

"Other than a massive manhunt for an elusive woman, I don't know."

"Then how about a cup of coffee? You look like you can use one." She slipped off the sofa and headed to the coffee tray against the wall. "Cream and sugar?"

"Yes, thanks." His cell phone rang. After a brief conversation, he replaced the phone to his pocket. "Kincaid's head count hit three. The female officer assigned to you has died. LVPD will have a vendetta for Anna now."

She glanced over her shoulder to see Jeff staring at the floor, shoulders hunched. "Did she have family?"

"A husband. No kids." He met her gaze. "I noticed you said *we*, Teegan. Are you still in?"

Should she? She had risked her life once for Budd. Actually, twice if she included the car crash. Anna might succeed on a third try. Was Budd worth the sacrifice?

Maybe that isn't the right question. Budd was a man who intended to remain a bachelor and enjoy the benefits of being a loose cannon. She had a fantastic weekend with him, but he was incapable of a meaningful relationship.

So no, she would not risk her life for Budd Richardson. She'd help Jeff apprehend a dangerous criminal, a cop killer. With a mug in each hand, she returned to the sofa. "Yes, I'm in. Anna missed me, but she may not miss Budd's next date." The statement tightened her throat. To picture him with another woman distressed her beyond anything she'd ever faced. She handed Jeff a mug.

"I'm curious, Teegan." He took the offered cup. "Anna hasn't gone after any of Budd's other dates. Only you. She must have a reason."

She sat and sipped her coffee, a frown creasing her forehead. "I have the strangest feeling it has something to do with my wealth. What do your profilers say?"

"That she's smarter than we think." He sipped his coffee while staring across the room. "Frank called me last night." He rotated his head, his gaze twinkling. "I told him he shouldn't threaten a Federal officer."

Teegan chuckled into her cup. "He called me, too. He wanted to be sure the surveillance team was outside and if all my doors and windows were locked."

"And herein lies the other reason I'm here." He looked at her, his expression serious. "You know the facts of life. We can save the department money by following your phone's GPS signal. I'd love to have eyes on you twenty-four seven, but we don't know when Kincaid will strike. She could stretch the days into weeks and maybe months." He placed his mug onto the side table and slipped a hand into his suit jacket. "Your father asked me to give you a list of good bodyguards." He extracted a folded sheet of paper and handed it over.

She placed the sheet on the nearby table without a second glance. "Anna will approach faster if she sees I'm unprotected."

"Budd said the same yesterday when I presented him with similar alternatives." He picked up his cup and sipped. "Mike Reeves has everything arranged for tracking your GPS. All I'm asking is you call him before you step outside…anywhere."

"Sounds reasonable."

"We confirmed the gun Kincaid used was the cop's service weapon, a nine mil. Anna won't hesitate to use it."

As evidenced by the twinge in her back.

"We have every cop in the city canvassing the neighborhoods. My gut says she's being sheltered by someone, a friend or relative, possibly the person feeding her information." He again placed his mug on the side table and ran a hand over his jaw. "She's good at hot-wiring a car. A few have been taken within minutes of a person walking away." His gaze flashed. "I'd rather she hot-wire than carjack. With a gun in her hand, she'll shoot first."

Mentally unstable with a gun at the ready? Hell, yeah, Anna had become a Vegas-most-wanted. Teegan smoothed her skirt without looking his way. "This case will be difficult for me, Jeff."

He reached across the sofa to squeeze her hand. "I know, Teegan. The expression on your face in the photo told me."

Oh, how she wished circumstances were different, that she had controlled her emotions and let Budd be like every man before him. But no, he gripped a part of her she had yet to understand, forced her to question her sanity. She'd fallen for him hard, and she had no one to blame but herself.

"Keep in mind, Jeff, I'm working to get this factory up and running. I've also got an important trip to Houston the day after tomorrow. My specs aren't together yet." Mainly because of a lack of concentration. Every line on the blueprint looked like a line with no purpose. She placed her cup on the table. "I can't neglect my real duties for this case."

"I understand. When I come up with something concrete in the way of Kincaid's capture, I'll give you a call." He slapped both knees and stood. "You might consider extra security around your building until she's caught. Kincaid got past us at the club. Who knows what she'll do with a wide-open place like this." He took her hand and urged her to her feet. "Remember, call Mike when you're ready to step outside and keep your phone and gun on you at all times. I don't want anything to happen to you, because your father will beat me to a pulp. Then I'll have to lock him away and contend with your brothers." His mouth drew into a tight line. "Above all, do not work after everyone goes home."

Teegan felt like a little girl being scolded by her teacher. She understood his concern. This assignment was beyond the scope of her training. Espionage was more up her alley, not the bang-bang-shoot-'em-up stuff. When the Feds had discovered her metal formulas appearing in foreign databases, Jeff recruited her with the notion of salvaging her reputation. He'd put her through an intense three-week training at the academy, an accelerated program because time was not on their side. He used her again for the stolen mercury case. A few others followed. Now, this.

Last case. No more. She was a metals chemist with no desire to continue her Federal agent role.

After saying goodbye to Jeff, Teegan sulked at her desk, feeling about as useful as a battery with no charge. She hadn't the foggiest idea what to do with Anna. *Will Anna believe Budd's newscast this evening?* He had promised to alert all the media to squelch any rumors about the mystery woman. If Anna believed the broadcast, what purpose would she have to come after Teegan Smith?

The photo in the newspaper, ding-dong.

All right, so she and Budd looked all lovey-dovey as they gazed into each other's eyes. People used the same facial expressions for their dogs.

No, Anna would come after Teegan for the jealousy factor. Nothing else explained why Anna waited for hours in a crowded club to ambush her. Nothing explained why Anna hadn't taken Budd the day she trapped him in the elevator. *I'm attempting to make sense of a woman's demented mind. And somewhere in that mind is the answer to her obsession with me.*

Definitely jealousy.

A strange numbing swept over her. The idea of

Anna on an incomprehensible mission to kill-hurt-maim a woman for dating her ex-boyfriend gnawed at every scrap of logic. Teegan hardly knew Budd…well, maybe she knew him better now, but at the time of Anna's first appearance, they had been mere acquaintances. The car crash was a warning, the restroom a trap. What was next? A duel at ten paces?

By afternoon, news had arrived about the fate of the conveyor system. Another week's delay. She threw up her hands in frustration, grabbed her purse, and marched out to Claudia. "Reschedule the EPA meeting." She'd snapped the words and immediately regretted them. After a long breath, she explained the situation with Budd and instructed Claudia to hire a top-notch security firm.

"What about for yourself, Dr. Smith? That photo in the paper probably made her see red."

Oh, she saw red all right. "Tell them to keep a man on standby for when I return from Houston."

She had to draw Anna into the open. *But how can I entice her without endangering anyone else?* She couldn't set a trap here and risk the lives of her employees. Even a nice walk in the park conjured images of Anna's bullet hitting an unsuspecting passerby.

No, her meeting with Anna had to be one-on-one. She would let Anna choose the time and place. *I simply have to make sure I don't occupy my mind with you-know-who.* Teegan called Mike Reeves and left the building.

Unfortunately, as soon as she stepped out the door and viewed the beautiful blue skies overhead, she thought of Budd's blue eyes. She missed him, damnit, missed everything about their wonderful weekend together, and for her to admit she missed a man in so short a time meant something special. Maybe she missed the sex. And his arms, his kiss, his smell, his taste—ah, shit, everything. *The relationship that will never be.* She approached her car.

A flyer, tucked under the wiper blade, flapped with the afternoon breeze. She yanked it with the thrill of having an object to rip into shreds.

Oh! Not a flyer at all. She read the scrawled print. *I know everything about you, Miss Fancy Pants. You think you're so smart with your swanky degrees, but Budd told me you rich bitches buy your way through college. You've humiliated him for the last time, and I'm the official payback queen. You won't be safe no matter where you go or how many cops surround you.*

Well, whatdoyaknow. Budd would waste his words tonight because Anna Kincaid was playing the avenger. Her note explained everything.

I am definitely dealing with a sick mind. Retaliation combined with jealousy. A dangerous duo. Her grip tightened, crushing the paper.

Well, guess what? Teegan had never scared easily, and no one, not even Anna, would change that. *So, go ahead, Anna. Make your move.*

Teegan scanned the parking lot for a car with an occupant. *Like Anna will stick her head out to be seen. Get real.* She started her car and drove from the lot with LVPD as her destination. Time to trade in the Beretta Pico for a Glock.

Since the factory was built outside the city in an area designated industrial, flat, open ground surrounded her, the brown desert sand dotted with palm trees—the city's attempt to beautify the area. Sod was ordered for the front and due in by next week. The landscapers had guaranteed a great-looking lawn, some type of genetically-modified grass that required little watering. *We'll see.*

Traffic on the two-lane highway bordering the industrial park was practically nil. Several sections were staked with red flags while large signs announced the construction company and possible start date. Only one sign mentioned the actual business moving in—a garment warehouse.

Whoa!

An old Chevy Nova came out of nowhere and cut her off, its rear end already crushed from a prior accident. Teegan slammed on the brakes to avoid adding to the damage.

An accident would top her day, and the woman driver was doing a good job trying. The Nova slowed, sped up, then slowed again. *Texting, no doubt.* Another driver incapable of doing two things at once. "Put down the phone and drive, bitch." Not like the woman heard a word.

The industrial highway eventually came to an end, and Teegan followed the Nova onto the main road leading to Vegas. The traffic was heavier, still a two-lane thruway, but the Nova crawled along, its driver oblivious to the cars lining behind, waiting patiently to pass. At the first opportunity, Teegan cut into the opposing lane, but the Nova matched her Audi's speed, effectively blocking a return. *Sonofabitch, she won't let me pass.* Teegan hit the brakes and retreated behind the Nova to avoid a collision with oncoming traffic.

Who the frig does she think she is?

When a second opportunity opened, Teegan floored the gas pedal, but this time, she glared at the driver before passing. Anna Kincaid stared back while a cruel twist lifted one side of her mouth. She hit the gas and sped ahead, forcing Teegan to once again retreat. *You friggin' cocky bitch.*

Teegan matched the Nova's speed as the car turned right, then left onto another straightaway. They were now heading away from Vegas with less traffic. She called Mike, using the car's phone controls. "I'm following Kincaid. What do you want me to do?"

"I'm in my office, Doctor. I'll head to the control room now. Where are you?"

"Oh, gosh." She searched for a sign. "I'm heading north. I don't know the road, but we're definitely heading away from Vegas."

"Stand by. My man's following your GPS. Let me take a look at the screen."

Teegan traveled a safe distance behind Anna, their speeds exceeding the limit by a good ten miles per hour. *Where's a cop when you need one?* Anna passed traffic when safe but made no attempt to lose Teegan since the road was flat and straight. Teegan eased up on the gas only to see Anna do the same. *Hmmm.*

The idea of another trap entered Teegan's mind. Why else would Anna be so blatantly obvious? No sooner had the thought flashed through her brain when the Nova suddenly skidded left into a turn, creating a cloud of dust.

The area was devoid of habitation. Nothing but flat desert sand right and left of a road that seemingly led to nowhere.

"Hey, Mike, Kincaid made a left onto a packed dirt

road. No sign with a name. Single lane, deep ruts. Looks like someone's old driveway." Her Audi hit a rut, and the sand scraped the underbelly. Teegan groaned. *My poor car.* "She's heading toward the mountains. I can see large boulders with the road cutting between them. I'm ending my pursuit." She lifted her foot off the gas pedal. "Do you copy, Mike?" No response. "Mike?" Teegan glanced at the phone's Bluetooth connection on the dashboard computer. *No service.*

Well, I'll be damned. Who's the sucker this time? Anna had lured her into a cellular dead zone. A planned trap. *Serves me right for the sudden burst of illogic by chasing her without backup.* She stopped the car.

A few seconds later, Anna did the same.

Now, what? Since the road wasn't wide enough, turning around wasn't an option. Budd had explained how car tires sank into soft sand once the wheels left a packed dirt road, and this road/driveway was far from being nicely packed. Without four-wheel drive, she'd be stuck in a no-call zone with a crazy woman.

But Anna was in the same predicament. Her Chevy waited in the middle of the road about one hundred meters ahead, unable to turn right or left. *How does she expect to get out?* For the lure to work, Anna needed an escape. That meant her trap was closer to the mountains and possibly a turnaround spot.

No matter. To go forward meant confronting Anna on her chosen turf. The only option remaining was to put the car in reverse and head back to the main road.

Retrieving her Beretta from her purse, she placed it on the center console before sliding the shift into reverse.

Anna jumped from her car, aimed her gun, and fired. The first bullet ricocheted off the car roof. The second struck the front grill.

Teegan instinctively ducked both times.

"All right, bitch, I've had enough of you." She stopped the car as the third shot busted the right headlight. Grabbing her gun, she threw open the door to use as a shield and stepped out. *Calculated odds of a direct shot with the power of a Pico bullet traveling one hundred meters, maybe twenty to one.* The bullet had an accuracy range of fifty meters. Anything farther and the bullet would be spent. *Damn. Who would have thought I'd have to shoot from such a distance?*

She centered Anna in the sight, raised the barrel one inch, and fired. The bullet struck Anna's arm who yelped and clamped a hand over the wound. *Not bad, all things considered.* Teegan cupped a hand near her mouth. "I was aiming for your friggin' head!"

With a fist shaking in the air and mouthing inaudible words, Anna jumped in her car and sped off toward the mountains, leaving a dust trail behind her.

As much as she wanted to chase after her, Teegan let common sense override anger. This was still Anna's ambush. Anna knew what was ahead. Teegan did not. With no choice and shaking from her brush with near-death, Teegan continued her drive in reverse until reaching the main road.

The bitch had to be stopped. One way or the other, this was Anna Kincaid's final shot at Teegan Smith.

Chapter Eighteen

For the second time within a week, Teegan's breath caught at the sight of Budd crossing her threshold. *Will I ever get used to this man?* The air crackled with sensuality every time he approached while her heart hammered against her rib cage like she'd ingested speed. All he'd said was hello with his beautiful smile, and her hormones went berserk. How could she give up a man who created so much stimulation with a subtle curl to his lip?

Well, I won't really be giving him up now, will I?

She'd made a decision to see him for the occasional liaison to reignite her libido. What she knew about Budd she liked. What they had she wanted. Budd could continue his most-eligible bachelor role as long as he recognized her need to date other men. She'd give him enough of a commitment to satisfy his ego and no more. Pride had a way of kicking her in the ass.

Tonight, he dressed informally in blue jeans and a pale yellow shirt, open at the collar, his sandy hair windswept from the warm evening breeze. She resisted the urge to jump into his arms, but she missed him so bad. Only two days had passed since she left his house, and the ache of not having him by her side tore at her self-control. After the incident with Anna in the desert, she had a long discussion with Mike and Jeff. Budd's very existence depending on Anna's capture, or no one would have any peace. Hence, the enticement in the form of a phone call to get him over to her house.

She kissed him lightly. "You had no need to hurry. Dinner won't be ready for another half hour."

"Are you kidding? I almost ran here because driving in traffic was too slow." He shut the door. "I think Jeff's psychic. He called not two minutes after your explanation of how my announcement to the press won't make a bit of difference. I told him about your car troubles and how you were home cooking up a meal. And can you believe it? He told me to go and have a good time." He sucked in a large breath. "Smells wonderful, Teegan." He wrapped her in his arms and nuzzled her neck. "*You* smell wonderful, too."

Like her mother always said, '*a little dab of chicken broth behind the ear will attract a man every time*'. Not that she'd done it, of course, but her clothes, her hair probably smelled of chicken and mushrooms. She touched a finger to his lips and smiled up into his face. "How about a drink?"

"In a minute." He swooped her into his arms and carried her to the sofa.

She shrieked from the sudden onslaught, pushing on his chest in a faked effort of resistance. "What are you doing?"

He settled on the cushions with her in his lap. "I'll nibble on you as an appetizer." He kissed the soft mound of her breast protruding from her tank top.

Shit, the man is turning me on already. "I don't have time for this!" Well, really now, what had she expected? Jeff needed to aggravate Anna into action, and Teegan needed a ride to the airport in the morning. Her intention to keep him overnight was obvious.

"Anna may burn down my house while I'm away." At this point, she didn't give a damn. *The man is hot, hot, hot.* She ran her fingers through his hair and kissed him hungrily.

He responded by sinking his tongue in deep. When he lifted his head, he grinned. "I'll give Anna the matches so you can come live with me."

Oh, right, that will go over real well for maybe a week. "I already refused the offer, counselor." She toyed with his shirt collar while fighting the urge to rip open the buttons to expose his chest. "Why didn't you bring Rommel?"

"Because I'm feeling selfish. I don't want to share you with anyone. I have a boy down the street who watches him when I go away. They get along great." He lifted a lock of her hair to the side. "Rommel certainly took to you, Teegan. He whined after you left. I joined him."

He captured her mouth, a lover's kiss, full of possessive greed, the kind that turned a woman into a puddle of goo.

"I missed you," he whispered. His blue eyes searched her face.

Joy emanated from his gaze, and the look surprised her.

"Did you miss me or the sex?"

"Both." He nuzzled her again.

He smelled fresh from a shower with a splash of his intoxicating aftershave circling like a funnel cloud, sending a shiver straight up her spine. A lifetime of this would put her in heaven. Even a simple touch of his fingers caused her insides to explode.

The timer dinged.

She nudged on his chest. "I have to get the casserole out of the oven."

"Let it burn." His hand slipped under her T-shirt and swept across her breast.

Oh, God help me! She pushed against him. "Come on, I don't want dinner to dry out."

He released an audible sigh and loosened his hold. She used the opening to roll onto the floor before jumping to her feet and hurrying to the kitchen.

As she grabbed oven mitts, she glanced over her shoulder to see the pout on his lips. Then, her gaze lowered to the bulge in his jeans. "Don't lose that, counselor."

He popped a black olive into his mouth. "You're the only woman I know who can create a rise with a single look. You should consider that a compliment."

"I'm flattered." She took the casserole from the oven and set it on the stove top then slid in a tray of dinner rolls. "What's Jeff got in mind?"

"He's working on a plan. Good thing, too, because his about-face floored me. One day, he tells me to restrict my time with you. The next, he's practically pushing me out the door." He popped another olive and wandered around the small kitchen. "You are full of surprises, Teegan Smith. You live like an ordinary woman without servants in a neighborhood I abandoned years ago. I vowed never to return yet here I stand in the old Bradshaw house." He pointed toward the kitchen window. "I used to cut through your back yard to get to the ball field three blocks from here."

The vision of a sandy-haired boy with beautiful blue eyes, yielding a baseball bat and glove caused a smile to tug on the corner of her mouth. She stirred a pot of boiling peas. "This is a nice neighborhood, Budd. People watch out for each other, unlike some swanky developments where people hide behind a facade of superiority." She set dishes on the table. "I understand what you went through where the haves picked on the have-nots. I saw it, too, but I wasn't one of them. I judge people by what I see, not what they have. If the woman cleaning the restroom takes pride in her work, then she's at the top on my list." She laid out the silverware.

"You're the exception. I still hear the taunts ringing in my ears." He gripped the back of the chair.

She placed the casserole on the table but paused to study him. "Did you talk to Anna about your rich classmates?"

"Oh, sure. She was my sounding board, and I vented a lot of anger. She talked about retaliation in some strange ways, but I told her my revenge comes from being best in the class."

After giving the table a last glance, she handed him the cork screw and pointed to the wine bottle on the table.

He popped the cork and sniffed. "I want to keep a neutral attitude about Anna, not judge her too quickly. What if her anger stems from being abused in the mental facility?"

Ah, getting to the nitty-gritty. She drained the peas and poured them into a serving dish with a quick glance in his direction. "Do you still love her?"

"I never loved her, Teegan. We were childhood friends, nothing more."

"A childhood friend wouldn't put a knife in you, Budd. She wouldn't come after me and aim to kill. I think you should listen to Jeff and Mike. Anna wants to kill you." She jammed a spoon into the peas and placed the dish on the table. "Please don't tell me you're under the assumption you can handle her."

He grunted in answer.

Was he serious? He might as well swallow nails.

He grabbed a carrot stick and crunched. "Part of Jeff's plan involves my cabin. He's got this elaborate idea of a trap." With practiced moves, he poured the wine. "For some reason, Jeff thinks your trip to Houston will lure Anna into the open. He wants us to put on a display at the airport. You know, big fight, a breakup kind of thing, like he suggested the other night."

His hand hovered over a dish of celery sticks as if debating.

"Have one." She nodded toward the table. "They're good for your nerves." She tossed a bamboo mat between their two plates.

He scowled but picked up a piece of celery and crunched. "You're not having good luck with vehicles these days. What's wrong with your car?"

"Radiator. It's still under warranty."

She'd barely made the drive to the call zone because of the coolant spewing all over the road. Anna's bullets busted a seven-hundred dollar headlight, a thousand dollar radiator, and scraped the paint on the roof. Served her right for buying such an expensive car.

Luckily, the cops were searching the area using her last-known coordinates. One of the cop cars was a four-wheel drive, and they took off after Anna only to report she escaped onto the connecting highway on the other side of the mountains. Mike's notification to all the medical facilities about a woman with an arm wound turned up nothing. She placed the warm casserole on the bamboo mat. "Jeff is using you as bait."

"He explained that. I'll try anything to get Anna back under medical supervision. Then she'll listen."

Like telling a rattlesnake not to bite. Teegan searched his face, looking for a glimmer of the love he denied for Anna. "She's a cold-blooded killer, Budd. She won't listen to you."

"Maybe not, but I have to try." He sipped his wine and lifted an eyebrow. "Good stuff."

She was no psychology expert, but she hadn't pictured Anna relenting for any reason. The woman had a cold, calculating mind. A dangerous precedent. Budd's assumption could get him killed.

She took the dinner rolls from the oven and placed them in a basket before returning to the table. "Let's eat." She placed the rolls near his plate and picked up a large serving spoon. "How much do you want?"

"A lot. I'm starving." He pulled out a chair and sat.

Men were always starving. Her brothers ate until they exploded. An hour later, they complained of starvation. She loaded Budd's plate with the chicken casserole then served herself and sat. "When are you leaving for the cabin?"

"Right after I drop you at the airport." He helped himself to the salad then handed her the bowl. "I'll swing home and pick up Rommel."

"Isn't your cabin isolated? How will Anna follow without being spotted?" She took the bowl, knowing full well how precarious Budd's cabin was. He'd be as far from civilization as an astronaut on Mars.

"I talked to Jeff about that. He's working on an

elaborate plan involving three teams of agents. Two in the cabin, two in the barn, and two down on the road. He also said he has an ace up his sleeve as a backup but never mentioned what or who." He buttered a hot roll. "Denise did her usual and marked her calendar so whoever is the informant will see the notation. We're only doing one day, Teegan. Jeff's convinced she'll show, but I'm not, and I won't stick around to wait. I've too much work at the office."

"You told no one, right?"

He munched on the salad, his brows creased in a frown. "Ed plodded in and interrupted my phone conversation with Jeff. He may have heard me talking about making a set of keys for the agents." He washed down his mouthful of food with a sip of wine. "The cabin and barn stay locked when I'm not there. I doubt Ed grasped any meaning."

Another dangerous assumption since Ed was at the top of her personal suspect list. "Nothing else?"

"Nothing. No one suspects a setup...except you, of course." He bit into the roll. "I hope Jeff has his head screwed on right. Anna isn't stupid."

No, Anna had a little help from a friend. Maybe Ed, maybe not. The man had been at the dance club and in Anna's old neighborhood. He also showed at the burger bistro while Anna was parked across the street. Too many coincidences. "She could have followed you at one time, Budd, and already knows where this cabin is. I'm sure Mr. Andrews is thinking along the same lines."

He shook his head. "The cabin's location makes it impossible for someone to follow without being seen, Teegan. The road is an open, packed dirt thruway and flat as a pancake. You can see a car's dust cloud for miles. Besides, I've only been to the cabin once since Anna started with her threats. I've been too busy to go."

"Does Ed know his way to this little paradise of yours?"

"Ed?" Shaking his head, he sat back, chewing a mouthful of food. "Lord, no. I'd never take him. He'd use it as some sort of harem." He swallowed. "So, if your next request is I take him along, the answer is no. I'll have Rommel and a rifle. I'll put a bullet in Anna if I have to. Can I have more?" He held out his plate.

"Help yourself."

Jeff's plan was too riddled with variables. Would the informant see the note and notify Anna? Had the bullet wound incapacitated Anna in any way? Even more important, would Anna take the chance of following Budd to the remote cabin? She'd smell a trap and counter with her own plan. *That* was the biggest variable of all.

Budd dug into a second helping. "I don't understand why Jeff considers your trip to Houston as Anna's incentive to make her move. He says with a little play-acting on our part, she'll perceive your departure as one threat out of the way."

She swallowed her food with a sip of wine. "The only reason Anna will make a move is if she feels pressed for time. Me being out of the way is one matter, but with every cop in the city looking for her, she'll have limited opportunity to accomplish her goal— namely you—before she winds up in a jail cell."

"Jeff had the same idea." He buttered another roll then held it up. "This is a good idea, Teegan. I don't often have a home-cooked meal."

The conversation shifted to lighter topics. Their last date was hot and heavy, full of sexual exploration, the first bedroom encounter over and done with. Now, they'd grow as any normal couple, hanging together for company, discovering details not found on any website.

Yeah, right, dream on. Her growing uncertainty about Budd's trip to the cabin weighed on her mind. The desert location offered the isolation to prevent any inadvertent injuries to innocent victims, but if Anna didn't show, she'd shoot Jeff's strategy into oblivion, and he'd have to start all over. As much as Anna wanted Teegan out of the way, Teegan felt the same toward Anna. Nothing would please her more than to explore a relationship with Budd without one shrouded in secrets.

Again, she'd considered the 'R' word and shoved a dinner roll in her mouth to muffle the anguish.

After cleanup, Teegan settled with Budd on the sofa, their wine glasses in hand, television on. She rested her back against his chest. His arm was around her with his hand scratching her belly. Contentment had returned intermingled with regret. Somewhere in the back of her mind was a picture of them spending the rest of their lives together. A fairy tale image. Reality was another subject. She lifted his hand from her belly and placed her palm against his to compare size. "Didn't you tell me you were building your cabin?"

"Yes, why?"

Her hand resembled a child's against his muscled fingers. "This is not what I call a typical lawyer's hand."

His fingers intertwined with hers. "I love carpentry. Once I get the cabin finished, I'll build furniture in the barn. I've collected a half dozen how-to books on the subject." He kissed her hair. "I want you to come to the cabin when my Anna problem is done."

If he survives. Oh, God, what a notion!

"I'm enjoying myself very much, Teegan. Thank you."

"For the record, this is one of our occasional dates."

"A little domestication to tame the wild bachelor, you mean?"

Inwardly, she jerked. Was this the odd feeling rolling around her gut? A subconscious desire to show him a happy family life? *Am I out of my mind*?

She only did what came natural, and relaxing on the sofa was part of a family tradition where everyone gathered to talk about their day. Heated sex was great, but the glue to true bonding began with trust. Once Budd discovered her involvement, he'd never trust her again.

"Is Houston a company trip?"

His words broke into her thoughts. "Yes. NASA. The tools for space exploration are the essential purpose of our new facility. Houston is only one branch of NASA, but Vegas is closer to Asia where a large percentage of our orders originate." She sipped her wine. "Asia is one of the reasons my father talked me into the job. I won't have to travel from Philadelphia all the time."

"Then you're staying?"

"I haven't decided yet. I miss my family and friends." Surprised at the wistful note in her voice, she stared into her glass. "It's hell being alone."

"You have me."

"For the occasional date and sex partner. That may be enough for you but not enough to fill my void. I don't expect you to understand."

"I don't, but that stems from being alone all my life. I have friends but no family. I'm happy enough. You'll get a roster of friends soon. Wait and see." He lifted a strand of her hair and sniffed before releasing. "My parents weren't the chummy sort. My dad was a hard-working carpenter whose biggest goal in life was to drink a case of beer every weekend. My mom worked two housekeeping jobs. We never did anything together like other families. So no, I have no need for a family, because I never had one in the first place. You won't change my mind."

She sat up to face him, leaving the comfort of his arm to make her point. "I've no intention of changing your mind as long as you realize my fundamental need for a family. We'll stay friends and have the occasional liaison, but we'll eventually go our separate ways."

The words hurt, but they had to be said. He was the perfect mate to fulfill her needs—only his path was different.

He peered through narrowed lids. "You're telling me you'll drop me like a hot potato should a more family-minded man come along?"

"Yes." She carried the wine glasses into the kitchen. If they pursued this conversation, they'd have a lover's quarrel. He'd storm out and ruin their plans. *Deal with the disappointment for now.* For tonight, she wanted this man in her bed. He'd leave the scent of his aftershave on her pillows, and she had vowed not to change the sheets until the smell dissipated, a reminder of a relationship that could have been.

He stepped behind her at the sink and squeezed her to his chest. "Don't be mad."

She loved the feel of him, at his male body pressing against hers, all muscle and hardness. "I'm not."

Resting hands on her shoulders, he rotated her to face him. "I'm a big boy. I can handle a setback. Consider me a man who understands your position."

"Good, because I don't want to destroy our brief friendship. Especially tonight. Let's go." She grabbed his hand and led him toward the bedroom, shutting off lights and TV along the way.

****

On the drive to the airport, Teegan listened to Budd humming in tune to a Bonnie Raitt song on the car stereo, his hand tapping the steering wheel in rhythm. He was a happy man, and rightly so. She had never taken without giving back, and last night, she gave everything she had because this was her last chance to love the man who would never be a part of her life.

Without a clue of what was to come, he responded.

Their relationship was based on secrets and assumptions, ambiguous at best. He assumed she'd enjoy the dalliances he offered without commitment. Occasionally, yes, but not as a steady diet. She wanted a more concrete bond, one full of the joys of a man loving a woman, unbreakable and permanent. Budd was content to live alone without ties. Consequently, reality mired their courtship. She had fallen in love with Budd, and the feeling could no longer be denied.

Which was why her lovemaking was intermingled with confusion. He had loved with an intensity of a man possessed, a heated fierceness, conjuring images of the happily-ever-after scenario. Was this his normal response to a woman in his arms, or was she digging to find meaning where none existed?

Oh, crap.

For now, she had a job to do and a flight to catch. Upon arrival at the airport departure terminal, Budd held her in his arms as he leaned against his car.

"Jeff said to make this obvious." He squeezed her close and whispered, "I don't have to pretend. I had a wonderful night." He kissed her, forcing her tongue to dance with his. When he lifted his head, he gave her a beautiful white smile. "I can't tell you how happy you make me feel, Teegan, a real king-of-the-world sensation. An awesome feeling."

Too bad they were mere words. He wouldn't be around to alleviate the dismal loneliness which had become so much a part of her life, especially out here in Vegas. Sure, her family and friends were a phone call away, but nothing compared to the physical contact, seeing the smiles on their faces, laughing at the dinner table. A real support system, not a virtual one over the web.

Maybe she should get a dog.

With one finger, Budd touched her chin. "I'm glad you'll be out of the way of this mess. I don't want you hurt."

"I don't want you hurt either. Make sure you're careful."

No one was certain if Anna followed to the airport. The surveillance team was conspicuously absent. Paparazzi were nowhere in sight. Anna had free rein to evaluate two lovers saying goodbye…assuming she watched.

He placed his forehead against hers. "I hope this is over by the time you come home. Will you call me?"

"I doubt it." She lifted her head and flashed a lop-sided grin. "If you remember, we're doing the occasional dating routine."

He clenched his jaw. "The vision of another man with you makes me angry."

"The vision of another woman with you doesn't please me either. But we're looking for different things, Budd. What I want is far from your mind. Last night was fun but hardly everlasting. It can be, but you're not interested."

His arms tightened.

She had hit a nerve. *Does he expect me to wait around for his call? Well, hard cheese.*

He pulled back. "You're saying goodbye?"

She placed her open palm against his cheek. "I can never say goodbye, but I am putting you on a back burner. I hope we can stay friends." Obviously, he had never heard this speech. His gaze widened, so she kissed him lightly, stepped from his arms, and held out a hand.

He stared at the gesture with raised brows. "A handshake?"

"For Anna's benefit. From a distance, I'm saying goodbye."

Budd took her hand and gave a limp shake.

For a brief second, she felt as if time stopped, that they were the only two people saying goodbye at the departure terminal. On many occasions, she'd given men the *adios* speech but not once had her throat tightened to a point where her breathe struggled…and it hurt like hell.

She reached for her backpack inside the front seat of his SUV and hoisted a strap over her shoulder. "I need to go. Watch yourself, Budd. Let the Feds do their job."

Teegan headed for the terminal and turned back just before entering to see Budd glaring after her.

He had the look of a man scorned with brows creased tightly together, lips thinned into pencil lines, just the way the Feds wanted. She'd played her act well, despite the powerful feeling of regret. Budd's reaction was a big part of the scene for Jeff surmised Anna would follow, see their goodbye, and gloat. Teegan presumed the opposite, that Anna set her own trap into motion and would once again fool the Feds.

Teegan waited in the shadows of the entrance until Budd sped off. Her heart sank to watch him go, not like she expected him to run after her and confess his love. He'd never make such a declaration, even more so after her little speech. The bond that was so much a part of them had snapped in two.

Yes, their affair was over. What she had to do now would finalize the breakup. Teegan walked past the check-in line and straight out a side door to a waiting car.

Chapter Nineteen

Teegan entered the six-bay garage as a man in blue coveralls slammed shut her car's hood and checked for a secure latch.

Another man with a yellow Mohawk sat in the driver's seat tuning the CB radio to the desired frequency. The antenna positioned at the rear of the roof extended a good six feet and looked totally out of synch with the sleekness of the Audi.

She had entered a man's world of grease and grime. Directional signs hung on the walls along with framed photos of sport cars and NASCAR posters. Recliners with padding popping from slits looked about as comfortable as barbed wire and dirty enough to make a woman cringe.

An old guy lounging on a grease-stained lawn chair munched on a sandwich next to a table covered with car parts, totally oblivious of his filthy hands smudging the white bread.

The place smelled of car exhaust and oil, odoriferous armpits, and surprisingly, pizza. She searched for the pizza box, ready to grab a slice and run. She'd had a light breakfast of toast and coffee with Budd, and her stomach growled for a proper lunch. She wouldn't be much help today if she passed out from hunger.

Jeff Andrews approached. "I sometimes wonder if

I should retire to a flower garden, you know, sit around and watch the roses grow. Tending to a bunch of roses beats going after nuts like Anna Kincaid."

Teegan kissed his cheek. "Think about retirement after we catch her. Are we ready?"

"Almost. The boys put in a new radiator and headlight, filled the gas tank, and double-checked all fluid levels. Budd uses the trucker's frequency, so I switched him to a less-trafficked channel. Temporary relay antennas were placed along the way to insure good communication. Off the road, of course. Everything was tested and works perfectly." He lowered his gaze to the greasy floor. "I still have misgivings about this." Hunching his shoulders, he shot her a glance. "Kincaid is about as unpredictable as weather. We don't know if she took the bait, if she followed you and Budd to the airport, or if her bullet wound has her laid up in bed dying." He crooked his finger. "Come over here."

He led her to a table where a topographic map covered the entire length. "Here's Budd's cabin." He pointed. "Four agents arrived an hour ago. They hiked in from over the mountain." He indicated the direction of their ingress. "One main road cuts through the area. It's a wide, dirt stretch common for the desert. Two agents are in position beyond the turn that is essentially Budd's driveway." He pointed to a rock formation. "These rocks allow them a good view of who comes and goes, even if Kincaid arrives from the Arizona side.

"This gas station here"—he tapped a square on the map—"is your turn-off. You'll see a large motor home with *Florida Here We Come* in black letters. That's our command post. Mike and I will arrive once I get the report you've passed. The motor home is also the beginning of the forty-mile cellular dead zone." Frowning, he paused to stare at the map. "Because of the open terrain, we can't move the command center closer until we receive word of Kincaid's presence. And here." He extracted papers from his breast pocket. "As you requested, Kincaid's high school transcripts. All four years, straight As. She applied for nine college scholarships. Nine rejected. Something about her attitude during the interviews."

Teegan studied the transcripts and raised a brow. The woman had aced differential calculus, physics, and complex trigonometry. "These are advanced classes, Jeff, all college-level courses. The woman has a brain in her head."

"A verifiable screwed-up brain. That makes her dangerous." He reached behind his suit jacket to retrieve a gun and holster clipped to his belt. "Here's your Glock. I'm grateful Mike qualified you after your last encounter with Anna. He saved us a lot of time."

Teegan checked the clip for ammo then slid the gun and holster onto the waistband of her blue jeans.

Jeff chewed his lower lip while his eyes stared at nothing in particular.

At the sight of his indecision, she touched his arm. "Things will work out, Jeff."

He rubbed his face with both hands. "I have six agents in close proximity to the cabin. All are good men with experience in field work. We're after one lone woman who is more unpredictable than some of the worst criminals I've locked away." He met her gaze. "But I'm popping antacids because of you, Teegan. I don't want to send you. This isn't what you're trained for."

A strange uneasiness swept over her. He was right. Three weeks at Quantico included the gun range, martial arts, and communication techniques, not the potential for a shoot-out at the OK corral. But the calculated odds of her coming face-to-face with Anna with six trained agents on the front lines…

She squeezed his arm before dropping her hand. "I volunteered, Jeff. She's made three attempts on my life, and I don't think she's done. If she walks into your trap, fine, but my gut feeling pits genius against genius. She's out to prove she's smarter."

"I hope you're wrong." He mussed his frazzled hair. "I'd like to send in thirty men, but we have no guarantee she'll show. I'm hoping LVPD turned on the heat to force her to make a move." His cell phone rang. He answered then turned his wrist and checked his watch. "Got it." He disconnected. "Budd's left for the cabin. We'll give him a good head start." With a finger touch, he took her elbow and turned her toward her car.

"Kincaid ditched the Chevy Nova. LVPD found it abandoned. Blood covered the driver's seat. She'll steal another to get to Budd. All cars heading in the cabin's direction will have license plates scanned." He sighed heavily. "If anything happens to you, I may have to lock away your father."

At his aggrieved tone, she smiled. "I'll be careful."

A technician, wiping his hands on a dirty rag, nodded toward Jeff.

Jeff responded with a similar nod. "Let the men give you a lesson on the CB. Remember, minimal communication. Kincaid could be listening. Main contact will come from the command center once you enter the no-call zone. If Kincaid is listening, she will hear you. Chose your words wisely."

"Understood." She headed toward the car.

"Teegan—" He stopped her. "I need you to be at your calculating best. If at any time you want to back away, do so. Don't be a hero. With that said, wear your vest. You'll find one in the back seat."

Twenty minutes later, Teegan slipped on a pair of sunglasses and maneuvered the Audi through the heavy Vegas traffic. Once she hit the Interstate, she activated cruise control. Her instructions were explicit. *Let the agents at the cabin do the job.* If they failed, she was the trump card.

More like the Joker. She shouldn't do this. If Anna didn't kill her, her father would.

'*Be at your calculating best.*' The words meant controlling the urge to floor the gas pedal. Surprise was her asset, but the probability of six trained agents failing to apprehend one woman had incalculable odds…unless Anna had help.

Teegan reached for the stereo control knob but hesitated. Maybe now wasn't a good time for a sing-along, even though music would be a wonderful diversion to calm her nerves. Somehow, she felt as if she was driving into a hornet's nest without bug spray. A thousand stingers were aimed at her body, injecting venom so she'd blow up like a balloon and die.

I must be out of my mind. Yes, all right, she had a level head and didn't frighten easily, but to confront a woman with a heart of lead smacked of vengeance. Teegan Smith wasn't Wonder Woman.

I can't ignore the transcripts.

Anna's academic history proved what Teegan had

felt all along. None of this I'll-get-the-rich-bitch for Budd's sake. So, Anna would show at the cabin, even knowing the Feds set a trap. With any luck, she'd be apprehended before reaching the driveway. The agents would broadcast the all-clear over the radio, and Teegan would turn around and head back to Vegas without Budd being the wiser. She'd catch a later flight to Houston and apologize like mad to the NASA engineers.

If everything proceeded as planned. The last trap wasn't successful at all. At the thought, she bit her lip.

She was making good time on the Interstate despite stopping for two burgers and soda along with a large cup of ice in case the desert sucked the moisture out of her skin. Once nearing her exit, she slipped behind an eighteen-wheeler that took the curve like grannie with a walker, forcing her to bite back the urge to jump the curb and risk the medium to get ahead.

Patience. Control the anxiety. She wished everything was over and done with, wished she had gone to Houston, and most of all, wished she'd changed her seat on the flight out of Chicago. Then, she'd have met Budd under normal circumstances, like maybe at a nightclub, or another conference…and missed the most wonderful weekend she'd ever spent in her life. At the first opportunity, she floored the gas pedal and left the truck in the dust.

Her directions after the Interstate were to turn right at the gas station with the blue sign. A sign color was unnecessary. The station appeared in the middle of nowhere with a big billboard declaring last chance for gas. Behind the dilapidated building, two tourists in beach chairs lounged outside a motor home sipping cold drinks while an awning shaded them from the hot sun. Teegan waved as she passed and reset her mileage counter.

Checkpoint cleared.

She glanced at the clock on the instrument panel. Several hours yet before dusk. *Try to relax. Drive like it's a field trip.* She was so anxious, feeling like she wanted to jump from the car and run the rest of the way just to dispense of this nervous energy. *If Budd gets hurt...*

Don't think in that direction. The agents are skilled. They know what they're doing. She sighed heavily and let her gaze wander over the desert.

In contrast to the east coast with its hills covered with forests of pine trees, the desert resembled a world unto itself. Desolation stretched in every direction. Not a house, a shack, not even an abandoned travel trailer rusting in the sand. The only movement was heat emanating in waves from the desert floor, creating a distortion with the sunlight. And the mountains, rugged and high in the distance, rose on both sides of the valley. As forbidden as the desert. Miles upon miles of scenic emptiness. If she wasn't on a special mission, she'd enjoy the ride.

Another day.

Jeff had wanted to pair her with an agent, but she'd convinced him to reconsider. What if, for some reason, Budd approached? How would she explain her sudden appearance in proximity to his cabin with another person in the car? Bad enough she had no idea what to say after her farewell speech at the airport.

Let him be.

With frustration levels reaching a peak, Teegan

opened every window plus the sunroof and let the breeze blow away thoughts of Budd.

No news yet on Anna. With a fingernail, Teegan flicked the CB mike in hopes it sprang to life. '*Be at your calculating best.*' Somehow, the words taunted her. Her Einstein brain calculated the odds of Anna knowing the way to the cabin, and the odds weren't good.

Anna had bypassed security in Budd's office building, bypassed the trap set at the nightclub, and so far, found every loophole in the Feds elaborate plans. She'd bypass the road and come in another way, possibly over the mountains, using the same path as the agents. The road beyond Budd's cabin led to Arizona, too roundabout from Vegas but a possibility for a murderer with time on her hands.

After a quick glance at the odometer, Teegan slowed the car as she neared her stop point. A small access road led to a crumbled homestead about a mile off the main thruway. Jeff had assured her of a safe turnaround spot near a wooden structure that collapsed inward eons ago. She headed toward it, saw the CB antenna behind the pile of wood, and also large boulders to the right, a perfect hiding spot. Steering the car to face forward, she cut the engine and stepped from the vehicle to look behind the boulders and pile of wood. A quick scan of the area and roadway. No dust clouds rising in the air. So, Anna hadn't followed. *Surprise, surprise.* Teegan removed her bulletproof vest and then popped the car trunk to grab her backpack.

Time to outsmart the devil.

****

Teegan said goodbye?

Budd gave a harsh laugh at her audacity, the sound echoing around his vehicle. No woman had dared say those words to him, maybe not spelled out in detail, but the meaning was clear. He didn't need a neon sign to fall on his head. In truth, she'd done him a big favor. He wouldn't have to endure the inevitable see-you-around speech when her novelty wore off.

He swerved to avoid a tumbleweed rolling lazily across the dirt highway. A glance in the rearview mirror told him he was still alone on his trip to the cabin.

But was Teegan a novelty? Last night, from the moment she'd opened her door, Teegan had incited odd feelings, emotions he hadn't felt before, that confused him and were impossible to shake. Like comfort when he stepped through her door to smell the aroma of the casserole, peace with her in his arms while sitting on the sofa in front of the television, happiness to converse with an intelligent woman.

The hours flew by, making his time with her too short. His reputation as a get-in, get-out man was well known, and he had little need to change. For some inexplicable reason, Teegan had forced him to question his lifestyle. His craving to explore every snippet of her life overwhelmed his thoughts and dreams, and never in his existence had a woman affected his psyche in such a profound way. Obviously, she hadn't felt the same.

This morning, she was quiet at the breakfast table, probably practicing her goodbye speech. She had laid her desires for a family on the line, but Rommel was his family. Anymore and they'd become a crowd.

Budd blared his horn at a desert fox strolling down the middle of the desert road. The creature acted like he owned the place and merely looked back with annoyance. As he passed, Budd stuck his head out the window. "We don't call this Fox Road!" *Like the fox understands English.*

All right, so I'm irritable. To think Teegan had the gall to terminate their relationship after three wonderful nights. The internal conflict was beyond anything he'd ever imagined and so foreign, he couldn't find a word to express how he felt.

I'm not feeling love, am I? For one, he hadn't any idea what the emotion entailed. He'd assumed they had something special brewing, and he enjoyed every second with her, but the description wasn't love in his book, just a wonderful time with a fantastic woman.

Many years ago, he thought he loved Anna Kincaid, but the experience was when his heart was young and his brain too small for his skull. By the time he realized his mistake, he was trapped in Anna's web of marriage demands and babies. He refused to go along and man, they fought like the dickens. The next thing he knew he had a knife in his liver and nearly bled to death on the street for the world to see.

Five days in intensive care. Fifteen days to regain strength. Two years to deal with the psychological scars. The anger of being so stupid covered his heart like a shield, never to be lifted for any reason. The shield had served him well over the years…until Teegan came along. She not only shattered the shield but melted the remaining pieces.

I can still get back on track.

He had a list of actress wannabes to call. Those women were perfect for sexual dalliances without strings because their ambitions included bright lights and autograph seekers. Of course, a few fooled him.

They were out to squelch his eligible bachelor label, and the paparazzi fueled the fire by pitting one woman against the other. He'd bought the desert property to escape to some solitude. The place was perfect now that the cabin was livable. Teegan would love it.

He slapped his forehead. *How could I think of such a thing?*

Because Teegan was unlike any before her. She hadn't a pretentious bone in her body and was as natural as unprimed wood. Walnut. Birch. Cedar. All beautiful like her. The relationship offer was a simple get-to-know-you gesture of which she wanted no part. *Her tough luck. If she expects me to crawl and beg her to marry me...*

Rommel gave a soft woof while fidgeting on the back seat of the SUV.

Budd threw a glance over his shoulder. "We're less than a mile away. Take it easy." He had to get the dog to the cabin before Anna made her grand entrance. Rommel's keen sense of smell would detect the agents already in position. By arriving early, he'd have a chance to get acquainted. *Yeah, his sense of smell was so keen he missed the intruder in the garage.*

Whoever had broken in that night understood the complex sensors within a dog's nose. Motor oil, rubbed at the bottom of the inside access door, distracted Rommel by disguising the scent of the intruder. Budd nearly broke his neck when he stepped over the threshold and slipped.

He slowed to turn onto the road to his cabin.

Jeff couldn't have picked a more perfect day. A bright afternoon sun lit the entire area, glowing off his cabin roof in an inviting way. Under normal circumstances, his problems would roll off his shoulders at the sight, but not today. He wasn't here to work on the cabin but to trap a woman who had plunged a knife in his back.

The whole Fed plan annoyed him. Anna wasn't an idiot to waltz into a trap. Hell, look what happened at the nightclub. She'd camped out all day. Who's to say she wouldn't do the same at the cabin? *Assuming she knows her way.* Anyone could have passed on the directions. The contractors who'd helped him erect the barn. The plumber who installed the water tower. Both more likely than the three friends who accompanied him with building material.

Jeff had assured him the agents would move in commando style and search the premises prior to his arrival. They'd radio the all clear only if Anna was captured. For some reason, Teegan's trip to Houston was the catalyst to draw Anna into the open. *What a crock of shit. Like Anna gives a frig where Teegan is.*

As he drove into the yard, he took a quick look around. The lock on the barn door dangled to the side so the agents were lying in wait. Two others should be inside the house. When he opened the SUV's rear door, he heard Rommel's low growl as the dog jumped from the seat. "We have company, boy. I'll introduce you."

Budd grabbed his suitcase and rifle from the hatch area, climbed the steps to the front porch, and opened the door, also unlocked.

Rommel barged past him, barking, only to return seconds later, snarling.

"Trouble?" Budd put down his case and searched the cabin. One room after another. No agents. While in his bedroom, he unlatched a window before returning to the living room to hear Rommel growling at the front door. "All right, let's check the barn." Before opening the door, Budd flipped a switch on the wall, which sparked the outside generator to life.

Rommel bolted ahead of him, down the steps, and around the back away from the barn.

A gunshot fractured the still desert air. Budd froze.

Rommel!

Pulse racing, he grabbed his rifle and ran out the door as a second shot fired.

Chapter Twenty

"Drifters, your status."

Teegan jumped and put a hand to her heart to calm the sudden pounding. *Holy crap, you scared me.* After listening to hours of silence, she hadn't expected to hear a voice on the radio.

"Come in, Drifters." Jeff sounded calm but concerned.

The Drifters were the four agents sent on foot. *Maybe they're having radio problems. Mountain range in the way, dead battery.* Weather shouldn't be a factor. A beautiful clear sky glowed overhead.

"Tiger Lily, status."

"Still here," said a male voice. "Carpenter on the premises. No sign of suspect."

"Acknowledged. Confirmation on suspect car. Dark blue Ford Taurus. Nineteen nineties model. Stolen this A.M. from a North Vegas residence. Metal One, come in."

Teegan lifted the mike from its holder. "Metal One." For some reason, CB'ers never used real names. They used 'handles'. Budd's was Carpenter. *Cute.*

"Copy the car description?"

"Affirmative."

"Maintain position."

"Understood." *For how long*? Under different circumstances, she'd be on a beach chair soaking up some of the afternoon sun.

Teegan checked her watch. Several more hours before dark and still no sign of Anna. What was the woman waiting for? *Even I know the desert gets freaky dark at night.* No lights. No sounds. A scary environment for someone used to a lot of city noise. *Like me.*

She tapped on the steering wheel, fighting the urge to do something, run, shout, anything to relieve the mounting jitters bouncing along her muscles. Instead, she threw her sunglasses on the side seat and stared at the mike, willing it to crackle to life. *Come on. Somebody say Anna has arrived.* She wasn't one to question Jeff's authority, but shouldn't Tiger Lily check to see if the Drifters were all right?

She grabbed her ice cup and shook. No ice. She had a few bottles of water in the trunk but no cooler. *What if Anna doesn't show? Then what?* Waiting in the middle of the desert in the dark wasn't her idea of a fun evening. *I'm a city girl, damnit.* Her knowledge of desert creatures equaled her knowledge about chess—two subjects of no interest to a metals chemist. She rested her head onto the seat cushion and looked off into the distance.

The desert had a way of making a human feel insignificant in the vast nothingness of its surroundings. Primitive was a good word. So oddly different from the mountains back home. Here, everything looked older, an area lost in time, a land where prehistoric giants had roamed, not a shred of civilization except for a rusted beer can or two.

What if Jeff was wrong about the informant in the office? What if Anna had a stroke of luck at uncovering

Budd's flight time and his date arrangements? Clairvoyance perhaps? *Oh, fish sticks, my brain is overheating.* She glanced up at the open sunroof and debated. The nearby boulders shaded the car from the hot sun so common sense said to leave it. Along with the open windows, a nice cross-breeze flowed through the car to keep her comfortable.

Had Anna worked with an inside informant? Who then? Budd's assistant was the most likely suspect with her total access to his whereabouts. The partners were also in a good position. *Ed Connors perhaps?* He'd overheard Budd talking about the keys to the cabin. A quick glance at the assistant's calendar would confirm any suspicions. He was at the restaurant, the nightclub, and the convenience store. *But Ed turned white when Anna drove by.* He was genuinely afraid.

So, back to the assistant. Why would she help Anna Kincaid get to Budd? *Oh, hell, the mystery person can be anyone.* The staff, the cleaning service, window washers, whoever had a frequent foot in the door.

Look at this logically. The informant had an incentive, an ulterior motive as yet undisclosed, not only to help Anna but to get rid of Budd. Perhaps a former client whose lawsuit had an unacceptable outcome? Or was someone jealous of Budd's success? His women?

Again, Ed Connors, the Budd Richardson wannabe. *Hmmm.*

All speculation with no supporting facts.

A cool breeze caused small goose bumps to rise on her arms. The desert was notoriously chilly after sunset, and with the sun approaching the mountain tops, she'd be in the dark soon enough. She stepped out of the car and reached into the back seat for her sweatshirt, slipped it over her vest, and tugged at the collar to get the material away from her neck. *Mental note: buy a larger-size sweatshirt to keep in the car.* She stepped from the shadows of the boulders to scan up and down the road.

Black smoke caught her eye, billowing skyward in the distance, maybe five to six miles. *The cabin?* No, the cabin was on a hill. The smoke was eye level. *Leave the investigation to Tiger Lily. They're closer and in a better position to evaluate the who and what.*

Unless—

She slid into the driver's seat and grabbed the mike, considered the consequences, and then replaced the mike to its holder. *Maintain position.* Instincts said move. Something wasn't right. A fire in the middle of nowhere shouldn't start on its own. Again, she grabbed the mike. *Anna could be listening. But didn't Jeff already reveal the presence of more agents? And if I told Jeff about the fire, I'd have to tell him where and give away my position.*

According to the odometer, her distance to the cabin was roughly five miles, the same distance as the smoke.

Not good. First, no communication with the Drifters, now a fire in the vicinity of Tiger Lily.

They're experienced agents. They know what they're doing.

And Anna Kincaid was an unrecognized genius. What if Anna had more than one person helping? What if she had a friggin' army behind her? *And what can I do except become part of another trap?* Every possible scenario flashed through her brain, but one prevalent detail stuck. Anna Kincaid was coming for Teegan Smith—whether here by the boulders, on the road, or near the cabin—regardless whether she'd captured Budd or not.

Teegan started the car and drove off. *Better to meet my adversary halfway rather than wait for her to come to me.* If she was wrong about the fire being Tiger Lily, she'd simply park her car on the other side of their position. *What's Jeff going to do, fire me?*

A bullet pierced the windshield. Startled, she jerked the wheel as a second bullet shattered the glass and sprayed shards at her face. An arm shot up to cover her face as her foot slammed on the brake. A third bullet missed her shoulder by inches and penetrated the headrest, the sound hissing too close to her ear. The car skidded on the packed dirt road, lost traction on soft sand, and flew airborne into a ravine.

I knew I shouldn't have taken this job.

Teegan stared in wide-eyed horror as the car careened down a steep incline, uprooting brush and rocks and knocking her in her seat like jelly in a bowl. The proverbial life-flashing-before-her-eyes happened. Her parents' relentless search to marry off their one remaining child, the FBI cases, her college graduation, Budd.

No way can I survive such a drop. She envisioned harps accompanied by angelic voices singing songs of heavenly praise with figures dressed in flowing gowns, floating around the clouds, guiding her upward. *I hope upward.* She shut her eyes, muffled a cry in her throat, and then threw her arms up to cover her face as a huge boulder refused to move out of the way.

The car impacted. An indescribable sound, a bang

combined with the shattering of glass and crunching metal. She lurched forward as the seatbelt locked against her chest, the force snapping back her head like a volleyball. Front and side airbags exploded and smothered her in white, robbing her air, the roughness of the material scraping her cheek. As the bags deflated, she stared dazed at the boulder occupying the passenger seat. She touched the rough surface with shaking fingertips, half expecting her hand to pass through the illusion.

I lived? How? Nothing in the car was where it should be. The boulder had pushed the center console into her right hip and jammed her other hip against the door. The steering column, bent at a forty-five degree angle, pinned her left leg in place. The metal combined with plastic squeezed her in the driver's seat with no space to wiggle free.

A quick physical assessment, both visual and palpation. No noticeable femur breaks, arms still intact. Both hips throbbed after bouncing back-and-forth between the console and door. Her neck hurt, too, probably from whiplash. Her pinned left leg—well, she was unable to move to determine damage, but she could move her feet without pain. Maybe if she twisted—

She froze, sucking in a breath.

A shadow had reflected in the cracked side-view mirror. A shadow on the ridgeline holding a rifle. Anna Kincaid! *I'm a sitting duck.*

Teegan squeezed her right hand between the console and her hip and lifted the Glock from her waistband. Would Anna descend the ravine to assure her target left the world of the living?

Three shots fired in rapid succession, forcing

Teegan to slither as low as possible in the bucket seat. One bullet pierced her door and shattered the steering column, freeing her leg. The second passed through the open sunroof and smashed the car's computer screen, missing her head by inches. The third penetrated the trunk. The odor of gasoline filtered into the cabin.

Aw, damn. She'd rather take a bullet than burn to death. Clenching her jaw, Teegan struggled with the seatbelt, using hands that shook more than grabbed then wiggled her legs from the dashboard and climbed toward the sunroof half crushed by the boulder. Gun ready, she peeked. No one on the ridgeline. *Where'd Anna go?*

Maybe she's waiting for me to pop my head through the sunroof like a Jack-in-the-box.

Teegan kicked out what remained of the windshield, squeezed between the boulder and the steering wheel to slide over the dashboard, across the hood before dropping to the ground with the grace of an elephant falling out of a tree. A quick roll across rocks and sand then an awkward jump to her feet when the car exploded and hurled her across the ravine. Heat and air propelled her from all sides, robbing her breathe. She hit the ground with a thud, ignored the whirl in her vision, and scurried behind the safety of a boulder to collect her wits. Her heart beat so hard and so fast, she swore she'd never hear again. Struggling with the confusion of events happening at a rapid pace with a world spinning out of control, she clamped her eyes shut to avert the sudden wave of nausea.

No time for this. Anna's waiting. Breathing deep, she opened her eyes and took a quick look around. Still no Anna.

Well, now what? Her head hurt. A warm ooze trickled from above her temple. A fingertip touch revealed a blood trail. *Not bad, all things considered. I'm alive and functional.*

Big deal. Her car was engulfed in flames and spewing black smoke like no tomorrow. The car had rocketed down a two-hundred-foot ravine before stopping at the boulder, its path marked by the deep ruts in the sand. Anna wasn't on the ridgeline pacing, but she was somewhere nearby, lying in wait.

Teegan lifted her cell phone from her back pocket to see the screen cracked but working. Her parents' photo smiled back. As expected, no service. Since the Drifters failed to communicate with Jeff, and smoke billowed from the direction of Tiger Lily, she had to assume the worst. *Can't deny it now. I am on my own.*

She studied the terrain for the possibility of avoiding the road, but the other side of the ravine rose toward a mountain. With her stomach jumping and heart racing, she blew the sand off her Glock, slipped the gun into her holster and stood but hesitated to move away from the boulder. Once she started up the ravine and stepped onto the road, she'd be an easy target yet knew she couldn't hide forever. She must meet Anna on Anna's terms in order to succeed.

I am out of my mind.

Teegan glanced skyward, said a silent prayer, and started her climb, disturbing soft sand that refused to allow a steady foothold. One step forward slid her two steps in reverse, and she fully understood Budd's description of car wheels sinking into the sand. This wasn't ordinary beach sand, more like ground-up rocks, the coarseness cutting into her palms like razors. She grabbed a rock or bush to stop any downward slide and paused several times to catch her breath.

At one point, the shadow returned. Anna stood on the ridgeline with a sinister smile plastered on her lips, her arm wrapped with blood-soaked gauze. She held a .308 rifle at hip level, its beautiful nickel-plated body reflecting the waning sunlight.

This just isn't my day. Teegan dropped her chin to her chest, heaved air into her lungs, and then forced herself into an upright position, matching Anna's steady glare.

"I've been expecting you, Miss Fancy Pants. A trap wouldn't be complete without you involved." She waved the rifle. "Why aren't you wearing a vest like the others? Not like it did them any good. I happen to know that a vest can't stop a rifle bullet." She caressed the side of the barrel. "This is Budd's rifle I'm holding. I consider it poetic justice to use one of his own bullets on you." A smug expression passed onto her face as she took two side steps along the ridge. "What are we, maybe fifty feet apart? I know you've calculated. It's what you do best."

"Approximately, fourteen meters or forty-two feet." *Nothing like taunting the woman.*

The rifle barrel pointed at her head. Since she had no intention of taking a head shot, Teegan stepped forward to allow a direct chest shot. Unfortunately, the move decreased the calculated distance. *This better work.* "Why didn't you descend the ravine while I was trapped in the car?"

"With this arm wound? Don't make me laugh. I'd never get out." Still holding the rifle at hip level, Anna slipped a finger onto the trigger.

Teegan reached for her gun as Anna fired. The shot hit center chest, knocked out her breath, and propelled Teegan down to the bottom of the ravine.

Chapter Twenty-One

How in thunder can one woman overpower four trained agents? And what about the two on the road? Are they friggin' deaf?

Budd asked the questions repeatedly while he struggled against the duct tape securing his limbs. The bitch had him taped like a mummy, propped against the sofa back, and facing the cabin's front door. She might as well wrap him in a lasso like a steer and press a branding iron to his ass.

Anna had fired when he ran onto the front porch. The bullet ripped through the outer portion of his thigh muscle, missed the femoral artery and the bone. The sting was like a hot iron burning from one hole to the other. Blood everywhere—on his new wooden floor and the sofa. Big deal, she'd put a towel over the wound before swathing him in tape, laughing at his excruciating pain. He'd probably be crippled for life or die from a massive infection.

Like he gave a shit. *She'll kill me anyway.* The insane look in her eyes had said it all.

He'd let his guard down and felt like a damn fool. Four experienced agents were assigned to protect him at the cabin, two down on the road to follow Anna as she drove in, and the crafty little bitch had outmaneuvered all of them—with a little help from a friend, but who, damnit? What deceitful bastard was screwing his back and smiling to his face?

Please don't let it be Denise. He trusted her with his most personal secrets. Josh or Ed? They'd been long-term partners and close friends, three buddies through thick and thin. Someone on the staff then, but who and, the bigger question, why?

Too many questions. He'd drive himself mad looking for answers. He strained against the tape, desperate to stretch the fibers.

Since the remaining two agents hadn't come running, despite the sound of the gunshots bouncing off the mountain, then they had wind direction to blame. If the wind blew toward the mountain behind the cabin, the breeze would carry off the sound, and no one would hear anything unless they had damn good ears. The same principle applied to sound created on the road or beyond. As in the two explosions. One was strong, as if it occurred outside in the yard, the other weak, probably a few miles away. Both had made him jump. At a guess, Anna's doing.

At voices on her handheld scanner, she had given a loud hoot and bolted out the door with his rifle, barking orders to someone in the yard. He couldn't hear the words through the radio static, but she heard clearly enough since her eyes turned into two flaming fireballs.

Damn duct tape. Strong enough to hold a building together. He wrenched and twisted to no avail, becoming breathless in the process.

The four agents at the cabin were now absent, possibly incapacitated or dead. If the two agents on the road met the same fate, that left Jeff's hidden ace—whatever that was. And Rommel. What had Anna done with Rommel? *My poor dog.*

The kitchen. Yes, gotta get to the kitchen.

Budd slithered across the wooden floor, biting his lip from the pain shooting along his thigh. *If I can get to my feet, maybe I can grab a knife from the drawer and cut myself free.* He paused to catch his breath. *So hard.* She used the whole roll and cut half the circulation in his arms.

Don't give up. Hurry before she returns.

The front door opened. A man stood in the doorway, waving a pistol, his thick lips twisting into a sneer.

Hoping to clear his vision, Budd blinked in rapid succession. *This isn't possible. He's an illusion.* Budd licked dry lips. "What are you doing here?"

Josh Feinberg stepped in. "I'm making sure you don't escape." He grabbed Budd's shirt collar and slid him back toward the living room, forcing him against the sofa. "Stay put."

His thoughts whirled. *Josh is my friend.* "Why are you helping Anna?"

"Why not?" His dark eyes flashed behind the thick glasses. "I'm in debt up to my ears because of my ex and that friggin' kid. Anna offered me a chance to take over the law firm. I'm second in line should you meet an untimely demise—thanks to the wording in our wonderful partnership agreement. That's a lot of money to come my way. I told Anna this was our best chance to get you before we voted on Bailey. The suggestion of a fourth partner signed your death warrant, Budd."

His thoughts raced. All he wanted was free time at the cabin. If Josh had said something…

What a dilemma. The man was willing to risk his entire career for more work. How friggin' crazy was

272

that? Budd pursed his lips. "But how did you know about the setup? I never said anything."

"Ed mentioned he overheard you talking about the keys to the cabin, so I checked Denise's calendar. Anna and I put two and two together and surmised another trap." He scratched his beard. "We didn't know how many agents were involved, but Anna figured we could handle five with surprise on our side. She was right, because we took the four up here easily enough by waiting for them when they arrived." He chuckled softly. "By now, she's taken care of the three on the road. You'll be next, and I'll move into the front office with no one the wiser. Clever, huh?"

What three on the road? The ace Jeff talked about, along with the two agents? He eyed Josh through narrowed lids. "How can Anna know so much about the FBI's plans? I certainly didn't tell her."

Josh tapped his temple. "She's smart, Budd, and wrote out two separate scenarios detailing every movement on our part and theirs. The Feds fell right into her hands."

How the hell could Josh be so gullible? Where was his common sense? He was one of the best defense lawyers in Vegas and building an enviable clientèle only to ruin it by being Anna's gunman. Budd groaned. "We've been friends a long time, Josh. Why didn't you level with me? I could have given you half my caseload."

Josh thrust the pistol into his pants belt. "That still meant a percentage going your way. I want your cases *and* your percentage."

All this time, he'd trusted Josh more than Ed. How in the world could he convince Josh of a better way?

He gritted his teeth at the pain radiating from his thigh to his groin, sending an uncontrollable shudder throughout his body. A quick glance at Josh showed a happy man with a crooked smile, enjoying the discomfort of his senior partner. *He won't listen to anything I say.* "Was Anna staying with you?"

"You bet. The perfect hiding spot. She's smarter than she looks, Budd. Whenever she left to do errands, she gussied up like the typical suburban housewife, using my car and being the pleasant neighbor without raising an eyebrow of suspicion. Whenever she tracked you or Teegan, she'd wear her standard outfit and hot-wire a car. This way, if she got caught, she'd leave me out of the picture. That was our agreement. But she never got caught." He scratched his beard. "The one detail I can't figure out is why she has such a personal vendetta against Teegan. I asked her, but she refused to say. Do you know?"

"Other than the fact we were dating, no." Every hair on his body stood on end. *A personal vendetta?* Thank God Teegan had gone to Houston, but what about when she returned? *I've got to get loose. If I could bend my elbow...*

Josh snickered. "I'd say Anna wrapped you pretty good."

Like a piece of sausage. His mind raced for a solution. *Stall for time. With no communication from his agents, Jeff is bound to move in.* "What's with Anna's arm? How'd she get hurt?"

"Bullet wound. She won't tell me any details, said she was too embarrassed. A through-and-through. Luckily it missed her bone." He ambled to the kitchen counter and leaned on an elbow while a smirk spread onto his lips. "I'm guessing your girlfriend put the bullet in her."

His eyebrows rocked. "Teegan? Don't make me laugh. She's a city girl from Philadelphia. What would she be doing with a gun?" *I'm making assumptions again when she's squelched every word out of my mouth.* He struggled to loosen his arms.

"Don't fight us, Budd. I'll make sure you go quick."

Like hell. He glowered at his one-time friend. "You're harboring a fugitive and a murderer. In the end, you'll lose everything."

Josh waved aside the comment. "No one will ever know. Anna assured me."

And Anna can be trusted with the nation's top secrets. Poor naïve Josh. And stupid, idiotic Budd Richardson. To think he believed Anna was a victim of the system.

Jeff was right. Anna had help. Josh knew his way to the cabin because he'd helped Budd transport a load of wood. Josh sheltered and kept her fed, relayed information, and screwed the one man who helped him through his divorce. *What a fool.*

More realizations hit, and Budd narrowed his gaze. "You were at the club that night. You delayed me on purpose to allow Anna time to reach Teegan. And you knew I arranged for Teegan to have a bodyguard. You deliberately endangered her life." The very words boiled like acid in his gut.

Josh removed the pistol from his belt and twirled it, imitating a gunslinger from the old west, shifting from hand to hand and even taking aim at the door.

The stupid shit probably doesn't have the safety on.

"The cop Anna attacked died, you know. Every cop in the city will have Anna's photo taped to the cruiser dashboard. Then what, Josh? They'll find her and piece everything together."

"I doubt it." With a jerk, he drew the gun from an imaginary holster and grinned. "After this, Anna will disappear to another part of the country. My objective is the front office. Anna's objective is you. If she's still after your girlfriend, then too bad." He walked across the open space of the living room to look out the front windows. "By the way, nice place you have here."

If I get my hands on him, I'll kill this friggin' bastard. Budd swelled his chest and arms to stretch the tape. "Aggh!" Instead, the tape pulled at his wound, and he grimaced from the pain.

Josh gave a harsh laugh. "Hurt yourself, Buddy boy?"

Anna strolled through the door looking like Annie Oakley with a rifle on her hip. She flashed a cocky half-ass grin.

"Success?" Josh asked.

"Oh, yes. Our way is clear. Amazing what can be done out in this forsaken desert." She walked to the kitchen counter and took a long swig from an open water bottle. "Did you get on the CB radio like I asked?"

"Yup. I told the guy we had radio problems."

"Good. That should give us time to get out of here." She held out her hand and waved her fingers. "Give me your gun and take this rifle." Once the exchange took place, she gestured toward the windows. "Keep an eye on the drive, will you?"

Josh did as he was told and strolled to the window,

dangling the rifle under one arm.

"What were the two explosions?" Budd asked, not sure if he wanted to hear the explanation.

"That was death to the Feds' elaborate plan." Anna wandered to his side and nudged his wound with her foot.

He bit the inside of his lip to hide the bolt of fire surging from his thigh.

"Does it hurt, honey-baby? I couldn't kill you outright, you know. We still need to have our talk."

What have I ever seen in her? Is she so full of hate that she'll kill anyone who gets in her way? Budd met her insane gaze and nodded toward Josh. "You played him. He can't shelter you after this."

"I don't expect him to."

Without a second of hesitation, she raised the pistol and fired two rounds into Josh.

The man dropped dead where he stood.

Anna sneered at the lifeless form. "His usefulness is over."

****

Teegan jerked awake. Alert, she darted her gaze, taking in her surroundings, searching for the shadow with a rifle. Crickets broke the desert silence, unseen in the faint light of dusk. No one about. Anna hadn't chanced the ravine to put a second bullet in her, a surprise considering the woman's intense hatred.

Now, that was a scary moment I don't want to relive. With shaking hands, she ruffled her hair to remove the sand, giving her scalp a good scratching in the process, silently cursing the time lost by passing out. *Yeah, like I'm wonder woman.* She rolled to a sitting position and winced.

The rifle bullet struck with the force of a sledgehammer against her breastbone. She looked down to see a large burn hole in her sweatshirt, exposing the form-fitted vest underneath—her own patented design, stronger and less bulky than the Federal-issue vest, and definitely one to wear facing a woman determined to kill. In test trials, her vest had withstood the impact of an AK-47 at fifty feet. Anna shot from about forty-two feet with a .308, and the vest still accomplished the job. *Time to put it on the market.*

Her watch was gone. A red scrape took its place. She had no idea how long she'd been unconscious but, considering the approaching twilight, no more than a half hour, three-quarters at the most. Her car was a burned-out shell still spewing a thin stream of black smoke, her second Audi in as many weeks. She grunted and groaned to her feet and shook the sand from her clothes, every movement shooting a pain in some weird path through her muscles.

Now, where is my gun? She hobbled about, searching from one spot to another until catching a glimpse of something black half buried under a bush. With a joyful cry, she snatched it and blew the barrel clear, kissed the cold metal, and tucked it into the holster. This time, she trudged uphill without staring into a rifle barrel.

She was alone, no sign of life in any direction, no headlights from Jeff coming to the rescue—nothing. The mountains stood ominous in the waning light, hiding their secrets, allowing predators to watch the terrain for their next meal. The road stretched flat before her, giving the impression one would fall off the edge of the earth at the end.

No way will I wait for Jeff. Anna had Budd, already captured or dead, and the agents were incapacitated or dead. Teegan had to do something. Jeff's plans were a shambles because Anna outsmarted them all.

Teegan began an easy jog up the road, limping at first from the ache of two hip joints refusing to cooperate and her left leg with a whooper of a lump on the thigh. With nightfall threatening, she wanted to be in the vicinity of the cabin. Hopefully, Anna left the lights on. *Or she has already escaped, gloating with victory.* Teegan cursed under her breath.

Her lungs hurt. She stopped to bend over and force air into a chest that refused to fully expand from a sore breastbone. *I really should exercise more.*

No, she should refuse these assignments, especially the ones with a bullet aimed at her heart. Espionage she could handle—anything to do with a paper trail, a desk, and a chair. No muscle movements, no car crashes.

Keep moving. Walk, jog. Cover the distance. Don't assume Anna's taken off with Budd. But logically, why would Anna wait?

Teegan continued her jog.

An eerie quiet surrounded her with her sneakers creating the only sound as they crunched on the dirt road. Odd shadows formed, conjuring images of childhood monsters ready to reach out and suck her into a void. One tall cactus looked like a traffic cop from center city Philadelphia with fat arms in the air and a wide straight body. Joey his name was. Nice guy.

A movement startled her. She jumped, spun, and reached for her gun as a jackrabbit, hidden in a sage bush, took off with a cloud of dust. "That's right. Give me a heart attack." She almost shot an unarmed rabbit.

With a shake of her head, she repositioned the gun in the holster and continued on the road.

Not too long afterward, a light glowing high on a hill caught her eye. The cabin, like a beacon in the darkness. *Thank you, Lord.* A welcomed sight for a woman contemplating hip and knee replacements.

As she neared the long, single-lane dirt road to Budd's cabin, she slowed her pace. With no plans on how to approach, she stared up the hill then down toward the direction of the agents' surveillance spot. The stream of smoke was no longer visible, but her nose detected the scent of a fire. *Best to be sure rather than approach the cabin alone.* She started toward the boulder formation, their hiding spot.

"Dr. Smith."

Teegan squatted and lifted her gun from the holster, not certain of the male's voice direction. "Show yourself."

A small light flashed to indicate his location.

She took several seconds to find him in the dark but recognized the shape of a human body partially hidden in a hole. With gun safely tucked back into the holster, she knelt beside him and smelled the strong stench of smoke—and something else. Her stomach rolled. "What was the light you used?" He handed her a key chain with a miniature flashlight. She took it and surveyed him.

He was an older man in charred clothing, face blackened from soot. Burnt skin dangled from his left hand, the fingers barely discernible. The right shook from the weight of his service weapon. If she hadn't eaten hours ago, she'd definitely upchuck her lunch all over the poor guy. She swallowed hard. "What's your name?"

"Watkins." He lowered his service weapon. "Kincaid snuck up behind us and tossed a Molotov cocktail into the car." He paused with a grimace contorting his face. "I managed to get out before the gas tank exploded. I don't think my partner had a chance to grab the door handle." He coughed. "Radio's destroyed. You've got to call for help." He coughed again with a distinct wheeze on the intake.

She returned his little light. "Kincaid ambushed me, too. My car's in a ravine, burnt to a crisp. I'll assume the agents at the cabin are incapacitated."

He elevated his charred hand. "Help me up. I'll go with you."

"No. You stay here and try not to die on me. I'll radio for backup as soon as I can, but Jeff should be on his way. If I fail, then Anna will be coming down this drive, and you'll be the last to stop her." She wanted to help him so badly, but she hadn't a piece of anything to use, not even a tissue. "Was anyone else with Anna?"

"I can't be sure. Everything happened too fast."

She pointed to the key chain in his hand. "You'll need the light to get Jeff's attention. Please, hold on."

Anna Kincaid was a friggin' mastermind. Six agents weren't enough. Teegan headed up the hill.

Nighttime in the desert. No moon to light the way. The sand reflected what little light it stored so she could run without tripping over her feet.

Aw, shit.

She tripped over a rock and fell to the ground with a roll, automatically reaching to check the security of her gun. *That's right, klutz. Break something.* She leapt to her feet, did a hop, skip, and a jump to put her bones back in order, and continued. When her gaze drifted skyward, she gasped at the abundance of stars overhead. Blues, whites, yellows—all twinkling with brilliance, unobstructed by light pollution from a city. She hadn't seen such a beautiful sky since her trip to a remote village in Peru. If time wasn't a factor, she'd stop to enjoy the view.

The interior cabin lights guided her. As she neared, she stopped to crouch behind a rock, searching for movement. Anyone could be on lookout and sneak up behind her to end the game. How many cohorts had Anna? Two, three, ten? *Still too many variables to consider.*

Gun ready, Teegan crept toward the cabin.

The front windows brightened the yard to show a log cabin with a wide, open porch. No window dressing. Not even a sheet on a hook. *Leave it to a man not to bother.* Four long wooden steps led to the porch, too high to see through the windows from ground level.

Budd had parked his SUV near the steps. No other vehicle was visible. Had Anna left already? *Am I too late?*

No, the agent in the ditch would have seen a car. Anna was still here, and Budd's SUV was the getaway vehicle. *Then, what is Anna waiting for? A parade?*

Teegan slipped her hand into the open drivers' window to feel for keys in the ignition. Empty. She reached for the radio mike and, with her finger nail, tapped a simple code before replacing the mike onto its holder. She dismissed the idea of peeking into the porch windows. The floor boards might creak. *How can I find out how many are inside?*

She tiptoed around the side to try a window or back

door, but a black form stopped her. A whimper followed. *Rommel!*

She knelt beside him. His head lifted but quickly dropped. His fur had a sticky feel, and the strong odor of blood surrounded him. She choked on a sob before leaning close to his ear. "Hang on, boy. I'll be back for you." *I'll kill that friggin' bitch.*

Teegan removed the safety on her Glock, approached a dark window, and pushed on the frame. Locked. The next window. A bedroom. The window slid open. Teegan climbed in and slid along the wall to a corner, crouched, and waited. The lights from the interior of the cabin showed a sparsely furnished room, a bed, end tables, and chest of drawers. No rugs to help muffle her steps, just bare wood. She crept to the open door.

A woman's voice echoed down the hallway. "Where are the keys?"

"In the ignition."

"You know damn well they're not. You tossed them somewhere, didn't you? Tell me where."

"You'll have to kill me Anna—oomph!"

"I like kicking you, you know. I've had five years to think about payback, and I can't decide what to do first. Tell me what you did with the damn keys!"

Now, she understood why Anna delayed. She planned on Budd's vehicle to get away, and Budd wasn't making it easy.

"All right, I've had enough of this." Anna's angry voice rose an octave. "Get up. You can still walk."

"You put a bullet in my leg. And how the hell do you expect me to walk with all this duct tape? Kill me now or carry me—oomph!"

Teegan inched toward the door to peek down the hall. They were around the corner out of sight, so she tiptoed to the end of the hall and stole a quick glance at a large living room. Anna loomed over Budd who was wrapped in a store's supply of silver duct tape. Blood covered his left pant leg, and he crouched on the floor, half propped against the sofa back. A wide area of open space stretched from the back of the sofa to the front door where a man lay dead under the front window. Black hair, black beard, a vaguely familiar face. Inwardly, she gasped. *The man from the nightclub!* Budd's partner. The informant.

Anna grabbed Budd's shirt collar and yanked. "Get up!"

He shrugged away her hand. "I won't make this easy for you. You drag me out because I'm not moving."

His face was white as a sheet despite the anger in his voice. Her heart ached to see his pain, and she fought the urge to jump into the open and shoot Anna dead. No warning. Just squeeze the trigger and be done.

Anna straightened to rub the blood-soaked gauze pad wrapped around her arm, her gaze glaring. "You've got no one to help you, Mr. Lawyer, not even your girlfriend. I finished her off along with the others." She shot a glance at the front door.

"You're full of shit. I put her on a plane for Houston."

"She works for the Feds, you idiot. I overheard one of your bodyguards sizing her up at the nightclub. Plus, I saw the cops coming out of her office building, the same cops who visited you." She leaned over him and tapped her temple, a cocky grin spreading onto her lips.

"She's good, but I'm better. I've figured out every possible angle." She straightened and again glanced at the door. "You're a bigger fool now than you've ever been, Budd Richardson, but no matter. The Feds will be swarming all over this place soon. We have to get out of here."

So, Anna had confirmed any suspicions by keeping her ears open. *Clever girl.* Teegan searched for the rifle and spotted it resting on the kitchen counter. A pistol protruded from Anna's back waistband.

Sweat trickled down Teegan's back. She plastered a shoulder against the hall wall, gun held with both hands, upright and ready. This was a now-or-never time, and she willed herself to move before it was too late. She had never been a coward, but this assignment was so different. Her love for the victim on the floor, for example. She prayed Jeff would barge through the front door and relieve her dilemma.

The sound of a distant helicopter filled the still air. *Yes!*

Anna's head snapped upward while her hand pulled out her pistol. "They're coming. I was hoping for a few hours alone with you, Budd, but not today." She pointed the pistol at him and sneered. "I had planned to kill you slowly to enjoy myself, but since you're so obstinate about the car keys, I'll have to escape without you."

He struggled to free himself. "You'll never get away, Anna. Give up. I'm your only hope."

She laughed, a guttural sound that sent chills throughout Teegan's skin. *The woman is pure evil.*

No way would Teegan allow the bitch another chance to kill. Even at the risk of losing Budd forever, she had her orders and owed it to the agents' families and everyone else who crossed Anna's violent path.

After a deep breath, Teegan rounded the corner into the living room, gun aimed and finger on the trigger.

Anna's head shot up. She cursed audibly but kept her gun pointed at Budd, her body rigid, her gaze like razors. The smile changed into a nervous twitch.

She's not so cocky while staring at the barrel of a gun.

Anna's nostrils flared. "If that damn rifle hadn't run out of bullets, I'd have pumped every last round into you from the ridgeline."

"Lucky me." Fate was on her side.

Anna's gun hand shook. "So, you wore a vest after all. You have a nasty habit of foiling my plans, Miss Fancy Pants." The cords on Anna's neck showed a heavy pulsing as she nodded toward the hallway. "The agents secured the house and barn when they arrived. How did you get in?"

That's right. Keep her talking. "Budd had instructions to unlock a back window the moment he arrived." She flashed a quick glance at Budd to see him staring, mouth ajar. *Oh, God, what he must think.* She approached, gun aimed at Anna's head. "You're finished, Anna. Give up."

Anna's gaze darted to the door. "Don't take another step, or I put a bullet into Budd's chest."

Teegan stopped. "You know I won't let you do that." Her finger itched to squeeze the trigger. *Come on, bitch. Make my day.*

The copter sound intensified, vibrating ground and cabin. Reinforcements were close.

Panic emanated from Anna's eyes as her gaze shifted from the door to the ceiling to Teegan. "They weren't supposed to come." She gasped and narrowed her gaze. "That was the strange tapping I heard on the radio. It was *you*!"

"Surprise, surprise."

Anna's shaking hands changed to a tremor akin to a severe Parkinson's condition. One false move and she'd blow out Budd's heart.

"Time's up, Anna. Drop the gun."

"Never." She stepped closer to Budd, her gun mere inches from his temple "You won't kill me. You don't have the guts."

"Try me, bitch."

Anna swung the barrel of her gun toward Teegan.

As soon as she spotted movement, Teegan squeezed the trigger and fired.

Chapter Twenty-Two

Helicopter blades vibrated the cool night air, rattling house and ground alike as it hovered, its search light turning night into day. Teegan stepped onto the front porch to wave the all-clear as cars with flashing lights raced up the dirt drive, a cloud of dust behind them. Budd's sanctuary was now a multiple crime scene.

Teegan re-entered the cabin to see Budd frowning at a lifeless Anna with a bullet hole in the center of her forehead. She thanked the Lord for the perfect shot which, gratefully, hadn't blown off the back of Anna's skull to splatter brain matter all over the cabin.

Budd lifted a cold gaze. "I feel betrayed. First Josh, and now you." He shifted on his butt and winced. "You're Jeff's ace?"

She grabbed a knife from the kitchen and removed the tape securing his body.

He sat propped against the sofa holding a towel to his leg, his face pale.

"That's what Jeff likes to call me. Technically, I'm a special ops agent." She knelt beside him to inspect his wound. He jerked away with a 'don't touch' maneuver that gripped her throat.

"You didn't give her much of a fair warning."

"I gave Anna as much warning as she gave everyone else, including you. Would you have preferred she shoot me first?" She leaned back on her heels and met his hard stare. "She's a cold-blooded killer, Budd."

He grumbled something inaudible.

The contempt passing onto his face hurt. She hadn't expected hugs and kisses, but she wasn't prepared for such a display of hatred.

"Rommel?" he asked.

"Anna put a bullet in him, but he's still alive. I threw your bedspread over him to keep him warm. We'll get him to a vet as soon as possible."

His jaw twitched as he glared at Anna's dead body. "And the other agents?"

"The two in the barn sustained facial fractures from a pistol-whipping, but they're alive. The two agents from the house weren't so lucky. I found both behind the cabin. One was beaten to death. The other suffered a similar beating and is barely alive."

The front door flew open, and Jeff, followed by Mike, hurried in. With a quick sweep of his gaze, Jeff surveyed the scene and then pointed to the body under the window. "I'll be damned. Josh Feinberg." He pursed his lips in a silent whistle. "So, he was Kincaid's insider. Who's rifle?" He indicated the rifle on the counter.

"Budd's," she answered. "Anna had a field day. Did you find the agent in the ditch?"

"Yes, I've got people with him now."

A medic entered with a large duffle bag over his shoulder. He checked pulses on Anna then Josh before kneeling alongside Budd.

Jeff crooked a finger at Teegan. "Can I talk to you outside?"

"Yo, wait!" Budd called. "Jeff, have one of your men get my car keys from under the porch."

Jeff's brow cocked. "What are they doing under there?"

A tired smile stretched onto Budd's lips. "You didn't expect me to hand them over to Anna, did you? After I hit the ground, I tossed them out of sight."

"I'll get them," Mike said and ran out.

Well, that answered the mystery of the missing car keys. Teegan followed Jeff onto the porch, grateful for the excuse to get away from Budd's piercing glare and into fresh air.

Once outside, Jeff turned and wrapped her in a tight hug. "I have never been so scared, Teegan." He kissed her hair. "I didn't want you this far involved, but you still turned into my hidden ace."

In anticipation of a good cry, she put her head on his shoulder, but the tears refused to come. She felt empty inside, totally devoid of any reaction to the night's events or the flurry of activity in the front yard. People and vehicles were everywhere. Medics, police, FBI. The porch lights, along with spotlights strategically positioned off the porch roof and barn, illuminated the yard as if daylight had arrived. "Budd won't forgive me anytime soon."

"Yes, I know. Right now, he's in shock. He lost his childhood friend and also a partner tonight. His world's in a spin." He loosened his arms. "Let him get over the bullet wound first. He'll come around."

She wasn't so sure. Budd's gaze flashed hate her way. Hate, not relief. And it had yet to ease.

Jeff held her at arm's length and jiggled the burn hole in her sweatshirt. "What are you wearing under this?"

"My own vest. The material is stronger than your government-issue, Jeff. I designed it to withstand a close-range rifle shot." The night breeze blew hair into her face. She shook the strand aside. "I knew Anna would come for me if she recognized my voice on the radio. She was after me from the beginning to prove she was smarter and nearly succeeded."

His mouth fell open. "Kincaid used the .308 on you? Damn, Teegan, you got specs?" Eyes wide, he released her.

She removed her sweatshirt and unfastened the vest. The cool night air hit the moist T-shirt underneath. She shook the shirt away from her body to let her skin aerate as she handed him the vest. "The size won't fit you, but you can show your superiors."

After digging into his suit jacket, he slipped on a latex glove, and extracted a bullet embedded in the center material. "My God, Teegan, this is a flat .308!" He turned the bullet over in his hand. "You better send me your test results."

"I'll have Claudia fax them over." With a nod toward the side of the house, she threw on the sweatshirt. "Rommel needs a vet."

"I'll make arrangements. Let me see about the other men. Mike!" Reeves stepped onto the porch, patting dirt from his trousers. "Supervise the copters, will you? We'll also need transport for the dog."

"Right." He tossed Budd's keys to Teegan.

Teegan re-entered the cabin as the medic finished with Budd. He'd cut Budd's pant leg nearly to his underwear and wrapped the wound with a thick gauze pad.

"A clean through-and-through, sir, and I don't care what kind of argument you have. You'll need stitches, and you're going to the hospital." He stood and turned toward her, running his gaze over her body. "Let me see your head, ma'am."

She hadn't realized she showed any visible injuries. Maybe she should strip and let him get a good look at her banged-up body. Lord only knew what else he'd find.

After stepping close, the medic lifted her hair. "Small cut. The blood made a mess." He moistened a gauze pad and cleaned the wound. Finished, he nodded his approval. "A bandage will do."

Once again alone, she met Budd's cold-as-ice blue eyes and held out the keys which he yanked from her fingers.

He struggled to stand, using the back of the sofa for leverage. "Take me to Rommel."

She wrapped his arm around her neck and, with her arm around his waist, helped him to his feet. "You're pale enough to pass out, Budd."

His body stiffened. "Don't care. Take me to him."

As they headed for the front door, Teegan grabbed a flashlight from the kitchen counter and helped Budd hobble out the door and down the porch steps. Rommel was in the same position as earlier with the bedspread tucked around him, leaving only his head exposed.

Budd dropped alongside with a soft cry.

She lifted the spread and swept the flashlight over the dog. "I'm no expert, but the bullet hit below the rib cage. I'm pretty sure it missed the vital organs."

"You pretending to be a vet now?"

Ouch. An unexpected zinger. Shock, hell. The man

hates me.

Two agents walked over with a board. With care, they slipped it under Rommel, strapped belts to hold him and the blanket in place, and carried him to a waiting SUV. She and Budd followed. From the SUV, they transferred the dog to a helicopter on the highway.

Budd turned before stepping into the copter, his posture rigid. "Your job is finished."

"I'm going with you." *A glutton for punishment, no doubt about it.* She could have said goodbye, chalked him up as another lost love, but no. Instead, she turned to the pilot. "What about the others?"

"Already airlifted out, ma'am."

The closest vet hospital was in Mesquite, Nevada, and Budd insisted it be their first stop. After landing in a ball field, they transferred to another SUV and arrived at the animal hospital fifteen minutes later.

Two attendants met them with a stretcher.

But the driver of the SUV stopped Budd.

"I've instructions to get you to the nearest emergency room, sir."

"I'll stay with Rommel," Teegan said. "Come back after you're finished. If they keep you, call me."

Budd stared at the two attendants rushing the stretcher toward a set of double doors. Without a glance in her direction, he lowered his gaze and stepped into the SUV.

Teegan stood in the middle of the parking lot and watched them drive away, her mind as empty as her heart. With a heavy sigh, she turned toward the main entrance and entered the animal hospital.

The veterinarian had advance notification of their arrival, and he, in turn, notified his surgical team. They set to work as soon as the attendants carried Rommel through the door.

Hours passed with the stress of the day taking its toll. Her limbs turned to lead, and she stretched across several plastic chairs, tucked an arm under her head, and fell asleep in the semi-lit waiting room to the cries of a cat behind the door and the soft scent of vanilla to hide the unmistakable animal odor.

A noise awakened her. A thump perhaps, as if something hit the floor. She forced open one eye to see Budd sitting opposite, watching her, a cane propped between his legs. Fatigue replaced his anger, and color had returned to his cheeks, but the gaze still held a chilly glare. She sat up with an effort and felt every muscle scream in response. "Why didn't you wake me? How's Rommel?" She suppressed a yawn.

"He'll be okay, but he has to stay at least overnight. They need to get his blood count up." He cupped a hand behind his left knee and lifted his leg several inches to the side, biting his lip in the process. "My ride back to the cabin will be here any second."

She rubbed her eyes. "You should go home and rest, Budd. Agents can take care of your vehicle since they have four separate crime scenes to investigate."

"They can camp out for all I care, but I'm picking up my SUV. I'll need the vehicle when the hospital releases Rommel." He thumped his cane on the linoleum floor and stood.

She suppressed another yawn. "I'll go back with you. I can drive while you rest." She stood and stretched, feeling every muscle recoil in protest.

His mouth opened but quickly slapped shut.

A good thing, too. She was too exhausted to

tolerate more of his barbs. Since he was antagonistic rather than grateful, he'd be better off keeping his yap sealed before she bopped him one.

On the return trip to the cabin, Budd sat in the front seat with the Federal agent. The two men conversed casually, leaving her to sit quietly in the back seat. Which was fine. She couldn't stop yawning. When the driver approached where her car entered the ravine, he slowed to maneuver around the abundance of cars on the road.

Budd leaned forward, craning his neck to see over the dashboard. "What happened?"

"That's where Dr. Smith's car ended up, sir. Another Kincaid ambush."

He snapped his head in her direction but said nothing more. No "my God, you almost died!". Nothing. Bad enough her insurance company questioned her first accident. This second one should win her a week at a driving school.

Oh, crap, let it be. The relationship was over anyway.

On the drive back to Vegas, Teegan encouraged Budd to sleep since his jaw was tight enough to crack a few teeth. He refused and gave curt directions, always glaring straight ahead. At four in the morning, no one was on the road, and they made good time. Vegas, of course, never slept. Once exiting the freeway and approaching the city limits, traffic increased. He directed her off the busy Vegas strip onto less-traveled side streets muttering little more than "turn here, turn there."

"You lied to me. I thought you were different."

Here comes the speech. She dreaded this final

confrontation, knew what he would say, and she had absolutely no retort. Her grip tightened on the steering wheel. "Let me explain a few things before your ears shut down." She gave a quick glance in the rearview mirror. "Jeff Andrews recruited me on several occasions over the years. They were mostly espionage assignments, nothing like tonight. When he saw the photo of us walking through the airport terminal, he approached and told me about Anna. I wasn't anxious to take on another assignment, but you had just kissed me in the conference room." Her throat tightened at the memory, and she swallowed hard to keep her voice under control. "I felt something in your kiss so I mulled over Jeff's request for a while. Anna's visit in the parking lot convinced me."

His head snapped. "She came to your office?"

That's right. He wouldn't know. She slowed for a turning vehicle. "Anna followed you to the Smith Tool Company and stayed to confront me when she recognized Jeff and Mike as the two men from your office. My original assignment was to keep you in Vegas, which I did."

Budd gritted his teeth. "You punctured my tires?"

"Yes, I'm sorry." She glanced his way.

He met her gaze. "How did you know I wouldn't pull out the Mercedes?"

"No CB." Shrugging, she gave him a sheepish grin. "The one in your SUV is mounted under the dash. To remove and then re-install into the Mercedes would take you hours. The tow driver was an FBI man who also made sure your size tires were not available for a little while."

"And the burger place? A coincidence or not?"

"You were under surveillance. They called and told me where you were then disappeared to allow Anna a chance to see me with you. The ploy worked."

The muscles in his jaw twitched. "She nearly killed you twice, Teegan, in the burger parking lot and at the club. Why didn't you tell me the truth?"

If he only knew how desperately she wanted to tell him, how much she resisted breaking the rules despite falling in love. She diverted her gaze by glancing into the rearview mirror. "I had to keep my part in this quiet, Budd."

He stared out the side window. "You're what I despise the most. Another rich-bitch having fun. Our entire relationship was a sham."

His comment shot a bullet into her chest. No vest for protection this time. Her heart was fully exposed to the assault. She gripped the steering wheel. "I faked nothing, Budd."

A cynical gaze scanned her. "Why don't I believe you?"

"Our time together was not a charade. I fell for you hook, line, and sinker, which made my job hard as hell."

"Yet, at the airport, you called it off."

With heat rushing through her body, she glared. "You left me no choice. I'm looking for a permanent man in my life, and you aren't ready for the role. I won't wait around for you to change your mind." She slowed for a stop sign. "Besides, this is my last case." Not like he'd believe her. She wasn't sure she believed herself. Either way, the flush of anger was unnecessary. She had known the outcome of their relationship before it began. Shaking off the mood, she attempted a smile.

"How about you stay at my place tonight? I have a spare bedroom. After we get some rest, we'll go see Rommel."

"No, take me home. I need to sleep in my own bed."

The emptiness returned. Her heart no longer pumped warm blood, only cold water to give the sensation of freezing from the inside out. She had fallen in love with a man who fulfilled her dreams only to, once again, be rejected and thrown back into the spiraling depths of loneliness. Even occasional dates were off the table.

But she felt more than the emptiness of losing Budd. She'd done a good deed tonight, risked her neck to save a man's life, and Budd had reduced the feat to a meaningless act and turned her into a hollow shell. He gave nothing but scorn in return, morphing the deed into a curse.

Thirty minutes later, she eased into his driveway, turned off the ignition, and handed him the keys. After she helped him into the house, she closed the door then faced him only to see a pair of glaring eyes cutting her in two.

"I don't need your protection anymore, Dr. Smith."

Formalities now? "No, of course."

"I suppose you'll get a big bonus for the successful completion of the job."

"Well, actually—"

"I'm sure Jeff already submitted the paperwork along with a recommendation for promotion."

She expected him to be cynical, but this much was getting on her nerves. She jutted her chin. "I was about to say I don't get paid."

He grunted. "Yeah, I really believe that. You're good at lying, Teegan Smith. You'd make a formidable opponent on the witness stand." He limped toward the hall. "I'm sleeping alone tonight."

Yeah, no shit.

He threw the keys in her direction. Surprised, she caught them and dangled the key ring with two fingers, a brow cocked in question.

"Take my SUV to your place. I'll arrange a tow for pickup from your house. This way, we won't see each other again." He headed toward the bedrooms without looking back. "Lock the door on your way out."

For the first time in years, tears stung her eyes. She had known this would happen, yet, deep down, she hoped to be surprised, that he'd show gratitude or even relief, but he was too stubborn, too opinionated, and too damn proud. Of all the audacity, a rich woman had saved his life. For a brief period, she had seen the real Budd Richardson, the man who gave everything he had with a love he refused to recognize. He couldn't fool her. Love poured from his soul with every touch, every kiss, causing her body to come alive like never before. But she wasn't sure which emotion shook her core the most—anger or sadness. Maybe both. Anger for his male pride and ungratefulness. Sadness for the same reasons. If she had to spin a positive aspect onto the experience, then she learned another of life's hard lessons.

At her age, she was so friggin' tired of new lessons. Teegan stared at his closed bedroom door then down at the keys in her hand. He wasn't the only one with pride. She placed the keys on the coffee table and stepped outside to call a cab.

Chapter Twenty-Three

"So, now what? You've been sulking all week and need to snap out of this mood."

Denise's voice jolted Budd since he had no idea she'd walked into the office. He'd been staring out the window, following puffs of clouds across the sky. His mind was so far away, he'd need a train to catch it. He swiveled in his chair to see her flop onto the chair opposite the desk, looking a little wind-blown with her normally perfect hair askew. He pointed to her head. "What happened to your hair? It's not windy out."

Her hand immediately reached to fix the strands. "Sorry. I should have looked in the mirror before coming in." She finger-combed the sides. "Men are working on the air conditioning, and the vents in the hall are off. I walked by as the air blasted. Does your leg still hurt?"

"No, my leg doesn't hurt." The words snapped from his mouth. Everything irritated him. The ring of the telephone. The squeaky floor board near his desk. The buzz of the gnat he swatted and missed a hundred times. Insomnia, of course, along with no appetite and irritable bowel—hell, he'd snap at an angel floating into the room. To boot, his leg stitches itched like mad. He wanted to rip them out, but he only had one more day, one more lousy day of the damn things driving him crazy.

While debating whether to tell her to mind her own business, he glared at Denise. "You're taking too many liberties these days, Mrs. Callahan. I need to remind you who your employer is."

She waved a hand. "Yes, I know who he is. He's a troubled man who stares into space day in and day out. And yes, I'm taking liberties because my feet are killing me." She took off a shoe to rub her foot. "I should get myself another pair of shoes."

Like I give a shit about her shoes.

Denise replaced her footwear then leaned forward, her gaze narrow. "Josh shocked the entire staff, Budd. He was such a mellow guy, not easily swayed even under the worst conditions. None of us can believe how Anna snared him, but the whole incident is more than that, isn't it? You're thinking of Teegan and all your nasty little assumptions bordering on the neurotic." She tugged on her skirt hem. "Women are not cut and dry these days. We have varied interests and skills, varied levels of intelligence. If you assumed in the courtroom as you do with your women, you'd be practicing law on the street corner." She sat back. "You don't know if Teegan does undercover work as a steady job."

"It's obvious. She's very good and fooled me completely. The whole relationship was a sham."

"Oh, bullshit. The old adage about a picture is worth a thousand words is true, you know. The photo in the paper captured the essence of your happiness." She pointed toward him. "You can't fake that."

"She's a good actress."

Denise cocked her head. "What about you? Take any acting lessons lately?"

The smart ass. I should fire her. But she was the

finest legal assistant in Vegas…and also a good friend with the womanly wisdom of fifteen more years of life under her belt. He bit the inside of his mouth to squelch an undeserved barb rising into his throat. "Teegan will find someone else."

"I suspect she already has. She was chatting with a hunk at a gas station a few days ago, but I'm not worried about her. You're my concern." She exaggerated a sigh while toying with her hair. "I suppose you can go back to your showgirls, but they aren't marriage material."

His head jerked so violently, his neck cracked. "Who says I want marriage?"

"Oops, my mistake. I'm falling into your habit of hasty assumptions. I guess you didn't read all the information on the web about Teegan. A reporter wrote an interesting article in *The Intimate Connection*, a woman's magazine. Teegan makes no pretense about wanting her own family. If you'd read that, you'd have thought twice about asking her out."

He hadn't seen any personal information, let alone a lame article in a woman's mag, and so what? The point was moot.

"You were a happy man with Teegan in your life, Budd. Now, you're back to your moody, grumpy self."

The chair squeaked when he straightened. "I am not grumpy." Actually, he was. He had convinced himself their time together was over, that he could never accept her lifestyle of chasing bad guys and shooting people dead, but he tossed and turned every night because her face drifted into his dreams. Even his bedsheets had held her scent to remind him of the wonderful weekend they'd spent together. His imagination, of course. His housekeeper had changed the sheets twice since then.

He'd also convinced himself her rich roots placed a permanent wedge between them. Another devil-may-care rich-bitch with no regard for right or wrong. For some reason, the wedge resembled his face, complete with the makeup of a clown. He blamed the vision on antibiotic hallucinations…an undocumented side effect. He shot his assistant a wary glance. "How chatty was she with this hunk?"

Denise pursed her lips and blew out a long breath. "Well, they were by the gas pumps when I went into the store. They were still chatting when I came out. I don't think she was in a hurry to leave." She fussed with her sleeve cuff while flashing him a cursory glance. "The woman has a beautiful smile."

Yes, damnit, Teegan had a beautiful smile. Her lips complemented the eyes, face, and body. Every part of her took a man's breath away.

She wagged a finger. "I'll bet if you combined all the women you've dated over the years and times the number by two, the total will not equal one Teegan Smith. Am I right?"

Dead on. He studied Denise with scorn. "Since when did you become a philosopher?"

With a wave of her hand, she ignored the question. "Think, Budd. When does Teegan have the opportunity to run around with the FBI? She has an unprecedented reputation in the chemistry field, lectures all over the world, and is now in charge of getting this new factory operational. Don't you think she told the truth about taking the assignment because of you? She sure as hell didn't do the job for money."

He tapped his pen on the desk. "For the excitement, more likely."

She shook her head while staring at the floor. "Men are so friggin' dense. I give up." Sighing, she slapped her knees and stood. "You have an appointment in an hour. Do you want Montgomery to handle it? He's itching to make a name for himself."

"Yes. Make my apologies to the client." Since he had no idea what client or subject. He wobbled to his feet, using the desk for leverage. "I'm going out." Maybe drink himself into a stupor. Or perhaps walk off the confounded emptiness that had smothered him since their fateful night. Something, anything to get his mind off Teegan.

The days passed with little change to the routine. Without Josh, the caseload had doubled, and he farmed off as much as possible to the associates. He wasn't in the mood for work. His mind stayed on the cabin and a beautiful, but focused, woman with a gun in her hand. The picture haunted his thoughts. He had a mountain of questions and no one to ask.

Luck hit the next day. Late that afternoon, Budd stepped out of the courthouse elevator as Jeff Andrews exited the one opposite. Both men stopped. Budd extended his hand, and they exchanged greetings.

Jeff placed a hand on Budd's shoulder to guide him away from the elevator traffic flow. "How's Rommel?"

"The bullet ran a trail through his gut, but he's coming along." Teegan was right about his condition, too. The bullet had missed the vital organs. Rommel had pulled through but hadn't acted normal from the moment he'd returned to the house. The vet said to give him time, but the poor dog moped around like he'd lost his best friend.

"And you?" Jeff indicated Budd's cane.

Budd shrugged. "The stitches are out, and I'm doing therapy to strengthen the thigh muscle." If he could get some much-needed rest, he might heal faster. "You have a few minutes to talk?"

Jeff looked around the large lobby. "I can use a strong drink. My whole afternoon involved legal bullshit, and I am officially off-duty."

Budd led him to Clancy's Taproom, a popular tavern down the street from the courthouse. Like most establishments with a bar, the room had too much dark wood and not enough lighting, making anyone with poor eyesight cautious about where they placed their feet. As was the norm, the tavern was packed with suits—male and female alike—most standing around the bar with drinks in their hands. Others sat at tables eating the tavern's famous deli sandwiches. Music played through overhead speakers, but no one listened, except for the bartender who whistled while he worked. Budd aimed for the two empty bar stools near the far wall away from the crowds. After ordering drinks, Budd hooked his cane onto the leather-covered bar lip. "We haven't had a chance to talk."

"All right, what's on your mind?"

The bartender served their drinks.

Budd swallowed a mouthful of beer while staring at Jeff's glass. "That's Irish whiskey, Teegan's drink."

Jeff sipped. "She got me addicted when I was doing my best to convince her to help out on a case. Good stuff." Another sip. "What do you want to talk about?"

"What happened to your carefully laid plans?"

Jeff popped a few peanuts into his mouth. "We anticipated every possible scenario including Kincaid waiting at the cabin. All doors and windows were locked when the agents arrived and performed their preliminary search, but Kincaid and Feinberg were already inside the barn, hiding in the loft. They jimmied a side window and broke the lock, then jammed a piece of wood so the agents felt it secure. Evidence indicates they spent the night—you know, food, water, sleeping bags." He glanced at Budd. "I take it Feinberg knew his way to the cabin?"

Budd toyed with the coaster under his drink. "Yes. I believed him more trustworthy than Ed for keeping the place a secret." Boy, was he wrong.

"Feinberg's involvement gave Kincaid an edge we hadn't expected." His facial muscles tightened while his gaze stared at his reflection in the bar's wall mirrors. "They devised their own trap and took the two agents in the barn. Kincaid held them at gunpoint while Feinberg cuffed them to posts. Ordinarily, the agents would make noise to attract the other two in the house, but Kincaid held a detonator in her hand and threatened to blow the barn and cabin to kingdom come. The agents complied only to discover the detonator was a plastic toy. Kincaid then pistol-whipped them into silence." He held his glass up to the lights. "I shouldn't drink this stuff." Giving a head shake, he sipped then continued.

"The two in the cabin weren't so lucky. We don't really know how she got them outside, but she cracked their skulls with a crowbar. One dead, the other still in a coma. All Kincaid had to do was wait for you to arrive."

And like a sucker, he waltzed right into her trap.

He shifted on the barstool. "She took a chance shooting me and Rommel. If the air was still or the breeze blowing down from the mountain…"

"Exactly, but I suspect she had no choice. She couldn't let Rommel get close since a Rottweiler has a powerful jaw. You, according to your statement, came running out with the rifle."

"But how had she known how many agents were standing by? I never said anything to anyone."

"Calculated odds." He shrugged. "Teegan called Kincaid an unrecognized genius. After what I've seen, I believe her."

A peanut missed his mouth, bounced off his chin and onto the bar where it rolled halfway down to the next customer. He stared, as if debating whether to reach.

The poor man must be starving.

Jeff ignored the stray peanut and, again, stared at his reflection in the mirror. "I received word last night the agent in the burn unit has died. That brings Kincaid's body count to six."

Unbelievable. Anna's hatred for him had transformed her into a stone-cold murderer. This from a woman he'd dated off and on for years. What had he seen in her? Availability? An object on which to practice his manhood? He'd screwed her for the first time after a high school pep rally in the team dugout, of all places. Several times in the backseat of his car. Never any place nice, like she was a free whore. Their dalliances lasted through college, but once he entered law school, he concentrated on his studies. In time, she'd become too possessive, demanding marriage, a big house, and children. "How did Anna and Josh get to

307

the cabin? I didn't see a car anywhere."

"We found their stolen vehicle a mile beyond our lookout's position. She and Feinberg trekked in. Lucky for you Teegan survived Kincaid's ambush."

Irritation surfaced at the mention of Teegan's covert role. He glared at the older man. "Why did you involve her, Jeff? The assignment was too dangerous."

Lifting a hand, Jeff caught the attention of the bartender and ordered another round of drinks. "I never meant to have her go any further than the nightclub, Budd. Unfortunately, Kincaid's third attempt on Teegan's life got the doctor's Irish temper up."

Budd's head snapped in Jeff's direction. "What third attempt?"

The drinks arrived. Jeff waited for the bartender to move on. Jeff frowned as he sipped and then set down the glass. "Kincaid lured Teegan into a cellular dead zone somewhere off Highway Ninety-three. By the time Teegan realized the trap, Kincaid put three bullets into her car. Teegan fired one shot and hit Kincaid's upper arm."

Anna's bloody gauze.

As with most Vegas residents, he knew about the dead zones along Highway Ninety-three. The road stretched clear up to Idaho and passed through some rugged mountain country. Teegan, being new to the area, wouldn't know, and Anna probably counted on that ignorance.

Three attempts. Four if he included the ambush near the cabin. Budd raised his beer to his lips but stared into the frothy foam. "Anna nearly beat the Feds at their own game, even with an injury." He watched Jeff's reflection in the mirror. "She made you look like inept fools."

Jeff's jaw twitched. "Don't remind me, I lost a lot of good people because of Anna Kincaid." He finished the last of the peanuts and motioned to the bartender for a refill. "I count my blessings that I had the good sense to listen to Teegan. She insisted on staying separated from the other men, and the idea for you to unlock a window was hers."

"Yeah, well, I thought it was an asinine idea, but now, I understand why. Teegan needed access to the cabin if all else failed." He slammed his beer mug onto the bar and turned toward Jeff, forcing words through clenched teeth. "Teegan killed Anna outright, Jeff. Why couldn't she just wound her?"

The older man studied him with a steady gaze. "My orders were shoot to kill. Teegan knew the situation going in, and even though she'd never faced carrying out such an order, she followed through." He toyed with the empty peanut bowl. "I'm sure you noticed the burn hole in Teegan's sweatshirt. She took a direct rifle shot at close range and felt the after-effects for a week. If she was wearing our vest, she'd be dead."

Pain stabbed his own chest. Budd nearly dropped his glass on the bar. "She invented her own vest?"

"Yep, designed and manufactured by Dr. Teegan Smith." He flashed a quick grin. "She incorporated the best vest material with her own special blend of treated fabrics, made the garment lightweight and affordable. The woman knows her chemistry. She sent me the specs. I'm taking a proposal before the committee for purchase approval."

He had seen the burn hole with the black garment underneath but never asked because he hadn't cared.

"She expressed no remorse, Jeff."

"She did with me. Cried on my shoulder for ten minutes. Her first kill, and she hated it." Jeff held the empty peanut bowl in the air and again waved to catch the bartender's attention. "What's a man gotta do for a refill around here?"

The bartender acknowledged with a wave and grabbed a bag from a cabinet behind him.

Jeff turned back to Budd. "Teegan was required to attend counseling, which she did. I guess your injury kept her off your shoulder."

More than his injury. His whole damn attitude. He wanted nothing more than to just get rid of her. Budd stared into his beer. "How often does Teegan do these undercover assignments?"

"Not as often as I'd like. I've used her on several occasions, but nothing like this job. Unfortunately, Teegan was the lure to get Kincaid out of hiding." He sipped his drink. "You've dated some beautiful women, Budd, but anyone with two eyes can see the special spark between you two. How's she doing?"

"I don't know. We broke up."

Jeff leaned back on the stool with eyebrows halfway into his hair. "Whose call?"

"Mine. I wasn't too forgiving after she shot Anna."

"Well, that's a fine how-do-you-do. She risked her neck to keep you alive, and you say *adios*? I'd say Teegan survived all Kincaid's ambushes because of divine intervention." He tapped the empty bowl on the bar. "You probably don't know this, but Teegan positioned herself to take a chest shot, a calculated risk for sure, but she had a better chance for survival with the vest than a direct head shot." He leaned close. "And another fact you don't know. Anna was after Teegan to avenge the torment you received in college from your rich classmates. I should let you read Teegan's report so you can feel more like an ass."

The bartender filled the peanut dish and placed it directly in front of Jeff.

Jeff dug in without hesitation.

Budd gulped half his beer. "What else do you want to say to make me feel bad?"

"Oh, I've got lots. When Teegan came in to sit before the review board, she told me afterwards how she climbed out of the car with only her Glock and cell phone. Once she got home from your place, she woke the neighbor to borrow money for the cab. Then, she had to wait for a locksmith to get into her house. I'd say the woman was ready for a breakdown by the time the frustration ended. If I were in your shoes, I'd never let her leave my house."

Budd used a finger to draw a line down the condensation accumulating on his beer mug. He had awakened several hours later to find the house empty and car keys on the coffee table, relieved to see her gone but with no thought as to how she'd gotten home. He gritted his teeth. "I'm sure you paid her well."

Jeff shook his head. "She never took money. Instead, she accepted the assignments because something had to be done, to right a wrong so to speak. She doesn't officially work for the FBI, Budd, but is more in the consultant line. God knows I've tried to get her on the payroll. Her father's the problem. The man has palpitations whenever his daughter puts herself in harm's way." He grabbed a handful of peanuts.

"Teegan attended the bureau's training course and

turned into a crack shot, but she only took special cases. Yours was one of them." He shrugged. "At least now, I understand her tears. She wasn't crying for Kincaid at all. She used her first kill as an excuse."

Aw, shit. He hadn't believed a word out of her mouth and effectively erased their time together by reverting to the asshole he'd been on the plane.

Just as well. The relationship was doomed anyway. Still...

He hung his head. "I'm the biggest jerk in Vegas. I was angry and in pain. My dog was near death, and I'm fuming because she shot Anna dead when I knew Anna planned to kill me."

"After she tortured you," Jeff added. "We found her stuff at Feinberg's house. She had books on medieval torture on her nightstand. The woman was seeking revenge big time. Where she planned to take you, we don't know." He twirled the liquid in his glass. "Teegan's worth a fight."

Tell me something I don't know. Budd glared. "I can't waltz up to her like every thing's forgotten."

"Why not? Pride getting in the way? Most men would cut off their arm for a woman like her. Have you thanked her for saving your life?"

"No, of course not."

He shook his head and curled his mouth to the side. "Then, you are a jerk. That's too much of a stubborn ego, Budd. Despite her training and genius brain, she's still a woman with a need to feel safe and secure. You can give her that security." He finished the last of the peanuts. "Saying thank you is a good reason to approach and start a dialog."

Budd sneered. "You make it sound simple. Before

this happened, we planned on cooling our relationship."

Jeff sucked in a large breath and coughed. "Damn near choked on that peanut." He met Budd's gaze. "Are you serious? Why?"

"I've got this aversion toward marriage. She doesn't want to waste her time."

The man's face creased into a frown. "Forget the word jerk. I'm sitting next to an idiot. I guess you like all the fame and notoriety they throw your way. If that's the case, Teegan doesn't deserve you. Now, if you'll excuse me, I have a lovely wife waiting at home." He gulped the last of his drink and stood.

"Teegan didn't have to be so secretive," Budd grumbled.

Jeff placed a hand on Budd's shoulder. "Then think of the outcome if you knew about her assignment and casually mentioned it to Feinberg. Her silence probably tore her up." He slapped Budd's shoulder and then dropped his hand. "Look, Budd, I've known Teegan for a while. She's strong. She'll get over you. One day, she'll meet a man who won't pick her apart. He'll accept her for what she is, a woman with strong principles who happens to be the most beautiful woman I've ever seen—besides my wife, of course." He leaned close, his gaze probing. "You owe your life to Teegan. Make sure you live a happy, productive one."

After paying the bill, Budd grumbled all the way back to the office. He should call it a day and go home, but he had dictation to do for letters due a week ago. Unfortunately, he remembered too late Denise's request to leave an hour early to take care of personal business. Determined to finish the task, he sat at his desk dictating into a hand-held tape recorder.

Ed popped his head through the open door. "Is Teegan fair game yet?" He stepped inside. "I've given you enough time to get back together."

The image of Ed with Teegan was enough to make his blood turn into lava. But what could he say in argument? Teegan *was* fair game, and he had no one to blame but himself.

"You expect me to understand your mumbling?" Ed flopped into a chair. "I won't approach her if you say so."

"I don't know what I want." He wanted lecherous Ed to stay away from Teegan, but she could wind up with worse. *The hunk at the gas station, for example.*

"Well, one way to make up your mind is to have a conversation. This way, you'll know for sure whether you can live without her." He crossed his legs. "You came back too soon, Budd. You need time to heal."

"I had legalities to consider because of Josh's involvement."

"I could have handled them. And if I was you, I'd sign on Bailey as partner like pronto. I've also got two new associates who look promising. I'd like to increase their caseload."

"Go right ahead." He hadn't enough concentration to tie his shoes let alone evaluate anyone on staff. Jeff's speech at the bar made him feel like a total heel. He had treated Teegan badly. If anything, he should at least apologize.

"Don't you think you overreacted with Teegan?" Ed brushed lint from his trouser leg. "She's a man's dream. Definitely not the type to hang on your arm pleading with the oh-woe-is-me stuff."

Budd studied him. "You like helpless woman."

"But you don't. Teegan's smart, beautiful, and a crack shot." He shuddered. "I'm getting chills thinking about her." He uncrossed his legs and leaned forward. "I can't believe you still loved Anna."

"I never loved Anna."

He wagged a finger. "That's not my interpretation. I suppose you'll tell me you don't love Teegan either. If so, I'm moving in." He sat back.

Every muscle in Budd's body tightened as he resisted the urge to jump over the desk to strangle Ed. He pursed his lips and glared. "You're not her type. She wants marriage."

"Then maybe it's time I settled down. She's perfect."

If he still had stitches in his leg, he'd be splitting them like old thread from the tension in his thighs. He wanted to hang Ed from the nearest rafter or at least stomp on him, but then, he'd be down two partners, and his caseload would triple. In frustration, he crumpled a piece of paper and tossed the ball into the trash bin. "Don't you have work to do?"

Ed stood while his lips stretched into a big grin. "I'll be busy for a while so Teegan will have to wait." After running a hand down the length of his tie, he headed for the doorway. "You can't hold onto her, Budd. I'll give her a call whether you approve or not. If you change your mind, let me know."

"Ed." No way in hell would he allow Ed or any man to move in on Teegan, not if he still had a shred of a chance for forgiveness.

Ed paused to look back, his hand on the door knob, one brow cocked in question.

"I changed my mind."

Chapter Twenty-Four

Budd stood at the curb, staring at the faded yellow siding on Teegan's house, half-hoping to see the door fly open and the woman from his dreams run toward him. The drapes covering the front bay window were drawn so unless she had X-ray vision, she wouldn't know he was standing here. Over the past week, he had called her several times, always getting voicemail where he'd left short, generic messages because—like the idiot Jeff called him—his pride wouldn't let him say more.

The dwelling looked lonely and without life, no car in the driveway, no trash can by the curb for pickup day like for the nearby houses. She wasn't home, probably at the office, buried in work, but he had to prove he could stand in this neighborhood without her, to rediscover his roots for if one thing he'd learned after the incident with Anna was that his old girlfriend was right. Too many years of women falling at his feet changed him into a snob, the very type of person he detested. Without question, fame and fortune had gone to his head, and he had to release the anger and frustration before he fell deeper into a hole.

That amazing revelation took a few swift kicks in the butt to sink in.

Teegan's house had a similar appearance to his boyhood home except his siding had been a faded pink.

Yellow was tolerable, but pink was ugly as vomit. The whole neighborhood grew in the nineteen sixties, a kind of build-it-sell-it development for the masses seeking riches in the new gambling mecca called Las Vegas. Not the best quality materials but not overly cheap either. Adequate for its day. The style unchanged from street to street with siding and door color as the only options.

Meeting Teegan had turned his life into a humbling experience. For the first time, he understood his biased opinion of rich people was based on certain assholes in college—two men, one woman, all attending law school—redefining the definition of arrogance by being as verbal as they pleased. None had any intention of working, but a law degree looked good on the wall behind an expensive desk, especially if their future plans included politics.

As a young attorney working for the city's most powerful law firm, he had witnessed how the super-rich defied the law, the catch-me-if-you-can mentality that pushed hard-working but frustrated lawmen into early retirement. From the first day, the firm's preference for the rich fueled his attitude, and the code traveled with him to his own firm. When Teegan had shot Anna, she'd given him every impression of another spoiled brat getting away with murder. Teegan, like all the others, had the money to fight whatever charges a DA slapped on her.

Except Teegan was like no other.

Funny how those words hadn't entered his mind until recently. He had pictured her as cold-blooded as Anna, but every one of the agents on the detail had the same orders. Surrender wasn't part of Anna's genetic

makeup. She had a way of taunting until a person
screamed with anger. He admired the trait when they
were younger, but over time, she grew into a bona-fide
harasser, a woman with a win-at-all-cost mentality,
never ceasing until she accomplished her goal.

Last night, after a quick sandwich, he'd settled on
the sofa with a pen and pad in hand and created a list.
Two columns—reasons to stay a bachelor and reasons
to marry. The bachelor side filled the page. Items like
peace and quiet, a bed all to himself, come and go
whenever he pleased, no one barking out orders—all
the stupid shit a bachelor believed essential to life. On
the marry side, only three words appeared—Teegan,
children, family. Somehow, that column had more
weight. Nothing else mattered. This remarkable woman
had opened his eyes to the possibility of love ever after.
She was different, so different he couldn't shut his eyes
at night without seeing her. She'd changed his
perspective on everything.

Her house, for example. He had sworn never to
return to this neighborhood. Yet, he stood on the street
where he and Tommy Ryan played whiffle ball. And
Betty Framer, his first crush, had lived at the end of
Teegan's block. He'd loved the girl with her straight-
cut bangs and rosy cheeks. She and her family moved
to Utah before the start of the fifth grade. Saddest day
of his young life.

So, yeah, his roots were here, firmly implanted,
and Teegan, a woman with a pure heart, had opened his
eyes. Standing now and staring down the street, he
understood why he loved his cabin so much. The place
gave him the happiness he'd lost as fame entered his
life.

The cabin, Rommel, nature, and Teegan. She belonged with them. For days, he had agonized over a decision, searching within his soul for clarity, what he wanted in life, what he needed to make him feel whole. The answer was to fill the incessant emptiness with the woman who'd turned his world upside down.

"She's not home," said a voice.

Budd pivoted to see a little old lady approach with a yapping poodle at her heels. The woman was as round as she was tall with a Shirley Temple face complete with dimples and a mound of curly white hair.

She bent over and shook a finger at the dog. "Shush!"

Of course, the dog refused to listen. Nobody trained their pets these days. "Do you know when she'll return?"

"She didn't say." She stepped closer, scrutinizing him with one eye half closed. "You're that eligible bachelor guy. You and Teegan were in the paper." The analysis continued as she crossed her arms over an abundant chest. "You're not playing games with her, I hope? She isn't one of your floozies, you know. Folks on this block don't want to see her hurt."

Floozies? Was that what people called his dates? Thinking back, he hadn't dated any woman with class—until Teegan. He smiled at the old woman. "I'm mending my bachelor ways because of her."

The woman pursed her thin lips while both eyes squinted up. "Why don't I believe you?"

Ouch. He'd spoken the same words to Teegan. To this day, they echoed in his ears. *God, I'll never fix this.* But he had to try, somehow convince Teegan to talk.

"Excuse me a minute." The woman turned to the

yapping dog. "Get back in your own yard or no yum-yums tonight." She pointed a shaky finger toward her front door.

The dog slapped his mouth shut but stayed by her feet.

The woman turned back. "I'm Lavania Lafferty. I knew your mother."

The news came as a surprise. Well, all right, not much of a surprise. The area had always been a close-knit community. Everyone knew everyone else eventually. *I'm the one who wanted to forget names and faces.*

Mrs. Lafferty waved to a neighbor across the street who had come out to toss another trash bag by the curb.

"After your mother retired, she volunteered at the Little League concession stand while I manned the first-aid table. She told me you wanted her to move near you, some senior center."

"Yes, after my father died, I wanted her closer, but she refused." He wasn't surprised to hear the old woman's words. His mother had often talked about the nurse at the concession stand and the lunches they shared.

The woman nodded knowingly. "I had the same argument with my daughter. This neighborhood might look a little rundown, but we've got some nice people living here. When she moved in, Teegan was like a breath of fresh air. All of us embraced her, and she needed our love, being away from her family and all. She fit right in, despite her wealthy roots. Not a snobby bone in her body." She glanced down at her now-obedient dog. When she looked up, she returned her one-eyed stare. "What took you so long?"

His brow lifted in question. "For what?"

"You haven't been back for a while. You don't look like a fool."

He smiled at her bluntness. "I am a fool, Mrs. Lafferty, a very big one. I came to beg her for a second chance."

He wasn't sure why he told the woman this. Maybe because she reminded him of his Aunt Helga, a woman who pounded the Bible at the dinner table.

"All right," she said, resting a hand on her hip. "I'll accept you at your word. I'm watching her place, collecting the mail, all that. She's been gone for two weeks now. If you want to know where she went, you might try her office. She works at the new factory outside of town."

"Thank you. I'll do that." He approached his car door but paused as a thought entered his mind. "Were you the one who gave her money for the cab?"

"Yes. She stayed with me until the locksmith arrived. The poor girl was beat. She fell asleep on the sofa, and I had to shake her awake. Then, she could hardly move. You know…" She wagged a finger in the air as she stepped toward him. "I've been a nurse for a long time, and never once have I seen such a bruise on a breastbone. She said it came from the steering wheel, but we have airbags to prevent those kinds of injuries, and I know the bags don't make such a concentrated bruise." She leaned against the SUV, a slight frown forming on her face. "She wouldn't explain the burn in her sweatshirt either, so I think she was in more than a car accident. I put an icepack on her while we waited for the locksmith."

A bruise on her breastbone. The impact of a .308

into a bullet-proof vest. He had noticed the cut on her head but hadn't cared if the wound sliced halfway into her skull. He was so friggin' self-centered that night. In his mind, he was riding with a woman no better than Anna. One shot had taken down Anna. One shot, and Jeff had to explain the necessity because Mr. Snobby Lawyer had shut his ears.

Twenty minutes later, Budd waited for a woman named Claudia to get off the phone. This was his second visit to the Smith Tool Company, but now, the employees watched him with more than curiosity. Maybe they recognized a certifiable idiot when they saw one.

They should be in cubicles, popping their heads up to see. But they weren't. The entire office was wide open. Six desks, six employees all typing on computers, others wandering from open doors just to look at the man pacing in front of Claudia. Teegan's secretary had a bigger desk and was separated only by distance, near a door marked private.

The woman put down her phone. "I'm sorry, Mr. Richardson, but Dr. Smith is out of town. I don't know when she'll be back. Hasn't she answered your calls?"

"We had a bit of a tiff."

"Oh." Claudia leaned forward on the desk. "That explains a lot. She usually flies to Houston, but this time, she drove. She said something about clearing her head." She folded a sheet of letterhead and slipped it into an envelope. "The engineers at NASA were gracious enough to reschedule since she canceled the last meeting so unexpectedly. That wasn't like her at all." She placed the envelope to the side and looked at him, her gaze guarded. "I thought the car crash shook her up, but I'd label a tiff as much more upsetting. I'm sorry."

"Not any more than me." He gritted his teeth.

Teegan's role in his rescue was not public knowledge. The media had a field day with the story, painting Anna as the vengeful ex-girlfriend out to kill Vegas' most popular bachelor. By all accounts, the FBI and LVPD had saved the day.

"Budd?"

At his name, he whirled to see Frank Smith standing in the doorway to Teegan's office.

The big man waved a beckoning hand. "Come in here so we can talk."

Budd approached Frank and shook his outstretched hand. "When did you get back in town?"

"A few days ago. Teegan doesn't know either." He pointed to Teegan's secretary. "Hold the calls, Claudia."

The office, like the conference room, was neither extravagant nor bland. Expensive mahogany desk, sofa against one wall, a wet bar on the other, several leather chairs with high backs. Functional, like his office. A large set of windows behind the desk showed a magnificent view of the mountains and desert. *Nice.* Better than his view of casino lights.

They settled on the sofa. Frank leaned back, relaxed.

Budd sat forward, feeling as if he might jump out of his skin. He wanted to do something, anything to find Teegan, not sit around and twiddle his thumbs.

"Teegan told me what happened," Frank began.

"You mean how I behaved like a total ass?"

Frank gave a gentle smile. "Not quite in those

words, but yes."

Budd turned to face him. "What exactly did she say?"

"That you weren't the right man." He fussed with his trouser crease. "I'm disappointed, but she'll find someone else."

Yeah, she was too beautiful *not* to find another man. Still, something wasn't right. He heard it in the older man's tone. Budd studied him. "Why are you here, Frank?"

"Oh, you know, I flew back to see what was going on with my little girl. She tells me she's finalizing the specs for a new space rover, but she never stayed in Houston before, always took the plans home to mull over the details." He lifted a leg onto his knee. "I'm guessing she can't concentrate."

An astute old man. His own father was a happy drunk most of the time and too inebriated to give advice, let alone talk to his only son. He wrung his hands. "I can't concentrate either. I was pretty harsh with Teegan."

"We all say stupid shit when we're upset. Do you love her?"

What a question! He wanted to shout it to the world, but she had to hear it first. "She's everything to me, Frank. I want a chance to tell her, but I don't think she'll talk to me again."

Frank studied him with a piercing gaze. "The match made in heaven got a bit tarnished, eh? You two are perfect for each other."

Budd gave a sick laugh. "She's perfect. I'm not. She's neither pompous, arrogant, nor opinionated—like me." He tugged on his tie to loosen the hold around his neck. "She's so incredibly down-to-earth when I've got my nose stuck in the air. I've become like the snobs I detested in college, the ones who flaunted their wealth and crushed every living being along the way." He lowered his head into his palms. "She doesn't deserve me."

"That's where you're wrong, son. I know for a fact she's in love with you. Telling me you weren't the one just about broke her heart." Shaking his head, he stared at the floor.

"How can I change her mind, Frank?"

The big guy pursed his lips and let out a slow breath. He glanced up. "By being honest. She's hurt, Budd. I can't tell you how many times she cried on my shoulder when some boy rejected her because of her brain. She learned to put up a shield early in life and hardly let a man get close for fear of the inevitable rejection. I was surprised to see how quickly she lowered the shield for you." He rested an arm onto the back of the sofa. "I guess you were special."

Budd jumped to his feet and paced. "Yeah, so special I nailed the shield back up by thinking she was a cold-blooded killer."

"What?" Frank's arm dropped back to his side as black bushy eyebrows creased together into a frown. "She only told me about the breakup. Does this have something to do with the FBI?"

Oops. She hadn't told her father. He ran both hands through his hair. "I don't know how much to tell you."

"All the facts would be nice. I already know she's a special ops agent, so you won't be telling me anything new."

Budd stopped pacing and thrust his hands into his

trouser pockets. "She was part of a covert operation. She alone took down my stalker, and I accused her of playing the bored rich-bitch role." He lifted his gaze and faced the older man. "She cried on Jeff Andrews' shoulder, Frank, not mine, because I wanted nothing to do with her."

"Oh." Frank drummed his fingers on the sofa armrest. "Now I understand her request."

Budd jerked, brows high. "What request?"

"She asked me to find her replacement. She wants out of Vegas, said she misses Philly too much." He rubbed both hands over his face and across his bald head before meeting Budd's gaze. "That's why I'm here. The entire facility is in protest. They're threatening to strike, and we're not even operational yet. No one wants to see her go."

And I'm at the top of the list. No way would he allow Teegan to step out of his life or even *think* of leaving Vegas before he said his piece. He had pushed her away and sure as hell would drag her back. That smart, good-looking genius had loved with a fierceness that ignited his soul. She was his ultimate mate. No other woman had made him feel so special so…loved.

The last word was the difference between Teegan and all the women before her. She loved him. He'd refused to acknowledge the feeling because of stubbornness, but every moment they'd spent together was like floating on a cloud. She loved him enough to risk her existence on the planet. *How big a fool am I to pass that up*?

Getting her to listen was the problem. If he had to crawl on his hands and knees to say the words, he'd do it. He loved her, damnit. His whole body came alive whenever she stood near. He would never, ever give her up.

Now, he needed to devise a trap of his own.

Chapter Twenty-Five

For the second time in a month, Teegan drove through the desert toward Budd Richardson's cabin. She had remembered the turn at the gas station easily enough. From that point, the odometer was her sole guide.

After her last trip, she'd finally gotten some smarts and bought an Audi SUV. Enough of this worrying about scraping the bottom of the car or inadvertently leaving the road and sinking into sand. Four-wheel drive, oyster white, with all the amenities. From the same dealer, of course. The salesman probably thought she was the world's worst driver.

The afternoon was beautiful. A warm summer breeze blew down from the mountains, swirling small funnels of dust across the ground. An occasional tumbleweed rolled by, a scene so peaceful she slowed to watch. As on the first trip, no sign of human life presented itself. No animals either unless they were lazing in the shade away from the hot sun. A cloudless sky as blue as—*aw, shit*—Budd's eyes.

Now why must I think of that? Bad enough the review panel had requested another meeting, but to face him again...

Before she'd left for Houston, she had endured the FBI's inquisition with their multi-layered questions full of innuendo. Two hours of steady questions, and as if that wasn't enough, Jeff called to say they had to see for themselves where she'd stood in relation to Anna's position and where Budd was. *I should have told them to take a long walk off a short pier.*

She wasn't on the payroll and had lost two vehicles because of Anna Kincaid. The second included her driver's license and credit cards. No one had offered to pay for the time and effort spent to replace them. Not to mention her dress from the nightclub and the high heels left in the ladies room. She could afford to replace everything, but it was a matter of principle. She'd risked her neck for a man who showed no gratitude, not even a simple thank you.

And now, this.

Well, hard cheese. Let them wait. Forever if necessary. She refused to break any speed limits just to get to the cabin. And for what? To relive that dreadful night, to reminisce how Budd's love turned to hate?

Love was a loose term and nonexistent in Budd's book. He'd never admit how much passion poured from him during their lovemaking, how he gave with an intensity beyond description. She hadn't felt anything so intense from any man, even men who admitted to being in love.

After NASA, she had spent the extra time on the road fighting to forget the contempt filling Budd's eyes. That fateful night, she'd felt a betrayal of sorts, a disbelief at such anger, but after considering the entire situation, she wasn't sure what she expected. He certainly wasn't a jump-with-joy kind of man because Anna was dead, his troubles over—that sort of thing. He simply hated Teegan Smith, the rich-bitch with time on her hands. She doubted his feelings lessened.

Her father had questioned the length of time she'd spent on her so-called mission to Houston. A mini-vacation she told him, an opportunity for a little sightseeing. A slow drive through one very big state to discover why Texans were such proud citizens. And shopping. A man always turned off his ears when a woman mentioned shopping.

Maybe the review panel plans to lock me away. Why else would they schedule an additional inquisition?

A worse thought, what if Budd had petitioned for murder charges? The man carried a lot of weight in Vegas with his political connections and criminal expertise. Jeff had assured her the panel performed the secondary review as a matter of procedure. All routine. *Uh-huh.* None of her other cases had gone before a second review board. Of course, this was the first time she had used a gun. Her other assignments were dangerous, but her proximity to the perpetrators was the distance of another room—none of the face-to-face stuff like this one.

Her first kill. A horrific experience and one she cared never to repeat. Jeff's orders were explicit, backed wholeheartedly by his superiors, the psych evaluation board, and LVPD. All the FBI experts had assured her of Anna's inability to surrender, that her final shot would be aimed at Budd's heart, because her ultimate objective was to remove him from the surface of the earth.

Mere words, of no help whatsoever, and she tossed and turned for nights. She'd known the odds going in, but to put a bullet in someone's brain, to see the instantaneous passing of life from her eyes was a memory she couldn't forget. Even a stop at a small church to pray had done nothing to alleviate the guilt.

Naturally, Budd would be in attendance at his own cabin. She had spent four extra days driving through the southwest after Jeff's call, stopping here, staying there, in no hurry to face more questions. Nothing kept her mind off Budd. Not even her sojourn at a Flagstaff spa for her first-ever mud bath. Never again. Washing the mud out of all her body's cracks was unreal.

She passed the road leading to the collapsed shack and boulders that served as her hiding spot. Anna's ambush occurred just a few miles ahead, so she slowed the car with a careful eye on the odometer.

Deep tire tracks caught her eye, cutting raggedly along the edge of the dirt road's surface. She stopped to step out and look down the ravine, her gaze following the line of deep ruts to a charred boulder. Bushes were either crushed or splintered from its roots to show the car's path. Her pulse jumped a notch, and a sick feeling settled in her stomach as she recalled the most frightening night of her life. The Audi was gone, towed to a junk yard somewhere. Thanks to the review panel, she'd relive her terrifying moment in detail. They couldn't take her word that survival was pure luck. Teegan sighed and slipped back into the car.

Jeff would need a snow storm in the desert before he talked her into another assignment. *Why add more aggravation when my COO position gives me enough acid reflux?* Whatever happened today, no matter what the outcome, should be the end of Budd, of her desert trips, and especially, the FBI. Enough was enough. She'd get the factory up and running then return to the lab in Philadelphia.

Without turning her head, she checked the clock on the dashboard. Jeff had said two o'clock sharp. Fifteen minutes to go. Not that she cared. *They can start without me. I won't mind.*

She passed a road and braked. A quick throw in reverse. Her gaze followed the road uphill where the cabin stood bright in the sunlight. *A now-or-never moment. Face Budd and then forever let him be.* Dreading the inevitable, she turned onto the drive.

The cabin took on a different appearance in daylight, a more peaceful, welcoming look. The sinister air created by a lurking crazy woman and darkness was gone. Sun rays glowed off the tan roof tiles, giving the rancher an immaculate shine while faint shadows between the logs brought out an inviting homeyness. The open porch stretched across the length of the front with wooden steps spanning a third of the width. Visions of lounge chairs and lemonade came to mind. Maybe a hammock. Lazy days on the porch with a good book.

The barn stood off to the side with two open doors facing the cabin. A tall, stainless steel tank protruded behind it, the one visible on Jeff's aerial photos. Only Budd's SUV was parked in the front yard. No evidence of anyone waiting impatiently for her arrival. She double-checked the time. Ten minutes past two. Jeff was late. *I'll be alone with Budd. What wonderful barbs will he throw today?*

How could one erase the pain of a lost love? She'd never fallen so deeply so fast and had no experience with the ensuing ache. Bad enough she couldn't eat—a rarity. She couldn't sleep either, and to see Budd again would only perpetuate the problem. *I should have refused.* With hesitation, she stepped from the car.

A quick glance skyward conjured visions of dark skies with stars forming their intricate patterns. They were beautiful that night, a sight rarely seen from a city. The scientist in her wanted to study the heavens through a large-diameter telescope, count the moons around Jupiter, and gasp at the rings of Saturn. As a child, she had a small white telescope, and she'd stayed out late in the backyard on a clear night. Her father always sat at the dining room window, pretending to read a newspaper, ever watchful of his little girl. Wonderful memories.

A weak woof-woof followed by a whimper brought her attention to the side of the cabin. Rommel lumbered over to greet her, his nub-of-a-tail wagging a mile a minute in contrast to his stiff body movements. "Rommel!" She squatted to give him a hug. Big mistake. He knocked her right over.

He whimpered and licked while she struggled to hold him at arm's length. A fruitless effort. She had known nothing about Rommel's condition or even if he'd survived. Budd had called her cell several times a few weeks later but never left a worthwhile message. She wasn't about to call him back just to say hello. "I'm glad to see you're all right, boy." A short re-growth of fur covered the surgical area where the bullet pierced. He'd lost weight, too, judging from the feel of his ribs under her fingers.

Heavy footsteps clomping on floorboards drew her attention to the front entrance. Her breath caught at the sight of Budd behind the screen door, his expression stern. He still had an effect on her, and her heart thumped against her ribcage. She stood while patting the dust from her T-shirt and jeans. "I'm hoping everyone came by helicopter."

He grunted in answer and stepped onto the porch. "You may as well come in. I've got coffee waiting."

Oh, right, and be alone with you? "No—thanks. I'll wait out here." She settled on the bottom step to scratch Rommel's head, her back to Budd. *A good excuse to avoid conversation. And him.*

Unfortunately, she had excellent peripheral vision and saw Budd as plainly as if he stood alongside. His tug was as strong as ever. If anything, their separation intensified the feeling, drawing her like metal to a magnet. *Will it ever cease, or must I suffer his loss forever?*

She knew the answer before she finished the question because the warmth of his arms was permanently embedded in memory. With every glimpse of his face or the sound of his voice, she'd suffer the inevitable pain of withdrawal. Even now. With him so close, dressed in blue jeans and T-shirt, he looked lean and rugged with sandy hair slightly mussed and falling onto his forehead, drawing her gaze even while she struggled to concentrate on Rommel. *If he would only turn into an ugly old toad with hair sticking out his nose.*

He leaned against a post. "What do you think of my place?"

Determined not to appear too interested, she looked off into the distance. "It's prettier in daylight." She loved the simplicity and charm, a house surrounded by a peaceful environment, in an area devoid of city noises and lights. Under different circumstances, she'd tell him so. She glanced toward him. "Why build so far from Vegas?"

He scuffed his boot on a board. "A friend had a thousand acres to sell. I bought the ground for the chance to get away from the glitz and glam. Let me show you the inside."

"I saw it."

"I doubt you took a good look around that night."

True. Her focus was to get Anna before she killed Budd. Everything else was secondary. *Hurry, Jeff.*

Why was Budd so calm, polite even? His gaze had shot daggers when they last spoke. *Weeks apart mellowed him, I guess.* Unless he wanted to save his contempt for when Jeff arrived. *Maybe he's afraid I'll shoot him.*

Budd thumped his boot on the edge of the porch as if to knock dirt from the grooved sole.

"I hired the best crime scene cleanup crew from Vegas to get the blood out of the floor. They did a good job."

"That's nice."

Boots? And sawdust on the legs of his blue jeans. *Great. A handsome lumberjack.* She avoided his inquisitive gaze.

"I can't believe how Anna turned so vicious," he said.

Well, golly gee, an acknowledgment of an avenging madwoman. From his tone, had he thought through all the danger everyone faced? She turned to meet his gaze. "She wasn't crazy, Budd, but she was unstable. She had unresolved anger issues stemming from childhood. Her case file told us everything."

He folded his arms across his chest. "I haven't read any of the psych evaluations, but I remember one nasty bullying incident from our junior year in high school where Anna lost control. She tried to hang one of the girls before someone stopped her."

She wasn't in the mood to listen to an analysis of Anna's behavior since a restless feeling had swept over her. Being alone with Budd was too hard. And he was being too pleasant, too friggin' polite. *The calm before the storm.* She had this uncontrollable urge to run away from him, from the cabin, but mostly, from Vegas. She sprang to her feet, startling Rommel in the process. "Can I see your barn?" She headed toward the building without waiting for an answer.

She'd seen the barn when she rushed in to check the two agents that night, but she had focused on their injuries with only a cursory glance at the surroundings. She remembered seeing wood and not much else. Daylight offered a better inspection of the interior. Not like she expected to see anything extraordinary. Big deal, a barn. She walked through the open doors.

The sweet smell of a woodworking shop greeted her nose. Pine, cedar, walnut. Several inches of sawdust covered the dirt floor along with snipped pieces of wood. Stacks of wood planks rested against the wall—short, long, fat, thin, arranged in easy-to-grab lines. Two bench saws were set up, a band saw, and something else—*ah, yes*—a plank sander.

She glanced upward at the loft. Anna and Josh had used the spot for their overnight accommodations. The Feds found two sleeping bags and water along with—literally—a pot to piss in.

A pegboard covered with Smith tools hung on one wall. Underneath the pegboard stretched a long workbench with a vise, well used. The barn smelled like a forest, and she sucked in several deep breaths to calm her nerves. *Not a bad place to wait for Jeff.*

Budd strolled inside with his hands thrust into his back pockets, scuffing at the sawdust with a swing of his boot while shooting her sidelong glances without moving his head. She had the unshakable sense that something was up. Either that, or he hadn't a clue what to say or do until Jeff arrived

Rommel, of course, hadn't left her side, always staring up with an adoring gaze.

"You're quite the carpenter." What else could she say? The situation was awkward. Jeff was late, and she and Budd were forced into small talk.

Jeff is never late.

That realization hit like a brick. Jeff was the most punctual man she knew. She faced Budd with an uneasiness churning in her gut, daring to meet his gaze. His eyes weren't full of the hatred from their last encounter. They displayed an intensity that took her aback, which made her wonder whether she needed glasses.

"I'm sorry, Teegan."

Tears flooded her vision, and she quickly turned away. She refused to let him see the emotions welling to the surface since she had no idea why he apologized. *The mess in the barn more likely.* "No one else is coming, are they?"

"No." He stepped toward her, releasing his hands from his back pockets and dropping his arms to the side. "You weren't answering my calls. I didn't leave a message because I didn't know what to say, and even if I said the words you wanted to hear, you wouldn't have called me back."

Right on that one, counselor. Throat tight, she faced him, head high. "What do you want, Budd?"

"You. For a lifetime." He dropped his hands to his side. "I don't want you to return to Philly."

Her breath caught, and her shoulders slumped. "Who told you?"

"Your dad. I went to your office to crawl on my hands and knees only to discover you were still in Houston."

Her heart took a flying leap. "You did?" Her father hadn't mentioned Budd's visit. She swallowed hard against the lump in her throat. "I thought you were too proud for something so demeaning."

"I'd crawl in front of paparazzi if it meant getting you back."

Is he joking? After all the hate he shot my way? She tapped the heel of her hand on the side of her head just in case she hadn't heard right.

"I behaved badly, Teegan. I never thanked you for saving my life. You risked everything for me, and I returned nothing but contempt." He kicked the sawdust, and the fresh scent of pine filtered through the air. He leaned toward her to force her gaze to meet his. "I am grateful—really."

Not certain what to believe, she searched his face, her pulse thumping double-time. Pride got in the way. She looked down at Rommel as a tear dropped from her eye and onto his nose. He licked the moisture, his gaze puzzled. "Why the change, Budd? I'm sure you didn't have this big, wonderful revelation."

"That's where you're wrong." He grabbed a rag and slapped the dust off the table saw, avoiding eye contact. "I used to think I didn't need anyone, that life was perfect, but everything changed when you were no longer with me. Food became tasteless. Comedians weren't funny. Judges were complete assholes and had no business being on the bench. I wasn't happy, and I made everyone around me miserable." He tossed aside the rag and faced her.

"When the situation with Anna was over, I had to contend with Josh's involvement. He never talked about his money problems. I'd have gladly given him my caseload for the opportunity to spend more time with you." Gaze focused on hers, he stepped closer. "Once I grasped what I had done, what I said, I felt sucker punched. I pushed you away, and I had no idea how to get you back."

She smelled his aftershave, and memories tore at her heart. She still loved him, had always loved him, but defiance set in. Men had a way of shattering her confidence, and the healing process was torturous. How many times in life must she question a man's motives?

She squared her shoulders and faced him. "All right, you tricked me, and you involved Jeff. Now what? I witnessed the hate in your eyes. You loved Anna, and I killed her."

Shaking his head, he wagged a finger. "Not the love that comes from deep within, Teegan. We were soul mates from grade school. We grew up poor and struggled our entire lives. So, my hate for you was real...then, until Jeff told me Anna's body count and his orders, not only to you, but the others as well. You alone survived her ambush."

Barely. Not without a broken heart. She wiped a tear from her cheek. "I waited as long as possible on the sidelines, Budd, hoping the agents captured Anna so I could return to Vegas and hop a plane to Houston. But I knew one way or the other Anna would come after me. I was part of her vendetta." She wiped another tear and met his gaze. "I had doubts about whether I could actually pull the trigger, but when I saw the barrel aimed at your heart, I knew what had to be done." She sniffed and stepped back to get away from his aftershave. The distance did nothing. The scent traveled with her. "You could have avoided this confrontation by apologizing via voicemail. Seeing this place and you hurts too much." She ran a hand under her nose to catch the drip. *Damn, I need a tissue, and I left my purse in the car.* She sniffed. "So, why are you telling me all this?"

"I think you know why. We belong together. I'm in love for the first time in my life, and I don't want to lose it."

Heart racing, she blinked away the tears. "You're in love with me?"

A faint smile tugged at his lips. "I needed a few swift kicks in the butt to admit it, but yeah, I'm in love." He took another step toward her. "You're the most extraordinary woman I've ever met."

A second tear fell from her eye onto Rommel's nose. The poor dog looked so confused. "I don't know what to say."

"Say you'll give me another chance."

With both hands, she wiped her cheeks. "I never expected this, Budd. I convinced myself we were done."

"And are we?"

Doubt clouded his face. Her heart thundered at the realization of his words. Budd loved her, but should she set herself up for another fall? He was still the confirmed bachelor with a bevy of women, and she wanted so much more, not the occasional date and sleepover but to be a permanent part of his life, now and forever.

She was wishing down the wrong well. "We should end things here and now, Budd. I can't take too many heartbreaks."

He held his right hand up in the three-fingered scout pledge. "I have no intention of breaking your heart ever again, Teegan, but you have to give me a chance to prove it." He dropped his hand.

She studied his face. The sincerity glowed from his gaze, and her breath stopped. But she was a realist. He would never propose anything beyond a liaison. *Should I allow him into my life? Enjoy him for however short a time?*

A heart-versus-brain debate again. *Time to tell my brain to take a hike.* She met his gaze. "I fell in love, too, Budd. I couldn't get over you at all."

Eyes widening, he sucked in a hard breath. "For real?"

Nodding, she choked on a sob. "For real." Teegan flew into his outstretched arms.

Chapter Twenty-Six

He felt so good, arms that held tight and possessive, intoxicating her with his strength. Soft sobs shook his shoulders, and he held her with his face buried in her hair. Her own tears flowed freely and saturated his T-shirt. Why she cried, she wasn't sure. Perhaps tears of joy intermingled with relief, the stress of weeks full of uncertainty falling from her mind. Doubts lingered about where they'd go with this relationship, but for now, she enjoyed the feel of his hard body pressing against hers.

After a long time, his embrace loosened, not much but enough for her to lift her head to look into his wet eyes. She sucked in a quick breath at the deep blue gaze staring back. "Are you going to kiss me?"

Without a word, he clamped both hands onto the sides of her face and kissed her lips, eyes, nose. He wouldn't stay in one spot nor give her a chance to respond.

"I love you so much, Teegan. I'll never let you go." He traveled from cheek-to-cheek until settling on her mouth with a soft moan. His tongue probed with the depth of a man ready to possess her soul and doing a damn good job, too.

He loves me. Don't that beat all. She slipped her arms around his neck and returned the kiss, relishing the warmth of his embrace, even the slight tremor of his hands caressing her back. If given a choice, she'd never leave his arms.

Rommel had other plans.

She felt a nudge on her leg. She looked down to see Rommel nuzzling his head between them, forcing their bodies to separate. "I think he's jealous. He wants part of the hugging and kissing."

Budd released her and yanked up the bottom of his shirt to wipe his face and eyes then stopped mid-wipe. "No, I'm not finished." He gripped her shoulders and kissed her again, ear-to-ear, eye-to-eye. He moved fast and furious in all directions, not allowing her a chance to catch a breath.

When he finally let go, he stepped back with a satisfied nod. "Come inside the cabin, Teegan. You need to see something." He caught her hand and urged her toward the cabin.

Teegan floated up the porch steps behind him, feeling so wildly light, like a cloud drifting in the heavens, and followed him through the door where he released her hand and stood to the side. She stopped dead in the center of the living room.

Directly in front of the sofa, hanging over a fireplace built of stones, was a huge blow-up of the newspaper photo in full color and framed in walnut. She cried out at the sight and slapped a hand over her mouth.

From behind, he slipped his arms around her waist. "I couldn't resist." He rested his chin on her shoulder. "That was probably the first time I appreciated paparazzi nearby. I have another copy hanging in my bedroom back in Vegas. It's a great shot."

Even more so in a blow-up. Blinking fast, she

choked on a sob. "It's beautiful, Budd."

He nuzzled her neck. "The newspaper thought I was storming in to sue them. You should have seen the look on the editor's face when I told him what I wanted." He kissed her neck before rotating her to face him. "I can't believe I ignored the look the first time around, but the picture shows how happy we are together. I was in love with you then. I'm in love with you now. I don't want to lose the real deal, Teegan."

He dropped his hands but rubbed his palms against the sides of his thighs, like he wanted to make sure not to overdo the hugging. She almost told him to put his hands back where they belonged—on her—but an impish grin curled the side of his mouth.

"I haven't had much of an appetite over these past few weeks, Teegan. Now that the weight of the world has lifted from my shoulders, I'm famished. Have you eaten?"

She'd lost eight pounds in the same time period but kept the news to herself. "I can eat. What have you got?"

"Chili."

"That's all?" She shook herself. "Sorry. I didn't mean to insult my host."

Smiling, he headed for the kitchen. "My housekeeper makes me a big batch whenever I come up here. Wait 'til you taste the stuff. It'll knock your socks off."

Oh, dear. That meant heat from too many jalapeños. But what the hell? She could eat a horse.

While she waited for the chili to heat in the microwave, she took a good look around the living room, a more enjoyable look this time. No pictures hung on the paneled walls, but a box of nails and hammer rested on a small table while a pile of pictures leaned against the table legs. A sofa with two matching side chairs faced the fireplace, giving her visions of cozy nights in front of a burning fire. No television but a stereo stood against the wall with a stack of audio disks propped against the side. The large front window remained undressed, and the wide expanse of emptiness from the back of the sofa to the front door remained unchanged. *A table will fit nicely in that area, a place to stare out the window to watch the lizards stroll by.* "For a man hounded by paparazzi, why aren't curtains your first priority? They'd be at the top of my list."

"I don't know a thing about curtains." He grinned broadly while placing two mugs on the counter. "That will be your job."

Her gaze wandered to the floor by the window, to the spot where Josh Weinberg fell, then to the back of the sofa, then, of course, where Anna fell. All three had left a pool of blood. Three different blood scenes and not a trace of the violence. "The cleaning crew did a great job, Budd."

He clanged silverware. "I refused to rip up the floor Frank and I installed, but I had to dispose of several planks. The cleaning crew did the rest."

And worth every penny.

The kitchen was about the size of her own with a counter and four stools for an eating area. Budd poured coffee into the cups while she slipped onto one of the stools and yawned. She hadn't eaten since crossing the Arizona border, and the half-cooked cheeseburger wasn't anything to brag about. Knowing she had to face Budd again hadn't activated any cravings. She yawned again with a haphazard attempt to hide it with the back of her hand.

Budd studied her as he took the bowls out of the microwave. "You look tired."

Yeah, and I feel like shit. She forced a smile. "I've had a long couple of days and haven't slept well. On my ride here, I envisioned facing handcuffs and a jail cell." She put her elbow on the counter and rested her head in her hand.

"Were you afraid to come?"

"Big-time afraid. I wrestled with the decision, not sure what type of reception you had planned. I considered dragging along a lawyer." She closed her eyes. A powerful wave of fatigue swept through her. With the anxiety of facing Budd over, she could sleep for a month.

"I considered charges against you, Teegan. I didn't understand why you hadn't just wounded Anna."

Hearing his terse tone, she peeked through one eye. "And now?"

He set small placements on the counter and then the two steaming bowls of chili but leaned on the counter, using both hands for support. His gaze stared at one of the bowls. "Re-thinking the scene brought new details. I looked up into Anna's gun barrel and saw her finger twitch on the trigger. I don't know why I reacted so harshly toward you when you shot her." He met her gaze. "You saved my life, Teegan." After a shrug, he extended a spoon. "Looking back, Anna always had to prove something, that she was smarter and faster than anyone else. I don't know why I ignored such a trait." He jammed his spoon into his chili bowl. "She harbored a lot of hate."

Well, he's finally admitted the truth. The mental institution had five years to modify Anna's vengeful behavior. Even though she had turned into a model inmate, she deceived everyone with her charade and developed a plan to escape. No one recognized the genius, but they had seen the hate.

Budd nudged the bowl of chili closer as if enticing a dog to eat. She smelled the aroma of too many jalapeños and sat up straight on the stool. "This might rot my gut, you know."

"It's great stuff. My housekeeper uses her own special recipe."

She yawned while digging in with the spoon.

Budd put his face close to hers until she glanced up to meet his gaze. He touched her chin. "I don't think you'll stay awake long enough to eat. Maybe you should rest first." He took her hand and urged her off the stool. "Come on, sweetheart."

Sweetheart? When had a man used such a term? "I'll be all right."

"I'm sure you will." From behind, he placed both hands on her shoulders and guided her toward the bedroom, the very room she'd climbed into and where she grabbed the spread to cover Rommel. A bright sun glowed through uncovered windows. The view outside was rugged mountains. Desert and mountains. As breathtaking as the view from her office window only here, the mountains were much closer, more majestic.

The bedroom was large and sparsely furnished. No clock to tell her the time of day. No mirror to show how tired she looked. Just one chest of drawers on the far wall along with two nightstands with lamps on opposite sides of the bed. The bed's headboard and nightstands matched. The chest of drawers looked like a yard sale bargain. He lowered her onto the bed.

"Too much driving," she said.

"Undoubtedly."

"Maybe a brief nap."

Budd slipped all ten fingers into her hair and kissed her like she remembered with the tenderness of a man in love, his tongue melting any resistance to fend off sleep. Her entire body relaxed in his arms, and she couldn't think of a better way to drift into la-la land. "Budd—"

He touched a finger to her lips. "Shhhh." He kissed both her eyelids. "I'll hold you until you fall asleep."

The feel of his warm breath on her cheek was enough to make her smile as she faded into slumber. "Wake me in twenty minutes."

"Whatever you want."

What she wanted she had—his arms holding her in a protective embrace, his lips close, the scent of his aftershave filling her nose. All wonderful.

****

The following morning, Budd stood in the open doorway watching Teegan sleep, marveling at the direction of his life. Without realizing, she had given him something he hadn't known was missing—a chance to feel love. A wonderful sensation. He learned how something so simple made him feel light-hearted and free. For weeks, he had denied the emotion like a fool and nearly let her get away.

Now, here she was, the weight of all that time without her lifted from his shoulders. The indescribable grief, the torment, the relentless guilt. All dissipated within seconds when he saw her standing in the middle of the front yard. The most extraordinary woman in the world was back where she belonged—with him, in his life, and in his cabin.

He had left her dressed but minus sneakers and socks. He'd held her as she slept. All night. The bedroom light stayed on. He had enjoyed every second with her in his arms, watching her chest rise and fall with slow, easy breaths. Even now in daylight, he couldn't take his gaze off her.

Rommel whimpered.

Budd glanced down and smiled. "Go ahead. Wake her."

His voice caused her to stir. Rommel used the opportunity to approach the bed and put his head on the blanket with a soft whine. Impatient, he lavished her face with licks.

She awakened with a jerk. "Oh, good grief, Rommel. Yes, I love you, too." She pushed him away. Undeterred, he continued his onslaught.

Between her struggle to avoid his tongue, she spotted Budd leaning against the door jamb.

"This dog will give me a bath if I let him." She kicked off the covers.

"That's my job." He stepped in. "Give Rommel a kiss before I chase him off. I want you to myself."

He loved his dog, but he had his limitations to their chumminess. After shooing Rommel onto the front porch, Budd kicked off his boots, walked back to the bedroom, and slipped alongside her. With his head propped onto one elbow, he traced a finger along her jaw line, savoring the softness of her skin. Sleep clouded her teal eyes, her hair was mussed, and he'd never seen a more beautiful sight.

She yawned. "You were staring at me from the doorway."

"Guilty as charged. I can stare at you all day and love every minute."

With a feather touch, she brushed a lock of his hair off his forehead. He took her hand and kissed the fingers.

"Did you sleep with me?"

He released her hand. "Of course, but that was quite a few hours ago."

Her eyes widened, and she attempted to rise. "What's the time?"

"Ten thirty in the morning." With one finger on her shoulder, he urged her back onto the bed. "I already accomplished a day's work plus showered and changed."

"Good heavens, Budd. That's nearly seventeen hours of sleep." She yawned again then grabbed his shirt collar and pulled his head down, brushing her lips against his. "You should have got me up."

"Why? We're not going anywhere." Savoring her taste but knowing he'd never stop, he lifted his head. "I have one question, however. Do you always sleep this late?"

She stifled a laugh and repeated the attempt to rise. "Hardly."

He placed a palm on her shoulder to keep her on the mattress. "Not yet, sweetheart." He kissed her again, deeply, relishing the softness of her tender lips.

This time, she stopped him by pressing a hand to his chest. "Wait a minute, Buster. We still have some unfinished business."

"No, we don't. The fact you are in my bed tells me

you accepted my stupidity and forgive me for all my past transgressions."

She grunted while running a hand through her hair. "You make me sound like a priest."

"I've had many dinners with your father. He's a wise man who kept me sane while I waited for you to return from Houston." He lifted her chin to gaze into her sleepy eyes. "The truth is I have never let a woman get so close to me before, and the whole experience was foreign. After all these years of keeping myself at a safe distance, I suddenly entered new territory by falling in love." He toyed with her hair, allowing the silkiness to run through his fingers. Even the thought of her strands grazing across his chest caused an uncontrollable shudder. "I sometimes wonder how I made such a success of myself when I can be so stupid. With you, I'm learning as I go." He kissed her nose and gazed into her eyes. "Without question, without debate, I love you, Teegan Smith, but I need you to teach me about relationships."

Eyes wide, she jerked to the side. "What makes you think I'm such an expert?"

In response, he pulled her close and captured her lips. A cry escaped from her throat, and he lifted his head to see a mist clouding her eyes.

"All right already. I forgive you."

He melted from the sound of her smooth voice. He would have a lifetime with this woman and hoped they both lived to be a hundred. "I emailed Denise to tell her you were here. She'll call your father and Jeff." He bent to kiss her.

Frowning, she pushed him to arm's length. "Don't try to divert my attention, pal. How'd you email

Denise?"

Even though she was highly educated, she still had the Philadelphia accent with its street-smart edge. He grinned broadly. "Satellite, my dear. I had the service installed two days ago. I emailed Denise to say you arrived safe, and you are here to stay. I won't let you change your mind."

"I won't." Her eyes twinkled. "Now, you can kiss me."

With his tongue, he counted every single one of her teeth. *Delicious. I'll never get enough of this woman.* He raised his head with a sigh. "Where would you like to honeymoon?"

"I don't recall hearing a proposal." She stared, unblinking.

"Oh—that's true. Another wrong assumption, unfortunately. Marry me, Teegan Smith. I love you too much to let you go."

She narrowed her gaze into slits. "What about your marriage hang-up, your no-need-for-a-family lecture?"

"I tossed the idea out the window. I want nothing more than you. If we have children, I hope they have your beautiful eyes. As big a family as you want, in whatever neighborhood you choose." Knowing what was at stake, he took hold of her chin with trembling fingers. "You belong with me in this cabin and forever in my life. What do you say?"

"I'm stunned."

"Then say yes."

"All right, yes."

"And the honeymoon?"

Her face lit up as she broke free from his arms and hopped onto her knees. "Here would be perfect, Budd.

We can buy a telescope and position it in the yard. Then, we can watch stars all night. We can take plenty of food and wine and make love whenever the mood hits us, maybe even out under the stars."

His heart swelled with pride at her suggestion to honeymoon at his cabin. *She loves it.* Another part of his anatomy swelled at the image of her naked on a blanket under the stars. "I love you, Teegan."

"I'm glad because I love you, too."

He drew her onto his chest for a lingering kiss. The little devil wiggled on top of him and deepened the kiss, causing a swelling that strained against his jeans. Her fingers slowly unbuttoned his shirt. "Don't do this, Teegan. You need to refresh yourself and eat."

"Nibbling on you is better. Low calorie, too."

She continued with the buttons then opened his shirt to expose his bare chest. She licked his belly.

Panic consumed him. What should he do? He wanted her so bad and yet, right or wrong…

Play it cool. "If I didn't know any better, I'd say you were horny as hell."

She kissed his nipple. "You assume right, counselor."

He grasped her shoulders to stop the nibbling. "Don't you need to use the bathroom?"

"Sure, in a minute."

Unfortunately, her hand slipped straight to his crotch. The warmth of her fingers and the ensuing massage sent him reeling. She undid the belt and snap, but he clamped onto her wrists to keep her from the zipper. "We have several areas of discussion before we proceed farther, Dr. Smith."

"Oh?" She hopped onto her knees again. "Like

what?"

"I don't want you working around heavy metals if you're pregnant."

Her brows rose. "All right. Not because you made the demand, but because I agree with the safety factor. What else?"

His fingers toyed with the bottom edge of her T-shirt. He slowly lifted the material to expose a bare midriff. When his fingers touched flesh, he experienced a strong ripple through his veins. He had a lifetime of this coming. With her. *Damn, I am a lucky man.*

"Out with it, counselor."

He traced his finger along her abdomen. "You have a beautiful belly button."

"*That* is not a topic of discussion."

"Attached to a fantastic body."

Shaking her head, she sighed. "You want to drive me nuts."

"Attached to a gorgeous face."

Her face furrowed into a frown. "I'm going to rip your clothes off any second."

"Rommel chewed up my box of condoms."

Their gazes locked. Teegan burst into laughter.

"I'm dying over here, woman!"

"I know. I feel it." She put her hands on his cheeks. "I should have one in my purse."

"One? Only one?" The world had stopped spinning, and he was about to fall off. "Teegan, that won't do! I almost killed Rommel. He was so bored. I came up here, you know, prepared in case you forgave me, but dummy me, I unpacked and left everything on the bed. By the time I realized why he was so quiet, I had a mess in here."

She chuckled as she sat back on her heels. "Let's look at this logically. I'm thirty-one years old. You're thirty-four. There's no time like the present to get this family started."

Smiling, he sat halfway up and grabbed her shoulders. "You mean that?"

"We'll have the wedding sooner rather than later. Do you approve, counselor?"

"Approve? My dear, I planned to love you into submission. Lovemaking, Teegan, not sex."

Eyes shining, she gasped. "You said the right word!" She shoved him onto the bed and kissed him.

He reciprocated by wrapping his arms around her and flipped her onto her back.

"Budd—"

"No more talking. We have a lot of catch-up to do."

And a lifetime to love and cherish the most wonderful woman in the world.

A word about the author...

Jane is a retired respiratory therapist who is married to a wonderful organic farmer. She has an extensive medical and science background and uses her knowledge in her books. She enjoys astronomy, has an amateur ham radio license, and is an avid people watcher. She loves to hear or read how two people meet, young and old. When she isn't traveling, she lives in southern New Jersey.

~

Other Titles by This Author

Ask Nothing in Return
Infinite Choices
Secrets by Necessity

Thank you for purchasing
this publication of The Wild Rose Press, Inc.

If you enjoyed the story, we would appreciate your
letting others know by leaving a review.

For other wonderful stories,
please visit our on-line bookstore at
www.thewildrosepress.com.

For questions or more information
contact us at
info@thewildrosepress.com.

The Wild Rose Press, Inc.
www.thewildrosepress.com

Stay current with The Wild Rose Press, Inc.

Like us on Facebook

https://www.facebook.com/TheWildRosePress

And Follow us on Twitter
https://twitter.com/WildRosePress